CAMPUS PLAYER

JENNIFER SUCEVIC

Campus Player

Copyright© 2020 by Jennifer Sucevic

Cover Design by Mary Ruth Baloy at MR Creations

Editing by Kate Newman at Once Upon a Typo

Proofreading by Sid Damiano of SD Editorial Services

Home | Jennifer Sucevic or www.jennifersucevic.com

ALSO BY JENNIFER SUCEVIC

Chapter One

DEMI

"Morning, Demi!" Gary, one of the stadium custodians, calls out with an easy smile and wave as he saunters toward me. "Up and at 'em bright and early this morning, I see."

My heart jackhammers beneath my ribcage from the twenty-minute run as I flash him a grin. "Always!"

"You have a good one! I'll see you tomorrow!"

Since I've already moved past him, I holler over my shoulder, "Same place, same time!"

Even with *The Killers* pumping through my earbuds, I almost hear the deep chuckle that slides from his lips. Our morning greetings are a ritual three years in the making. I've been running through the wide corridor that leads to the stadium football field since I stepped foot on campus freshman year. This will be something I miss when I graduate in the spring. Five days a week, I'm up at six, logging in a four-mile run before returning home, jumping in the shower, and heading off to class.

At this time of the day, the stadium is still relatively quiet, with only a few people wandering the hallways. There's something both serene and eerie about it. I've been here on game days when there are thirty thousand fans packed shoulder to shoulder, rooting on the Western Wildcats football team. Three-fourths of the stadium filled with black and orange is an amazing sight to behold. Football is a religion at Western. Unfortunately, the same can't be said for the women's soccer team. We're lucky if there are a couple of hundred spectators in the stands.

I've come to terms with it.

Sort of.

I keep my gaze trained on the light at the end of the tunnel and push myself faster. As soon as I burst out of the darkness, bright sunlight pours down on me, stroking over the bare skin of my arms and shoulders. It's late August, and summer is still in full swing. A whistle cuts through the silence of the stadium, and my gaze slices to the field. Nick Richards has been head coach of the Wildcats for the last decade. He also happens to be my father.

Two days a week, the guys are up at six in the morning for yoga. Dad is a big believer in flexibility. Even though I'm winded, a smirk lifts the corners of my lips. Watching two-hundred-and-eighty-pound linebackers contort their bodies into Downward-Facing Dog, the Warrior II Pose, and the Cobra is enough to bring a chuckle to my lips. Some of the guys actually like it, but most grumble when they think Dad isn't paying attention. Little do they know that he sees and hears everything.

My father catches sight of me and flashes a quick smile along with a wave in my direction. He has a black ball cap pulled low and aviators covering his eyes. There's a clipboard in one hand as he paces behind the instructor.

When I point to the field, he shakes his head. He might make the guys do yoga, but he refuses to participate. Something about old dogs and new tricks. Every once in a while, I'll tell him that he needs to get out there and set a good example for the team. He usually shoots me a glare in return.

Every Wednesday night, Dad and I get together. Our weekly dinners became a thing when I moved out of the house and into the dorms freshman year. He's busy coaching football, and my schedule is packed tight with school and soccer. Getting together once a week is the best way for us to stay connected. It doesn't matter if we're in the middle of our seasons; we always make time for each other. Especially since Mom lives in sunny California. After eighteen years of marriage, she got fed up with being a distant second to the Western University football program. She packed up her bags and walked out. I hate to say it, but Dad didn't notice her absence for a couple of days. Which only proved her point. Now she's remarried, learning to surf, and is a vegan. I visit for a couple of weeks during the summer before soccer training camp starts up at the end of June.

Even though it's only the two of us, our weekly dinners are set for three people.

I tell myself to stare straight ahead and not glance in his direction.

Don't do it!

Don't you dare do it!

Damn.

My gaze reluctantly zeros in on him like a heat-seeking missile. Long blond hair, bright blue eyes, sun-kissed skin, and muscles for miles. And he's tall, somewhere around six foot three.

I'm describing none other than Rowan Michaels.

Otherwise known as the bane of my existence.

My dad discovered the talented quarterback the summer before we entered high school and took him under his wing. Which has been...aggravating. In the seven years since, Rowan has become an irritatingly permanent fixture in my life. He's the brother I never wanted or asked for. He's the gift I wish I could give back. He's the son my father never had but secretly longed for.

On a campus with over thirty thousand students, one would think that avoidance would be easy to accomplish. That hasn't turned out to be the case. Somehow, we ended up in the same major—Exercise Science. I get stuck in at least one class with the guy each semester. This time it's statistics, which is a requirement. Three times a week, I'm forced to see him. And then there are the weekly dinners at Dad's house.

Every Wednesday, Rowan shows up without fail.

It's so annoying.

No, *he's* annoying!

Our gazes collide, and electricity sizzles through my veins before I immediately snuff it out and pretend it never happened.

I am not attracted to Rowan Michaels.
I am not attracted to Rowan Michaels.
I am not attracted to Rowan Michaels.

Maybe if I repeat the mantra enough times, it'll be true. That's the hope I cling to. I've made it through the last seven years trying to convince myself of this. I only have to get through our final year together, and then we'll go our separate ways—me to graduate school or maybe to the Women's National Soccer League, and Rowan to the NFL. He's one of the most talented quarterbacks in the conference. Hell, probably the country. There is little doubt in my mind that he'll be a first-round draft pick come next spring.

Trust me when I say that Rowan Michaels fever is alive and well at Western University. His fanbase is legendary. The guy is a major player.

Both on and off the field.

Girls fall all over themselves to be with him. They fill the stands at football practice, show up at parties he's rumored to be at, and basically stalk him around campus.

It's a little nauseating. Don't these girls have any self-respect when it comes to a hot guy?

I wince at that unchecked thought.

Fine...I'll begrudgingly admit it; he's good-looking.

I shake my head as if that will banish the insidious thoughts currently invading my brain. Enough about Rowan. It's time to focus on the reason I'm at the stadium at this ungodly hour. I rip my gaze from him as I hit the cement staircase. After half a flight, all thoughts of the blond quarterback vanish from my mind. How could they not when my quads, glutes, and calves are on fire, screaming for mercy as I force myself to the nosebleed section. By the time I finish, my legs are Jell-O, and I still have a two-mile run back to the apartment I share with my best friend off-campus.

I give Dad a half-hearted wave before leaving. It's the most I can muster. His lips quirk at the corners as he shakes his head. He thinks I'm crazy. At the moment, I can't argue with his assessment of the situation. Although, it's the extra training I put in that helps me run circles around the other team in the second half of the game.

The jog home feels like it will last forever. By the time I unlock the apartment door, I'm ready to collapse. I beeline for the shower and jump in before it's fully warm. My skin prickles with goose flesh, but it feels so damn good. Twenty minutes later, I'm dressed and ready to take on the day. My hair has been thrown up in a messy bun, and I'm making a protein smoothie that will fuel me for my morning classes.

Just before taking off, I poke my head into Sydney's room. I know exactly how I'll find her, and that's buried beneath a small mountain of blankets. She doesn't disappoint. We met the summer before freshman year in training camp and have been besties ever since. She's the yin to my yang. The peanut butter to my jelly. The Thelma to my Louise. Where I'm more introverted and cautious, she's loud and boisterous. She's been known to leap without necessarily looking at what she's jumping into. Every so often, it gets us into trouble. Sydney and I have lived together since sophomore year. I gave up trying to cajole her ass out of bed for a six o'clock run after the first week of us cohabitating when she nearly took my head off with an alarm clock.

"It's that time again," I sing-song obnoxiously, "rise and shine."

There's a grunt and then some shifting from under the blankets that tells me she's alive.

When I chant her name repeatedly, each time escalating in volume, she growls, "Get the fuck out!"

"Awww," I mock, "that's so sweet. I love you, too."

Sydney snorts before a hand snakes out from beneath the blankets to give me a one-fingered salute. Then she grabs a pillow and tosses it in my general vicinity. It falls about five feet short of its mark.

I stare at the dismal attempt. "If you're trying to cause bodily harm, you'll have to do better than that."

"Piss off."

"All right then." I shrug. "See you after class." With that, I close the door behind me.

My farewell is met with another indecipherable mouthful. If this weren't something we went through on the daily, I'd worry she was in the midst of a stroke. Sydney is definitely not a morning person. She's more of an early afternoon person. Another thing I've learned over the years? The action of waking up to a brand-new day is a gradual process.

She's like a bear rousing prematurely from hibernation. It's not a pretty sight. She's lucky I don't take her insults personally.

I grab my backpack from the small table crammed into the break-fast nook area along with a coffee before heading out the door. The apartment I share with Sydney is located three blocks from campus, which is highly sought out real estate. We're fortunate Dad is friends with the guy who manages the building. It's probably one of the only perks of having a father who is a head coach of a college football team.

You'd think there would be more, but you'd be wrong. Honestly, being Nick Richard's daughter is more of a hindrance than anything else. People assume you receive special treatment on campus, from professors, or that you have an in with all the football players.

Or worse...

Much worse.

After a bunch of ugly—not to mention untrue—rumors circulated freshman year, I've done my best to distance myself from the Wildcats football team. They're a great bunch of guys, but I don't need all the ugly gossip and speculation that comes along with being friends with them.

As I reach Corbin Hall, the mathematics building for my stats class, my gaze is drawn to a clump of students standing around outside the three-story, red-brick building. In the center of that crowd is Rowan. I don't have to see him physically to know that he's close. The muscles in my belly contract with awareness. It's like a sixth sense. One I wish would go away. He's the last person I want to be cognizant of.

As I jog up the wide stone stairs to the entrance, my gaze fastens on him. A smirk twists the edges of his lips, and my eyes narrow before I drag them away and yank open the door to the building. Relief rushes through me as I step inside the air conditioning and disappear from sight.

"Hey, Demi, wait up!"

I turn at the sound of my name before slowing my step. The dark-haired guy jogging to catch up smiles before falling in line with me.

Justin Fischer.

He's a baseball player and teammates with Sydney's boyfriend,

Ethan. We've been seeing each other for about a month. It's still casual at this point. With school and soccer, I don't have a ton of time to invest in a relationship. He seems to understand that and isn't pushing to be more serious.

When he leans in for a kiss, I angle my head. At the last moment, he tilts in the opposite direction, and we end up bumping teeth instead of locking lips. With a grunt, I pull away and chuckle. My fingers fly to my mouth to make sure I haven't chipped a tooth.

Maybe I've been reluctant to admit it to myself, but that kiss sums up our relationship perfectly.

Awkward and a step out of sync with each other.

"Sorry," he murmurs with a slight smile. I search his face and wait for any telltale sign of sexual chemistry to ping inside me. Unfortunately, my insides remain completely unfazed, which is disappointing but not altogether unexpected. I had a sneaking suspicion when we first got together that it might turn out this way.

"No problem," I say, hoisting my smile and brushing aside those thoughts.

"I haven't seen you for a couple of days," he remarks as we turn a corner and continue walking.

"It's been busy." Which isn't a lie. School might have recently started, but the academics at Western are rigorous. And being a Division I athlete is more like a job. If you're not ready to put in the work, don't bother showing up. There's no half-assing it around this place.

"When's your next game?" he asks.

"Tomorrow at six." My gaze flickers in his direction. Not that I expect him to come, but...

Fine, so maybe I do. If he wants to be my boyfriend, then he needs to show a little support.

His dark brows draw together. "That sucks. I've got a mandatory study hour I have to attend."

I shrug off the disappointment. It's another nail in the coffin of this relationship as far as I'm concerned. "That's cool. It's not a big deal."

"But I'll see you tonight?"

Oh. Right.

Tonight.

Well, damn. In a moment of weakness, I threw out an invitation to join our Wednesday evening dinner. It's one I now regret. If only there were a gracious way to rescind the offer.

"If you're busy, I totally understand—"

"Are you kidding? No way." With a grin, he shakes his head. "I wouldn't miss it for the world. I'm looking forward to meeting Coach Richards."

Great. So this is more about my father than me? Exactly what every girl wants to hear.

I force a brittle smile. "Awesome. He's excited, too."

That might be something of an overstatement.

Justin nods toward the end of the corridor. "I better get moving. Professor Andrews is a real stickler for punctuality."

"Yup. See you later."

This time, when he leans in, our lips align perfectly. The kiss is nothing more than a fleeting caress. There and gone before I can sink into it.

And I'm left feeling...absolutely nothing.

I bury the disappointment where I can't inspect it too closely before giving him a wave as he takes off. For a moment, I stand rooted in the hallway and watch as he disappears through the crowd. There's nothing to distinguish Justin from the thousands of guys who look exactly like him on campus. He's of average height and build with dark hair and espresso-colored eyes. He's nice enough. Although, if I'm completely honest, he's a little self-absorbed. He talks about baseball all the time. If Ethan hadn't introduced us, he's not someone I would have looked twice at. We don't have a ton in common.

As much as I hate to admit it, this relationship has probably reached its expiration date.

Now it's a matter of pulling the plug.

Ugh. I hate breakups. Although, it's doubtful this will end up destroying him. I'll have to make it through tonight and figure out the rest.

With a sigh of resignation, I head to the classroom and find a seat tucked away in the far corner of the small lecture hall. A lanky guy I recognize from a few of my other classes settles beside me. He flashes a dimpled smile as we empty our backpacks.

The tiny hair at the nape of my neck rises seconds before Rowan enters the room. It's like my body knows when he's within a thirty-foot radius. I glance at him from beneath the thick fringe of my lashes before shifting away. Air becomes wedged in my lungs as I wait for him to take a seat. And it won't be next to me because I'm—

"Hey man, would you mind moving?"

Surrounded on both sides.

Damnit. I'm hoping the cutie next to me will tell Rowan to go take a flying leap.

What? It could happen. Not everyone at this university is enamored of the football-playing god. Although I realize the odds aren't stacked in my favor. Rowan is the most recognized athlete on campus. People fall all over themselves to accommodate him.

It's a little sickening.

Okay, maybe more than a little.

"Sure, no problem, Michaels." The guy next to me hastily packs up his books before vacating the desk. Unable to ignore him any longer, I glare as Rowan slides onto the seat next to me.

"Did you really think you could evade me that easily?" Laughter brims in his deep voice. A voice, I might add, that does funny things to my insides.

"One can always hope, right?"

"Oh, answering a question with a question." He leans closer, eating up some of the much-needed distance between us. "I like it."

I roll my eyes as his lips stretch into a satisfied grin. Irritation bubbles up inside me when sexual tension blooms at the bottom of my belly. Or maybe that tension has settled a little lower.

It's definitely lower.

I'm tempted to swear like a sailor. How is it possible that I feel nothing for the guy I'm actually dating, and yet my pulse skitters out of control for someone I don't even like? It's so freaking ironic. It's been this way since we met, and nothing I do stomps it out. I can try to fool myself into believing it's not there, but that doesn't make it any less true.

It's a relief when Professor Peters takes his place at the podium and clears his throat. Once he's captured everyone's attention, he delves headfirst into the probability of dependent and independent events.

Grateful for the excuse to ignore Rowan for the next fifty minutes, I open my textbook and concentrate on the lesson. Just as the blond boy fades into the background, his bare knee bumps into mine. Electricity ricochets through my entire being. I glance at him to see if he's noticed the strange energy we always seem to generate and find his ocean-colored gaze fastened to mine.

My guess is that he does.

Damnation.

Chapter Two

DEMI

"All right, folks, I think I've imparted enough information on you for one morning. I can see that your brains are on the verge of exploding. Please remember that today's assignment needs to be turned in online by midnight. Late work will be downgraded fifty percent."

A chorus of grumbles and groans follow that announcement.

Professor Peters lips twitch in amusement. It's no secret that he doesn't give a damn whether students pass or fail this course. Statistics is a requirement for all health science degrees. If you don't understand the material and refuse to seek out help, you're screwed and doomed to repeat it. Over and over and over again. And Professor P is the only instructor who teaches this specific course.

I've heard tales of students having to retake his class three or four times to eke out a passing grade. That would be seriously soul-sucking. Luckily, I've always been advanced in mathematics and took statistics in high school. So far, we're a couple of weeks in, and I haven't found this class to be a challenge. I've got an A.

By the time Professor Peters dismisses us for the day, I've packed up my belongings and am ready to bolt from the room. I need to escape from Rowan's presence. I was ridiculously aware of him the entire period.

What makes no sense is that there's a group of girls in this class who constantly fight for his attention. If the guy is looking to get laid, he needs to explore other options. Instead, he ignores them and sits next to me every time.

It's maddening.

Without a word, I haul my backpack onto my shoulder and wiggle past him. As I make it to the aisle, a puff of relief escapes from my lungs, and I take the carpeted staircase two at a time. A few people say hello as I fly through the double doors and into the already crowded hallway. The more space I'm able to put between myself and Rowan, the sooner I can find my equilibrium. Rowan Michaels has the nasty habit of throwing it off every single time. I'm unwilling to examine the reason for that.

The guy is totally annoying.

Case closed.

Midway down the corridor, my shoulders loosen from around my ears. The rest of the day should run smoothly from here on out. As soon as that thought pops into my head, a muscular arm is thrown around my shoulders, and I'm hauled against a hard body. A clean fresh scent, which is a strange concoction of sunshine and the ocean, is a dead giveaway as to who has a firm hold on me. It's one that is purely Rowan Michaels.

Damn.

Damn.

Damn.

This guy will seriously be the death of me. Just like he taunted an hour earlier, I should have realized he wouldn't let me escape that easily.

"Hey, you took off before I could ask if you needed a ride to dinner."

A kernel of dread fills my belly and I'm not sure why. It's not like we're going out, and we're certainly not friends. Not really. I can barely tolerate the guy. So, what does it matter if I tell him about Justin joining our threesome tonight?

I wince. That just sounded plain wrong.

I suck my lower lip into my mouth and gnaw on it. Rowan is going to find out sooner or later, so what does it matter if it turns out to be sooner? Already I know that he won't be thrilled with the slight deviation from our normally set plans.

"That's not necessary." I clear my throat and brace myself for his reaction. "Justin is going to pick me up."

Uncomfortable silence rains down on us as he digests that bit of news. It goes over exactly the way I suspected.

Like a lead balloon.

"Wait a minute," the smile disappears only to be replaced by a scowl, "you invited *Justin* to dinner?"

"Yeah," I mutter, unwilling to add that it's an offer I now regret, "I did."

"Why would you do that?"

Good question. Clearly it was an error in judgment on my part. But I won't be admitting that to Rowan.

"He hasn't met Dad yet." The thought of that occurring makes me queasy. My father has the tendency to go into over-protective mode, which is precisely why he isn't introduced to most of the guys I go out with.

Now I'm having second thoughts.

More like third and fourth thoughts.

Unfortunately, the wheels have already been set in motion, and it's too late to cancel our plans.

"So...this *thing* between you two is pretty serious?" He sounds decidedly unhappy about the predicament.

I remain silent, reluctant to confess the truth. It's none of Rowan's business who I date. Just like it's none of mine who he bangs. In the three years we've been at Western, not once have I heard of Rowan settling down with a girl. But I've heard a shit ton of gossip regarding his sexual conquests. Every Monday morning, there's a new set of salacious stories floating around campus.

That thought makes me as nauseous as introducing Justin to Dad. Maybe a little more.

Needing to distance myself from Rowan, I shrug in hopes of dislodging his arm. It doesn't work. If anything, he only tightens his hold. Most girls would be thrilled by his attention. They would be burrowing against the solid strength of his chest. Admittedly, I have to fight my own body's natural inclination to do exactly that.

He turns his face until his warm breath can feather across the delicate shell of my ear. I have to steel myself against the shivers that attempt to skitter down my spine. "You didn't answer the question."

"I guess so." That's a lie, but since he can't prove otherwise, I'm sticking to it like my life depends on it. More like my mental state.

"Hmmm. That didn't sound very convincing." His grip intensifies. "Want to give it another shot?"

I swivel toward him, not realizing how close we are. It doesn't take much to get lost in the various shades of blue that dance in his irises.

Rowan has gorgeous eyes.

It's one of the first features that snagged my attention. They're so watchful. As if he sees everything going on around him and there's no hiding. It's the directness of his examination that makes my insides tremble. I don't want him to catch a glimpse of the feelings I've buried within. I don't want him to realize how much he affects me. Or how much willpower it takes to fight the magnetic pull I feel toward him.

As we reach the glass doors that lead into the fresh air, Rowan pushes it open before we move down the short stone staircase. We don't make it more than four steps before he's swarmed by a handful of girls. As the crowd surges around him, I slip from beneath his arm and hightail it down the pathway that winds through campus.

"Demi," his deep voice resonates over the chatter of voices.

Unable to stop myself, I glance back until our gazes collide. A surge of unwanted jealousy gnaws at my insides as jersey chasers paw at him like he's a piece of fresh meat thrown into a den of starving lions. It's equal measures aggravating and disturbing that he's the only one able to make my pulse race in this manner. This campus has tens of thousands of people on it. There has to be at least one other guy who can provoke the same kind of reaction from me.

I just need to find him. Then I can stop thinking about the blond quarterback.

"I'll see you tonight."

I gulp.

Why does that sound more like a threat than anything else?

Not bothering to answer, I force my gaze away before fleeing from the vicinity like the hounds of hell are nipping at my heels. It's only when I'm a block away that I'm able to once again find my equilibrium. The only way I'll make it through the rest of the day is to force all thoughts of Rowan from my head.

Unfortunately, that's easier said than done.

Chapter Three

DEMI

A couple of hours later, I shove the key in the lock and push open the apartment door. Even before it swings wide, loud voices assult my ears. Honestly, if I didn't need to stop at home before practice, I would carefully back away.

"That's not what I said," Ethan grumbles. "You're putting words in my mouth again."

"Ha!" Sydney snaps. "Do you think I'm deaf?"

Uh-oh.

If Ethan has any sense, he'll proceed with extreme caution when answering that question. Kind of like a bomb tech handling explosives that could detonate at any second.

Ugh. My guess is that Ethan and Sydney are at it again. They've only been dating for four months, and I've already lost track of how many times they've broken up and gotten back together again. I was over their drama after the first few times it happened. It's a vicious cycle that neither seem willing to pull the trigger on. Hell, I'd be more than happy to end it for them if they'd let me. They need to go their separate ways and never look in each other's direction again.

Individually, they're both great people. I love them.

As a couple?

They are a total nightmare.

"You know what? Forget this," Ethan yells, not bothering to answer her question which is probably the shrewdest move he could make. "I'm out of here! Call me when you calm down, and we're able to have a civil conversation!"

I peek around the doorframe before reluctantly inching my way inside. I'm just in time to see Sydney rear back as if she's been slapped.

Her fists settle on her hips. "Excuse me? Are you implying I can't hold a civil conversation?" From where I loiter in the tiny entryway, I'm able to see the sparks of anger that flash in her vibrant, grass-colored eyes.

The last thing I want is to be pulled into another one of their arguments. Been there, done that way too many times to count.

Ethan plows a hand through his short blond hair before his shoulders slump. "I'm gonna go. We'll talk later when we've both calmed down."

Instead of waiting for a response, he stalks toward the door, passing me on the way out. I give him a tentative smile in greeting.

"Hey, Demi," he mumbles before closing the door behind him.

"Bye." By the time I raise my hand to wave, he's gone, already disappearing into the hallway. I turn toward my friend. "Um—"

"Yes, we broke up," she snaps before I can ask.

"I'm sorry?" It's more of a question at this point. From one day to the next, I'm never sure if these two are a couple or not. It's exhausting, and it's not even my relationship. I'm a spectator—or maybe hostage would be a more accurate term—sitting on the sidelines, trying not to be hit by friendly fire.

My bestie rolls her eyes before throwing herself onto the couch in our living room. "I think we're really over this time."

Sure...whatever you say, crazy.

Sydney says this every time they have a fight. After a few days of separation, they somehow find their way back to one another. Kind of like a guard and an escaped prisoner with a tracking device. It's maddening. They can't be together, and yet, they can't be apart. I have no idea what they'll do, and I've stopped doling out unsolicited advice that goes unheeded.

I've come to the disturbing conclusion that the two of them are gluttons for punishment.

How else do you explain the constant drama?

"What happened this time?" The question pops out of my mouth before I can rein it in again. My backpack is set on the table before I plop down on the chair and settle in across from her. We've got roughly thirty minutes before practice. Their fight probably lasted ten minutes tops, but the dissection of it will take four times that long.

Sydney wrinkles her nose as she squints at the ceiling. "You know what? I don't even remember what started it."

Not surprising.

"I just know he doesn't get me," she continues.

"Then maybe this breakup is for the best," I say gently, hoping the remainder of senior year doesn't follow the same pattern that has already been set. If so, I might end up moving home, and I really don't want to do that. As much as I love my dad, we need our own space.

"Maybe. We'll see." Sydney rolls onto her belly and rests her chin on clasped hands before waggling her brows at me. "So...dinner with daddy tonight, huh?"

"Ewww!" I scrunch my face at her wordage. "That's gross. Rephrase, please."

"What's wrong?" She grins as her shoulders shake with unconcealed mirth. "You didn't like that?"

"God, no. In fact, I just threw up a little bit in my mouth." I'm not kidding either. Every once in a while, Sydney likes to torment me by talking about how good looking my father is. When that happens, I go into self-protective mode and tune out the conversation. I suspect she does it more to rile me up than anything else. At least, I hope that's the reason.

"I can't believe you're bringing Justin to dinner. It hasn't even been that long. I can't remember the last guy you brought home to meet Coach." She eyes me speculatively. "You must really like him."

I bite my lower lip and shake my head.

Her brows skyrocket. "Seriously?"

"Yeah."

"I don't understand." She pauses for a beat. "Why did you invite him to dinner if you're not into the guy?"

It's an excellent question. One I don't have an answer for. I give her the best response I've got. Even if it doesn't make sense. "In the moment, it felt right. But now? Not so much."

"Well, that'll be uncomfortable. I can just imagine it—Coach, Rowan, Justin, and you. All sitting around the dinner table getting to know one another."

Ugh. She's right.

"That sounds horrific." I slump on the chair, dreading the evening ahead before perking up enough to ask, "Hey! Want to come and help run interference? You'll get a hot meal out of it."

"Hell, no. I've had your dad's cooking enough times to know that it's not worth the price of admission," she says with a laugh. "Sorry, you're on your own with that one."

"Bitch," I mutter.

Her shoulders shake with undisguised amusement as she steers us back to the original topic. "What happened to change your mind about Justin? I thought everything was going well."

I shrug, unwilling to tell her that the one guy who makes my heart beat into overdrive isn't necessarily the one I'm going out with. There is nothing about Justin that makes me want to know him on a deeper level. And that's a problem.

"Oh, come on, there must be *something*."

My gaze shifts to the picture window that overlooks the tree-filled courtyard. "I thought it might take some time to feel a spark, but so far, it hasn't happened, and after a month, I've lost hope that it will."

"You know better than that. Sparks are instantaneous. They're either there or they aren't." Still sprawled on her belly, Sydney swings her bare legs back and forth.

Reluctantly, I acknowledge she's spot-on with her assessment. Even the memory of Rowan throwing his arm around my shoulders and hauling me close is enough to make my pulse skitter out of control.

Not wanting to dwell on it, I shove those thoughts away before they can infect my brain like a deadly virus. I've got enough to deal with tonight. The last thing I need is to invite more complications.

And Rowan is nothing if not a complication.

One I can't afford.

Chapter Four

DEMI

Justin parks his Honda Civic in front of the two-story brick residence I spent my childhood in. After the divorce, Dad considered downsizing, since it was only the two of us, but I begged him not to. There's something comforting about the knowledge that you can go back to the house you grew up in. Even though my parents are no longer together, and the divorce was hard on all of us, our home was a happy one, and I have a ton of fond memories. Plus, I love the rectangle-shaped pool in the backyard. It's always nice to pop over in the summer and take a dip after soccer practice.

Justin reaches over and lays his fingers across mine. I wait for a little buzz of sensation. Any indication that will sway me into giving him one last shot. Other than the slight clamminess from his perspiring hand, there's nothing. "You ready to do this?"

Nope, not at all. Instead of admitting that I've made an epic mistake, I nod and hoist my smile.

After he releases my hand and exits the vehicle, I swipe my palm across my thigh before giving myself a quick pep talk and doing the same. As we meet on the sidewalk, I smooth down the navy-colored shorts I've paired with a cap sleeved white floral wrap top.

Butterflies wing their way to life within the confines of my belly.

The nervousness crashing around inside me is ridiculous. This isn't the first boy I've brought home and introduced to my father. Although, admittedly, it's been a while. Most of the guys I've gone out with get irritated when I'm not available to hang out at their whim. If they are athletes, then their schedule is as jam-packed as mine, and the relationship ends up fizzling out on its own.

Sometimes it feels like a lose-lose situation.

"You look seriously hot," Justin says, interrupting the whirl of my thoughts.

"Thanks." I glance at my outfit. What I'm wearing isn't dressy, it's just not my usual athletic shorts paired with a T-shirt.

He gives me a wink and a grin before clasping my hand again. I wince as his damp palm comes in contact with my skin and resist the urge to tug it away. Hand in hand, we walk up the brick path to the front door. I rap my knuckles against the wood before pushing it open and stepping inside the entryway. As I glance around, my gaze lands on Dad and Rowan. They're sitting on the couch, heads bent together as Dad draws out plays on the whiteboard.

I almost roll my eyes. There is never a time when these two aren't talking football.

Dad glances up. "Hey, honey!" When I raise my brows, a sheepish smile breaks out across his face, and he tosses the dry erase marker onto the coffee table before rising to his feet. "Just squeezing in a little chalk talk."

And this would be exhibit A as to why Mom walked out five years ago and never looked back. As much as I love my father, I can't blame her for wanting to be with a man who was capable of leaving his work at the office. Or, in my dad's case, on the football field.

My father's gaze slides from mine to the guy at my side before he steps forward and extends a hand to shake. "Nice to meet you, Justin. Demi's told me a lot about you."

Actually, I've been very tight-lipped about our relationship. In all honesty, there hasn't been much to say. And after tonight, there will be even less.

From the corner of my eye, Rowan rises to his feet before making his way over to us.

"It's a pleasure to meet you as well, sir. Thanks for inviting me to dinner."

"We're happy to have you." Dad lays a hand on Rowan's shoulder as if he's the proud papa. "I'm sure you already know who this guy is."

You would have to live under a rock not to realize who Rowan is, and even then, if you had access to the internet, you'd probably still recognize him. At Western, he's treated like a celebrity with all the perks that come with his fame. There are huge posters of him plastered everywhere on campus. You can't go anywhere without seeing his handsome face.

I mean ugly mug.

"Of course." Justin extends a hand to Rowan. "Good to see you, man."

The blond football player gives him a chin lift in acknowledgment.

I can't help but compare the two as they stand next to one another. Even though Justin is four or five inches taller than I am, he's still a handful of inches shorter than Rowan. And where Rowan has thick, chiseled muscles, Justin is leaner. Almost boyish.

Wait a minute...what the hell am I doing?

The moment I realize that I'm comparing them, I shove those disturbing thoughts from my brain. There's no reason to do that. And I don't even want to acknowledge that Justin has come up sadly lacking in the evaluation.

Ugh. This evening can't be over with quickly enough.

"Dinner should be ready in about twenty minutes," Dad says, surprising me when he throws an arm around Justin's shoulders. "I was thinking the two of us could have a little chat in the study and get to know one another better. What do you say, buddy?"

Buddy?

That doesn't bode well.

"Oh." Unease flickers across Justin's face before his gaze settles on mine. I get the feeling he's looking for me to throw him a lifeline. "Um, sure."

"Is that really necessary?" I ask with a scowl.

"Of course it is, sweetie. I want to make sure Justin has the right intentions as far as my little girl is concerned."

How is it possible this situation went from bad to worse in two seconds flat?

"Dad..." I groan. "If I'd known you were going to give Justin the third degree, I wouldn't have brought him to dinner."

"I guess you'll know better next time." He chuckles before slapping Justin on the back. The dark-haired baseball player stumbles forward before quickly righting himself. "Calm down, I'm kidding. I have no intention of hurting the boy." There's a pause. "*Yet.*"

Silence descends before Dad barks out another laugh. "I'm joking! Sheesh. Everyone is so serious. There's no reason for concern." The smile drops off his face as he narrows his eyes at the baseball player. "There's no reason to be concerned, is there, Justin?"

Justin shakes his head. "No, sir."

"Good."

This was a mistake.

Before I can offer up a protest, Dad steers my date from the living room into the study, sealing them inside his home office. I jump when the lock clicks into place and gape at the closed door for about twenty seconds. I'm tempted to stalk over and bang on the wood until Dad opens it so I can drag Justin out again.

I never should have brought him home. This will definitely be the last time it happens. The only guy Dad doesn't mind having around is—

I glance at the tall boy with the long blond hair.

Boy is probably the wrong term to use as a descriptor. Rowan Michaels is definitely all man.

Please tell me I didn't just think that.

Guilty.

Oh, so guilty.

"So," he says, stuffing his hands deep inside the pockets of his khaki shorts.

I clear my throat, unable to rip my gaze from his. I'm caught in the crosshairs of those ocean blue depths. It's disconcerting. "So."

He points to the couch. "Want to sit down?"

My brow furrows as I throw another concerned glance toward the study. "I guess." Hesitantly I move toward the well-worn tan microfiber couch that has seen better days before settling gingerly at one end. Instead of sitting at the opposite side, so there's a fair amount of distance between us, Rowan drops down next to me. He's so close that his thigh grazes mine. A little zing of unwanted attraction scampers down my spine, and I grit my teeth in a feeble attempt to ignore the sensation.

Over the years, I've made it a point to never be alone with Rowan. Now that I am, I have no idea what to do. I search my brain for something to say, but it comes up empty. The silence that stretches only ratchets up my nerves.

It's almost a relief when he says, "Big game tomorrow, huh?"

Whatever you do, don't look at him.

Even though I tell myself to resist the temptation, it's like an involuntary reflex. Staring at Rowan feels suspiciously like gazing at the sun. It's dangerous to my health. Any moment, my retinas will turn to dust.

"Yup." I fiddle nervously with the hem of my shorts, wishing they stretched further down my legs. "UNC."

"I've watched a little bit of game film," he throws out casually. "Lookout for number fifty-five, and you'll do fine."

My eyes widen before flicking to his. "You watched game film?"

Of soccer?

Why would he do that?

His admission sends a cascade of warmth flooding through me. It takes everything I have inside to stomp it out.

He shrugs, and his muscles dance beneath his T-shirt. "I had a little time between classes, and I was curious to see what UNC looked like this season."

I...have no response to that.

"One of their midfielders, number thirty-one, is out with an injury."

Ummm...yeah, I know. Coach and I had a lengthy discussion about it this afternoon. I just never expected him to realize it, too. I blink and attempt to regain my equilibrium. At every turn, Rowan manages to throw me off-balance. He shifts, stretching his arm across the back of the couch. When the tips of his fingers brush against my shoulder, it sends a thousand tiny shivers scurrying across my flesh.

What the hell is going on here?

Why is my body reacting like this?

"It won't be an easy win," he continues, as if unaware of the anxiety spiking through me, "but I think you guys will pull it off in the end if you play with an offensive strategy in mind."

Soccer.

Right.

We're discussing soccer. Tomorrow's game, to be specific.

Focus, Demi!

I blink, attempting to rein in all the strange, out of control feelings he stirs up inside me.

Nope. I can't do it. I can't sit here and nonchalantly shoot the shit with Rowan. He makes me nervous. Twitchy. I have a difficult time concentrating when he's this close. More than anything, I don't want to feel this way about him.

Before I realize it, I'm popping off the couch like a Jack-in-the-Box and jumping to my feet. "I need something to drink." That being said, I race out of the living room like my ass is on fire. "Want anything?"

"Nah, I'm good."

I don't have to turn around to realize there's a smile lighting up his face as I haul ass to the kitchen. Once there, I exhale and attempt to collect myself.

This is ridiculous.

I am *not* attracted to Rowan.

I don't even like the guy!

What?

It's true, I don't!

My nerves are jangled because Dad has sequestered Justin in the study, and I can only imagine the kind of grilling that is taking place. I rub my temples and suppress the groan fighting to break free. I really hope he hasn't opened the safe and brought out his rifle in an attempt to scare Justin.

He did that once before. Other than my father, no one else found it the least bit amusing.

It takes a few minutes to lock down all of the emotions rushing around inside me. If Dad isn't out of the office in approximately three minutes, I'm storming the room and busting Justin out. With a firm game plan in mind, everything inside me settles as I yank open the refrigerator door and grab a bottle of water before slamming it shut again.

I spin around, only to find Rowan standing a foot away. A squeak of surprise escapes from me. He's so close that one step would have me bumping into the wide expanse of his chest. The plastic water bottle gets bumbled, falling to the hardwood at my feet before rolling away.

Rowan doesn't release my gaze as he drops to the floor. I'm held spellbound as he reaches out and grabs the bottle before straightening to his full height. Only then does he hold it out for me to take.

When I remain frozen in place, he smiles. "I changed my mind about that drink."

The deep scrape of his voice jostles me from my paralysis, and I reach out, nipping the plastic from him before stumbling in retreat. It's only a step before my back hits the stainless-steel door. Electricity crackles in the air as he moves closer, invading my personal space until his warm exhalation is able to feather across my lips. I flatten against the fridge as my heart pumps painfully.

His gaze holds mine captive as he yanks open one of the doors. His forearm brushes against me as he reaches inside and grabs a water. His chest is so close that I feel the suffocating heat wafting off him. Once the bottle is wrapped in his fingers, he closes the door but doesn't back away. He continues to crowd me. When my tongue darts out to moisten my lips, his attention drops to the movement. The black of his pupils dilate, and a punch of arousal hits me.

For a sliver of a moment, I wonder if he'll close the distance and kiss me. Only now am I willing to acknowledge how much I want to feel the soft pressure of his lips coasting over mine. Maybe I've always wanted it. This isn't something I've ever allowed myself to admit. Not even privately.

Especially privately.

Everything in me becomes whipcord tight as I wait for what will happen next. It's the opening of the study door that shatters the tension-filled silence that has fallen over us and knocks me out of the thick Rowan-induced haze.

Holy crap!

The air escapes from my lungs in a rush as I duck beneath his arm and flee to the safety of the living room where Dad waits with Justin. My gaze arrows to the dark-haired boy, and I feel—

Nothing.

It's disappointing but not surprising. It only solidifies my decision to pull the plug on this relationship sooner rather than later. From the corner of my eye, I notice the smirk on Rowan's face. It's like the bastard knows exactly what I'm thinking and couldn't agree more.

My shoulders collapse.

There's only one thing I know for certain and that's tonight will be a long-ass night.

Chapter Five

DEMI

Can you stop by the office when you get a chance?

I glance at the text from Dad before pocketing my cell phone as I head from my last class for the afternoon and onto the cement walkway that winds through campus. It's three o'clock, and I need to go home, grab something to eat, and get my butt to the field.

Lucky for Dad, I pass by the stadium on my way home. Less than ten minutes later, I'm strolling down the corridor. One left and then a right turn brings me to the guy's locker room where Dad's office is located. The moment I pull open the door, boisterous male voices greet my ears. That might deter some girls from stepping inside, but not me. A quick scan of the interior solidifies my suspicion that the team has just finished up practice. There are guys in various states of undress. Some already have underwear on while others have small white towels draped around their waists. I catch sight of a few naked ass cheeks before jerking my gaze straight ahead.

"Hey, Demi!" a few guys call out, unconcerned with their nudity. That just goes to show you the difference between males and females. Most girls I know wouldn't willingly parade around in front of the opposite sex.

I throw up my hand in a quick wave, not bothering to glance in their direction. I've been in the locker room dozens of times. It's not really a big deal. I've known these guys since freshman year, so most of the players see me as one of the boys.

Coach's daughter.

As I move past another set of lockers, that telltale tingle of awareness scampers down my spine. There's only one person capable of instilling that kind of sensation in me. I don't have to glance over to confirm my suspicions.

Although that doesn't stop my eyes from snapping in his direction. What I find is the blond quarterback lounging in front of his locker with a small towel wrapped across lean hips. His attention fastens on me, and I feel the connection straight down to my toes. Almost as if it's a physical caress. Before I can stop myself, my gaze dips to his bare chest.

Damn.

Why does he have to be so gorgeous?

The sculpted, sinewy strength that stands out in sharp relief is enough to make my mouth turn cottony. How is it possible that his muscles have muscles?

All of the raucous laughter falls away as my focus drifts from perfect pectorals to tight washboard abdominals. It's like I'm having my own not-so-private moment with him. Even though I'm wearing shorts and a thin cotton T-shirt, my body is seconds away from bursting into flames. I'm tempted to pick up the collar of my shirt and pull it away from my chest in an attempt to cool myself.

My attention sinks to the towel, and I narrow my eyes, wishing for the first time in my life I had X-ray vision.

What the hell am I doing?

Mortified by my shameless perusal, I rip my gaze away and race into my father's office before slamming the door and collapsing against it. My inhalations turn labored as I squeeze my eyes shut in an attempt to banish the nearly naked image of Rowan from my mind.

It doesn't work. The last minute has been singed into my memory for all eternity. And my panties...yeah, they are embarrassingly damp.

"Hey, sweetheart," Dad says, knocking me out of those disturbing thoughts.

My eyelids fly open, locking on him. Thank God he can't see the X-rated images rolling through my head. The man would have a heart attack if he realized I was sexually attracted to his star quarterback.

We've always been more like siblings who barely tolerate one another. All right, so maybe that's not a hundred percent true. I'm the one with a problem, not the other way around. Rowan doesn't seem to have an issue with me.

It would be so much better if he did.

It takes everything I have inside to shove those thoughts away and paste a smile on my face. "Hey, Dad."

"Thanks for stopping by on such short notice." He shuffles around a few documents on a desk exploding with paperwork. He tells me there is a method to his madness. I think he's full of crap. He grabs the remote from a drawer and clicks off the game film he's been watching. The man must pour over a hundred hours of film each week. He's obsessed. It's what makes him one of the best coaches in Division I football. It's also what makes him a terrible husband, which is precisely why he's still single after being divorced for five years. Mom is now happily married to a man who caters to her every whim.

"It wasn't a problem. I've got a couple of hours before the game."

"Yup," he sits back on his swivel chair and folds his hands behind his head, "I'll be there. Should be a good one."

A fresh wave of nerves slide through me. I always get ramped up before a match, especially when we're playing UNC. They are a Division I powerhouse who have had a number of players turn pro. Playing for a professional women's team has been my goal since I was a little girl. With scouts in the stands, there's a lot riding on today's game. As soon as that thought enters my mind, I shove it away. If I focus on it, I'll end up psyching myself out. And I can't allow the pressure to get to me.

"You'll be great," Dad says, voice filled with conviction as if sensing my sudden burst of anxiety.

"Thanks." I've done everything possible to prepare myself for this evening's match. Now I just have to get out there and let instinct take over. "Why did you want to see me?"

"Right!" He drops his arms and sits forward, closing the distance between us as he sifts through a small mountain of paper before opening up a manilla folder and glancing at the top sheet. "I know you've got a lot going on this semester, but would you have time to work with one of the players?"

"For which class?" In the three years I've been at Western, I've tutored half a dozen guys. I'm a four-point student, academics have always come easy to me.

"Statistics."

A prickle of unease flares to life in the pit of my belly as I push away from the door and slide onto the chair parked in front of his desk before dropping my backpack to the linoleum tiled floor.

Before I can respond, he quickly adds, "It would only be a couple hours a week for about a month or so. Just enough time to make sure he is over the hump. And you're so good at math..."

Dad wouldn't ask unless it was absolutely necessary. While I don't have a ton of extra time, carving out a few hours a week shouldn't be a hassle. "Sure, I can probably work something out."

"Great!" A relieved smile breaks out across his face. "You know what it's like trying to find someone who is actually interested in tutoring rather than talking football."

It's not the *talking football* that turns out to be the problem. It's the girls who are interested in hooking up with a football player and then trying to turn it into a bona fide relationship. It's an occupational hazard that comes with being an athlete at a school obsessed with everything football. And that certainly won't help with eligibility requirements.

I grab my backpack from the floor and rise to my feet, ready to take off.

"Hey," he says, "I really enjoyed meeting Jackson last night."

I narrow my eyes and wonder if the name slip is purposeful. "It's Justin."

"Right." He points a finger at me. "*Justin.* Anyway, I really enjoyed meeting him. Seemed like a nice guy. You should bring him around more often."

"Really?" My forehead furrows. This...isn't what I was expecting to hear from him. Normally, when I introduce Dad to a potential boyfriend, he nitpicks, finding something not to like about the guy.

I'm not going to lie, I'm a little thrown off by his easy-going demeanor.

With a grin, he lounges back in his chair again. "Yup. I really enjoyed our chat in the study."

"You did?" With a frown, I drop my chin and search his face for any indication that he's messing with me.

"Sure." Innocence enters his dark eyes. "Why wouldn't I?"

Hmmm. Something feels off about this conversation. "I don't know. Normally you don't like the guys I introduce you to." Which is precisely why I don't do it unless I'm certain they'll be around long-term. Most of the time, it's not worth the hassle.

Last night's dinner went well enough. On the surface, everyone got along fine. It was the undercurrents that almost suffocated me. Specifically, with Rowan. Even though I refused to make eye contact after what transpired in the kitchen, I could feel his gaze crawling over me the entire evening. It was a relief when eight o'clock rolled around, and we got the hell out of there.

"Will Jasper be at the game tonight?"

"Justin," I correct automatically, blinking out of those thoughts and shifting my weight. "I don't think so. He has a mandatory study hall for baseball."

Dad shrugs before adding pleasantly, "That's too bad. But don't worry, Rowan and I will be there to cheer you on. On the off-chance Justin shows up, he can sit with us, and we can pick up where we left off last night."

All right, it's official. The man is seriously frightening me. As I stare, trying to figure out what game he's playing at, a grin stretches across his face. Yup, he's definitely enjoying this.

"*What?* Is it a crime to want to get to know the guy my daughter is dating?"

Possibly.

Ugh. I should probably give him a status update so he can knockoff this weird behavior. It's a little freaky. I'd thought it would be better to have that discussion with Justin before I tell my father. And since I didn't want to slide into the car and have that uncomfortable convo on the way back to campus last night, I kept my mouth shut. It's also not something I'm going to delve into before my game. So...tomorrow. I'm going to end it with Justin tomorrow. There's no point in letting this relationship limp along when my feelings aren't there.

"You can stop pretending to be so nice," I finally grumble. "I don't think it's going to work out with Justin."

He straightens in the chair as his lips tug down at the corners. "What? Are you serious?" Before I can verify the information, the frown disappears, and he's throwing his arms in the air. "Oh well, that's a shame."

Please...I am totally on to him. "Uh-huh. You seem heartbroken by the news."

"Trust me, I am." He taps his chest. "On the inside, where you can't see it."

With a shake of my head, I readjust the strap of my backpack on my shoulder and head to the office door. As I reach for the handle, it occurs to me that Dad never mentioned which player is in need of tutoring. I pause and glance over my shoulder. "Who needs help with stats?"

There's a beat of silence.

"Rowan."

And just like that, my belly goes into freefall, dropping to my toes where it settles.

When I remain silent, he continues, "Row mentioned that you two are in the same class. I figured that would make it easier."

Easier for who?

Certainly not me.

FML.

Chapter Six

ROWAN

From the corner of my eye, I watch Coach's closed office door. Barely do I hear the guy next to me yapping my ear off. Every once in a while, I grunt to let him know I'm paying attention even though I have no idea what he's talking about. More than that, I don't care.

What the hell is Demi doing sauntering into the locker room? She doesn't belong in here with a bunch of half-naked guys. Anger slides through me as I take in the scene. Some of them are full-on naked, standing around with their junk hanging out for all to see.

For fuck's sake, she doesn't need to be looking at that.

"Dude, are you even listening to me?"

The question snaps me out of my Demi-filled thoughts, and I reluctantly drag my gaze to Brayden Kendricks. This is our fourth year playing together. He's the best wide receiver the Wildcats have. Like me, he's a senior who will enter the draft come the spring. He'll leave a huge gaping hole in the program when he graduates.

"Yeah, I heard you."

He crosses his arms against his chest and jerks a brow. "Really? What did I say?"

Busted.

I drag a hand through my hair in annoyance and jerk my shoulders. "Dunno."

He flicks a glance toward Coach's office. "Does your distractibility have anything to do with a certain dark-haired soccer player?"

Fuck.

I don't make a habit of talking about my feelings for Demi. It's something I avoid at all costs. Although, I shouldn't be too surprised that Bray has figured me out. He's an astute dude. It's what makes him so damn good at his position.

Well, there's two ways I can tackle this situation. I can man up and come clean or—

"Nope."

Deny.

Deny.

Deny.

He snorts before grabbing a T-shirt from his locker and dragging it over his head. "Whatever you say, man."

The door to the inner sanctum opens and out walks the girl we've been discussing.

"Speak of the devil," he murmurs, smile simmering in his voice.

If it were possible to force my attention away from her, I'd shoot him a death stare.

"Hey, Demi," Brayden yells in order to be heard over the raucous noise inside the locker room. When she glances in his direction, he adds, "Good luck with your game tonight."

Her expression softens as she smiles. "Thanks."

When I remain silent, Brayden clears his throat. "Is there anything you want to say, Rowan?" A shit-eating grin spreads across his face. Barely is he able to suppress the laughter attempting to break loose.

Her gaze skitters to mine, and I feel the intensity of her dark depths like a punch to the gut. Getting sacked by a defensive tackle doesn't addle my brain nearly as much as being in her presence. It's as if everything around us falls away before she rips her gaze from mine and hastens her pace, silently disappearing from sight.

"Wow, that was a super smooth move, Casanova. Your rep as a player has clearly been well earned."

"Shut the fuck up," I grunt before scowling.

"You might have a thing for her, but she *definitely* wants nothing to do with you."

Tell me something I don't know.

"You have to admit, it's an ironic situation." My glower doesn't stop him from continuing to share his thoughts. "You can have any girl you want on campus with the exception of that one." He spears a finger at the spot where Demi last stood.

Again...tell me something I don't know.

"Plus, I can't imagine Coach would be cool with you sniffing anywhere around her."

Precisely the reason I haven't made a move in her direction.

"Damn, but that girl is fine!" a freshman yells, interrupting our one-sided conversation.

"Yeah, I'd sure love to get my hands on that," another bonehead chimes in from the other side of the wide space.

"When the hell did she grow up so nice?" Arron McKinley shouts.

Unable to listen to another word, I snap, "Shut the fuck up!" Silence descends. "That's Coach's daughter you're talking about!"

Arron grins before holding up his hands in a gesture of surrender. "What? I'm just stating the obvious." He glances around as if expecting the others to chime in and agree with him. Most are smart enough to keep their traps shut. "We're all thinking the same thing."

"Well, don't," I growl. "Have a little fucking respect."

I'm about to lay into a couple of the younger guys when Coach opens the door to his office and hollers, "Michaels, see me before you leave."

With one last glare around the room, I grab a T-shirt from inside my locker and yank it on. The blood rushes through my veins and pounds in my ears. I don't like these guys looking in Demi's direction, much less talking about her. The whole thing pisses me off. They better not let me hear them spouting off like that again, or I'll be cracking some skulls together. I don't care if we're on the same team or not.

"Uh-oh, looks like someone caught wind of the little crush you got going on," Brayden snickers like the asswipe he is.

I certainly hope not. Coach wouldn't be pleased about my interest in his daughter.

Instead of responding to the taunt, I give him the finger. Brayden flashes me a grin before hauling the athletic shorts up his thighs and snapping the elastic band around his waist.

A knot of tension settles in the pit of my gut as I make the walk to the office. I hesitate outside the door for a moment before rapping my knuckles against the frosted glass and popping my head inside. "Hey Coach, you wanted to see me?"

Air gets trapped in my lungs as the older man glances up from the shit pile of paperwork on his metal desk. He waves me in, pointing to the chair on the opposite side of him. "Yeah, have a seat. This'll only take a moment."

Well, fuck.

Maybe Brayden was right, and Coach has finally figured me out. Since the very beginning, I've done my best to cover up my feelings when the three of us are together. I can't imagine what Demi's father would do if he discovered my dirty little secret. Probably boot my ass right off the team. He would stop inviting me over for Wednesday night dinners and letting me hang around like I'm part of the family. I don't think I could stand that. It's not only about my need to be close to Demi but because of Nick Richards. The man is like a father figure to me. More so than the sperm donor who spawned me.

"Yeah, Coach?" I slide tentatively onto the chair.

He glances up after studying the manilla folder in his hand. "Your statistics grade is slipping. I spoke with Professor Peters this afternoon, and you're clinging to a C-."

My shoulders loosen in relief. I should have realized that was the issue. Stats is a massive pain in my ass. I have no problem wrapping my head around most of my classes. That one, for whatever reason, evades me. All Professor P has to do is lecture about quantitative data, inferential statistics, and parameters, and I go a little lightheaded. It's like he's talking in a foreign tongue. If I could avoid the damn class altogether, I would gladly do so.

Unfortunately, it's a requirement for my major. Some guys in my position might skip it and not bother to finish out their degree but I've come this far; I'm sure as shit not going to let a statistics class stand in the way of being the first in my family to graduate from college. I'll need something solid to fall back on if the NFL doesn't work out long-term.

I'm sure that Demi's presence in the same section doesn't help matters either. I have a difficult time concentrating on Professor Peters and his monotone lectures when she's seated next to me. Especially when the scent of her floral shampoo teases my senses. It's all I can do to stop myself from scooting closer and inhaling a giant lungful of her. If I weren't so masochistic, I'd sit my ass elsewhere. But that isn't going to happen.

I've seen the way some of the other guys eye her up in class like she's a juicy steak they want to sink their teeth into. Sitting next to her every class period is my way of staking my claim. Maybe she doesn't realize what I'm doing, but yeah...that's *exactly* what I'm doing. I'll be damned if some other dude hits on her right in front of my face.

I can't imagine Demi would be overly thrilled if she realized my intentions.

From what I can tell, I rub her the wrong way. It's been like that ever since I met her the summer before freshman year of high school. I've never seen any girl go to such great lengths to avoid coming in contact with me. It would be funny if it weren't so damn sad. She's friendly enough with most the other guys on the team, but with me, she's always careful to maintain a distance. Like I'm a leper fresh from the colony. I can't get most of the girls on this campus to leave me alone and yet, like Brayden said, she won't give me the time of day.

As much as I hate talking about stats, I'd rather discuss that than the hard-on I sport anytime his daughter is near. I drag a hand through my damp hair and shove it out of my eyes before shifting on the chair. Even thinking about her is enough to give me wood. "Yeah, I need to put a little more time into that class. The last quiz didn't go so well."

That's an understatement.

Homework is the only thing saving my ass right now.

And it's not by much.

Coach shakes his head and points to my hair. "You got a real mop going on there, Michaels. Maybe you should consider cutting it." A smile tugs at the corners of his lips. "I got a razor around here somewhere. I'd be more than happy to buzz it off right now. All you have to do is say the word."

The familiar conversation settles something inside me, and I smile. "Nah. If I cut the hair, I'll lose all my power. You really want to be responsible for that?"

He snorts and pulls off his ball cap, plowing his fingers through his thinning strands. "Must be what happened to me." He clears his throat and shuffles the papers in front of him. "If you can't get this grade up, you won't have to worry about your power. You'll spend part of the season riding the bench." He raises a brow. "I can't imagine you want that to happen."

"Nope." The thought is enough to have my blood curdling in my veins. With the upcoming draft, all eyes will be on me this season. I need to be stacking up those passing yards and lead the conference in touchdowns which will help me win a Heisman.

"Good. Let's nip this in the bud before it gets any further out of hand."

I tilt my head. "How are we going to do that?"

With a grin, he stabs a finger at me from across the desk. "I'm glad you asked."

Uh-oh. That doesn't sound good.

"I found a tutor for you."

Great. The last thing I want is to work with some starstruck fan who is more interested in riding my dick than improving my stats grade. Been there, done that. Not interested in a repeat performance.

Before I can ask if there are other options we can consider, he continues. "Demi has agreed to tutor you for the next month or so. With a little hard work, there's no reason you can't lift that grade."

Fuck. That's even worse.

Everything inside me goes whipcord tight. "Demi?"

"You two are in the same section, right?"

"Ummm, yeah. She's in there."

He tosses the folder onto the desk and claps his hands together like he solved both world peace and hunger in one fell swoop. "Then it works out perfectly."

I wouldn't go that far. Even though I'd like nothing more than to spend a little alone time with his daughter, it's a shit idea. I can barely keep it together when she's sitting next to me in class. Working one-on-one will probably kill me. Or I'll break the promise I made to myself long ago to keep my hands off her.

My mind goes to what transpired in the kitchen last night. It took every ounce of my willpower not to haul her into my arms and kiss her. I'm walking a thin line here. I've done my best to bury my feelings for Demi, but it hasn't done a damn bit of good. If anything, they've only continued to grow and flourish. Seven years is a long time to hold a torch for a girl. At some point, the dam is going to burst, and all hell will break loose.

That's not something I want to happen.

"You can set up a schedule directly with her," he says, interrupting the whirl of my thoughts.

Well, hell. Maybe I should suggest working with Professor Peters. Except...he bores the shit out of me. It's like my eyes are conditioned to glaze over as soon as he opens his mouth. Talk about being trapped between a rock and a hard place. I'm damned if I do and damned if I don't.

I mull over my choices before finally mumbling, "Yeah, all right. Sounds good." Decision made, I rise from my seat and trudge to the door. As I reach for the knob, I pause.

Don't say anything, asshole. It's none of your damn business.

Maybe not, but still...

Before I can stop myself, the word is shooting out of my mouth. "Coach?"

"Yeah?" He glances up from his desk to meet my gaze.

"It's probably not a good idea for Demi to be walking through the locker room when the guys are in the middle of changing."

Silence descends. I probably should have kept my big trap shut.

His brows furrow as he swipes his tongue carefully across his teeth. "You're probably right."

Relief floods through me as I slip from the office.

If that girl is going to be checking out anyone's junk, it'll be mine.

I wince.

Fuck.

Maybe Coach thinks he's doing me a favor by having me work with his daughter, but all he's done is the opposite.

Chapter Seven

DEMI

Ten seconds remain on the clock. Time slows, and I feel the tick of every millisecond as I dribble the ball between my feet and race toward the goal at the opposite end of the field. The fans in the stands, the coaches on the sidelines, and the other players fade to the background. My breath comes hard and fast before echoing in my ears. There's a UNC girl flanking my side, looking for an opportunity to steal the ball.

The game is tied, and it's down to the wire. A kind of tunnel vision occurs, and my focus narrows on the opponent's net. The goalie watches me with slitted eyes. She crouches, shifting her weight from side to side, waiting for me to make a move. Her gaze stays focused on my hips.

It's just like Shakira claimed in her song—hips don't lie. Although, in this instance, it's the hips that will tip her off as to which direction I'll move in, where in the net I'll try to place the ball.

She knows it, and so do I.

The player at my side pushes into me as she tries to take the ball. With a grunt, I elbow her away to get a little more room.

It's not going to be that easy, girlfriend. You're good, but so am I.

As I close in on the goal, she makes another attempt, and I decide that it's now or never. I'm running out of time. If the buzzer rings before I get a kick off, the game will end in a tie, and that's no good. In a nanosecond, I assess the situation and try to place the ball where it has the best chance of going into the net. Time slows as I pull my foot back and send the ball flying. The girl keeping pace with me attempts to stop it with her head but she's a tick off, and it hurtles forward. The goalie springs into motion. With her arms outstretched, she sails gracefully through the air.

My hands go to my head as I wait and watch. The goalie's fingers graze the ball, but it's not enough to stop the force of it from hitting the net. Time, once again, speeds up and the cheers from my teammates and the fans fill my ears, overloading my senses.

Yes!

We did it! We pulled off a win.

I glance at the stands. Dad is on his feet, clapping and whistling. There's a humongous grin stretched across his face. Rowan is next to him, also cheering. As our gazes lock and hold, something warm spreads unwantedly through my chest. I tell myself it has nothing to do with Rowan or the obvious pride on his face. But even I know it's a lie. Without fail, the football player has attended every home game since freshman year. And, depending on where our away games are, he shows up for them as well. I'm sure he's there because it's another opportunity for him and Dad to discuss strategy on the football field. I don't want to believe it has anything to do with me. If I did, I'd have no other choice but to acknowledge there's something between us, and I'm nowhere near ready to do that.

Eye contact is cut off as I'm swallowed up by my teammates, both the ones from the field and the ones from the bench. Twenty-five girls swarm me, patting me on the back as they jump up and down with excitement. There's a jubilant feeling that permeates the air as we go through the line and shake hands with our opponents. A chorus of *good game* is repeated as we move down the field. Then we gather around Coach Adams for a brief talk before being released to the locker room to shower and change.

With a whoop of excitement, Sydney jumps on my back and wraps her arms around my neck. "That last play was so awesome! You are so the freaking woman!"

Giddiness bubbles up inside me. The adrenaline rush from a hard-fought win is like nothing else. Not even sex can top it.

"Did you notice that the campus hunk was in the stands?"

It would be impossible *not* to notice. There is an energy surrounding him that sets the fine hair on my arms on edge. Without searching him out, I would know he was there. That being said, there's no way in hell I'll admit that to Sydney.

"I'm sorry, who are you talking about?"

"Please girl," she snickers, not fooled in the slightest by my nonchalant attitude. "Nice try."

I snort as the edges of my lips curl upward.

She cranes her head. "I guess Justin put the final nail in his coffin by not showing, huh?"

"The nail was already there. It's better this way. I don't want to feel bad about breaking things off." I scour the stands one last time to make sure he didn't show up late and notice that Ethan is sitting with a couple of other baseball guys.

So much for study hours. It only reinforces my decision to cut him loose and move on.

"You didn't tell me that you worked everything out with Ethan."

"That's because I didn't." All of her previous excitement drains away.

"And yet he still showed up." See? Now *that's* a guy who is interested. One who takes the time out of his own busy schedule to support his girl.

Sydney shrugs before glancing over her shoulder. "Yeah." Her voice softens. "He did."

"That deserves a few brownie points in my book." I wince and slam my mouth shut. What the hell am I doing? I shouldn't be encouraging those two. They need to go their separate ways.

"Maybe."

As I cart Sydney to the locker room, someone knocks into me from behind, and I stagger a couple of steps before righting myself. With my roommate clinging to my back like a baby rhesus monkey, that could have ended disastrously.

I stare at the leggy auburn-haired girl as she strides past us. Her lips curl with scorn.

Annica.

The junior soccer player has turned out to be a real pain in the ass. I'm unsure what happened for her to direct so much hate my way. When Annica came in as a freshman, I took her under my wing and mentored her. We got to know each other pretty well and spent a lot of time together. We're both forwards, and for a while, we worked really well together. We were an unstoppable duo.

Until we weren't.

I blinked, and suddenly everything was a competition both on and off the field. It's gotten to the point of uncomfortableness. I've tried ignoring her, hoping she would grow up and realize we're on the same team, but my silence has had the opposite effect and emboldened her.

"Oops, sorry." The smirk tells me that she's not the least bit remorseful and her bumping into me wasn't an accident.

"Watch where you're going," Sydney snaps.

As captain, I try to lead by example. That tactic hasn't worked with Annica. She's mistaken my silence for weakness. I'm not delusional enough to think that all twenty-six girls on this team will mesh, but we need to work together for the greater good. I've attempted to put the best interest of this team above my own personal feelings for any one individual.

A couple of younger players flank Annica. I've noticed that she's become the piped piper for the freshman and sophomore girls. It's like she's carefully gathering forces for a coup. Any day, they'll come for me, and I'll be beheaded.

"Didn't I tell you from day one that girl would be a problem?" Sydney mutters.

It's warily that I watch both her and her minions strut their stuff to the locker room. Even though it pains me to do so, I have to begrudgingly give Sydney credit where it's due. She was spot on in her assessment. My bestie took an instant dislike to Annica and kept trying to tell me that the younger girl was playing me like a fiddle. I thought Sydney was paranoid (maybe a little jealous) and refused to listen.

"Yup, you did."

"One of these days, you're going to have to knock her down to size."

A sigh escapes from my lips with the realization that she's not wrong. As much as I'm dreading a confrontation with the other girl, it's been brewing for a while. And I can't let it go much longer. Teams that are fractured from within don't bring home championships.

And this is my senior year. Maybe the last one I have to play soccer. So, coming in second or losing in the playoffs isn't an option.

We either get our shit together or we don't bother at all.

End of story.

Chapter Eight

DEMI

Sydney throws open the front door to the house and yells over her shoulder, "Now this is what I'm talking about!"

There's a massive off-campus party in full swing on Spring Street. It's only one of many happening tonight. There are six players who live at this residence, including Rowan. This particular group of guys are well known for their out of control victory celebrations. I expect total craziness to ensue since the Wildcats football team crushed their opponents this afternoon on the field. It's nine o'clock, and this place is already standing room only.

Sydney throws her arm around my neck and pulls me close before blazing a trail through the thick crush of bodies. Music pumps, reverberating off the walls and inside my skull. People are drinking and laughing, cutting loose after a long week of classes.

Not only is Western University renowned for its rigorous academics, it's also known as one of the top party schools in the country. The students here like to blow off steam as much as they study. Maybe more so. I've never been much of a partier. As you might suspect, Sydney is more of a social butterfly than I am. She's the one dragging me out most weekends. It's not like I don't enjoy going out, but I'm just as content to order a pizza and watch a movie in my pajamas.

Maybe I'm too aware that most of the student body knows who I am, and my behavior is a direct reflection of my father. I make it a point to never get trashed or out of control. Those are the last things I need making its way around campus or getting back to Dad. Most of these kids don't have to worry about their parents finding out about what they're up to. They're able to live by that old adage of—what happens at college, stays at college.

Unfortunately, the same can't be said for me. Dad is on campus as much as I am. Probably more. It's easier for all concerned if I stay out of the limelight. I've gotten burned in the past when girls have gotten jealous and spread rumors that I was screwing around with some of the football players, which is precisely why I keep everything strictly platonic with them.

In true Sydney fashion, she plows her way to the front of the beer line and grabs us two red cups of golden frothiness before shoving one in my hand. We tap the rims together.

"Salut!" she says before rather impressively downing the entire container in one thirsty gulp.

I raise my brows and take a dainty sip.

"What?" She swipes the back of her hand across her lips. "It's been one long-ass week."

Even though Ethan made a point of showing up at the game, Sydney still isn't talking to him. We'll have to see how this one plays out. Although, I have my suspicions as to what will transpire. These two are like Kourtney Kardashian and Scott Disick. They can't be together, and yet they can't be without one another.

"I'll be right back, I'm going to grab another one," she says.

As she turns away, I shout, "Hey, I don't want to carry you home tonight. You're like dead weight when you pass out."

She flashes a grin before returning in record speed. "I needed that first one to take the edge off."

Mission accomplished. The edge has clearly been taken off.

When a song that has been playing all summer long comes on, Sydney whoops and throws her hand in the air before moving her body to the rhythm. Several guys in the vicinity take notice. Unable to resist joining her, I follow suit and let the beat flow through me. One song bleeds into another, and we dance in the tiny bit of space we've managed to carve out for ourselves. When a pair of male hands wrap around Sydney's waist and spin her away, I peek around to view the culprit. Her shoulders tighten, and all the lightheartedness she had managed to find in the music drains away, leaving a pissed off Sydney in its place.

I should have known...Ethan.

"Can we talk?" His voice is barely audible over the chatter of people and music pumping around us.

Emotion flickers over Sydney's face before she shrugs. "Is there really anything for us to talk about?"

It feels like we've reached the point in the evening where I should make myself scarce. I'm not looking to referee this conversation.

Sorrow fills his eyes as his face falls. "I'm sorry, Syd. I was a jackass. I care about you, and I'm not ready for this to be over."

She takes a tentative step toward him before tucking a stray lock of hair behind her ear. "I don't know. Maybe we're better off as friends. All we do is fight when we're together."

The girl makes a valid point. He should really listen to her.

"Yeah, I know. But I still want to make this work." There's a pause. "Don't you? Don't we owe it to ourselves to give this one last shot?"

When she remains silent, he closes the distance between them before cupping her cheeks with his hands. Then he leans in and plants a kiss on her lips.

If I know Sydney (and I do), she'll react one of two ways. One, she'll scratch his eyes out or two—

She'll melt beneath his hands, and they'll start sucking face.

When her mouth opens under the pressure of his, I know exactly how the rest of this night will go. And that's with the two of them playing an intense game of tonsil hockey while I stand around feeling like an awkward third wheel.

Sydney tosses her empty cup over her shoulder before twining her arms around his neck. From somewhere behind her comes a disgruntled—*hey!*

I take another sip of my now lukewarm drink and wince. Icy cold beer goes down a lot easier than room temperature hops and barley.

Yuck.

As I step away to give them a bit of much needed privacy—even though they're making out in the middle of a crowded party—Ethan pulls away and stares at me with a dazed expression.

"Ummm, Justin is around here somewhere."

Great. Exactly the person I wanted to contend with. This night has officially gone down the tubes. Justin and I haven't spoken since he dropped me off Wednesday night. There's been a text or two, but otherwise, we've both been busy.

I jerk my thumb over my shoulder and point to nowhere in particular. "I guess that would be my cue to leave."

Ethan flashes me a lopsided grin before his lips return to Sydney's. With one last look at the pair, I shake my head and take off. It's even more jampacked than when we arrived an hour ago. People are crammed into the first floor of this house like sardines.

As I move into the dining room, I notice a couple of guys from the football team. They wave me over, and since I have nothing better to do, I join their small group, relieved to find a few friendly faces in the crowd. Nothing says loser more than standing around by yourself in the middle of a rager.

"Congrats on the win!" I shout to Brayden Kendricks before he pulls me in for a quick hug. I've known him since freshman year. He's like a big brother to me. Even though he's hot as hell, I've never felt anything more than friendship for him.

He glances around before his gaze returns to mine. "What? No roommate? I was under the impression you two were surgically attached at the hip."

"She's currently attached to someone else's hip at the moment," I joke.

The smile disappears, only to be replaced with a frown. "She still with that guy?"

I shrug, surprised he's been following the whole Sydney-Ethan romantic rollercoaster.

Which is...kind of interesting.

"For the moment. Check back tomorrow. We could have a different answer."

With his brows beetled together, his gaze coasts over the throng. Almost as if he's searching for her.

Even though that seems doubtful, I can't resist teasing, "Hmmm, am I sensing a bit of interest on your part?"

He lifts a bottle of beer to his lips and takes a long swig. "The girl is seriously hot, but she's way too much work."

I snort and shake my head.

Here's the thing about Brayden—he doesn't chase girls, they chase him. With his dark hair and eyes, the guy is a real heartbreaker. He's funny, has a great personality, and is intelligent. Not to mention muscular. In other words, he's catnip for the females on campus. He's been voted campus heartthrob three years running. And I have no doubt he'll receive the distinction for his fourth and final year, a Western University first.

Before I can investigate the situation further, a leggy blonde with humongous breasts squeezes her way between us before pressing her double D's against him. He grins, his attention homing in on the groupie.

I've watched this scene play out too many times not to know how it'll end. He'll flash his signature panty-dropping smile, and she'll sigh, fall onto her back, and spread her legs wide.

Someone hand me a barf bag before I'm sick.

For a flicker of a moment, I'd actually thought he might be interested in Sydney. I glance at him again. The blonde is now clinging to him like a barnacle, and he's certainly not fighting her off. I can all but guarantee that girl will be taking a ride on the Brayden express this evening.

I'm knocked out of those thoughts when one of the younger guys comes up behind me and grinds. Mitch Harrison is a sophomore. He's a defensive tackle and a teddy bear of a guy, weighing in at three hundred pounds. We had a class together last year. As far as dudes go, he's pretty harmless. I'm about to bust out a move when a muscular arm slides between our bodies and hauls me away. Air gets trapped in my throat as I'm pressed against a hard chest.

I don't need to glance at the person holding me to realize who it is.

My skin is abuzz with recognition. There's only one guy capable of producing that kind of sensation within me.

Rowan.

As if to solidify my suspicions, he growls, "Knock it off, Harrison." He pulls me so close that I'm able to feel every hard line of his body. Another punch of awareness hits me before settling in my core. "Leave her alone."

The deep rumble of his voice ties my insides up into a series of complicated little knots. As much as I want to pretend I'm stone cold inside and feel nothing where Rowan is concerned, I can't. The attraction is too explosive to ignore.

What the hell is wrong with me?

Why can't I control my body's reaction to him?

It's frustrating to want someone you know you can't have. Someone who isn't good for you. And yet, that knowledge does nothing to stop the surge of hormones from flooding through me, lighting me up from the inside out. Since day one, when we were fourteen years old, I've been all too aware of Rowan Michaels. He's ridiculously good looking. I can acknowledge that. At least privately to myself. And from the attention he garners, I'm certainly not the only one who thinks so.

Up to this point, I've been successful in pushing all thoughts of him to the back of my brain, where I can ignore them. That doesn't seem to be the case anymore, and I don't understand why. Something indelible has changed, but I'm not sure what it is. It's like we've reached a tipping point.

What I need right now is for our relationship to go back to the way it's always been.

Is that even possible?

For some reason, I don't think so.

And that, my friends, is a huge freaking problem. One I have no idea how to solve.

With no other choice but to confront the situation, I spin around in his arms before pressing my palms against his chest.

What is it about him that makes my pulse race?

I've never been attracted to guys with hair that nearly brushes their shoulders. I've always gone for clean cut boys. And yet, my fingers itch to tangle in the thick length. And when he wears one of those hair band thingies at practice?

A shiver slides through me just imagining it.

The intensity of his gaze burns into mine, and it takes a moment to find my voice. "You're kind of a buzzkill." I exhale as everything spinning gradually resettles inside me. The last thing I want or need is for him to realize how easily he's able to knock me off-kilter.

Rowan quirks a brow. "Is that so?"

"Yes. We were dancing. It wasn't a big deal."

He doesn't move, and yet somehow manages to loom closer, obscuring everything in my line of sight except for him. The raucous party fades as I'm trapped in the blueness of his eyes. They remind me so much of the ocean. Of waves crashing against the shoreline. It takes everything I have inside not to glance away and reveal how much he unnerves me. Even when my knees turn to jelly and I'm in immanent danger of sliding to the floor, I hold myself upright.

"It's doubtful Coach would approve of his players grinding up on his daughter."

He's right. Dad wouldn't care for it at all.

But that doesn't stop me from firing back with, "Do you think he would approve of you holding me like this?" His hands burn into my bare skin, making me wonder if I'll be sporting marks for days.

His lips thin as his eyes darken. "Probably not."

When his arms reluctantly fall to his sides, I take a hasty step back, needing distance to regain my bearings. I don't fool myself into believing it's anything less than full-on retreat. I need to distance myself from Rowan before something happens. There's an explosive energy brewing in the air. It feels as if one strike of a match could blow us all to hell. I can't take the chance of our relationship shifting anymore than it already has.

"I need to find Justin." Before Rowan can deter me, I swing away, shoving through the crowd that presses in on me. The more space I put between us, the easier it is to think straight. No one has ever affected me this way. Certainly not Justin. If I'm lucky, I won't run into Rowan again for the rest of the night. It's bad enough I see him three times a week in stats, and he insists on parking himself next to me every class period. Now I'll have to spend time tutoring him.

Alone.

I gulp down the strange mixture of nerves and excitement that burst inside me like an overinflated balloon.

When I set out this evening, I had no desire to meet up with the dark-haired baseball player. I figured we would talk at some point over the weekend, and I would gently break off our relationship. But right now, he feels like the safest alternative. Once I find him, I plan on sticking to the guy like glue.

For the next ten minutes, I scour the first floor of the house before moving to the backyard where the party has spilled out, but there's still no sign of him. Maybe Ethan was wrong, and he isn't here. Or maybe he took off for a different party. There are enough of them happening around campus.

I'm about to call off the mission and make my way back to Sydney when I spot Sasha, one of our goaltenders. I wave, and we end up chatting for a few minutes. I didn't realize other girls from the team were here. I've combed the entire place and haven't come across another teammate. Sasha informs me that a group of them are party-hopping, and they showed up thirty minutes ago. Most of the girls are like me— they like to go out and have a good time, but they don't need to get shitfaced in order for that to occur. A number of them have athletic scholarships that pay for a chunk of their tuition and don't want to jeopardize it. This may be a party school, but the sanctions for getting caught, especially if you're an athlete, are severe.

"You haven't seen Justin around, have you?" I yell over the music to make myself heard. Why am I even bothering to ask? It's not like I really want to meet up with him. Now that I've found Sasha, I can hang with her for the rest of the night. Or I can try to find Sydney and hope they're done sucking face.

That thought brings a snort to my lips.

Sasha's brows draw together as confusion flickers across her expression. "I didn't realize you two were still a thing."

"Yup." At this point, it's more of a technicality. I really need to talk to Justin before I tell anyone else that's no longer the case.

"Oh." A troubled look fills her eyes before she glances away. "Um, yeah," she mumbles, "I saw him about ten minutes ago in one of the back rooms."

"Great, thanks." Her less than enthusiastic reaction has a prickle of unease blooming in the pit of my belly. Before it can take root, I shake it off. "I've been looking for him but haven't had any luck. This place is a total madhouse." I shrug. "I suppose if he's here, I should say hi."

"Yeah." Sasha gives me a slight smile in return. "I guess so."

Decision made, I take a step toward the back bedrooms when she reaches out, wrapping slender fingers around my forearm. While Sasha and I are friends and teammates, we've never been close. Although we've always been cool with one another.

"I'm sorry, Demi. I didn't know."

Her comment is so out of left field that I have no idea what it means. "What are you sorry about?"

Before I can ask anything more, she releases me and disappears into the crowd. I blink, and she's gone.

That was a really bizarre thing to say. Maybe Sasha is more drunk than I assumed.

Even so, my brain churns, trying to come up with an answer that makes sense.

I'm tempted to go after her and get to the bottom of this, but it would be like searching for a needle in a haystack. I'll pull her aside on Monday at practice and figure out what she meant.

It takes effort to shake off her cryptic words as I push my way through the mass of bodies toward the back hallway off the kitchen. The first bedroom I peek inside has about eight people sitting around, smoking a bowl. A thick haze permeates the air. A cursory inspection tells me Justin isn't here. And since I'm not looking for a contact high, I quickly back away. The last thing I need is to test positive for pot. All athletes at WU are drug tested throughout the year. They agree to random testing when they sign their NCAA eligibility paperwork before stepping foot on campus. Most of us have worked our entire lives to reach this level of play and aren't willing to throw it away over a couple hours of mindless pleasure.

I check two more bedrooms, but Justin is nowhere to be found.

It's always possible that Sasha was wrong about seeing him, and it was simply a case of mistaken identity. At this point, I'm not even sure it matters. I've had enough and am more than ready to call it a night.

I'm about to take off in the opposite direction down the hallway when a noise catches my attention. It's barely audible over the pumping beat of music that echoes off the paper-thin walls.

I'm not sure what has me creeping around the corner. A sixth sense maybe. Even though there are more shadows where the light from above doesn't reach, plunging the narrow area into darkness, there's enough illumination to make out the guy standing with his back pressed against the wall. A rough groan slides from his lips as my widened gaze drops to the girl on her knees in front of him. It's fairly obvious what's going on here. My lungs fill with air as the girl works him with her mouth, sucking him deep into her throat before sliding nearly to the tip and repeating the maneuver.

I'll tell you what, this chick is a total pro. She knows how to give a BJ. The polite thing to do would be to carefully back away and disappear down the hall, but I'm unable to do that. My feet are rooted in place. I wish this were a faceless, nameless guy but it's not.

It's Justin.

Unfortunately, the look on Sasha's face now makes perfect sense. She knew he was fooling around with someone else.

The growl that escapes from my boyfriend is enough to have me blinking back to the present. His eyes are squeezed tight and there's a slight gape to his parted lips. His fingers are tangled in thick hair.

Auburn-colored hair, if I'm not mistaken.

Annica.

Why am I not surprised?

Although this is an all-time low, even for her.

As if realizing she has an audience, Annica cracks open her eyes and locks them on me. Instead of flaring with surprise, embarrassment, or even guilt, a victorious light fills them. As if this is what she wanted all along. For me to find them together. It might be dark and shadowy in the cramped hallway, but the look she sends me is blatant. Much like the shove on the field after the game on Thursday, this was intentional.

I'm sure if her mouth wasn't stuffed full of Justin's dick, she would be grinning ear-to-ear.

What a bitch.

She really has no shame. I've never met a girl like her. And to be clear, I've dealt with my fair share of bitchy mean girls throughout the years, but this one takes the cake.

When Annica's movements become more frenzied, Justin's fingers tighten on her scalp before he pulls her closer. Even though I don't give a damn about him, it's not in my nature to skulk away with my tail tucked between my legs. I want the dark-haired boy to know that he's been caught with his pants around his ankles.

Literally.

The fact that he chose to cheat on me with one of my own team-mates makes him beyond despicable. I fold my arms across my chest and wait for the perfect moment to interrupt.

His face scrunches as he throws his head back, exposing his throat. *"Yeah, just like that. I'm gonna—"*

"I have to admit, I was expecting a little more in the length depart-ment." I point to his groin. "That's seriously disappointing."

His eyelids fly open as he jerks to awareness. His mouth gapes momentarily before he quickly shoves Annica away from him. The younger girl lands on her ass with a grunt.

A thin smile curves my lips as I hold up a hand. "Please don't stop on my account. I wanted to interrupt for a brief moment to tell you that we're over." I glance at the auburn-haired girl who, at one time, I'd considered a friend. "You two are perfectly suited for one another."

"Demi!" he yells.

I turn away, not bothering to look over my shoulder as I stalk down the hallway. And here I'd thought it was possible to remain friends after our breakup.

Ha!

That's no longer happening. With any luck, I'll be able to avoid Justin for the remainder of the year. Unfortunately, the same can't be said for Annica. The level this girl will stoop to in order to hurt me is almost unbelievable. And a little bit scary. I should have listened to Sydney from the beginning.

At some point, my vindictive teammate will have to be dealt with. But it won't be this evening. Tonight, my plan is to go home and drown myself in a pint of chocolate ice cream. The name of the flavor—death by chocolate—now makes so much more sense.

I snort and continue to push my way to the living room, only wanting to leave this party—and the memories—behind.

Chapter Nine
ROWAN

I lift the bottle of beer to my lips and take a swig. It goes down smooth but does nothing to alleviate the discontent that brews beneath the surface. There's only one person capable of that, and it's not the sad imitation currently hanging on me.

"We should get out of here." Her slim hands stroke over my chest as she stares up at me with dark eyes. "We can go back to my place and talk."

Right. I think we both realize that conversing is not this girl's end goal. The only thing she wants to better acquaint herself with is my cock.

Why pretend otherwise?

What I've come to learn over three years at WU is that most of these girls are a carbon copy of each other. The hair, eyes, and body size might be different, but beneath the exterior features, they're all the same. They want the notoriety that comes from being with a high-profile athlete on campus. Throw in someone who has a chance of turning pro and making millions, and you got yourself a stage five clinger.

That's the last thing I want.

Or need.

But this girl—if I squint hard enough and suck down a couple more drinks—bares a striking resemblance to a certain someone else. Thinking along those lines will be precisely what gets me into trouble.

"Rowan?" When I don't answer, she presses closer, pushing her breasts against my chest. "Did you hear me?"

Yeah, I heard. If I end up leaving with her, it'll be for all the wrong reasons. She might resemble Demi with her dark hair and eyes, but her body is a lot softer instead of being tight and athletic.

I'm five seconds away from giving in when my skin prickles, and I glance around, knowing that she's somewhere in the nearby vicinity. Call it fucked up Spidey senses. I scan the thick crowd until my gaze homes in on her dark head. Her lips are a tight slash across her face, and there's a hollowed-out look in her eyes. Even from this distance, I realize something is wrong.

Without thinking, I yell, "Demi!"

Even though the music is obnoxiously loud, and I'm unsure if my voice carries, her gaze slices to mine as if she knew I was standing there the entire time. It only reconfirms that I'm not the only one who feels the strange gravitational pull. Whether she wants to admit it or not, there is a bond that connects us to one another.

For a fleeting moment, our gazes lock and hold. Pain flares in her eyes before it's blinked away. She drags her gaze from mine before pushing steadily through the mass of bodies toward the front door.

I don't realize I'm on the move until the girl previously wrapped around me calls out, "Hey! Where are you going?"

Barely do I stop to throw the words over my shoulder. "Sorry, a friend needs me."

Although that statement is highly debatable. It's unlikely that my *friend* wants any assistance from the likes of me.

"I thought we were leaving," she whines, unwilling to throw in the towel just yet.

"Maybe another time."

Or...more like never.

My size and notoriety on campus make shoving my way through the crowd unnecessary. If you're not looking to get mowed over, move your ass out of the way. Within thirty seconds, I've cut a direct path to

Demi. I wrap my fingers around her bicep, effectively halting her escape.

"Hey." I spin her around until she has no choice but to meet my searching gaze. "What's going on?"

"Nothing." She shakes her head, but the fib is there, lurking in her dark depths.

"Why are you lying?" I drag her closer. "Tell me what happened."

"I'm just tired." Demi jerks her arm, attempting to break free from the hold I have on her. "I want to go home."

I study her tightened features for the truth. "Why don't I believe you?"

A crack of anger flashes across her face. "I don't care what you believe." For a second time, she tries to wrench her arm free, but I refuse to let her get away that easily. I don't like the pain reverberating in her eyes, and I want to know who put it there. "Let me go!"

"Demi!"

Our heads swivel as Justin crashes onto the scene, interrupting our conversation. Any struggle Demi had been putting up ceases as every muscle in her body goes rigid.

"I'm sorry," he blurts, gaze focused solely on her.

It shouldn't come as any surprise that I'm not much of a Justin fan. Even before they got together, I never had much for the guy. He always struck me as a conceited tool. And I've become even less enamored since they've been seeing each other. He's nowhere near good enough for her. I was hoping Coach would put the kibosh on their relationship the other night, but that didn't happen.

My eyes narrow as I pull Demi closer. "What exactly are you apologizing for?"

Justin tears his gaze from her long enough to shoot me a glare. Heat flags his cheeks. "That's none of your damn business." He waggles a finger between himself and the girl pressed against me. "This is between the two of us." He shifts from one foot to the other before dropping his voice. "Please, Demi, can we go somewhere and talk in private?"

A gurgle of disbelief bubbles up from her throat. "You didn't seem too interested in privacy a couple of minutes ago."

What the hell does that mean?

Justin grits his teeth as the flush staining his cheeks creeps further down his neck. "Would you hear me out?"

When she presses herself against me, I realize that whatever she's upset about has everything to do with him. That's all the incentive I need to snake my arm around her shoulders and tuck her carefully against my body.

Justin plows a hand through his hair as frustration flashes across his face. His voice drops, taking on a pleading note. "I made a mistake, all right? Don't make such a big deal out of it."

Demi's brows skyrocket across her forehead. "Are you being serious?" Before he can answer, she says, "Clearly you don't understand that sticking your dick in another chick's mouth is a *huge* deal. And for that girl to be one of my teammates makes the situation even more unforgivable."

"You cheated on her?" Why the hell would Justin do that? Doesn't he realize how fucking special this girl is? Any guy lucky enough to have Demi should be worshipping the very ground she walks on. I knew this guy was a douche but somehow, he's managed to jackhammer to an all new low.

A potent mixture of fury and irritation swirl through Justin's eyes as his gaze swings to me. "Fuck off, Michaels," he growls. "This doesn't involve you. Why don't you take a hike?"

Ha! He's legitimately insane if he thinks for one damn moment I'm going to walk away and leave Demi alone with him. All he's done is hurt her, and it will be over my dead carcass that he inflicts anymore damage.

"I'm not going anywhere, so get used to it."

"This isn't the first time you've done this, is it?" Demi cuts in, drawing Justin's attention to her.

"What?" His voice falters as surprise flickers in his eyes.

She levels a hard look at him and repeats, "This isn't the first time you've cheated on me."

When a bead of perspiration breaks out across his brow, and his gaze falters, I realize Demi is right. He's been hooking up with other girls the entire time they've been together.

Goddamn it!

It takes everything I have inside not to punch that stupid mother-fucker in the piehole.

"Well?" There's a pause before she snaps, "I'm waiting for an answer!"

When it becomes apparent that Demi won't drop the subject, he clears his throat. "Maybe I've gotten a few BJ's here and there, but that's it! I wanted to take things slow with you."

She scrunches her face and straightens to her full height like someone rammed a two-by-four up her ass. "Wait a minute, are you really trying to," one hand slaps her chest, "blame *me* for this?"

He blinks a few times before muttering, "No, I'm saying that we weren't totally serious, and I didn't want to rush you. I thought you would appreciate me being respectful."

"So...I was supposed to *appreciate* you getting blow jobs from other girls?" She doesn't wait for him to respond. "You know what I would have *appreciated* even more? If you would have kept your dick in your pants."

"That's not what I meant! You're taking everything out of context and twisting it to make me the bad guy in this scenario."

"Newsflash, asshole—you *are* the bad guy! As for taking everything out of," she uses her fingers to make air quotes, "*context.* I don't think so. You never asked if I wanted to take things slow. You just assumed. Why would any girl want the guy she's seeing to hookup with other people behind her back?" She shakes her head as another realization dawns. "Even after we got serious, you would have continued to screw around on me." When he opens his mouth to argue, she raises a hand. "I'm done with this conversation and more importantly, I'm done with you!"

"What?" His voice rises and several people in the nearby vicinity turn in his direction. *"Wait!"*

When he steps closer, attempting to reach for Demi, I shove him back a couple of steps. It takes everything I have inside not to get more physical. "Demi already told you that she's not interested. Take the hint, buddy, and leave her alone."

"Give me a damn break, Michaels," Justin snarls. "Like you're not getting your dick wet every damn night of the week?" He jerks his arm to encompass the party. "You've probably nailed every ass in the place. Shut the fuck up and stay out of my business!"

Revulsion flashes across Demi's face as she shoves out of my arms. "Maybe you two should become friends. It seems like you have a lot in common."

With that last parting shot, she pushes her way through the crowd.

Once Demi is out of earshot, Justin growls, "The only thing we have in common is that we both want to get in her pants." He smirks. "Although, I'm sure all you'd have to do is talk to Coach Richards, he'd probably hand his daughter right over. I've heard that's one of the perks to being a baller around here."

The fuck he said!

Rage clouds my better judgement. I yank my arm back and slam it into the asshole's face before anything else can come out of his stupid piehole. With any luck, that'll shut him up.

He squeals like a little pig as his hands fly to his nose.

"You had the one girl worth having on campus, and you fucked it up because you couldn't keep your pecker in your pants." I step closer, getting in his face. "You and I are *nothing* alike."

When Justin fails to respond, I swing away, striding after the only girl I've ever cared about. The very same one who wants nothing to do with me.

Chapter Ten

DEMI

I'm still fuming as I stride down the sidewalk. It seems unimaginable that Justin would attempt to pin the blame for his cheating on me.

On me!

As if I had *anything* to do with him whipping out his dick and stuffing it in someone else's mouth.

Nope. Don't think so.

The temperature might have dipped into the low seventies, but it does nothing to cool my temper. It's as if the conversation is playing on a constant loop in my head, and I can't make it stop.

The nerve of that guy!

Instead of apologizing—not that it would have done any good—he had actually tried to justify his cheating! I've never met two people who deserve one another more. Justin and Annica are a match made in hell.

It's the heavy fall of footsteps from behind that snap me out of my thoughts. I swear to God, if it's Justin, I will totally lose my shit. I can't deal with anymore of his asinine behavior. Had I been smart, I would have pulled the plug on our relationship on the way home from dinner Wednesday night. Instead, I waited.

With my hands clenched, I swivel around. I'm not normally a

violent person, but tonight, I've been pushed past my limit. Except it's not Justin. My gaze collides with concerned ocean-colored eyes. A soft puff of air escapes from my lips as my muscles loosen.

Rowan.

He was there to witness my humiliation and is the last person I want to see or talk to.

It takes a second for him to fall in line with me. For half a block, we walk in silence before he asks, "You okay? That was brutal."

I keep my gaze focused straight ahead. "I'm fine."

Lie.

What hurts most is that one of my own teammates despises me enough to inflict that kind of damage. I had already decided to cut Justin loose. My feelings for him weren't that deep.

But Annica?

Someone who I'd taken under my wing and considered a friend? Someone who should have my back as a teammate?

That one stings more than I'm willing to admit.

Drunken students loiter on the lawns of houses where multiple parties are in full swing. A few people yell out Rowan's name as we pass by.

Instead of responding, his attention stays solely focused on me. "You sure about that?"

My skin prickles under the intensity of his stare. Can you even imagine falling for a guy like him? He would ground your heart to a fine dust beneath his cleat.

Instead of answering, I snap, "Why is every guy on this campus a cheating bastard?" The question escapes before I have a chance to rein it back in. I flick my gaze in his direction to get a read on his thoughts before adding begrudgingly, "At least you don't pretend to be faithful. That would involve dating, and you don't do that."

In all the years I've known Rowan, not once have I seen him with the same girl more than once or twice. His adoring fan base is legendary. A kernel of jealousy blooms in the pit of my belly before I quickly stomp it out.

"Wait a minute," he says, breaking into my thoughts, "you think I'm a womanizing asshole like Justin?"

Ummm...*yeah*. That's exactly what I think. If you asked anyone at Western who the biggest player on campus was, the answer would undoubtedly be Rowan Michaels.

Are we really going to pretend otherwise?

"Look, I don't think you're an asshole, but we've gone to school together for the past three years." I shoot him a—*who are you trying to kid* look. "The tales of your conquests are legendary."

"Maybe you shouldn't put so much stock in the gossip you hear around campus, Demi."

Seriously?

I've heard *way* too many stories for at least *some* not to be true. It's a little hard *not* to believe when the information comes straight from the horse's mouth. And by horse, I mean the girls he bangs.

"Oh, please." I snicker before shoving at his arm. Why is he trying to bullshit me? Just own it. "You're like the manwhore all other manwhores look up to and want to emulate. You should wear that badge of honor with pride."

"You don't know what the hell you're talking about," he growls.

After the night I've had, all I want is an honest conversation and to figure out how to better discern the jerks from the guys worth getting to know. Right now, I'm at a loss.

I'm ripped out of those thoughts when Rowan's fingers lock around my upper arm as we grind to a halt on the sidewalk. Before I realize what's happening, he drags me closer. I stumble a few steps before crashing into his chest. My gaze goes wide as it locks on his. A harsh look fills his eyes. One I've never seen before. It has all the saliva drying in my mouth and nerves skittering along my spine. When my tongue darts out to smudge my lips, his attention falls to the movement. A mixture of excitement and fear bloom inside me as a strange energy crackles in the air.

These are exactly the type of feelings I've always tried to keep at bay where Rowan is concerned. It's as if he's trying to break through all of my defenses, and I have no idea why. Emotion crashes within, leaving me to feel off-balance and confused.

"What are you doing?" It takes effort to force the question from stiff lips.

Rowan's face looms close enough for his warm breath to feather against my skin. The feel of it shouldn't be this intoxicating. It shouldn't make me want to suck in greedy mouthfuls of him and hold it deep inside. Anticipation coils tightly in the pit of my belly as everything inside me goes silent.

"As much as you think you know me, you don't know shit."

That's not true!

"We've known each other for seven years," I whisper. "How can you say that?"

"Have you ever taken the time to figure out who I am? I'm talking about the guy buried beneath all the hype." He searches my eyes with narrowed ones. "Sometimes, I think it's more comfortable for you to pigeonhole me into the persona you've created rather than the guy I actually am."

I gulp down a fresh burst of nerves.

This conversation is ridiculous. I understand *exactly* who Rowan Michaels is. I've been forced to endure dinner with him once a week for the past three years. I've listened to him and Dad discuss football ad nauseum. We've had classes together almost every semester.

There is no question in my mind that the guy standing before me is a total player. Like most of the athletes at Western, he's spent the better part of his college years partying and sleeping with groupies. He gets by in his classes because he needs to retain eligibility to play football but has no intention of ever using his degree in the real world.

So...do I know who Rowan Michaels is?

Yeah, I'm pretty sure I do.

I open my mouth to blast him into next week and realize that our faces are scant inches apart. Air becomes lodged in my throat at the heated look that fills his eyes. It's anger mixed with something more potent. My gaze falls to his lips and everything inside me coils tight. An image of us in the kitchen on Wednesday forces its way into my brain. We were standing so close, and I'd wondered if he would kiss me.

As much as I hate to admit it, I'd wanted him to do it.

Just when I think Rowan will lean in, and I'll finally feel the slide of his lips against mine, he takes a hasty step in retreat. The strong hands gripping my arms fall away, leaving behind an odd kind of regret to fill the emptiness. I'm so tempted to reach out and drag him closer. Instead, my hands tighten at my sides.

I want to say something.

Something that will smooth over the suffocating tension that vibrates in the cool night air between us, but my mind remains frustratingly blank.

"Maybe you should take the time and get to know me instead of assuming things that aren't true. If you would give me even half a chance, Demi, I might just surprise you."

With that, he swings around, stalking down the sidewalk in the direction we'd come from. For a long moment, I can only stare after him as a strange concoction of emotions crash inside me.

There's definitely relief. And if I'm being honest with myself, a fair amount of disappointment bubbles up as well.

It's almost enough to make me forget what I stumbled across at the party.

Almost.

But not quite.

Chapter Eleven

DEMI

I'm startled out of a sound sleep when something—or more likely, *someone*—lands on my chest. My eyelids fly open, and I stare groggily up at vibrant green eyes that are entirely too awake for—I glance at the digital clock on the nightstand—good lord, it's not even seven in the morning.

Sunday morning, I might add. One of two days I take off from running and allow myself the luxury of sleeping in. And Sydney ruined it.

"Why are you awake so early?" I slur.

"Please, I could hardly sleep a wink last night."

"Ugh." I attempt to push her off my body and roll onto my side, but Sydney refuses to budge from her perched position on top of me. "I really don't want to hear about your sexcapades."

"Please, girl." She rolls her eyes. "You would have heard that loud and clear firsthand."

She's right about that. Her and Ethan are loud as fuck. It's like they're shooting a porno every single time.

"I'm talking about what happened with you last night."

"Me?" Any sleepiness I'd been clinging to vanishes in the blink of an eye. "Nothing happened. What are you talking about?"

She gives me a—*exactly how drunk* were *you* look. "Um, hello. There are a *shit ton* of stories flying all over the place. I heard about them before I even left the party."

Awesome. Exactly what I want to hear at the butt crack of dawn. When I remain silent, she pokes me in the chest with a pointy finger.

"Ow!" I rub the spot. Damn! That hurt.

She folds her arms across her chest. "Oh, and thanks for letting me know you were taking off. Do you have any idea how worried I was about you?"

"Please," I snort. "The last time I checked, Ethan had his tongue shoved so far down your throat, if was like he was doing a strep test."

A sly grin curves Sydney's lips. "All right, so maybe we went at it a little hard. But still, you should have let me know."

"You're right, I should have sent you a text." I'd been so angry with Justin that it hadn't occurred to me to inform Sydney I was walking home by myself. Probably not the smartest decision I've ever made. Usually we stick together at parties. Girls are always safer when traveling in pairs.

"Apology accepted." Then she redirects the conversation back to the original topic. "Want to hear the stories?"

"Are you really giving me a choice in the matter?"

"Nope." Sydney holds up a finger. "The first one is that you walked in on Justin having a threesome."

After last night, I wouldn't put anything past him, but that definitely didn't happen.

"Two." A second finger joins the first. "Rowan beat the shit out of him, and Justin spent the night in the ICU and is now pressing charges."

Seriously, people?

That's pure lunacy.

"Neither of those things occurred." There wasn't even a fight, for goodness' sake. This is a perfect example of the rumor mill at Western running amuck.

"Three," another finger joins the first two, "Justin found you with another guy and went berserk."

The corners of Sydney's lips tremble when I burst out laughing.

Jeez. Who makes this shit up? "Trust me, there's more, but those are the ones I thought could have a shred of truth to them."

"It's all a bunch of bullshit."

"Hmmm." Her shoulders fall. "That's disappointing."

"Really?" I quirk a brow. "You were hoping Justin got beat up, or one of us was caught up in a cheating scandal?"

"Maybe." She shrugs unapologetically. "You have to admit, it's getting kind of lame around here. We need something to spice things up."

There's no point in holding back what transpired last night. "Then you'll be delighted to hear that I walked in on Justin getting a blowie."

Her eyes widen. *"From a guy?"*

"No, not a dude! It was none other than our very own Annica Weber."

"No way!"

"Yup." The whole sordid mess leaves a bad taste in my mouth. Although, not nearly as bad of a taste as Annica had in *her* mouth last night. God only knows where his you-know-what has been.

Sydney collapses onto the mattress next to me before rolling onto her back. "What a dirty little bitch."

"My thoughts exactly." There's a pause. "Honestly, I don't give a crap about Justin or what he does. We weren't going anywhere as a couple but if he felt the same way, he should have been straight with me instead of hooking up behind my back." More like right in front of my face. "It's Annica's behavior that bothers me the most." I swivel my head to meet her gaze. "You know what I mean?"

"Yeah. That's some super shady shit right there."

Tell me about it.

An image of Annica on her knees forces its way into my head. "You should have seen the way she looked at me, Syd. It was like she was thrilled that I'd stumbled upon them as if it had been her intent all along. She didn't even bother to stop blowing him. Kept right on going until he pushed her away." A shudder of disgust works its way through my body.

"Seriously?" Sydney's brows rise as if even she's shocked, which is saying something. She doesn't bat an eyelash over much.

"Yup." My voice softens. "I don't understand what her problem is." My brain trips over the past two years. When Annica had come in as a freshman, she'd been so sweet and nice. Eager to soak up everything she could learn on the soccer field. She had shadowed my every move around campus. She was like the little sister I'd never had but always wanted. Fast forward two years, and I could have never imagined our relationship would be so contentious. I've done nothing to her. Certainly nothing to incite this kind of single-minded hatred. I'm at a loss as to how to change the path we're careening down.

A contemplative expression settles over Sydney's face as she chews her lower lip. "Do you want my honest opinion?"

"Of course." I steel myself for what will come next. Sydney isn't the kind of girl who pulls punches. Ask her for the truth, and she'll give you the unvarnished version. Her unflinching honesty is one of the things I love about her.

"I think Annica has been eaten alive by the green-eyed monster. She wants your position on the team." When I remain silent, she continues. "If that girl could skin you alive and wear you as a coat, she would."

I scrunch my nose at the vivid image she paints. "That's fairly disturbing."

"You know what?" She doesn't bother waiting for a response. "*Her* behavior has been pretty disturbing."

Sydney's right about that. The situation with Annica has spun out of control. I'd hoped that if I gave it enough time and didn't give her the reaction she was looking for, the girl would get bored and move on, but that has yet to happen. If anything, her behavior has only become more spiteful and ruthless.

"Dem," she says, cutting into my thoughts, "you can't let this slide anymore. Some of the younger girls already seek her out for advice and look up to her as a leader. She'll continue to wreak havoc on this team if you let her."

That's exactly what I'm afraid of.

When did it all go so wrong?

When I was named co-captain last season? Our relationship was definitely tense last year, but I have no idea if that's what caused the rift. Now I'm captain and Annica is my co-captain. I suppose I'd been holding out hope that it would appease her, and she'd settle into her leadership role with more grace. That hasn't happened. At every turn, she attempts to undermine my authority. I haven't taken this issue to Coach because I should be able to solve this on my own. That's part of the responsibility of being captain.

What a fucking mess.

"I'll talk to her," I mutter, not looking forward to the conversation.

Sydney reaches out and tangles her fingers with mine. "Good. Now...what do you say to making me breakfast?" With her other hand, she rubs her toned belly. "I'm starving."

I laugh and shake my head. "I say you're crazy."

"You've known that for a while, and you're still here. So, I guess that means you're stuck with me."

I wrap my arms around her and squeeze tight. Honestly, there's no one else in life I'd rather be stuck with. Sydney is my ride or die, which means, I'm on the hook for making breakfast.

"Eggs or pancakes," I ask.

"Both!"

A chuckle slips free as I shake my head.

Why am I not surprised?

Sydney is an all or nothing kind of girl. And I wouldn't have her any other way.

Chapter Twelve

DEMI

"Hey, Demi! Wait up!"

I stiffen, immediately recognizing the voice. Instead of slowing down, I tuck my chin against my chest and haul ass, hoping to lose him in the herd of students moving across campus like cattle. I'm not usually one to run and hide, but I'll make an exception in this case.

"Demi!"

The voice grows louder, and I realize he's closer than I had originally suspected.

Crappity...crap, crap, crap.

When a heavy hand lands on my shoulder, I silently acknowledge that escape isn't in the cards for me this morning. A potent concoction of disbelief and anger shoots through me as I attempt to shrug him off. After finding Justin and Annica together Saturday night, he's the last person I want touching me. Honestly, I'm a little surprised he has the nerve to seek me out in the first place. I had assumed by unspoken agreement we would avoid each other for the rest of the year.

"Justin." Reluctantly I flick my gaze in his direction only to discover that his nose is bruised and swollen.

That's new. It certainly wasn't like that when I left the party. My brain whirls, silently trying to figure out what happened. Is there any truth to the rumors Sydney heard? Did Rowan get into a fight with Justin after I took off Saturday night?

He must notice where my attention is focused, because his fingers brush self-consciously over the battered flesh. Instead of acknowledging the injury, he asks instead, "Do you have a minute to talk?"

"Not really." I hasten my pace. "I have to get to class."

Not taking no for an answer, he quickly says, "I'll walk with you, and we can talk on the way."

Awesome.

Thankfully, Corbin Hall looms on the horizon. If I speed walk, I can be there in five minutes, tops. The less interaction I have with Justin, the better off we'll both be. After discovering his extracurricular activities, there's nothing left to discuss.

"So," he clears his throat when I remain stoically silent, "I wanted to apologize again for the other night."

The guy is delusional if he thinks we're going to brush this neatly under the carpet and move on. What happened wasn't an accident. Any hope of us remaining friends has been obliterated. I don't even want to look at him.

"You mean when I stumbled on you getting a blowie from Annica?"

He has the good grace to flinch at my blunt description. "Yeah, I'm sorry. It shouldn't have happened."

No shit, Sherlock.

"I'm over it." I shrug, only wanting to move on with my morning and my life.

You know what the definition of insanity is?

Doing the same thing over and over and expecting a different outcome.

The lesson I've learned from this experience is to steer clear of the athletes on campus. Maybe it's unfair to paint them all with the same broad-brush stroke, but I've been burned too many times in the past. The guys around here have too many options available. Every men's team at Western has their own set of jersey chasers, cleat sniffers, or puck bunnies.

I'm over the womanizing jocks. I've dated a couple different athletes throughout the years.

Luke, a hockey goalie.

Logan, a soccer midfielder.

Ashton, a breaststroker.

And Justin...a baseball pitcher.

And they've all turned out to be players.

In one regard, it's nice to be with someone who understands the physical demands of playing a sport at a high level. There's a dedication that other people can't comprehend. But the cheating is the ugly side of it.

I'm officially tapping out.

Unaware of the thoughts circling through my head, Justin says, "I wanted to reach out yesterday, but I figured you needed time to cool off."

Is he actually suggesting thirty-six hours is enough time to put his cheating into perspective and forgive him?

That's not going to happen. In fact, the more I think about it, the angrier I get.

When I remain silent, lips pressed into a thin line, he continues. "I was hoping we could move past my," there's a pause, "lapse in judgement and work this out."

He's joking, right?

"I'm sorry?" My gaze jerks from the math building to Justin who remains tenaciously at my side. There's no way I heard him correctly.

"I want to move forward with our relationship. We were really good together." He gives me a hopeful smile. "Instead of letting my indiscretion tear us apart, let's work to overcome it. We'll be a stronger couple in the long run."

Holy crap, the guy is serious. Well, color me stunned. I didn't think it was possible for Justin to shock me anymore than he already has, but I was mistaken. This conversation has totally thrown me for a loop.

"Why would we do that?" My brows beetle together as confusion spirals through me. "It's not like we were seeing each other for that long." I wave a hand in his direction. "In fact, you're the one who said we weren't serious. And you obviously didn't like me enough to remain faithful. So...why bother? Why not move on?"

"You're right, I did say that. I thought I was being considerate by getting my needs taken care of elsewhere."

A snort of disbelief escapes from me. I just can't with this guy.

"I like you, Demi. *A lot*. And I'm human."

Is he really playing the human card?

"I made a mistake," he continues. "Can't you find it in your heart to forgive me?"

No, I really can't. Once trust is broken, it's almost impossible to earn it back again. Why is he even fighting for this relationship?

"Look," I huff, only wanting to pull the plug on this conversation. At this point, I regret ever giving Justin a chance. It was a lapse in judgment on my part. Deep down, I suspected it wouldn't work out in the long run, but even I couldn't have imagined how it would implode. "I appreciate your apology, but our relationship is over." Sure, I could tell him that I was planning to end things before I found him with Annica, but what good would that do? He needs to accept that my answer is final and move on.

Relief bursts inside me when I realize we've reached Corbin Hall and this conversation, whether he wants it to be or not, is over. Just like our relationship.

My gaze reluctantly flickers to Rowan, who lounges outside the brick building. It's hardly a surprise to find him swarmed by a group of students vying for his attention. There's something about the blond football player that attracts both men and women. He's like the sun, and they want to be in his orbit, even if it's for a moment. I would be lying if I didn't admit that I feel the same gravitational pull myself. There's an unrelenting energy that refuses to be subdued. I've spent years struggling against the force of it.

Images from Saturday night crash unwantedly through my head. Days later, I can almost feel the warm drift of his breath across my lips, and the hope that had spiraled through me when I'd thought he would kiss me.

Thankfully, that didn't happen. It would have only complicated matters. Already it feels like we're walking a fine line.

And yet...it's not relief that floods through me.

Our gazes collide, and Rowan's eyes narrow before shifting to Justin who continues doggedly at my side.

"Instead of making a snap decision, one you'll probably regret, why don't you take a few days to think it over."

"That's not nec—"

My voice is cut off as I'm yanked against a hard body.

"You heard her, Fischer," Rowan snaps, "she doesn't need more time. It's over."

Justin presses his lips into a tight line as his expression turns stony. "Why are you always hovering around, Michaels?" His narrowed gaze fills with suspicion as he waggles a finger between us. "Oh. I get it. Maybe the reason you're not interested in working things out with me is because you've been sneaking around behind my back! Maybe that's why you weren't interested in spreading your legs." Justin stabs a finger in Rowan's direction. "You've been screwing around with *him*."

My jaw drops at his sudden turnabout, and I rear back as if I've been slapped. I didn't think it was possible to feel more hurt by his behavior.

"Do you really believe that?" My chest constricts, and I'm barely able to force out the question.

An ugly glint sparks to life in his eyes as he jerks his shoulders. His voice grows louder, booming over the crowd, attracting more unwanted attention. "Who are you trying to kid? Everyone knows you've been making your way through the football roster for years."

Even though Justin doesn't mean a damn thing to me, hurt and humiliation flood through me. Those rumors have always floated around campus. Every once in a while, they rear their ugly head. It's the reason I don't date football players. As I glance self-consciously at the people gathered around us, a dull heat creeps into my checks.

"You know that's not true." It takes effort to keep my voice from trembling. I straighten to my full height, refusing to give Justin the satisfaction of seeing how much damage he's inflicting.

Fuck him. And fuck all these people who think they know *me* or the *truth*.

Justin's voice escalates as if he sees the writing on the wall and wants to alter the demise of our relationship.

Rowan's hands fall from my shoulders as he takes a step in Justin's direction. "Keep running your mouth, Fischer, and I'll give you a shiner to go along with your busted nose."

I grab hold of Rowan's arm to keep him from advancing any further. The two of them getting into a fight will only draw more unwelcome attention to the situation. And I don't want Rowan suffering any consequences on my behalf. I'm more than capable of handling my own problems. And Justin has turned out to be one hell of a problem. One who wasn't worth nearly the trouble he's set on causing.

"Don't," I whisper, attempting to keep my voice devoid of emotion, "he's not worth it."

Rowan's gaze snaps in my direction. "You're right...he's not, but *you* are."

Justin snorts, reluctantly drawing my focus to him. "Maybe if I were a football player, you would be more willing to spread those pretty thighs."

That ugly comment is all it takes to snap the last of Rowan's control. Without warning, he leaps forward. Before he can get his hands on Justin, the baseball player retreats, disappearing through the throng of onlookers. My heart thunders painfully under my breast.

"That guy is a real douche," Rowan mutters, narrowed gaze searching the thick crowd as if he's contemplating going after him.

Yeah, tell me something I don't know. Although, I didn't realize what a complete jackass he was until this latest confrontation. Had I understood it sooner, I could have saved myself a shit ton of humiliation. Lesson learned the hard way. After this debacle, it's going to take a long time for me to trust another guy. In fact, maybe a lengthy break from the opposite sex would be the best thing.

"Are you all right?" Rowan asks, knocking me from my turbulent thoughts.

Before I can summon an answer, his strong arms wrap around my body before tugging me close. It's oh-so-tempting to sink into the warm comfort, squeeze my eyes shut, and pretend this has been nothing more than an ugly nightmare that will disintegrate in my memory come morning. Unfortunately, doing that will only feed the gossip that is probably, at this very moment, spreading across campus like wildfire.

Instead of burying my face against his steely strength, I force myself to glance at the people who continue to stare wide-eyed. Embarrassment flags my cheeks, flooding them with heat. Loud whispers ripple through the group.

Don't these people have anything better to do than stand around and gawk?

Apparently not.

Knowing that I can't stay in his arms, I push away from Rowan, needing to separate myself. Ugly speculation is already running rampant. I certainly don't need to add fuel to the fire. I've suffered enough mortification for one morning.

"We should probably get to class," I mutter.

With my head lowered, I slink toward Corbin Hall. Rowan stays steadfast at my side. Somewhere in the back of my brain, I realize he's trying to be supportive, but his attentive manner only makes matters worse. The knowing whispers and snickers burn the tips of my ears.

As we reach the doors, Rowan stretches around me, grabbing hold of the metal handle before pulling it open. My brain churns as we silently move through the crowded corridor. Relief fills me as we make it to the small lecture hall, and I'm able to slip into the last row. At least I won't have to feel a dozen pair of eyes drilling into the back of my head for the next fifty minutes. With any luck, this will blow over in a day or so. A huff escapes from my lips as I slump onto a chair.

When Rowan moves to settle next to me, I mumble, "Would you mind sitting somewhere else?" My gaze flickers over our classmates who already fill the room. Half of them are swiveled around and staring in our direction. Speculation fills their eager faces as if they're waiting for us to add to the drama that unfolded outside. I'll be damned if I give them anything more to salivate over.

Hurt flashes in Rowan's eyes, leaving me to feel like a first-class jerk. It's on the tip of my tongue to apologize, but I can't push out the words.

When I remain silent, he mutters, "Yeah, sure. No problem."

From the corner of my eye, I watch as he slides to the end of the row before walking down the carpeted staircase. A few girls wave, trying to capture his attention before calling him over to an unoccupied desk.

My belly pinches with unwanted jealousy. His expression transforms and he smiles, focusing on the trio of girls. It should be a relief that he's taken the hint and is no longer at my side. Without us putting on a show, people have already lost interest and are turning away.

Whether Rowan understands it or not, I did what needed to be done. Neither of us want the rumor mill churning at our expense.

And yet, that knowledge only makes me feel worse.

Chapter Thirteen

DEMI

This has turned out to be one hell of a shitty day. Someone needs to explain how Justin is the one who cheated, and yet, he's managed to turn everything around and make me the bad guy in this fucked up scenario. Instead of his name being on everyone's lips, it's mine.

The sidelong glances I've been getting from people I don't even know is ridiculous. At first, I told myself it was nothing more than my imagination. But it's become clear throughout the morning that isn't the case. I keep hearing my name paired with Rowan and the team. Apparently, I've been a busy girl and screwed every single one of them. Lord knows how I have time for so much sex with both school and soccer.

Unsure what to do, I escaped to the only place capable of making me feel better.

I lay on my back in the middle of the stadium field and stare up at the bright blue canvas of sky stretched out overhead. Normally, I would grab something to eat between my second and third class, but there was no way I was walking into the Union without reinforcements.

My fingers stroke absently over the turf as I try to settle all of the rioting emotion inside me. I've never been one to let petty bullshit bother me, but what's happening right now stings. I foolishly allowed the person into my life who set all of this into motion. Instead of being apologetic and taking responsibility for his bad behavior, Justin would rather make me out to be the villain in this scenario.

Every once in a while, the football rumors will rear their ugly head. When they do, I'm always worried that Dad will catch wind of them. He's never come out and said I couldn't date any of the guys on the team. It's more of an unspoken rule. If I were to get together with one of his players, it would only complicate matters. Not only between me and my dad, but him and the guys. So, I've always done what's best for everyone and steered clear.

And yet, here we are.

Again.

A heavy sigh escapes from my lips.

"Is it really that bad?"

Rowan's deep voice knocks me from my thoughts. I blink against the harsh sunlight, shielding my eyes as he drops down beside me. An uncomfortable silence settles over us. One I'm unsure how to break. I'm embarrassed by my earlier behavior. I know he was only trying to help.

"Why are you here?" Practice is never scheduled for this time of day.

His voice softens. "Because I know you're upset about what that jackass said, and I wanted to make sure you were all right."

The concern filling his voice only makes me feel worse. Rowan is being so damn nice, and I don't deserve it after the way I treated him.

The guilt nearly swallows me whole, and I force myself to say, "Sorry for asking you to move in stats. I shouldn't have done that."

Rowan stretches out beside me. His head is only a few inches from mine. The tips of our fingers touch but don't entwine. And yet, I'm acutely aware of them.

Of him.

All it would take is a slight movement, and we would be holding hands. The temptation that crashes over me only serves to confuse me more. If I'm being completely honest with myself, I'm ridiculously aware of Rowan on every level. I'm hyperaware of the way his chest rises and falls with each inhalation. No one has ever made me feel like this, and I'm uncertain what to do with it.

"It wasn't a big deal." His voice drops, becoming rough and low. "I understand why you did it."

And yet, the hurt that had flashed across his face tells a different story.

"I shouldn't have. You were only trying to help. The rumors have circulated before, and I'm sure they'll make the rounds again before I graduate." I've enjoyed going to school here and playing soccer, but the gossip is one thing I won't miss.

"Justin is an asshole for turning everything around on you."

True story.

"Yup, he is." For the umpteenth time, regret flickers through me. "I wish I'd realized it sooner."

"Don't say I didn't try to warn you."

I rotate my head until our gazes can lock. A small smile simmers on his face.

"Please, you've never liked any of the guys I've dated."

"Can I help it if you have terrible taste in men?"

"Oh, really?" My brows shoot up across my forehead. I'm about to argue when I slam my mouth shut. He's right. I have shitty taste in men which is exactly why none of my previous relationships have worked out.

"Fine. If there comes a time when I'm ready to date, I'll let you pick out the next victim. You couldn't possibly do any worse than me."

"I'll hold you to it," he shoots back. "Although, you might be surprised by who I choose."

The scrape of his deep voice sends a fresh wave of nerves cascading down my spine. The way his blue eyes sharpen on me has the bottom of my belly hollowing out.

A heavy silence descends.

He raises a brow in challenge. "Not going to ask who I have in mind?"

It's a loaded question, and we both realize it. I'm not quite ready to go there. Not when I'm still licking the wounds Justin needlessly inflicted earlier this morning. When neither of us takes the conversation further, the thick tension permeating the air gradually recedes, leaving behind a surprising tranquility as we lay stretched out in the middle of the football field. It feels as if something unidentifiable has shifted but I'm not sure what; or even how it happened.

After about five minutes, I clear my throat and force out the rest. "I also wanted to thank you for coming to my defense. You didn't need to get involved."

When he turns his head, I do the same until our gazes collide. Confusion furrows his brow. "Why wouldn't I?"

I jerk my shoulders and try to come up with a plausible explanation before finally admitting the truth. "I guess we've never really been friends."

"Yeah, I've noticed." A heartbeat passes. "Why do you think that is?"

I suck my bottom lip into my mouth and chew it thoughtfully before refocusing my attention on the cloudless sky overhead. It feels as if I'm walking through a minefield. One wrong answer could blow me to smithereens.

When I remain silent, he says, "Demi?" A strange urgency fills his voice. One that brings the tension that always seems to simmer beneath the surface back full force. He rolls onto his side so that his head is propped up by his palm, and he's able to stare down at me.

My tongue darts out to moisten my lips. "I don't know..."

How can I explain that I'm frightened by the intense energy we always generate? That I've never experienced this level of attraction with anyone else. Maybe it's one-sided, and he's unaware of it. Somehow, it would be worse if he did feel it because there's not a damn thing that can happen. Rowan is Dad's star quarterback. And I'm the coach's daughter. I'm not the type of person who believes rules are in place to be broken.

"I think you do, and I want you to tell me," he urges. When I fail to respond, he continues. "You've always kept me at arm's length. Are you finally going to tell me why?"

"That's not true," I whisper. But Rowan is right, that's *exactly* what I do.

A knowing smile settles on his lips. "Yeah, it is. And I get the feeling it's purposeful."

It's shocking to realize how much he's noticed throughout the years. Too scared to reveal the truth, I scramble to come up with an alternative that's believable. "I'm not sure you'll understand..."

The intensity of his stare never wavers. "Try me."

I inhale before carefully expelling it from my lungs. "Sometimes it feels like we're in competition with each other."

When that statement is met with a deafening silence, I flick my gaze nervously to him.

His brows slam together. Whatever he was expecting, that wasn't it. "I don't understand. How are we in competition?"

If only it were possible to abort this uncomfortable conversation. One look at his face tells me that he won't drop it easily. So, I force myself to continue, only wanting to get it over with. As much as I don't want to share this with him, it's better than revealing the truth. The little bit of peace I had managed to find at the stadium has now been shattered by Rowan's presence, and it's doubtful I'll be able to find it again.

"Throughout my dad's career as a coach, players have come and gone from his life. Once they graduate, he always stays in touch, but none have become a part of our lives the way you have." I shrug self-consciously. "You're probably the closest thing my dad will have to a son." The sentiment is like an arrow through my heart because it is unflinchingly true.

Emotion crashes over his handsome features.

Happiness.

Longing.

And finally, understanding.

"Demi." The way he says my name strums something deep inside. His voice drops, sounding as if it's been scraped from the bottom of the ocean. "You have to know how much Coach loves you."

"I do," I cut in, cheeks flaming with humiliation. I sound like a jealous, spoiled brat, and I hate it. That's not who I am.

There has never been a time in my life when I didn't think my father loved me. But I also realize that he probably wishes I'd been a boy. One who he could share his passion for football with—a son who would follow in his footsteps. That's the kind of relationship he has with Rowan. There's an unbreakable bond between them. One I'm not part of.

I startle when Rowan strokes his fingers against the curve of my jaw.

"No one means more to him than you. He's always talking about what an amazing soccer player you are, and that you might try out for the National Women's Soccer League. Or how smart you are, and that you have a near four-point GPA." Before I can interrupt, he continues. "*You* are the most important person in his life."

My heart swells, and a thick lump settles in my throat, making it impossible to suck in oxygen. I know my dad loves me but to hear everything Rowan is saying is like a balm for my soul. Especially after the morning I've had.

"You might not realize this, but I owe everything to your father. Coach was there when I needed a strong male hand to guide me. Without him," he jerks his shoulders as uncertainty fills his eyes, "I don't know where I would be."

There's a naked vulnerability in his expression. One that knocks me off-balance and takes me by surprise. There has never been a time when Rowan and I have opened up to one another like this. I've always been so careful to keep our relationship at a surface level. It was so much easier that way. But that, I realize with a punch to the gut, is no longer possible.

It's only now that we've torn down some of the walls, and I'm able to see him with clear eyes, I realize how little I know about Rowan's background. I search my memory, going back to when my father first scouted him. The only thing I remember hearing about was the four-teen-year-old kid with one hell of an arm. I met him right before freshman year of high school, and Rowan has been a permanent fixture in my life ever since.

I've never questioned the reason for that.

Is his family in the picture? Does he even have one?

If you asked me about his football stats, I could rattle them off because I've heard him and my father discuss them ad nauseum. But personal information? I don't have a clue. It's a giant void.

"What about your parents?" He mentioned needing a strong male hand, does that mean his father wasn't in the picture?

All of a sudden, curiosity eats away at me, and I'm hungry for more information.

A dark shadow flickers across his face before his expression turns guarded. "What about them?"

I blink, surprised by his reaction. Now that we're finally digging deep and sharing personal information, I wasn't expecting him to clam up. "I don't know...do you see them often?"

"Nope." He bites out the word and shifts as if uncomfortable with the direction our conversation has swerved in.

"Why not?" I'm slammed with a thought, and my eyes widen. Barely can I force out the question. "Are they...*dead*?"

"No." He shakes his head as his voice softens. "They're both still very much alive."

From his expression, I can't tell if that's a good thing or not.

"But you don't have much contact with them?" What I really want is for Rowan to open up on his own and explain to me why my father is a surrogate to him when it's obvious he has his own family.

Instead he says, "It's a complicated situation."

"Oh."

What has become clear from our brief conversation is that Rowan isn't comfortable when it comes to discussing his past. I suppose I should respect that. It only proves that Rowan and I aren't friends. If we were, opening up wouldn't be so difficult. And maybe that's for the best. The two of us becoming all buddy-buddy—or *more*—would only complicate matters, and that's the last thing I need.

Another silence descends, and I allow my eyelids to drift closed. The heat of the sun strokes over my cheeks. There's something soothing about the warmth. It's like getting a straight shot of vitamin D.

I'm startled out of my drowsy state when he says quietly, "If you don't want me to come to dinner anymore or hang around with your dad, I get it." There's a pause. "I don't have a problem backing away. I didn't realize it bothered you so much."

When my eyelids feather open, it's to find Rowan staring down at me. There's an intensity filling his eyes that leaves me feeling slightly winded. It blows open the door I was attempting to slam shut.

"I don't want to cause a problem between you two," he adds when I remain silent.

The possibility of him withdrawing from our lives—*from my life*—is enough to send a sliver of fear scampering down my spine. "That's not what I want."

He searches my gaze carefully as if it's possible to sift through my thoughts and discover the truth for himself. "Are you sure?"

"Yes."

A sigh of relief escapes from my lips when he changes the subject. "Can we meet up at the library tonight and work on the stats assignment?"

Right.

Tutoring.

"Yeah." Mentally I go over my schedule for the remainder of the day. "Does seven o'clock work?" When he nods, I add, "East wing of the second floor near the Curriculum Collection?"

He gives me a bemused look, and I shrug self-consciously. "What? I've studied there enough times to know it's quiet."

I spend a lot of time at the library. There's something about the peacefulness and being surrounded by all those books that helps me focus. When Dad asks me to tutor some of the guys, that's my go-to place.

"All right," he says, "it's a date."

My eyes widen, and I shake my head. "What—no! We're just studying—"

"Relax, Richards." A grin flashes across his face. "It was a figure of speech."

"Oh." I force out a nervous chuckle. "Right, I knew that."

Rowan pops easily to his feet. The way he stares down at me makes my skin buzz. Our gazes lock and hold. Some unidentifiable emotion flickers in his deep-blue depths before disappearing, and he stretches out a hand for me to take hold of. The moment I place my fingers in his, a zip of electricity sizzles through me. With barely any effort at all, he pulls me to my feet. My hand stays enveloped in his larger one as my gaze searches his.

Does he feel the connection humming between us, or is it only in my imagination?

Then again, does it really matter?

Nothing can happen.

Those thoughts are like a bucket of cold water dumped over my head, and I take a hasty step in retreat. As I do, our hands drift apart before falling back to our sides.

I have a strict no-footballer rule in place, and it's more important than ever I stick to it.

Chapter Fourteen

DEMI

"Can you believe that girl?" Sydney mutters as we sit on the turf and stretch before practice.

I don't bother to ask who she's talking about; I already know. She reserves that particular level of disdain for very few people.

Unable to help myself, I glance toward the sideline only to see Annica talking with Coach Adams. Every once in a while, the auburn-haired girl will reach out to touch his bare forearm. It's a harmless caress, barely perceptible.

Except...I know it's not.

The way she smiles, tucking a stray lock of hair behind her ear and laughing, tells me it's anything but innocent.

When I remain silent, Sydney continues to seethe next to me. Any moment, she'll begin to foam at the mouth. "Does she seriously think that if she flirts hard enough with Coach, he'll make her a starter?"

Yeah...that's exactly what she thinks. I only hope our coach isn't gullible enough to fall for her doe-eyed behavior. It's not in my nature to see the worst in people, but over the last year, Annica has proven herself to be manipulative. I would be an idiot not to keep a close eye on her. Maybe Sydney is right, and I can be too trusting where my friends are concerned, but she's burned me enough times to warrant my caution.

"Ignore her." It takes effort to drag my gaze away and focus on stretching out my quads. I've got enough to worry about without adding Annica to the mess. Rumors are still swirling through campus.

Coach blows his whistle, and we get to work. For the next two hours, we run through drills and then scrimmage. Even though Annica and I are on the same team, she continuously knocks into me, trying to steal the ball before I have a chance to get off a good kick. The last one I send toward the net is easily caught by Sasha.

Goddamn it!

My placement would be better if I hadn't been trying to fight off the redhead.

"You need to work together, ladies!" Coach bellows from the sidelines. "Teamwork makes the dream work!"

It might be a cheesy cliché, but it's true. We won't get anywhere if we're battling each other instead of the other team. I place my hands on my hips to catch my breath. Annica shoots me a nasty look as she stalks past.

We scrimmage for another twenty minutes before Coach blows his whistle. "That's enough for today. Hit the showers."

A few of the younger girls gather around Annica as we walk to the locker room. I've had enough of her antics. Instead of being one team, there are factions.

We have *Team Annica* and *Team Demi*.

This behavior is so immature. If Annica and I can't come together and find a way to coexist, I'm not sure we'll make it to the playoffs, let alone championship. As much as I hate the idea of a confrontation, there's no longer a way around it.

"I'll meet you in the locker room," I tell Sydney. When she raises her brows, I add, "There's something I need to take care of."

"It's about damn time. Are you sure you don't want me to stay? I can be the muscle." She makes a show of cracking her knuckles. "Your intimidation factor."

I snort at the image she makes. Sydney can definitely be daunting.

As much as I appreciate the offer, I shake my head. "No. It would be better if Annica and I had a private convo."

"All right," she mutters, as if unsure that's a wise choice.

Before Sydney is able to talk me out of my decision, I seek the other girl out on the field and raise my voice. "Annica?"

My auburn-haired teammate turns and glares. The icy look is full of hatred. A shiver of unease scuttles down my spine. For the umpteenth time, I can't help but wonder what I did to have all this loathing aimed in my direction. I've never been anything but nice to her and all the girls. I dealt with enough cliquey behavior in high school and never wanted it to be like that on this team.

I jerk my head toward the empty field. "Let's talk." It's not a question. We're too far beyond that.

Annica purses her lips as if she wants to give me the finger and tell me to get bent. One glance at our coaches has her stomping over to me.

When she's five feet away, she grinds to a halt and folds her arms across her chest. "What do you want?"

All right then. If I were under the delusion that she might actually apologize for sucking my boyfriend off last weekend, that notion is thrown right out the window. There's not a trace of regret or embarrassment in her expression. If anything, it's like I'm the one who has done something wrong. I really don't know what to make of this girl. I've never dealt with anyone like her before.

"Well," I clear my throat, momentarily thrown off by the sparks of anger flying from her eyes, "I wanted to talk to you about what happened on the field."

She shifts her weight as boredom settles over her expression. "Okay. What happened?"

Seriously?

Is it really too much to expect that we act like the grown-ass adults we're supposed to be?

I draw in a steady inhalation and fight for patience. I'm not someone who easily loses my temper, but Annica pushes every single one of my buttons. In a perfect world, I would simply avoid the girl, but that's not possible when we play for the same team. She won't be the reason I quit soccer. Once the season is over, we can part ways. Until then, we have to peacefully coexist.

Maybe Annica likes to play games, but that's not how I operate. I refuse to be dragged into any more of them. The only way to handle this is to cut right to the chase. "You've made it more than obvious that you don't like me." Before she can cut me off, I continue. "And that's fine. We don't have to be best friends or even like each other, but we do need to play together. I think we both want the same thing, and that's to win as many games as possible this season and take home a championship." I pause, allowing the sentiment to sink in. "Is it possible for us to put aside our differences and work together as a team from here on out?"

Not that Annica deserves it, but I'm trying to be a good leader and extend an olive branch. Unfortunately, I can't do it alone. Annica needs to let go of her anger and meet me halfway.

Thick tension crackles in the air as a myriad of expressions flicker across her face. I have no idea if anything I've said has resonated with her. A tiny burst of hope rises in me as she takes a step forward, closing some of the distance that separates us. Instead of giving me a tentative smile, the edges of her lips sink into an ugly scowl as her eyes narrow.

Any hope I'd been harboring bursts like an overinflated balloon. I don't need to hear her response to realize my words have fallen on deaf ears. I should have known that sorting out our issues wouldn't be that easy. Nothing with this girl is simple. By the furious expression twisting her normally pretty features, it becomes clear that I underestimated how deep her loathing goes. I would be lying if I didn't admit I'm a little taken aback by the hatred.

My muscles stiffen as she takes another quick step in my direction until we're practically standing toe to toe. I'm tempted to retreat but refuse to give her the satisfaction of thinking she can intimidate me.

"You're right. I don't like you. I've *never* liked you." A nasty smile flits across her face. "Guess what? Most of the girls on the team don't. You think you're so damn special, but the truth of the matter is that you're not nearly as good as you think you are. If you had any brains whatsoever, you would do us all a favor and quit."

What the fuck?

My mouth drops open as my heart riots painfully beneath my ribcage. Her behavior on Saturday night pales in comparison to the vitriol pouring from her mouth.

My mind blanks.

When I remain silent, a victorious light fills her eyes. "The fact that you're a captain and a starter is the biggest joke of all." Her upper lip curls maliciously. "You strut around like you're some big shit when you're really nothing. It's pathetic. Know what the funniest thing is?" Before I can answer, she continues. "Everyone seems to know it but you."

Air gets clogged in my throat. It's as if I'm being suffocated from the inside out.

Ever since I started playing soccer when I was four years old, I've poured my heart and soul into the game. I wasn't one of those kids who tried a bunch of different sports before finally settling on one. It's always been my first love. I've played on a handful of different travel teams and then for my high school. When I was applying to college, I had several offers from Division 1 schools. I chose Western because the academics were top-notch, and the women's team consistently ranked in the top two programs in their division. I didn't come in as a starter freshman year. I earned my position through hard work and dedication.

How dare she insinuate otherwise!

It takes a few moments before I'm able to find my voice. "Excuse me? Who the hell do you think you are?"

"Oh, I know exactly who I am. I also know I'm more talented than you." She shoves a hand against my shoulder, knocking me back a step. "The only reason you're anything on this team is because of your daddy." She smirks. "Not only does everyone know it, but they also resent the hell out of it."

Heat slams into my cheeks. "My father has *nothing* to do with my position or being captain!"

"Is that what you really think?" She rolls her eyes and waves a hand toward the locker room. "Everyone knows that daddy is the one who secured you the spot."

Rage bubbles up inside me.

I take a step forward, unwilling to back down or be intimidated by this girl who is nothing more than a loudmouth bully. "I've spent three years earning my position on this team. No one handed me anything. I've put in the time, and I've worked hard. Maybe you should try that instead of flirting with the coach and causing dissension on the team."

Her eyes narrow as if she wasn't expecting me to slap back. "I've got more talent in my pinkie than you'll ever have."

"Oh yeah?" I raise my brows. "Then prove it! If you're so damn good, take my position away through talent on the field instead of constantly running your mouth and trying to turn my teammates against me."

She bares her teeth like a feral animal. "When I'm done with you, you'll wish you never picked up a soccer ball in the first place."

"Good luck with that, Annica. Right now, the only thing I wish I'd never done is befriend you."

Unwilling to argue with her anymore, I stride away, leaving her to stand alone on the field. It's only after I distance myself that I realize my hands are shaking. Even though it needed to happen, I hate confrontations. The only good thing to come out of this conversation is that we know exactly where we stand with each other. For better or worse, it's all out in the open. If I'd hoped we could put our differences aside and finish out this season as a united team, that notion has been blown to shit. Annica won't be happy until she wipes me off the face of the earth.

And I refuse to go down quietly without a fight.

Chapter Fifteen

DEMI

After the day I've had, the library is the last place I want to be. I feel like hammered horseshit. My run-in with Justin this morning and then Annica this afternoon has wiped me out emotionally. As tempting as it was to cancel my tutoring session with Rowan, I couldn't bring myself to do it. The conversation at the stadium this afternoon has shifted our relationship. He was there when I needed someone and stood up to Justin. If he needs help with stats, then the least I can do is return the favor.

As soon as my confrontation with Annica pushes its way into my brain, I'm once again taken aback by the viciousness of her comments. Over the last year, I've become increasingly aware that there was a problem between us. Never in my wildest dreams did I realize she harbored so much hatred for me. It's a little disturbing. All right, maybe more than a little.

Even though I know exactly how hard I've worked to get where I am and that I've earned my position on the team as both a starter and a captain, the ugliness she hurtled earlier gnaws at my insides. Doubt mushrooms up inside me. It's stupid. I've never questioned myself before. So why am I listening to anything she has to say now?

And yet, the vitriol she spewed circles viciously at the back of my brain, refusing to be banished.

"Hey."

The deep voice has me blinking out of my thoughts as Rowan slides onto the chair situated next to me. For the first time in my life, it's a relief to see him. His presence forces me out of my own head. And right now, I need that more than ever.

"Hi." I hoist my smile and attempt to shove everything to the outer recesses of my brain.

Rowan settles on the chair and pulls out his book and notebook from his backpack before carefully searching my eyes. His brow furrows. It's as if he's able to pick through all of the private thoughts I'm trying to shove deep down inside. He doesn't know me that well. He shouldn't be able to read me so easily. "Are you all right?"

His unexpected concern throws me off-kilter. "Yeah." Rather than tell him the truth, I say, "I'm fine."

A hard glint enters his eyes, and the easy-going expression he had been wearing vanishes. "You didn't have another run-in with Justin, did you?"

"No."

"What then?" His jaw tightens as stubbornness settles over his features. "It's obvious something happened."

Even though some of the barriers standing between us have been chipped away, that doesn't necessarily mean I want to spill my guts. Maybe, deep down, I'm afraid that Annica is right, and my father has something to do with the success I've found at Western. Not once have I ever considered the possibility. Now that she's breathed life into the idea, I can't stop from worrying there could be a kernel of truth to it.

"Demi, answer me." His voice drops, becoming more commanding.

My teeth sink into my lower lip as I glance away. "It's nothing."

His fingers wrap around my thigh before giving it a gentle squeeze. Electricity sizzles through me at the innocuous contact. "Why don't you tell me what's going on and let me determine that for myself?"

I huff out a breath and try to steer the conversation back to safer terrain. "We're supposed to be working on statistics, not talking about all the crap going on in my life."

"I thought we'd decided earlier that we're friends?"

A second ticks by as I consider the prospect. Is that what we are now?

Friends?

After spending so many years holding him at a distance, it's a strange concept to wrap my mind around.

When I remain silent, he continues, "Friends talk to one another when there's a problem. And we're friends, right?"

I don't know...are we?

I jerk my head into a tight nod. For better or worse, I suppose that's the path we're now careening down.

He squeezes my thigh for a second time. The heat of his handprint becomes singed into my bare flesh for all eternity. "Then tell me what's going on."

I press my lips together, fighting the strange need I have to confide in him. When I can't hold it in any longer, all the details pour out. Every poisonous dart that Annica hurtled in my direction. Heat flames my cheeks as I purge it from my body. Sydney had drilled me for the details on our way home from practice, and while I told her most of it, I'd glossed over the ugliest parts. The ones that leave me questioning my own talent. It sucks how one little comment can fill you with so much self-doubt.

When my shoulders finally slump and everything has been released into the atmosphere, Rowan's expression turns thunderous. "She really said all that to you?"

I jerk my head.

"You know it's a bunch of bullshit, right?"

Is it?

Dad is the highest-paid coach in the conference. Every two years, the university renews his contract. It's important they keep him happy. The football team brings in a lot of money for Western. Money that allows professors to continue with their research. Over the years, Dad has fielded offers from several top-notch programs throughout the country. He's always been happy here, so he's never given them any serious consideration.

But...what if I'm part of the equation?

What if Dad hasn't considered leaving because deals were made under the table on my behalf?

My heart stutters at the possibility. As much as I'm loath to admit it, Annica has done the one thing I never thought possible. She's shaken my confidence.

If I found out that Dad had something to do with me being a starter or a captain, I would be beyond humiliated. I wouldn't deserve to play the game at this level and would be forced to quit. It would take away all of my achievements.

When I remain silent, Rowan closes the distance between us. "Demi?"

I snap back to the conversation. "Yeah, I do."

"But?" He raises his brows, clearly picking up on the uncertainty weaving its way through my voice.

I hate that I've let her fuck with my head. As an athlete, the worst thing you can do is allow an opponent to get to you. Even though we're on the same team, we're adversaries.

"Ninety-nine percent of me doesn't believe it, but there's that tiny one percent that can't let it go. That wonders if my father is part of the reason I'm on the team or was made a captain." My heart lurches as I give voice to the thoughts racing through my head.

"I've watched you play. There's no way that's possible. Everything you've achieved is because of your hard work and commitment to the sport. It has nothing to do with Coach."

Rowan's voice is filled with so much certainty. I wish I felt that secure in my own abilities and could easily brush off the comments. Let them go in one ear and out the other.

"This girl sounds jealous. She's trying to knock you off your game. Don't let her do it."

My lips lift into a slight smile. "Now you sound like Sydney."

How is it possible that Rowan Michaels—of all people—has made me feel better about this situation? A week ago, I could have never imagine confiding something so personal. And yet, here we are. It's a little unnerving how quickly relationships can morph into something different.

He flashes me a grin. "Sydney is a smart girl. Maybe you should listen to her. She seems to know what she's talking about."

I snort as some of the heaviness weighing me down vanishes, leaving a surprising lightness in its place. "I doubt you'd say that if you knew what she's encouraged me to do over the years."

"That might be so, but in this instance, her assessment is spot-on. This Annica chick sounds jealous."

"I don't know." That's the one thing I can't wrap my head around. Annica is a talented player. There's no reason for jealousy. If she spent more time focusing on soccer and stopped trying to create drama where there is none, she could be better than I am.

When the younger girl came in as a freshman, I was blown away by her raw talent. I figured at some point; she would surpass me in skill. Instead of being threatened, I befriended her and tried to help her grow as a player. If she's fallen short of her own expectations, that's on her.

"Well, I do. Hopefully now that you've pulled her aside, she'll lay off."

As much as I want to believe that Annica will let go of her animosity and let bygones be bygones, I don't think that will be the case. This seems more like a battle to the death.

Much like earlier this afternoon when we were stretched out on the football field, a strange calmness falls over me. Hashing out this problem with Rowan has helped me to feel more settled. Nothing has been solved, but all the noise in my head is more of a whisper.

How is it possible that in the course of one day, I've had two conversations with Rowan that have had more depth than any we've had in the seven years we've known each other?

And it's actually been...dare I say...*nice*?

Yeah, I just admitted it. We're spending time together, and I'm actually enjoying it. Trust me, no one could be more surprised by this turn of events. And it kind of makes me want to...I don't know...spend more time with him?

Oh, boy.

I clear my throat and try to banish all the peculiar feelings attempting to take root inside me before I force my gaze to the statistics book splayed open on the table. "It's getting late. We should probably get started."

For the next hour, we move painstakingly through each problem that Professor Peters assigned this morning in class. Rowan scoots his chair closer until his thigh brushes against mine. I become hyperaware of his woodsy aftershave and the cedarwood scent of the shampoo he must have used after practice. The combination is oddly distracting, and I find myself leaning in to suck in a greedy lungful of him. When I catch myself doing it for the third time, I jerk away and refocus my thoughts.

The realization of why I've gone out of my way to avoid him hits me like a Mack Truck. He makes me feel things I'm not necessarily comfortable with. In the past, I've convinced myself that I found him annoying. Now that we've scratched beneath the surface of our relationship, I can finally admit that it's not true. It was all a smokescreen. A way to keep myself separated from him. What I've come to understand is that I actually like Rowan.

More than I thought possible.

More than I want to.

And definitely more than I should.

Today, unfortunately, has been a day for revelations.

"There." Unaware of the disturbing thoughts crashing around inside my head, Rowan slides the notebook toward me to check his work.

I blink and focus on the problem that swims before my eyes. It takes far more effort than necessary to work through the steps. "Yup," I say, slightly rattled by the emotions flooding through me, "you got it."

When the edges of his lips quirk, something dangerous pings at the bottom of my belly. His eyes darken, and my breath gets trapped at the back of my throat making it impossible to breathe. He draws closer until I'm able to decipher all the stunning flecks that make up the ocean-like color. Saturday night slams into my consciousness, and I recall what it felt like to be pressed against the steely strength of his body.

How I'd wanted him to kiss me, and the disappointment that had flooded through me when he backed away. The library, with its rows of shelves and desks that line the perimeter, fade to the background until it's only the two of us. He's all I see. All I'm aware of. My head turns fuzzy from lack of oxygen. It's a strange sensation, but one that's not entirely unpleasant. Almost like being drunk.

Everything in me becomes whipcord tight. Time stretches as the distance between us is eaten up. He's so close that I can feel his warm breath as it drifts across my lips.

This is it. He's going to kiss me.

And you know what?

I'm going to let him.

After all the crap today, I need it. I need to feel the firm pressure of his mouth coasting over mine, dragging me under so I no longer have to think. As my eyelids feather shut, a chirpy chorus of voices knock me from the strange paralysis that has taken hold.

"Hi, Rowan!"

I lurch back so fast that I almost give myself whiplash.

His gaze reluctantly shifts from me to the two girls who have sidled up beside our table. A smile curves his lips, but the intensity isn't the same as the one that had been aimed in my direction. "Hey. What's up?"

I release a steady puff of air and try to get a grip. My heart is thumping like it'll explode from my chest. I can't believe that almost happened. What the hell had I been thinking?

The brunette slinks closer, all the while flashing him a wide grin. Those pearly whites are nearly blinding in their intensity. She has the look of a hungry shark. I think we all know what she would like to gobble up in one tasty bite.

"Mandy and I were heading over to a party at the Sigma Kappa house." She invades his personal space before fluttering a hand over his shoulder. "You should come with us." She shoots her friend a sly look. "It'll be so much fun!"

I know *exactly* what that look means. Apparently, the three of them know each other well.

Intimately so.

Since it's doubtful an invitation will be extended my way, I take this as my cue to get the hell out of Dodge. It only goes to show what kind of day I had if Rowan Michaels was able to burrow beneath my skin so easily. I've spent the last seven years keeping the handsome football player at a distance. If I've learned anything today, it's that I'm going to have to work a little harder to resurrect the walls that have been knocked down. Especially when he's every inch of the player I suspected.

I don't need someone like that in my life.

"That sounds fun but—"

Before he can get the rest out, I shoot to my feet. "I'm going to take off."

"Wait—"

With my eyes averted, I shake my head. "I've still got my own work to finish up. I need to get moving."

"Oh." His voice drops, disappointment coloring the deep timbre.

Even though I tell myself not to do it, my gaze flickers in his direction. "I'll see you in class on Wednesday."

"Yeah, sure." Before I can get trapped in the blueness of his eyes, I shove my materials into my bag and hightail it to the staircase. It's a relief when I push through the glass doors on the ground floor, and the cool night breeze wafts over my heated cheeks.

All I know is that what occurred in the library can't happen again.

I've put Rowan in a little box marked *do not touch,* and that's exactly where he needs to stay.

Chapter Sixteen

DEMI

"There are so many parties happening tonight. And girl, I need it. I plan to cut *way* loose."

I glance at Sydney as she barges into my room and flops onto my bed.

A frown settles on her face as her gaze drops to the canvas bag I'm filling with clothes. "What are you doing?"

"Dad is out of town for the weekend, so I thought I'd head home and chill out."

"What?" She jerks upright from her prone position. "You're leaving?"

"Yeah," I sigh. It's been a tough week. Instead of the rumors dying down after a couple of days, they're flying all over school. When I'm on campus, people point and whisper. It makes me feel like a bug under a microscope. None of the stories I've heard are accurate. Some are plain outlandish. It's like the headlines of my life have been ripped straight from the storyline of *Gossip Girl*.

"I need to get out of here for a while." If I'm lucky, someone else's life will implode this weekend, and when I return to Western on Monday, everything will magically be back to normal.

Dinner on Wednesday with Dad and Rowan was awkward. I spent

most of the time worrying that my father had not only caught wind of the rumors but might actually believe them. If he had, he never mentioned them. The rest of the time I spent avoiding Rowan, which is difficult to do when there are only three people in attendance. I stuck to Dad's side like glue before taking off as soon as the dishes were done.

"Running away won't solve anything."

"That's not what I'm doing." Okay...so that's *exactly* what I'm doing. I deserve a break. This whole week, I held my head high and ignored all the sly comments and knowing looks sent my way. I can't do it any longer. "Want to come with me? We can chill and catch some rays by the pool."

"Can't." She shakes her head. "I told Ethan that we would have dinner and hash out some stuff, and then we were going to meet up with a few girls from the team. I figured you'd need a drink as much as I do."

"I think what will help the most is to get away from this place." I don't mention that I need to put a little distance between Rowan and myself.

Sydney stretches out on the bed and stares at the ceiling. "Annica better hope I don't run into her tonight. I know that little bitch is behind all this."

Her and Justin are running their mouths all over campus.

The dynamic duo.

What's hilarious—not to mention ironic—is that I'm not the one who cheated. It was the two of them. And yet, I'm the one being talked about. It's my name being dragged through the mud.

I toss a black bikini into the bag. This weekend is supposed to be gorgeous. I plan to spend at least part of Saturday and Sunday laying out by the pool relaxing. With any luck, I'll forget all about this mess. At least for a few days. "Please don't do anything that will get you in trouble, okay? Annica isn't worth it."

Sydney waves a hand. "Please, you know me better than that."

My gaze slices to her. "Yeah, that's why I'm saying it."

She snorts. "I'll try to control myself to the best of my ability."

"And don't drink too much. I won't be around to talk you off the ledge." The one weekend I was gone last year, Sydney got into a wicked fight and punched some girl who had been making moves on her man.

She sits up and points a finger at me. "Hey! I told that skank what would happen if she kept it up. It's not my fault she didn't take the warning seriously. I have zero regrets!"

"That's part of the problem. You're damn lucky Coach Adams was able to get you out of that mess, or you would've had to take anger management classes."

She grumbles at the reminder.

I've known Sydney for three years, and I learned quickly that she's not someone to be messed with. The girl is a bad bitch. She may look all sweet and innocent with her blond hair and vibrant green eyes, but beneath the doll-like exterior lies a temper that explodes as easily as dynamite. That's what happens when you have five older brothers. You learn to kick a little ass. Sydney is accustomed to sticking up for herself and fighting for what she wants.

When I'm done filling the duffle bag, I zip it up and hoist it over my shoulder. "I'll be back late Sunday afternoon. Call me if you change your mind and want to stop over."

She rises to her feet. "Are you sure about this?"

"Yup. A break will do me good."

Fine," she mutters, "but I'll miss you."

I pull her in for a quick hug. Sydney has always been a good friend. I'm lucky to have her. "Plus, you'll have the apartment all to yourself. You can be as loud as you want."

"You know that I'm always loud." She squeezes me before stepping away. "It's never good to hold your feelings inside. It messes up your Chi."

She's right about being noisy. The girl has no shame.

Sydney walks me to the door. With a wave, I slip into the hallway and out of the building. Once I settle in the front seat of my white Jeep and start the engine, relief courses through me. Every mile I put between myself and campus has the tension leaking from my body. By the time I pull into the driveway of my house, I feel almost normal again.

My plans for the weekend include—ordering pizza, binge watching

Supernatural, and taking a dip in the heated pool. Dad will be closing it up in a few weeks, so I want to enjoy it while I can.

As I shove the key in the lock and walk through the front door, I realize that I made the right decision. This is exactly what I needed. A little time to myself to relax, rewind, and reset.

With any luck, by the time I head back to campus, my perspective will be restored.

Chapter Seventeen

ROWAN

I lift a bottle of beer to my lips as my gaze coasts over the crowd. The music is pumping, a group of frat guys is playing a game of cups near the makeshift bar, and some underclassman threw up all over himself in a corner. In other words, it's another weekend here at WU. Under normal circumstances, my ass wouldn't be out on a Friday night. I would have eaten a carb-loaded dinner to give me energy and hit the sheets early. But it's a bye week, so there isn't a game scheduled. I spot a few teammates, it's only nine o'clock, and a couple of the younger guys are already shitfaced.

It's not a good look. Coach would have their asses if he realized they were out partying it up. Bye week or not.

During the season, I'll have a beer or two. But no more than that. Getting tanked lost its appeal a long time ago. Maybe when I first stepped foot on campus, I went a little crazy and enjoyed the freedom, but it didn't last long. I have too much riding on the line to throw it away on partying. I've spent years working toward my dreams of turning pro. Now that I'm so close to making it a reality, there's no way in hell I'm going to jeopardize it.

There's one particular face I've been looking for. So far, she's remained elusive. This week has given Demi a swift kick in the ass. I wouldn't blame her for sitting this one out. Although, for obvious reasons, I'm hoping that's not the case.

As I continue to search from where I've taken up sentinel, slender arms snake their way around me from behind. A moment later, breasts are squashed against my back. "Hey, Rowan," comes a silky voice against my ear, "I was hoping to run into you tonight."

Great...Harper Davenport. Just who I *didn't* want to see.

"Hey, Harp."

Now I need to figure out an extraction plan. Sooner rather than later. There are definitely times when an escape hatch would come in handy. This is one of them.

"I haven't seen you around lately." As she presses closer, her nipples pebble through the thin shirt she's wearing. "It's almost like you're avoiding me."

Yeah, well, there's an excellent reason for that.

I made the epic mistake of fooling around with Harper freshman year, and she's been stalking my movements ever since. That's not me being egotistical. It's the truth. I've tried my best to let her down gently, but she refuses to take the hint that I've moved on and am not interested in a repeat performance.

When her fingers migrate south of the border, I grab hold of them to stop their descent before they reach their intended destination. Maybe some guys are cool with getting a handy in the middle of a crowded house party, but that's never been my style.

"Wanna take this somewhere private?" she asks, voice full of sultry promise.

Hell, no. That's the last thing I want. I've given this girl zero encouragement, and she refuses to leave me alone. There are plenty of guys who would give their left nut to spend a little one-on-one time alone with her. She's gorgeous with a banging body.

But I'm not one of them.

"Sorry, Harp. Not tonight." I unwind her arms before pulling her around in front of me. I'm careful to keep her at arm's length. She's like a snake; once she gets ahold of you, it's damn hard to get her uncoiled.

She thrusts out her bottom lip in a pout meant to be sexy but comes off as toddler-ish. "You say that every time."

The girl's got me there.

"Why is that?" She squeezes her arms against the outer sides of her breasts, pressing them together so I get a good look down the front of her cleavage. "Aren't you interested?"

Hard no.

"Well..." I'm about to level with her for the umpteenth time when I catch sight of Sydney. Anticipation shoots through me as I comb the immediate vicinity for Demi. Those two are usually attached at the hip. "I need to talk with someone. I'll catch you later."

"What?" Harper's voice escalates. "We were in the middle of a conversation!"

"Sorry about that." I don't bother waiting for a response as I shove my way through the crowd to reach Sydney and her boyfriend.

Right as I catch up to them, she whips around to Ethan. "Oh my God, that's not what I said! Why do you have to take everything so literally?"

Great.

They're fighting.

Again.

I've seen them out enough times to know that these two are either going at it hot and heavy or are bickering like an old married couple. There's no in-between with them.

It's tempting to disappear through the crowd so I don't get dragged into their argument—except I can't walk away. I want to know where Demi is. If there's a problem or something else happened with fuck-wad, I want to know about it. I'd be more than happy to have another convo with Justin.

Using my fists.

I've heard all the shit going around campus. I have zero doubts it's originating from him. Someone needs to shut him up before he does anymore damage.

"Hey," I say loudly, cutting into their conversation before it can escalate any further.

With their mouths open, they swing toward me.

"Oh, hey," Sydney says.

Ethan grumbles something about grabbing a drink before stalking away. A mixture of sadness and irritation fills Sydney's eyes as he takes off.

I clear my throat, drawing her attention to me. "Trouble in paradise?"

"Is it that obvious?" Her voice softens, turning almost pensive. "Have you ever liked someone and kept trying to make it work, but you couldn't do it? It was like trying to shove a square peg into a round hole? It just didn't fit?"

I glance at Ethan as he grins at a few fellow baseball players. The tension filling his expression has already dissolved.

If Sydney is looking for romantic advice, she's come to the wrong person. I pull something out of my ass and hope it's helpful. "Can't say that I have. I guess you'll know it's time to walk away when the bad outweighs the good."

She contemplates my nugget of wisdom. "Yeah, I suppose that's something to consider." Then she blinks, and all of the emotion filling her gaze disappears as if it had never been there in the first place. "Sorry. It's Friday night, and here I am, getting all maudlin. Must have already had one too many drinks." With a tilt of her head, her attention zeros in on me. "So...what can I do for you?" A sly expression morphs over her features. "As if I didn't already know."

My guess is that Sydney realizes exactly where my interest lies. But still...I'm not about to confirm or deny my feelings. Not yet, anyway. "Just wondering where your trusty sidekick is."

The humor falls away as she glares around the room. "She decided to go home for the weekend. These assholes are giving her hell."

Home?

I'm pretty sure Coach is away on a recruiting trip, which means Demi is there alone.

"Is she all right?" It pisses me off that she felt the need to escape from campus because of it. Sydney nailed it on the head when she said these people were assholes.

A good number of them are.

"She's hurt and embarrassed by all the rumors." Anger flashes across her face. "I'd like nothing better than to kick Justin's ass."

From everything I know about Sydney, that's not an idle threat.

Justin better hope he doesn't run into her this weekend. It could be detrimental to his health.

"If it makes you feel better, I rearranged his nose last Saturday."

Her lips reluctantly hitch at the corners. "Yeah, I heard all about it. Too bad you didn't inflict more damage."

Before I can ask any further questions, her eyes narrow as she gives me a shrewd look. "Exactly what are your intentions with my girl?"

"Just being a concerned friend." Even though it's probably too late, I glance away and try to play it cool. "Is that such a crime?"

"Friends?" She steps closer before driving a finger into my chest. "Yeah, I don't think so." There's a pause. "I think you like her."

I roll my eyes and try to make light of her suspicions. "What? Are we in middle school now? You want to know if I *like* her or *like-like* her?"

"Oh, sweetheart." A knowing look settles across her face as she pats my cheek none-to-gently. "Don't be ridiculous. I think you *like-like* her. I was just curious if you had enough balls to admit it."

Sydney's got enough on her plate with Ethan. She doesn't need to worry about me. "Maybe you should—"

"Well, well, well...look who it is. Just the girl I was hoping to see."

My voice trails off as Brayden sidles up beside us. He's got eyes for one person, and it isn't me. Sydney straightens to her full height which is still nine or ten inches shorter than Bray. The teasing expression vanishes from her face. Whatever information gathering mission she had been on is now forgotten.

My gaze flickers to my teammate as I assess the situation. His attention is solely focused on the blonde.

Hmmm. Interesting.

"Great," she snaps. "Just who I was hoping *not* to run into."

His smiles stretches into a full-on grin as if her less than enthusiastic greeting is exactly what he was hoping for. He makes a show of glancing around. "What? No boyfriend tonight?"

Her cheeks pinken. "Not that it's any of your business, but he's here."

"You run him off already?"

She gnashes her teeth before baring them like a rabid animal. "He went to grab a drink. He'll be back any minute. What's it to you?"

Brayden shrugs before closing the distance between them. "If you were my girl, I sure as shit wouldn't leave you to your own devices."

"Fortunately, I'm not your girl," she fires back.

"Never say never."

"Are you totally delusional?" Her eyes flare wide. "There is no way in hell that I would ever be," she uses air quotes, "*your girl*."

My surprised gaze flickers from one to the other as the tension rachets up between them. It's almost enough to choke on.

What the hell is going on here?

As interested as I am to see how this interaction plays out, now seems like the perfect time to slip away undetected. I suspect a bomb could go off and neither of them would notice.

Not bothering to say goodbye, I take off through the crowd, pushing my way toward the front door. I'm not sure what Brayden is up to. I've known the guy since training camp of freshman year. Sydney isn't his usual type of girl. He's used to jersey chasers and cleat sniffers who hang all over him and stroke his ego.

Sydney is the complete opposite of that. She'll chew him up and spit him out if he's not careful.

Chapter Eighteen

DEMI

The doorbell chimes, and I pause the movie before jumping off the couch and grabbing the money from the credenza by the front door. Looks like the pizza has arrived. Thank God, I'm starving. Dad doesn't keep a lot of snacks stocked in the pantry, which is exactly why I ordered a large pepperoni with extra cheese. There should be enough left over to get me through the weekend. Most of the time, I try to eat healthy. But after the week I've had, that's been thrown out the window. Tonight, I'm going to eat my feelings. One slice at a time.

Thank you very much, Justin and Annica.

My belly rumbles in anticipation as I yank open the front door, ready to hand over the money in exchange for some ooey-gooey deliciousness. Hands down, One Hell of a Pizza is my favorite restaurant. It's New York style with huge floppy pieces.

The more I think about it, the more my mouth waters.

Except...it's not the pizza delivery guy I find waiting on the other side of the threshold. It's the blond football player who has been occupying way too much of my thoughts lately.

"What are you doing here?" The question shoots out of my mouth before I can rein it in again.

His lips twist. "And a good evening to you, too."

"Sorry." Heat singes my cheeks as I shift uncomfortably from one foot to the other. "You're not who I was expecting."

"Oh?" His brows slowly crawl up his forehead as his expression turns harsh. It disappears before I have a chance to decipher exactly what it means. "And just who were you expecting?"

"Pizza," I offer in the way of clarification. Not that I owe him any. But still...the sudden tension crackling in the air feels stifling.

I hug the edge of the door as he shoves his hands into the pockets of his jeans. It's almost painful to admit how good he looks in the navy T-shirt that hugs the swells of his biceps and molds perfectly to his chest.

Focus, Demi!

Right.

I shove those distracting thoughts from my brain before they can cause anymore mischief. "You didn't answer my question." I pause for a beat. "Why are you here?"

He shrugs as his voice softens. "You've had a crap week, and I wanted to make sure you were okay."

"Oh." That's the second time he's made a point of checking on me. Even though I want to stay strong, everything inside me melts. "How did you know I was here?"

"I ran into Sydney at a party, and she filled me in." Silence descends as we cautiously watch one another. He clears his throat and shifts his weight. "So, you gonna let me in?"

That doesn't necessarily seem like the best idea. This has been an odd week, and everything in me is still raw and churning. Under normal circumstances, I have no problem keeping Rowan at a safe distance, both mentally and physically. But our relationship has recently shifted in unexpected ways. I think about our talk at the stadium and when we worked together at the library. The emotions he'd roused had left me feeling strange and uncomfortable. What I need is for my relationship with Rowan to shift back to what it's always been—little more than strangers who are forced to interact upon occasion.

Before I can voice a decision, a hunk of junk with muffler issues rolls to a stop in front of the house. It backfires before the engine dies, and a plume of smoke belches from the tailpipe.

Holy crap. How the hell did that clunker pass emissions?

Rowan turns, and we watch a kid who can't be more than sixteen years old jump out of the car and sprint to the passenger seat before pulling out a red carrying case and jogging across the front lawn.

"Hi! I'm here to deliver a pizza to—" he glances at the order form before looking at us. His eyes widen. "Hey! You're Rowan Michaels, QB for the Wildcats!"

Rowan's lips lift. "Guilty."

"Wow!" The kid pulls off his red ball cap with the One Hell of a Pizza logo on it before plowing a hand through his ginger-colored mane. "I was at the game last weekend, and you were so awesome! I couldn't believe you threw that eighty-yard pass right to Brayden Kendricks!"

"Thanks. We all had a great game."

"*You* had a great game, Michaels." The pimply faced kid stares at Rowan in a worshipful manner, as if totally starstruck. It's kind of amusing. But then again, I'm famished, so not really.

When the delivery guy continues to stare in awe, Rowan clears his throat before digging around in his front pocket. "How much do I owe you for the pizza?"

"No, I got it." I offer up the twenty I grabbed off the credenza. "Here you go."

The kid shakes his head. "No way, Michaels! The pizza is on me." He steps closer and lowers his voice as if he's divulging state secrets. "Free pizza is one of the few perks this crap job has."

Even though the guy hasn't bothered to look at me since he realized he was in the company of Wildcat greatness, I push the money toward him. "I insist on paying."

"No can do, it's on me." The kid shakes his head. "No one is going to believe I bought Rowan Michaels a pizza!" His eyes pop wide again. "Hey! Can I take a selfie with you?"

"Um, I don't think—"

"Sure you can!" I step forward and grab the insulated bag from the kid before unzipping it and sliding out the box from within.

"Awesome!" the delivery guy gushes.

Rowan shoots me a pleading look, which I promptly ignore before stepping inside the house with my large pepperoni pizza and slamming the door closed. That's what he gets for showing up on my doorstep unannounced and sending my hormones into further chaos.

Five minutes later, I've got a plate and have opened the box on the dining room table. I'm about to lift a massive piece of deliciousness to my mouth when the front door swings open, and Rowan steps inside.

He glances around until his narrowed gaze lands on me before jerking a thumb over his shoulder. "Thanks for leaving me out there. I barely escaped with my life intact." When I say nothing in response, he continues. "Do you know that he wanted to take me to the restaurant so I could meet the gang?"

I can almost imagine the kid pleading with Rowan to come back with him. My shoulders shake with silent laughter.

"It's not funny!" he grunts with a scowl.

"It kind of is." Actually, there's no *kind of* about it. It's funny. There hasn't been much to laugh about this week, and that definitely does the trick.

He spears a finger at the open box. "I hope you appreciate that pizza. I feel dirty right now. Kind of like I prostituted myself."

"I tried to pay," I say with a shrug. "He wouldn't accept it."

"The least you could do is offer me a slice."

I wave my hand toward the kitchen. "Be my guest. You know where the plates are." Rowan probably knows the set up of this house as well as I do. He's certainly been here enough times.

He takes one step toward the kitchen before grinding to a halt. With more interest, his gaze slides over the length of me. It's a physical caress I feel straight down to my bones. Only then, do I become aware of my fashion choices for the evening. Since I wasn't expecting company, I'm wearing tiny pajama shorts and an oversized Wildcats jersey.

Minus a bra.

Did I mention that Rowan's name is stamped across the back?

"Huh." The frown he had been wearing morphs into a smirk. "Nice shirt."

A bolt of heat hits my cheeks. I could kick myself for giving in to the urge when I came across the jersey stuffed in my dresser drawer. "Don't read anything into it. Dad gave it to me a while ago. He mentioned something about there being a lot of extras they needed to get rid of."

"Is that so?" With a grin, he strokes his fingers over the sexy five o'clock shadow that lines his jaw. For a moment, I get caught up in the movement. "Usually, the campus bookstore can't keep my jersey stocked on the shelves."

I shrug, feeling very much like a groupie with a Rowan Michaels crush. This guy already has a massive ego. The last thing I want to be accused of is stroking it.

"Looks good on you." His voice drops, strumming something deep inside as heat fills his eyes.

There is no way I'm touching that comment with a ten-foot pole.

When I remain silent, he disappears into the kitchen, presumably to grab a plate and something to drink. An army of butterflies wing their way to life in the pit of my belly as I migrate to the couch, settling at the far end to give him enough room in case he decides to bypass the armchair. Instead, he takes a seat directly next to me, barely leaving a few inches of space to separate us. I'm ridiculously aware of his muscular body next to mine. Even though I try to tamp down the sparks of attraction shooting through me, they flare to life like fireworks on the Fourth of July.

He points to the big screen television mounted over the fireplace. "What are we watching?"

We?

When did this situation turn into a we?

"A psychological thriller that came out last summer." I clear my throat and stare at the frozen screen. "You, ah, don't have to stay." My gaze flicks to his. "I'm fine. I just needed to get away from campus for a bit."

"I don't mind hanging out." He shrugs as his gaze collides with mine. "Plus, I could use a breather. It would be kind of nice to chill for the evening."

I gnaw my lower lip with indecision. The two of us spending more time alone together sounds like a disaster waiting to happen. All of my usual defenses have been beaten down, which has left me feeling unusually vulnerable where Rowan is concerned.

When I remain silent, his voice drops. "No one knows I'm here, if that's what you're worried about."

Those butterflies now feel more like an uncontrollable horde trying to fight their way out by any means necessary.

Is that my concern?

That people might find out we're spending time together? It would only feed the rumors and speculation already running rampant. And yet, I'm strangely torn. There is something comforting about his presence.

"Demi?"

The scrape of his voice jostles me from the internal struggle being waged within. "It's fine."

"Are you sure?" Carefully he searches my face. "If you want me to take off, I will."

Even though I'm confused, I shake my head. All we're going to do is eat pizza and watch a movie. What could possibly go wrong?

It's probably best not to answer that question.

In no time at all, we polish off the pizza. Apparently, Rowan is as hungry as I am. While he runs the plates to the kitchen, I restart the movie. It takes about fifteen minutes to lose myself in the plot and forget about the handsome football player sitting next to me. When he shifts, slinging an arm across the back of the couch, I don't pay much attention to it. My focus remains on the screen. My muscles coil when the violins of the musical score grow more pronounced. I shutter my eyes before peeking through the cracks between my fingers.

Something's about to—

I yelp when the villain jumps out.

"How did you not see that coming?" Rowan chuckles, stroking my shoulder with his fingers.

"I knew something was going to happen," I mumble as my heart beats into overdrive, "just not that."

The arm wrapped around me tugs me close until I'm pressed against the steely strength of his chest. My body molds to his as I inhale a greedy lungful of him.

He smells so damn good that my eyes nearly cross.

Wait a minute—

I jerk to awareness.

What the hell am I doing?

Please tell me that I did not sniff Rowan Michaels.

Again.

This is exactly why I shouldn't have allowed him to stay. My emotions are a little too raw. A little too exposed. I'm not acting like myself. This was a mistake. One I need to rectify before it spirals any further out of control.

Even though it's the last thing I want to do, I jump to my feet in order to put some much-needed distance between us before pointing toward the kitchen. "I'm going to make popcorn."

As I scramble back a step, he reaches out, snagging my fingers with his own. The unexpected touch has my eyes widening, and my pulse skittering.

He leans forward and a bolt of nervousness slices through me. When I try to slip free, his fingers tighten around mine. "Why are you always running away from me?"

I gulp and force out the lie. "That's not what I'm doing." Even as I release the words into the atmosphere, I know he won't believe them.

The way Rowan's brow arches tells me that he's all too aware of the truth. No good will come out of this forced conversation. It's like a capsizing ship. Someone needs to save us. When I make a second attempt at freeing myself, he tows me toward him until I have no choice but to tumble onto his lap. Air rushes from my lungs as his arms band around me, anchoring me securely in place.

"Come on, Demi," he says softly, warm exhalation feathering against my lips, "be honest."

Part of me is scared to death to admit the truth. He's done the unexpected and found a chink in my armor. If he continues, the crack will turn into more of a gaping chasm. I can't afford for him to wedge his way in there anymore than he already has.

"I am being honest." The lie sits on my tongue like bitter ashes. I'm not someone who tells falsehoods. Life seems less complicated when you stick to the truth. And yet, I can't bring myself to do that with Rowan. I *am* always running away from, or at the very least, trying to avoid him. If he comes into a room, I promptly leave. If there's a choice in where to sit, it's as far from him as I can get. Distance is my best defense against him. This behavior was never a conscious decision on my part. It was more of an instinct.

Self-preservation.

The truth is that Rowan frightens me. He makes me feel things I'm not necessarily ready for. It's been that way from the moment I laid eyes on him.

His fingers rise, brushing the hair away from my face before tucking it gently behind my ear. A shiver of awareness scampers down my spine. Our gazes lock and hold until everything around us fades, and he's all I'm cognizant of. The blueness of his eyes is almost hypnotic, and I find myself falling effortlessly under his spell.

"Are you sure about that?" he asks.

My tongue darts out to moisten parched lips. His gaze drops to the movement. When he finally meets my eyes again, there is enough heat in them to scald me alive.

Unsure how to respond, I remain silent.

"You're always holding me at a distance. What are you so afraid of?"

I have to gulp down the nerves bubbling up in my throat, threatening to choke the life out of me.

He's right. I *am* afraid. I've always assumed that if I held the mask firmly in place, he would never figure out my secret. But he sees right through me.

"Tell me, Demi." The world around us falls away. "Tell me what you're so afraid of."

"*You.*" The admittance is a relief. It's been there, simmering beneath the surface for years. I never realized until now how much effort it took to keep it buried deep inside where it couldn't see the light of day.

His lips quirk as if he doesn't believe me. "You can't possibly be afraid of me. You're the most fearless person I know."

Laughter gurgles up in my throat.

How can he say that?

Maybe that's how it appears on the outside, but that's not how I feel inside. I've always been scared of making a mistake and fucking up. Of embarrassing my father. Or taking a chance and giving my heart to someone who will crush it. When it comes down to it, I'm a puddle of insecurities. It might not be how I project myself to the world, but it's still the way I feel. Maybe I'm just better at faking it than other people.

He strokes his fingers through my hair, and it's so tempting to close my eyes and lean into him. When he touches me like this, all the noise buzzing around in my brain goes strangely silent. It's an addictive sensation.

"Rowan?" The husky way his name escapes from my lips sounds nothing like me.

His gaze flicks to mine. "Yeah?"

"What's happening here?"

Tension ratchets up until it reaches a fever pitch and becomes almost too much to withstand.

"Something I've wanted for a long time."

Before I can suck in a lungful of air, his hand slides from my face to the back of my head. His fingers splay wide across my skull, cradling it in his palm. As if in slow motion, he drags me forward. My heartbeat stalls as his lips slant across mine. First one way before tilting his head the other. We fit perfectly. There are no awkward angles. No bumping of noses, mouths, or teeth. He caresses my top lip before nibbling at the bottom. A groan builds in my chest.

When I can't stand another moment of this sweet torture, his tongue darts out to lick at the seam of my lips. There's only so much of the gentle yet demanding touch I can take before I capitulate, opening under the firm pressure. As soon as I give in, his tongue delves inside to tangle with my own.

I expect his exploration to turn aggressive. Like a triumphant hero who has thrashed his opponent. Instead, his movements remain measured. Slow and languid. As if Rowan wants to take his sweet damn time to savor every single part of me. Within a heartbeat, I lose myself in the drugging caress. I don't realize my arms have snaked around his neck until I'm pulling him closer. With a groan, he tightens his hold, pressing my body against his.

"You taste so damn good," he mutters before dragging me to the bottom of the ocean where rational thought becomes impossible. The only thing I'm aware of is the way his mouth coasts over mine.

Everything about Rowan's touch is masterful and sexy. I totally get why the girls on campus clamor for his attention. If he screws anything like he kisses—

That thought is like a bucket of frigid water dumped over my libido.

What the hell am I doing?

Rowan is even more of a manwhore than Justin. Barely have I extracted myself from one shitty situation only to fling myself head-first into another.

No. I'm smarter than this.

Correction...I'm usually smarter than this.

Even though breaking physical contact is the last thing I want, my palms settle against the steely strength of his chest before pushing until our lips part, and there is enough distance between us for logic to once again rush in.

By this point, we're both winded. Like we've run a marathon. I have no idea how much time I've spent wrapped up in his arms. It could be hours or mere minutes. And I would be lying through my teeth if I didn't admit that everything inside me is screaming to feel the soft slide of his lips over mine again. Never have I been kissed quite so thoroughly. And I want more of it. I want to keep reality at bay for a little longer and forget all the reasons this is a terrible idea that will come back to haunt me in the not-so-distant future.

But I can't do that.

No matter how tempted I am.

"Why did you stop?" he asks, eyes still hazy. He licks his lips, looking as if he's a second away from delving back in and giving us what we both want.

"This is wrong," I force myself to say. "It shouldn't be happening."

His brow furrows. "Why not?"

"Because I can't be with another guy like Justin."

The sexual fog clouding his expression evaporates. His eyes widen in shock before disgust flashes in them. "Is that what you really think?" The chill of winter whips through his voice, turning it hard and unforgiving. "That I'm no better than Justin?" He doesn't give me a chance to respond before biting out, "You should know better than that."

A heavy wave of guilt crashes over me. Deep down, I do realize it. But still...the guy has spent three years cultivating a certain reputation. And I've been burned too many times to take another chance. "Why would I know that?"

We've never been friends. Not really. It's the reason why I've been able to hold him at a distance with such ease and pretend we're nothing more than strangers.

Hurt flickers across his features.

Even though doubt creeps in at the edges, I straighten my shoulders. There's too much evidence for there not to be a shred of truth to it. The rumors that have swept through campus. The girls who have bragged about their sexual exploits with him. I've seen groupies hang on him with my own eyes. Not just one. But two or three at a time. He hasn't exactly pushed them away. In fact, like most athletes on campus, he seems to accept the attention as if it's his due.

"We've known each other since we were fourteen years old. We eat dinner together once a week. We've been in the same classes since freshman year. I attend all of your home games. How can you *not* know me better than that?" Tension swirls through the air. "How can you not know who I really am?"

For reasons I don't quite understand, I'm loath to see him in a different light. It's easier to cling to my perceptions rather than acknowledge that I could be wrong about him. "Why does it matter?" When I attempt to climb off his lap, his hands tighten around me.

"Because it does. We're going to get this out in the open once and for all. I won't allow you to run away from me again."

Rowan has never frightened me, but in this moment, he does. Not because I'm afraid he'll hurt or force me into something I don't want. I'm terrified he's going to rip through the last of the barriers I have in place to protect myself against him. Running and hiding is so much easier. And that's exactly what I want to do. My fight or flight instinct has kicked in.

"Don't try and deny it. We both know that's your modus operandi." Before I can defend myself with another lie, he says, "You know me, Demi. Even though you've done everything in your power to pretend otherwise, you know who I am at a fundamental level. You need to think about that."

A thick shiver works its way through my body as everything stills. It's as if I'm standing in the eye of a hurricane. The center is calm while everything outward is in chaos.

When I fail to respond, he tilts his head, continuing to batter my weakened defenses. "I know things about you."

My mouth goes bone-dry, making it impossible to swallow. "Like what?"

"I know you've been playing soccer since you were four years old, and you started travel when you were eight. Your favorite food is carbonara and eggplant parmesan. You love chocolate chip cookies fresh from the oven, and your favorite place to vacation is Maui because that's the last trip your family took before your mom decided to leave."

My eyes widen as my mind cartwheels.

I'm at a loss.

Even though Rowan has been in my life for seven years, I had no idea he was paying such close attention to the details. The realization leaves me winded as warmth reluctantly flares to life inside me.

His face looms closer until he's all I see. Until my world begins and ends with Rowan. "Whether you want to believe it, I *know* you, Demi." He presses his palm to the middle of my chest. "I know *you*."

My heart clenches before jackhammering into overdrive.

How did I miss all this?

While I've been busy pushing him away, he's been here, patiently waiting for me to see the real Rowan Michaels.

And I didn't.

Couldn't.

I lift my hands until my palms can cradle his cheeks. "Tell me something no one else knows."

A long pause stretches between us. It's one that leaves my nerves jangled. Just when I wonder if he'll refuse to answer the question, he knocks me off-balance once again.

"I'm still a virgin."

Chapter Nineteen

ROWAN

A heavy silence descends as her hands fall away from my cheeks, and her eyes widen to the point of being comical. Except there's nothing amusing about this moment. Far from it. I definitely made an error in judgment. One of epic proportions that I can't take back. For better or worse, my secret is out there.

Fuck.

Why the hell did I think it was a good idea to tell her the truth?

It takes a few heartbeats before her expression morphs into one of confusion. A frown settles on her face as she hesitantly shakes her head. "No, you're not."

Relief floods through me as I consider lying.

Almost got you! Ha, ha, ha. I've banged more girls than I could possibly keep track of. Just listen to all the gossip on campus. My stats with the ladies are legendary.

But I can't do that. I'm tired of pretending to be something I'm not. More than that, I'm sick of the way Demi looks at me. Like a manwhore who is no better than that fucko Justin. The reality is that I am *nothing* like him. And it's important she understands that. I want her to know me. *The real me.* Not the one everyone whispers about.

Not the one girls make up stories about to make themselves look better. As if sleeping with me will somehow bolster their popularity.

It's pretty fucked.

"It's true, Demi. I'm a virgin."

Emotion crashes over her pretty face as she digests that bit of information, gradually coming to terms with it.

Disbelief.

Doubt.

Astonishment.

And finally, acceptance.

Demi may not realize it, but her face is so damn expressive. Her thoughts are there for all to see. I always know what she's thinking. She would hate it if I told her that. She would hate that I could read her so easily.

"I don't understand." Her features contort as she shakes her head for a second time as if to clear it. "What about all the rumors?"

This is an uncomfortable conversation I never imagined having with her. It's tempting to bolt from the couch and out the door instead of baring my soul and exposing myself as a fraud. "That's all they are," I force myself to admit, "rumors."

She blinks a few times as those thoughts circle in her head. Understanding floods her expression as her delicate hand drifts to my cheek for a second time in a matter of minutes. It's a rarity for her to reach out and touch me. Only now am I able to expel the air being held captive from my lungs. I squeeze my eyes shut before sinking into the warmth of her palm.

"Thank you for telling me," she whispers. "I appreciate you entrusting me with the truth."

I open my eyes and meet her steady gaze. "Honestly, it's a relief that you know."

"I'm sorry you ever felt the need to hide your authentic self not only from me but the rest of the world. All this time you've been living a lie."

Well...I wouldn't go that far.

"It's not really anyone else's business."

"You're right. No one should judge you." There's a beat of silence. "What about your teammates? Do they know?"

My eyes widen. "Hell, no! Can you imagine their reactions?"

"Oh, Rowan." Sadness fills her voice before she closes the distance and presses her lips against mine in a chaste kiss. When I go to sink into the caress, she pulls away. "That must be so difficult! I wish you'd told me sooner so I could have supported you through this."

Supported me?

How would she have done that?

"Huh?" My brows jerk together.

Her other hand rises to cup the side of my face. "There is absolutely nothing wrong with being gay."

Of course there's not.

Why the hell is she bringing that—

Wait a minute...

She thinks I'm—

"Demi! I'm not gay!" I bark out a disbelieving laugh. "Trust me when I say that I like women." My gaze drops to her parted lips which are still swollen from our kisses. *"A lot."*

Her expression becomes pinched. As if I've confused her all over again. "I don't understand. Then...why haven't you had sex? Clearly you've had *plenty* of opportunities."

For such a smart girl, Demi can be kind of dense. Apparently, I'm going to have to spell it out for her. And here I thought revealing that I was a damn virgin would be the hardest part of the evening.

"I've always had my eye on someone. Since I've never wanted anyone more than her," I jerk my shoulders, "I waited." Even as the words tumble out of my mouth, they sound absurd and farfetched. No one on campus could get laid easier than me and yet, I've chosen to remain celibate.

What red-blooded, college-aged guy does that?

None I'm acquainted with.

Then again, I don't exactly broadcast my status. Demi is the only person who knows I'm a virgin. It's always been a well-kept secret. Not one I'm ashamed of, but still...

Our gazes cling as the tension simmering in the air ratches up a couple hundred notches. Demi becomes perfectly still as she sits perched on my lap. My hands fasten around her waist to keep her in place. Now that I've made the big reveal, I'm half-afraid it'll be too much for her to take in, and she'll bolt.

When I can't stand another moment of the suffocating silence that blankets us, I blurt, "Aren't you going to ask who the girl is?"

She shakes her head, and all of the hope rising inside me bursts like an overinflated balloon before crashing back to earth with a painful thud. Not only have I made it obvious that I have feelings for her. I told her I'm a virgin.

Fuck me.

This isn't good.

Especially since it's pretty damn obvious by her refusal to ask who the girl is that she's not interested. And that's cool. If I've learned anything over the years, it's that you can't force feelings that aren't there to begin with.

"You know what?" Regretting my overshare, I clear my throat. "It's late. I should probably take off." I want to go home and lick my wounds in private. After this debacle, it's doubtful I'll ever put myself out there again. Who the hell needs this shit?

So, yeah...I'm more than ready to flee the scene of the crime. And the way she continues to gape at me like I've grown a horn on my forehead isn't helping matters either. It only makes me feel like a humongous dumbass for choosing to disclose the truth.

Seriously, what the hell had I been thinking?

For once in my life, I allowed the wrong head to make the decisions.

When I can't stand the oppressiveness for another moment, I tighten my grip on her hips and lift Demi from my lap before carefully setting her down next to me. Then I pop to my feet, ready to fly through the front door like a bat out of hell. I need distance from the pain and humiliation pumping through me.

As I take a hasty step toward freedom, her voice halts me in my tracks. "Why don't you stay here for the night?"

Surprised by the offer, I flick my gaze over my shoulder.

"It's late," she clears her throat, "I'll sleep in Dad's room, and you can take mine."

No way. It's a shit idea. The best course of action is to return home and drink enough to forget this incident ever transpired.

Blackout drunk is the new plan for the evening.

"All right, I'll stay."

Goddamn it.

I'd really like to kick my own ass right now.

Chapter Twenty

DEMI

I stare sightlessly at the ceiling as the conversation from earlier plays through my head as if it's on a constant loop. There's no way that Rowan Michaels is a virgin.

How is it possible that I've slept with more people than the campus player?

And to be clear, I've had sex with a whopping five guys.

Five.

That's it.

No matter how many times I squeeze my eyes closed and try to turn off my thoughts, they refuse to be banished. They circle through my head like hungry sharks.

Aren't you going to ask who the girl is?

Instead of having the balls to hear the truth, I'd shaken my head, too frightened to take the conversation any further. Deep down, I had known what it would be. Once everything was out in the open, there would be no going back. We would only be able to move forward. And I'm unsure how to do that.

In the hour since I left Rowan at the threshold of my childhood room, I've come to realize that I *need* to hear him say the name.

I need to hear him say *my* name.

Before I can reconsider the wisdom of my actions, I throw off the comforter and pad into the darkened hallway before arriving at my bedroom. I stumble to a halt when I find the door slightly ajar. I pause, tentatively laying a hand on the wood as my heart riots painfully under my breast. If I push the door open and step inside, everything will change. I'll be forced to acknowledge that my feelings for Rowan have always been smoldering beneath the surface, waiting for the chance to break free.

Am I ready for that?

The tiny voice at the back of my brain tells me to run before it's too late. But I can't do that. This feels much too important to back away from. With trembling fingers, I reach out and push the heavy wood door wider before stepping over the threshold and into the dark space.

A fresh wave of nerves crashes over me, threatening to drag me under. It takes everything I have inside to force out the question. "Are you awake?"

"Yup." As my eyes adjust to the darkness, I realize his hands are stacked behind his head.

I take a cautious step toward the bed. It's like there is a magnet drawing me to him. One I can't escape from.

"Who?" Even though it's only one word that falls from my lips, he understands the question. And the gravity behind it.

As he straightens to a seated position, the sheet slithers down his bare chest before settling around his waist.

"I think you already know the answer." There's a pause. "Don't you?"

Yes.

When he extends his hand, it never occurs to me *not* to close the distance. I find myself gravitating toward him before carefully placing my fingers in his. As soon as his hand fastens around mine, he tugs me toward the bed until I'm settled on the mattress next to him.

"In case there was ever an ounce of doubt, it's always been you, Demi."

My heart melts. As much as I've tried ignoring him, thick tension has always smoldered in the air between us. It's the reason I was so intent on keeping my distance. I was afraid to open up and let someone in.

Especially a guy like Rowan.

It doesn't seem possible that one little secret has the power to change everything, but that's exactly what it's done.

Rowan draws back the sheet, and without hesitation, I slide beneath it, curling up beside him until my head can rest against his chest.

"I don't understand how you could wait for something," I glance at him, "or someone if you weren't sure it would ever happen."

Silence descends as he wraps his arm around me and tugs me closer.

"I never set out to wait; it just kind of happened. I've always had feelings for you, and even though there's been plenty of other girls, they never held my interest. It seemed pointless to be with another girl when you were the one I couldn't stop thinking about."

Emotion explodes inside me, and I shift, maneuvering until my face can hover over his. "I'm not sure what to say."

"You don't have to say anything. As embarrassing as it is to admit I'm still a virgin at twenty-one, it was more important you understand that I'm nothing like Justin."

Guilt slices through me like a burning arrow. "I don't think that." How did I get it so wrong? Why didn't I see through to the truth?

He raises his brows. "Yeah, you did."

"You're right, I did. There have always been so many rumors floating around. How could I not believe them?"

"They never came from me."

That's the ironic part. It's the girls who spread the lies far and wide. As if there was prestige to be had if you'd slept with Rowan. An exclusive club that drives up popularity.

When I was a freshman and even a sophomore, my older teammates would brag about hooking up with him. My chest would tighten as I was forced to listen to a blow-by-blow of the encounter. It made me sick to my stomach to think about him messing around with other girls. Instead of admitting I liked him, I convinced myself that I was disgusted by his sexual antics. That he was nothing more than a manwhore coasting through college on his athletic prowess and good looks. Every time he tried to get close, I pushed him away.

Guys get a bad rap for bragging about sexual encounters, but sometimes...*sometimes* it's the girls who make stuff up to look better. Until now, I didn't realize it could go both ways.

"I've heard so many girls boast about hooking up with you."

"Yeah, I know."

When he doesn't say anything more, I prompt, "Doesn't that bother you?"

A sigh escapes from him. "I guess the answer to that would be yes and no."

"I don't understand." There have been plenty of times when people have spread rumors about me. Not only does it suck, it's humiliating. It's the reason I decided to leave campus for the weekend; I couldn't take the scrutiny for another moment.

"It's not like I wanted people to talk about me, but if girls were bragging that we'd hooked up, then no one was speculating as to the reason I wasn't sleeping around like most of the guys on the team."

Wow. I never considered that.

"Look at your reaction." He pauses for a heartbeat. "The moment I told you that I was a virgin, you immediately thought I was gay."

Heat slams into my cheeks. He's right, that's *exactly* what I'd thought. I couldn't understand why a perfectly healthy and attractive male wouldn't want to sleep with as many girls as he could. Especially when they were throwing themselves at him left and right. From a young age, males are told that in order to be a man, they need to have sex with as many women as possible. If a guy doesn't adhere to that, then there's an assumption something is wrong with him. As painful as it is to admit, I'm as guilty of perpetrating the notion as everyone else.

"I'm sorry." Now I feel even more like an asshole for jumping to conclusions. No wonder Rowan didn't bother to correct the gossip. "I shouldn't have assumed that."

He brushes a kiss against the crown of my head. "You don't have anything to apologize for. In our society, that's the way people are conditioned to think. There must be something wrong with a guy if he decides to wait. No matter what the reason might be." He adds with a touch of humor, "I'm probably the only virgin on campus."

His comment lightens the mood. "Nah, there might be a freshman or two."

"Thanks," he says with a snort. "I feel much better now. Maybe we can start a club or support group."

I twist in his arms until my mouth can drift over his. As soon as it does, his lips part, and my tongue slips inside. He pulls me close and rearranges my body until I'm stretched out on top of him and able to feel all of his hard lines pressed against me.

It's all too easy to lose myself in him. The way his mouth sweeps over me. The velvety softness of his tongue as it tangles with mine. The feather-light touch of his fingers as they dance along the sides of my breasts before skimming down my sides.

Almost reluctantly, he pulls away. "You feel so damn good."

When I swoop in for more, he gently pulls away until his gaze can fasten on mine. "You realize that I'm not looking for a quick fuck, right?"

How could I not?

But what does that necessarily mean?

That we can't have sex?

Like right now?

Because I'm more turned on than I have been in a long time.

Maybe ever.

His lips twist as if he has mindreading capabilities. Carefully he repositions me until I'm snuggled up against him instead of draped across his body.

I guess that answers the question, now doesn't it?

"You're kind of a tease," I grumble.

Even though a chuckle rumbles up from his chest, it's scraped raw as if he's as tortured as I am. "That wasn't my intention."

"Doesn't matter." At this very moment, hormones are raging through my body, singeing me from the inside out.

He drops a kiss against the top of my head as his arms tighten around me. "Go to sleep, Demi."

A snort escapes.

Like that's going to happen anytime soon?

I don't think so.

Chapter Twenty-One

DEMI

Sunlight slants across my face as I wake with a stretch. My eyelashes flutter open as I focus on the ceiling overhead. For a sliver of a moment, a sense of calmness fills me, which is odd. I escaped home because of all the bullshit at school. So, I don't understand why everything feels kind of—

Perfect.

That's when the memories from last night crash through my head like a ton of bricks. One moment I'm blissfully unaware and the next— boom! They're there. I'm suddenly wide awake and jackknifing to a seated position.

Holy crap! My gaze flies around the empty room. Except for the masculine scent clinging to the sheets, there's no sign that Rowan slept in my bed. With a deep lungful of air to prove I'm not delusional, I collapse against the pillows.

Last night...

Did that really happen?

My fingers drift across my lips.

Did I kiss Rowan?

Hold on a second...did he actually admit to being a virgin?

Mind.

Officially.

Blown.

My breath gets clogged in my throat at the thought.

Rowan Michaels.

Campus player.

Hot commodity with a golden ticket to the NFL.

Now we're adding *virgin* to that list?

And he's seriously been holding out for me?

Me?

It seems a little too farfetched.

And yet...

I believe him. There's no reason not to. I've known Rowan for a long time, and the one thing I can unequivocally say is that he's never lied to me. I trail my fingers over the cold sheets. We talked. And kissed. Then fell asleep wrapped up in each other's arms.

And now he's gone.

Does Rowan think he can dump all that on me and then take off at the crack of dawn?

Are we supposed to pretend it never happened?

Rowan could have allowed me to finish out senior year blissfully unaware of his true feelings, but he didn't. He took a chance and disclosed everything. At the same time, forcing me to acknowledge what I've always kept bottled up inside. Now, knowing what I do, how can I pretend it doesn't exist?

With a huff of frustration, I throw off the covers and pad over to the window before drawing back the gauzy curtain to peer outside. It might be early September, but it's absolutely gorgeous out. My gaze lands on the now empty spot where Rowan's pickup truck had been parked last night. I draw my lower lip between my teeth before chewing on it, dropping the sheer material back into place, and taking a step in retreat.

I'm confused as to what his absence means. Is the ball now in my court? Am I supposed to make the next move? What *is* my next move? Do I even have one?

Not really.

Well...it appears I've got some thinking to do this weekend. I can mull over the issue with a steaming cup of coffee. Hopefully, that will get my neurons firing.

Since I have the house to myself, I don't bother to throw a robe over my tank top and panties. I've never been self-conscious about my body. I've been an athlete my entire life. I'm used to changing in a locker room full of girls.

With my mind full of Rowan, I pad down the staircase to the entryway before turning toward the back of the house. Sunshine pours in through the eastern facing windows as I pull open the refrigerator door and peer inside.

Yup, it's like I suspected—a barren wasteland. Since Dad lives alone, he doesn't keep up on domestic chores like cooking, cleaning, and shopping. After the divorce, he hired Mrs. Granger, an older woman in the neighborhood to stock the fridge once a week, tidy up the house, do the laundry, and prepare a few quick meals for when he's running late. Otherwise, the guy would probably camp out at the stadium and subsist on cafeteria food.

What he needs is a girlfriend. Every once in a while, I make noises about him dying alone. With a roll of his eyes, he'll remind me that he's perfectly content living a bachelor lifestyle. His excuse is that he doesn't have enough time to devote to a girlfriend, and no woman wants to be a distant second to football. He's not wrong about that, but maybe if the right woman came along, it would change his mind and his priorities.

What?

It could happen. Although, I won't be holding my breath.

It takes seconds to scour the entire contents of the fridge. There's not even a single slice of pizza to be found because Rowan and I polished it off last night. Had I known he would be making an unannounced appearance, I would have ordered two larges. My plan had been to nibble on it throughout the weekend.

Guess that idea has been shot to hell.

As I slam the fridge closed, the front door opens. Which is...odd. There's no way Dad is home. He shouldn't return until late Sunday evening, and if, by chance, his plans changed, he would have called or texted to let me know.

My muscles tense as I cautiously move to the middle of the room, giving me clear sightlines to the entryway. A puff of air escapes from my lungs when I find Rowan. As our gazes lock and hold, something pings unwantedly at the bottom of my belly. For so many years, I ignored the physical attraction, doing my best to convince myself it didn't exist. His confession last night makes that impossible. The floodgates have been opened, and there's no chance of resurrecting them again.

Only now do I realize how disappointed I was to find him missing this morning.

His lips quirk into a lopsided smile as he holds up a paper bag with a familiar logo stamped across the front. "I ran out for bagels and coffee."

Fresh bagels are my absolute favorite. Before his admission last night, I would have assumed it was nothing more than a coincidence. Now, I know differently. It only proves that Rowan has always been there, hovering at the edges, paying attention to the details. It's such an insignificant gesture, and yet, it means so much. No other guy has ever bothered to run out and grab breakfast in the morning.

My heart lurches, and it takes effort to clear away the emotion struggling to take root deep inside. I'm not ready for that yet. Instead, I clear my throat and lift my lips into a smile. "I thought you took off."

"Nope."

Warmth blooms inside me as I drag a hand through my disheveled hair. Unsure what to do or say, I shift my weight and point toward the patio. He makes me feel emotions I'm not entirely comfortable with. "Want to eat outside?"

"Sure."

His easy response makes the tension vibrating in the air dissipate. Needing a moment to collect my scattered thoughts, I turn away, grabbing napkins and plates before carrying them out through the slider to the stamped cement patio that surrounds the pool. We settle at the iron table beneath an over-sized navy-colored umbrella. Rowan sets an extra-large travel container of coffee in front of me before opening the bag. As soon as he does, I catch a whiff of fresh bagels.

Yum!

In silence, we arrange our breakfast on our plates. A burst of anxiety explodes in my belly, and my gaze skitters across the backyard. Rowan's confession last night has changed everything. Nerves hum beneath my skin as I focus on slathering cream cheese onto my bagel.

When he clears his throat, I nearly jump out of my chair.

"What are your plans for the day?"

"Umm..." My brain blanks. *Plans?* Oh...right. "I have a couple of assignments to finish up," I glance at him, "otherwise chill out."

There's a brief pause before he asks, "Mind if I hang with you?"

A thrill shoots through me, and it takes effort to tamp down my excitement at the notion of spending more time together. "Not at all."

The edges of his lips curl before he reaches out and snags my fingers, pulling me to my feet and onto his lap. His arms wrap around me, anchoring me securely in place. Barely am I able to find my bearings before his mouth slants over mine. My brain clicks off as my arms wind around his neck. Much like last night, it's a slow exploration of lips, teeth, and tongues. Most of the guys I've been with are in a hurry to reach the finish line, which is apparently in my pants. This couldn't be more different. As his wide palms stroke over my back, his fingers leave an explosion of delicate shivers in their wake. When I whimper, he swallows down the sound as if starving for it.

"You're so fucking sexy," he growls, the low vibration rumbling in his chest.

Before I realize what's happening, Rowan rises to his feet. His arms are locked around me, securing me in place as he turns and sets me down on the chair he had been occupying. I blink as his fingers go to the hem of his Navy T-shirt, yanking it up his body and over his head before tossing it to the concrete.

Holy cow...

From a distance, I've seen Rowan without a shirt dozens of times. Just last night, I caught a glimpse of his chest, but this is different. It's broad daylight. Up close and personal. With the bright light beaming down on him, he looks very much like a Greek god. Which is corny as hell but nonetheless true.

We're talking sun-kissed flesh and ripped muscles.

At this point, I'm pretty sure I'm drooling.

When my eyes finally meander to his, a knowing light fills them. "Like what you see?"

It takes everything I have inside to swallow past the thick lump that has settled in the middle of my throat. "What's not to like?"

No, I'm serious.

What's not to like?

The man is utterly gorgeous. He should be advertising expensive underwear on a billboard somewhere. This is *exactly* why girls come out of the woodwork and offer up phony stories about him.

His fingers drop to the button of his jeans, where they hesitate long enough to send my heart pounding into overdrive before a metal snap breaks the silence of the morning. Only then do I become aware of the air trapped in my lungs and have to make a conscious effort to force it out again.

With a ridiculous amount of leisure, he lowers the metal teeth of his fly. Rowan Michaels is giving me my very own private strip-tease. Do you have any idea what most girls on campus would give to be in my position?

We're talking first-born sons.

The denim material is shoved down muscular thighs before it puddles around his ankles, and he's standing in nothing more than a pair of form-fitting black boxer-briefs.

My mouth turns cottony as a knowing smirk curls around the edges of his lips.

And you know what?

I couldn't give a crap.

He deserves every ounce of ego where his body is concerned. It's a thing of beauty. I get a few moments to eat him up with my eyes before he stalks toward me. Once he closes the distance, he places a hand on each armrest of the chair, effectively caging me in. His lips hover over mine, stroking back and forth. When he finally draws away, it feels as if I'm burning up inside. My panties have dampened. I don't have to wait long for his next move. He slides his arms around my body and scoops me up. It's an effortless movement. As if I weigh nothing at all. My legs tangle around his lean waist as my arms do the same with his neck. Awareness sizzles through me as my core is pressed against his tight abdominals. When he hoists me higher, the grinding motion nearly sends my eyes rolling to the back of my head.

"Are you ready for this?" he asks, his voice barely penetrating the loud rush of the ocean that fills my ears.

Oh, my God...

Is he talking about *sex*?

Instead of walking toward the sliding door and inside the house like I expect, he swings in the opposite direction.

I don't understand. Are we going to do it outside? It's not like I'm opposed to the idea, but I thought—

"Hang on," he murmurs.

Hang on?

Too late do I realize his intent. With me secured tightly in his arms, Rowan jumps into the deep end of the pool. Not that it does any good, but a protest bursts from my lips as we hit the water.

Chapter Twenty-Two

ROWAN

Demi sputters as we surface from the crystal-clear liquid. Tiny waves lap at our bodies. Eyes wide with shock, she stares at me with a slack-jawed expression. My shoulders shake with silent laughter. Mentally, I prepare myself for the ass-chewing I'm about to receive.

It takes a moment for the edges of her lips to tremble and laughter to bubble up from her throat. Just when I think all is forgiven, she slaps her palm against the water, splashing me in the face.

"I can't believe you did that!" She untangles herself and sprays me again.

That makes two of us. Things were just starting to heat up, and who knows what would have happened had I walked us into the house instead of the pool. Actually, I know *exactly* what would have transpired. I want this girl in the worst possible way. But I also want to take this slow.

I shield my eyes with one hand before retaliating. Hey, what's good for the goose is good for the gander, right? Or some shit like that.

With a squeal, Demi swims away from me. As she puts more distance between us, she kicks a steady stream of water in my direction. In case you might have forgotten, her legs are muscular. She can easily keep this up for days. The grin on her face tells me that she knows it as well.

"Now you're in trouble," I bellow, rising up from the water like the Loch Ness Monster, and leaping at her with outstretched arms.

She yelps and tries to twist away. The operative word in that sentence being *tries*. I get my hands on her for a moment before her slippery flesh slides through my fingers, and she sprays water in my eyes. For the next fifteen minutes, we splash around and play. I've swum in Coach's pool dozens of times. He usually invites the team over for a barbeque during the season, and Demi is always there to help out.

Do I necessarily like the guys ogling her in a bikini?

Hell, no.

Is there anything I could do about it?

Other than crack the back of a few skulls when they stared a little too long, nope—not a damn thing. It was both heaven and hell.

When our breathing turns labored, I finally say, "All right, I give. You win."

Demi snickers. She's an endless bound of energy. It's one of her strengths on the soccer field. Even in the final minutes of the game, she's still going strong, running circles around the other team. It's all the extra conditioning she puts in. I've never met anyone more single-minded and dedicated to the sport they play. And that, my friends, is sexy as hell.

She tilts her head and beams. "You sure about that?"

"Yup."

When she rises from the water, the tank top gets plastered to her lean upper body, molding to her breasts like a second skin. Her nipples tighten into hard little buds that poke through the thin fabric. The dusky color is clear as day through the pale pink material.

My mouth dries as I stare. Pulling my gaze away is impossible. I've been rendered powerless. I'm totally at her mercy. Does this girl have any idea how damn sexy she is? Or how much I want her?

How much I've always wanted her?

She can't possibly know. I've spent so many years, holding all these feelings deep inside. It's both scary and a relief to finally release them.

Her body stills. Like a prey animal scenting a predator. She doesn't move a single muscle. Instead, Demi stands under bright shafts of sunlight and allows me to look my fill.

Time stretches and lengthens along with my nerves. With a deliberateness that leaves my heart stuttering, her fingers drop to the hem of her shirt before carefully dragging it up her body and over her head. With her gaze locked on mine, she tosses the sopping wet material to the edge of the pool. It lands against the concrete with a thunk.

Holy.

Shit.

If I didn't realize it before, I certainly do now. Demi Richards is utter perfection. Her breasts are high and tight with a slight roundness to them. The nipples are pink and tiny. All I want to do is wrap my lips around one and suck it into my mouth.

Do you have any idea how long I've dreamed about doing exactly that?

Since the day I met her when I was fourteen years old.

As if in slow motion, Demi raises her arms before running her fingers through her long dark hair, sluicing the clear drops of water that run in rivulets down her naked skin. With her arms stretched high, her breasts stand at attention, and my cock stiffens painfully in my boxers.

I'm so fucking turned on right now.

"Don't you want to touch me?" Her voice drops to a husky whisper that strums the need buried inside.

Is she serious?

I want nothing more than that. It takes effort to rein in the beast trying to break free beneath the surface of my skin. But I can't allow that to happen. I can't allow him to claw his way out and lose control. I won't scare Demi with the desire bottled up inside me.

With my need tightly harnessed, I close the distance that separates us. When I'm no more than a foot away, I reach out and wrap my fingers around one puckered bud before tweaking it gently with my fingertips.

Her head falls back, exposing the narrow column of her throat as a guttural sounding moan slides from her mouth. Excitement rushes through my veins as my other hand rises, needing to play with the other perky little nipple. Pinching and tweaking, elongating each one. She arches her back as if offering herself up to me. I palm the soft weight of each breast, needing to learn the feel of her. My hands slide from her chest, around her ribcage, until I'm able to drag her close. Close enough to suck one delectable nipple into my mouth. The deeper I draw her in, the louder her moans become.

With a soft pop, I release her. My tongue dances around the areola before lapping at the hard little tip. Demi squirms in my arms as her hands drift along my biceps, over my shoulders, before tunneling through my hair and dragging me to her.

"Mmmm, that feels so good," she murmurs.

Damn right, it does.

I could spend an endless amount of time adoring her sweet little titties with my mouth.

Before I realize it, my leg is wedged between her thighs, and she's riding me. Grinding her panty-covered pussy against me. If I'm not careful, I'll go off like a shot. I need to get ahold of myself, and the only way I can do that is to put a little distance between us.

Fuck!

It's the last thing I want right now.

I lift my head and take in the sight. Demi looks so damn wanton in my arms with her chest bared under the bright sunlight. A dazed expression fills her eyes as her long wet hair clings to her shoulders and back. Her lips are parted so sweetly. She's like a fucking goddess come to life. I couldn't want her anymore than I already do.

Several heartbeats pass before the sexual haze clouding her eyes clears. "Why did you stop?"

Does she have any idea what that question does to me? How it forces my control to the breaking point? If I had my way, I'd take her like a fucking animal. I want to bury my cock so deep inside her that I have no idea where she begins, and I end. But I can't do that.

Demi means too much to me.

She always has.

My fingers tunnel through her hair until I'm able to cup the sides of her head. I wait until her gaze fastens onto mine, and I have her complete attention. "When I have you, it won't be a quick fuck in some damn pool. It'll be long and slow and perfect."

Her dark eyes turn smoky with need.

"Yeah, it's gonna be *exactly* like that." It's important that Demi understands what she's getting herself into. It can't be an impulsive decision that means nothing. An itch that needs to be scratched. "You have to know that once I have you, you'll be mine, and I won't let you go anytime soon." I pause for a beat, allowing everything I've said to sink in. Carefully, I search her eyes. "Do you understand?"

She jerks her head.

The tightly coiled tension sitting in the pit of my gut gradually dissipates. "Good. I want to take my time with this. *With you.*"

She releases a steady breath as her shoulders loosen. "Okay."

Now that we're both on the same page, I drag her body closer until her breasts are pressed against my chest. It takes a moment for her muscles to relax. With a deliberateness that belies the harsh need running rampant through me, I trail my fingers up and down the length of her spine, and for the first time in my life, I realize what contentment feels like. It's both strange and unexpected.

Foreign in nature.

There have only been a few times I've experienced it. The first was when Coach came into my life and took me under his wing. The second was when I realized that my dreams of playing in the NFL were more than a pipe dream like my old man had beat into my head. And the third was when my father pleaded guilty and was sent away. Hands down, that was the best fucking day of my life because it meant that Mom and I didn't have to deal with him or his constant bullshit any longer. He wouldn't be coming home drunk at two in the morning, knocking Mom around, and stealing her hard-earned cash. Other than booze, I have no idea what he spent her rent and food money on, but I have my suspicions.

"Rowan?"

It's a relief when Demi's husky voice pulls me out of those unpleasant thoughts.

"Yeah?" My past is ugly and dark. I don't want it to ever touch Demi. She's everything that is light and happy. Maybe that's why I've always been so attracted to her. She's the opposite of everything I grew up with. She's like the vibrant store window I had my face smashed against as a kid. Always looking in from the outside. Not quite good enough. Always dirty and hungry and left wanting.

A groan slides from me when her teeth sink into her lower lip. I'm so fucking tempted to nip the plump flesh and suck the fullness into my mouth. With her topless in my arms, I want to rewind our conversation and tell her that I have no intention of taking this relationship at a leisurely pace. I want fast. I want to delve in headfirst and take it all. I'm like a kid in a candy store who intends to gorge himself on all the sweetness laid out before him.

"Were you serious last night?" she whispers.

Those thoughts buzz around in my brain, making it difficult to focus. "Hmmm?"

When she remains silent, I force my gaze to hers and realize there's a flush staining her cheeks.

Some of the sexual haze clouding my better judgment evaporates. "Serious about what?"

Her gaze darts away.

"Don't do that," I growl. No longer will I allow her to hide from me or what's unfolding between us.

Her wide gaze snaps to mine before she blurts, "Were you serious when you said that you've liked me for years?"

My hands tighten around the sides of her head. "Don't you understand?" A second or two tick by. "Where you're concerned, I'm as serious as a fucking heart attack."

She gulps. "And I'm the reason you've held off on sex?"

I draw her closer, resting my forehead against hers. "Since the moment you came into my life, you've been my reason for everything." Not once do I break eye contact. "Does that freak you out?"

She remains silent for a long stretch of time, and I panic. Fuck...I probably shouldn't have dumped all that on her last night. It was too much, too soon. Unfortunately, there's no way to back-peddle. For some stupid reason, I decided it was a good idea to be honest and totally strip myself bare.

When she shakes her head, the tension filling my muscles evaporates.

"The last thing I want to do is scare you," I mutter, feeling self-conscious.

"I'm not scared." She presses her lips together before admitting, "I like that you waited because you wanted to be with me. It only makes me want you more."

Heat fills her eyes, and it is so damn sexy. A groan rumbles up from my throat as my cock stiffens. All I want to do is sink inside her.

"You have," her tongue darts out to moisten her lips, "*done stuff*, right?"

"Yeah, I'm not a total nube," I mutter.

"Like what?" Her eyes light with undisguised interest. "Tell me."

Heat floods my cheeks as I shrug, embarrassment swamping me, threatening to drag me under. This is a humiliating conversation to have with the one girl I've always fantasized about. I don't want Demi to think I'm not man enough to please her because I haven't screwed a ton of girls.

Or, in my case, *any*.

With my hands cupping the sides of her skull and our foreheads touching, she tilts her head until her mouth can slide over mine. As soon as her tongue brushes across the seam of my lips, I open until they can tangle. I'm about to lose myself in the caress when she pulls away.

Her breath comes out in short sharp pants that drift across my lips. It's almost drugging. "There's no reason we can't have an open conversation about this, right?"

Ugh. The sexual haze surrounding me disintegrates.

"Yeah, I guess." Like I want her to realize just how inexperienced I am? I've already put that out there. Is there any reason to rub it in?

"Don't be embarrassed."

It's much too late for that. Somewhere, deep inside, I'm dying. *Slowly.*

"I want to be upfront about everything." Quickly she adds, "You can ask me questions, too." With our bodies fused together, she pulls away until there's a bit of distance between our chests.

Mentally I steel myself for the oncoming humiliation. If this is what it will take to make this girl mine, then I'll do it. "All right, fire away."

And that's exactly how it feels...like I'm standing in front of a firing squad with no chance of escaping unscathed. She's either going to find my inexperience a turn-on or not. I can't help but wonder for the umpteenth time why the hell I blurted out my virginal status. That wasn't something she needed to know.

"Have you ever had a blow job?"

I jerk my head into a nod.

When I remain silent, her voice drops. "A lot of them?"

"Yeah." It's not something I've ever kept track of, but there has been a good amount. The first time a girl went down on me was sophomore year of high school. She bore an uncanny resemblance to Demi. I'm not proud of it, but with the girl's head buried in my lap, I could stroke my fingers through her long dark hair and pretend she was someone else. I remember exploding in her mouth and her sucking me down until every muscle turned limp.

Best fucking feeling in the world.

Maybe I wasn't out boning every girl I could get my hands on, but when I needed a release, that did the trick.

Carefully I pick through the thoughts that flicker across her face. "Does that change the way you feel about me?"

She shakes her head. "Of course not."

Time to turn the tables. "What about you? How many guys have you blown?"

Her gaze darts away as heat rises in her cheeks.

"Hey." My hand settles on the curve of her jaw. "It goes both ways, remember? There's no reason to be embarrassed. We can be honest with each other."

"A couple." When I raise a brow, wanting specifics, she adds, "Three." Her shoulders jerk. "Oral sex seems so much more intimate than..."

"Actual sex?"

"Yeah."

The question shoots from my mouth before I can stop it. "How many guys have gone down on you?" I want to know everything about this girl—all the nitty-gritty details.

"None."

"Really?" My brows shoot up. From my limited experience, girls seem to enjoy it. *A lot.* Hell, some like it more than sex. I'm a little surprised but, then again, I like that she hasn't done it with anyone else. It's something new we can explore together.

A blush hits her cheeks as she shakes her head. "I've slept with five guys, and the relationships never lasted more than three or four months. Most of my boyfriends were more interested in getting off rather than making sure it was good for me."

I hate to admit it, but college-aged dudes are selfish assholes when it comes to sex. There's a reason they say—young, dumb, and full of cum. Because most of them are.

"Have you," her voice drops, "gone down on a girl before?"

"If you're asking if I've returned the favor, then yeah...I have. It only seemed fair." The edges of my lips curl into a smile as I whisper against the shell of her ear, "I don't want to brag, but I've got some serious tongue skills in that department." I suck the delicate lobe into my mouth before biting down on it. "I love everything there is about eating pussy." When her breath catches, I continue. "I love thrusting my tongue deep inside and hitting that little spot that drives girls crazy."

Demi moans, grinding her pelvis against mine. Her response only ramps me up even more.

"That's exactly what I'm going to do to you. I'm gonna spread your lips wide and lick your pussy until you cream all over the place. Then I'm going to suck that little clit into my mouth until you scream my name over and over again."

"*Oh, God.*"

"You know what else I like?"

With a shake of her head, she whimpers.

"I love talking dirty."

I've barely touched this girl, and she's on the cusp of splintering apart.

So.

Damn.

Responsive.

How did Justin let her slip through his fingers? How did any of the guys she's been with allow her to get away? Didn't they realize what they had?

Too fucking bad for them. Their loss is my gain. And once I make her mine, I won't ever let go.

I squeeze her ass in the palms of my hands. So damn muscular. And that's a huge turn-on. Some guys like their women to be soft and curvy. That's never done it for me. Maybe it's because this girl has always dominated my thoughts. I've never been able to see past her. Even though her body is tight and athletic, Demi has curves where it counts. I can't wait to strip her bare and learn every inch of her body.

"I want you so much right now." Her eyelashes flutter open, and need fills her eyes. "Are you sure about waiting?"

Hell, no.

As I capture her lips, my tongue plunges into her mouth to tangle and dance. I pull her against me until she can feel how hard I am. "I want you more than you could possibly know, but it needs to be right. I want to take my time, and I want you to be certain."

She grinds her pelvis against me. "Remove those boxers, and I'll show you how certain I am."

Even though it feels like the tip of my cock is going to explode, the comment makes my lips twitch. Did I ever think there would come a time when Demi Richards would practically beg me to fuck her?

Nope. Never in a million years.

"Slow," I whisper as a reminder to both of us. "We need to take this slow."

Although that doesn't mean I can't give her a preview of what she can expect. A little something to look forward to. One hand slips from her ass to the front of her panties before delving inside. I groan as my fingers brush over the soft lips of her pussy. She widens her legs as I push two fingers inside.

Once they are completely seated inside her warmth, a moan escapes from her.

"Feel better?"

"Yes." Her eyelids drift shut as her head lolls back.

I don't think I've ever seen anything as sexy as Demi gyrating against me, getting off on my fingers. Slowly I drag them from the heat of her body before plunging inside again. It doesn't take long for us to find a rhythm. A flush stains her cheeks as her teeth sink into her lower lip.

She's so fucking beautiful.

When a furrow creases her brow, I know she's hovering at the precipice. I pump my hand, giving her everything she needs to find her release. Her body tightens as her movements become frenzied. As she opens her mouth to scream, I seal my lips over hers and swallow down her pleasure. I continue thrusting my fingers inside her until her muscles turn lax. Only then does satisfaction fill me as I slip free from her body.

If I have my way, that will be the first of many orgasms I give this girl.

Chapter Twenty-Three

DEMI

We spend the rest of Saturday morning working on a statistics assignment and kicking around a ball in the backyard. The QB may be hot stuff on the stadium turf, but on the soccer field? I run circles around his ass. Since the refrigerator looks like Mother Hubbard's cupboards, we decide to make a run to the grocery store and pick up a couple of necessities to get us through the rest of the weekend. On the way home, Rowan detours, swinging into the paved parking lot of Twist 'N Dip, a small ice cream stand in the center of town.

He doesn't realize it, but this place holds a lot of fond childhood memories for me. When I started playing soccer, Dad would bring me here as a special treat after each game. It was something I always looked forward to. Once I started playing with higher-level teams, and we started traveling more, we'd stop when we were in the area, but that became less frequent. I haven't been here in ages. Probably since middle school.

"I love this place." Nostalgia fills me as I study the small white brick building with a sliding glass window. It looks exactly the way it did ten years ago.

Rowan flashes me a grin. "Yeah, I remember you mentioning it."

Huh...I don't recall that conversation.

"Really?" My brows lift as I sift through my memories.

"It was a while ago." He shrugs. "You said your dad would bring you here after games. You loved the dipped cones."

That's exactly what I'd order.

Every single time.

My heart flutters beneath my ribcage at the realization that he tucked away such an insignificant piece of information. It's another reminder that Rowan has been quietly hovering at the edges of my life, paying attention to the minute details, while I was intent on creating walls to keep him at a distance. I pegged him as a player who would only end up hurting me.

How did I not see him for the person he truly is?

Why was I so stubborn about giving him a chance?

I don't realize I've become trapped in a web of my thoughts until Rowan reaches over and gently strokes his fingers along the curve of my cheek. "Does it weird you out that I know so much?" Concern and embarrassment weave their way through his voice.

If it were anyone else—yeah, I might find it creepy or stalkerish. But how can I possibly feel that way when this is Rowan we're talking about? Someone who has been a part of my life for so long? He and my dad have formed such a strong bond. We sit down for dinner every Wednesday night. We've had at least one class together every semester. Had I paid more attention, I'd probably know as much about him as he does about me.

"No." If I'm being honest, I like that he knows me so well. Rowan understands what's important to me. I've been with enough self-absorbed guys who didn't ask one thing about me. Some couldn't even be bothered to discover what position I play on the field. They talk about themselves ad nauseam and barely ask any questions. They don't care about my thoughts or feelings. Sometimes, I think they would prefer I didn't have any. "It doesn't."

"Good." The pad of his thumb grazes my bottom lip. "The last thing I want to do is scare you away."

"I'm not scared." Which is strange. I've spent so many years keeping him at a firm distance, and now, all I want to do is pull him close. I want to rip away the last of the barriers that keep me from him. "I wish I hadn't been so stubborn," I admit. Guilt slices through me as my gaze drops to my fingers as they twist together in my lap. "I wasted so much time."

"I think we went through everything we needed to in order to get to this place. Our relationship grew when it was meant to."

His response sends a little shiver scuttling through me, and the fine hair on my arms prickle. "Do you really believe that?" My gaze locks on his as interest careens through me. "That everything happens for a reason?"

Emotion flashes in his blue eyes. For a split second, they deepen with a vibrant color before vanishing. It's there and gone like a crack of lightning before I can decipher what it meant.

"For the most part, I do." His fingers strum my cheek, and I'm tempted to sink into his touch.

His take on life surprises me. I wasn't expecting it.

Fate.

Kismet.

Destiny.

Whatever you want to call it, it all means the same thing.

I tilt my head and study him, intrigued by the notion. This isn't the kind of conversation I expected to have with Rowan while sitting in the Twist 'N Dip parking lot. All thoughts of ice cream flee as I delve headfirst into the topic. "Isn't that more of a yes or no question? You either believe everything happens for a reason or you don't?"

A slight chuckle escapes from him. "Is anything in life ever that black and white?" The emotion I'd caught sight of moments ago comes back full force, and it feels like we're drilling a little deeper beneath the surface of our relationship. He's revealing a tiny piece of himself that not everyone else gets to see. "Is *your* life that black and white?"

Good question.

"I've never thought about it before in such simple terms." As the words tumble off my tongue, I realize there's never been a need for me to examine such an existential question. Even though my parents are divorced, and our family has gone through some challenging times, my life has been stable and fairly easy. My parents have good jobs, we've had plenty of money, and have always had a nice place to live. And I was loved. Most of the girls I grew up playing soccer with came from the same kind of upper middle-class background. Travel soccer is surprisingly expensive; you have to have a disposable income to practice, train, and travel. This little bit of introspection makes me realize how blessed I am. Perhaps if my life hadn't been so cushy, those are questions I would have reflected upon at an earlier age.

For Rowan to have already formed an opinion about the topic makes me wonder about his upbringing. I had assumed he grew up much like I did—in a solid middle-class neighborhood in suburbia with two loving parents who supported his dream of playing football. My mind tumbles back to the conversation at the stadium and how guarded he'd become when I asked about his family. Only now do I realize that maybe I jumped to the wrong conclusion.

"But it kind of sounds like you have," I say softly, hoping to tease out a little more insight.

For a long moment, he remains silent. Just when I wonder if he'll respond, he says, "When you grow up with very little, and you see people around you with so much more, it makes you question the reason for it." Rowan jerks his shoulders. "So yeah, maybe I have examined if there's a purpose to the things that happen to us or shape us into the human beings that we are. It's kind of depressing to think the struggles we go through in life are pointless and don't ultimately push us toward our purpose or goals."

I blink, surprised and yet somehow not by the depth hidden behind Rowan's pretty façade. There is so much more to him than being a handsome football-playing jock. It's doubtful most people take the time to get to know him on this level; or that he gives them the opportunity to see him in this light.

"I guess I never thought about it like that."

He strokes my face. "Maybe that's why it took so long for you to open your eyes and see me standing in front of you. Maybe we both had to change and grow before we were ready for that next step."

Everything in me stills as I consider the possibility. Maybe Rowan is correct, and life works out the way it's supposed to when the time is right. The challenges we work through and ultimately overcome are there to help shape us into the people we were always meant to be.

It's a dizzying thought.

He shrugs, and the seriousness filling his eyes melts away. "You ready for that ice cream?"

When I nod, he closes the distance and brushes his lips across mine. "Good. Then we can go back to your place and have a little rematch. FYI—this time I won't go so easy on you."

Laughter bubbles up in my throat, banishing our previous discussion, and lightening the atmosphere. "Oh, please! We both know I kicked your ass fair and square. But hey, it would be my pleasure to crush you all over again."

He raises a brow. "You always this cocky?"

"That's not cockiness," I snort. "It's confidence."

"Whatever it is," his fingers trail over my bare thigh toward the vee between my legs, "it's sexy as hell."

My gaze drops to his hand before flicking to his face. I point to the offending appendage. "Yeah, that's not going to work, bruh. I'm not that distractable."

"*Bruh?*" He bursts out laughing. "Is that what I am now? Your bruh?"

"When we're on the field, and I'm wiping it with your ass, that's *exactly* what you are."

"Have I mentioned how sexy the confidence is?"

I flash him a grin. "Does that mean I'll be getting lucky afterward?"

A cagey look enters his eyes. "Guess we're going to find out now, aren't we?"

Oh, you're damn right we are.

Game on.

Chapter Twenty-Four

DEMI

My eyelids flutter, and I blink, focusing on the guy stretched out next to me. His bare chest rises and falls with every inhalation. I glance at the window and realize the sun is peeking over the horizon, painting the sky in splashes of pink and purple hues. As beautiful as the sight is, it's not nearly enough to hold my attention, and my gaze returns to Rowan. His blond hair is spread out across the pillow. His skin's sun-kissed hue glows against the snowy white sheets, giving him a rich color.

I almost shake my head.

A week ago, I could never have fathomed waking up in bed next to him. Or that he had wanted me this entire time—enough to remain a virgin. Even now, it all seems farfetched. The past thirty-six hours have irrevocably altered our relationship. We can never go back to what it once was.

As swiftly as this has happened, Rowan wants to take our physical relationship slow. After we fooled around in the pool yesterday morning, all I wanted was to feel him inside my body. Even though I gave it my best shot, Rowan was adamant about taking our time and waiting.

It's kind of funny. And a bit of a role reversal. In most of my past relationships, I've always been the one to pump the brakes. And now that I've finally found a guy I want to tear the clothes off of and get naked with, he's the one slow tracking sex. I've read enough novels to appreciate the irony when I see it. And this situation is chock-full of it.

I inch closer to the warmth that emanates from his lean body. His arms are stretched above his head, making his chest stand out in sharp relief. The rigid slab of muscle and sinewy strength makes my mouth go dry. Even though his hair is the color of freshly harvested wheat in bright sunlight, his thick eyebrows and lashes are dark—the latter sweeps in twin crescents across his cheeks. Any girl would be envious of their length.

His softly parted lips draw me closer. I'm tempted to press my mouth against his. No one has ever kissed me with so much skill. And the way he takes his time...

It's as if we have an eternity to explore and discover each other.

A horde of butterflies erupts in my belly as I study him in fascination. I've spent so much of my life pretending Rowan wasn't there that I never stopped to look at him without my prejudices coloring the lens.

My teeth sink into my lower lip. It's like I'm seeing him for the first time. I'm totally bowled over by the man I find in front of me. And make no mistake, Rowan Michaels is all man. Deliciously so. There's something about him that captivates me and draws me like a bee to honey. Maybe this is why I went to such great lengths to avoid him in the first place. Deep down, I knew this was the one guy who could wreck me, and I wasn't ready. His admission Friday night has peeled away every protective layer of my resistance. I now find myself strangely powerless where he's concerned.

It's as frightening as it is freeing. Almost as if I've shed all of the constraints that have kept me firmly in check all these years. I can only liken it to jumping out of an airplane and not knowing if your parachute will open before you smack into the ground.

Here's hoping my parachute opens.

My gaze scours the chiseled lines of his face. He's all hard angles with sharp cheekbones, pouty lips, and a strong chin. For a second time in a handful of minutes, his good looks hit me like a sly sucker-punch to the gut.

What I've learned in the past thirty-six hours is that Rowan is so much more than a hot, football-playing jock. There is a hidden depth I never imagined existed. I'm having a difficult time reconciling the guy I thought I knew with the one he actually is.

Ever since I stepped foot on campus freshman year, I've been inundated with the whispered rumors of his sexual conquests. Stories swirl through the hallowed corridors and lurk around every corner. Pictures of him surrounded by busty sorority girls flood Insta after every weekend. Over the years, I've heard dozens of girls brag about hooking up with him. And they were all a bunch of lies. It blows my mind that these chicks would fib about having sex with Rowan.

For three years, I steered clear because of those lies. It turned my stomach to hear about his sexual exploits. Like he was somehow incapable of keeping his dick in his pants. Only now do I realize that I've never heard him talk about a girl or even flirt with one. They were the ones always running their mouths.

He has a reputation as a manwhore and the guy has never had sex before.

How messed up is that?

I almost snort but bite back the sound at the last minute, not wanting to wake him. I'm enjoying my silent perusal with the light that streams through the windows and across the bed. My room faces the eastern sky and gets a ton of sunshine in the morning. I used to hate it and would drag a pillow over my face so I could sleep.

At the moment, though?

I'm loving it.

My gaze travels from the planes and angles of his face before sliding to the powerful lines of his chest. Even in repose, his musculature is a sight to behold. Rowan works hard to look the way he does. This is not simply a case of good genetics. This kind of muscle tone and hard, sinewy strength takes years of rigorous weightlifting to achieve. As a fellow athlete, I can totally appreciate the dedication. To sculpt your body into a machine takes single-minded focus and determination.

My fingers itch to reach out and trace over his flat male nipples. I want to draw each one into my mouth and nibble at them with sharp teeth. The need to drive him as crazy as he makes me thrums through my blood.

Is that even possible?

For the umpteenth time, I'm bowled over by the thought of Rowan holding out for me. That knowledge only stokes the hunger that demands I explore every firm inch of him. My gaze slides to his lower abdomen, where the sheet lays crumpled. There are so many tantalizing muscles on display.

Rowan Michaels is more sculpture than actual man.

A light trail of hair arrows from his lower abdominals before disappearing beneath the cotton sheet. My gaze drops to the tented material. It looks like someone is sporting a little morning wood. Although, by all appearances, there's nothing *little* about it.

My teeth sink into my lower lip as I tentatively reach out and tug the sheet down his body until the waistband of his boxers comes into view. Gradually the cover slithers further until his boner is revealed. Sharp shafts of need explode in my lower belly before settling in my core. Unable to resist the impulse, I reach out and stroke my fingers over the thick curve. Even beneath the cotton material, heat radiates off him as if he's burning up with a fever. It sends goose bumps skittering along my skin.

Once.

Twice.

Three times I caress the hard length. Another punch of arousal slams into me. So badly do I want to delve beneath the thin material and wrap my fingers around him. A groan rumbles from Rowan's chest as he shifts beneath my touch. I glance up, only to find him watching me through slitted eyelids still clouded with sleep.

"Good morning," I whisper, continuing to stroke his length.

He stretches beneath my fingertips, becoming impossibly hard. "Yes, it certainly is."

His voice is all deep and growly. It sends another arrow of lust straight down to my core before exploding like a firework. Already my panties are damp with need. The way I'm touching him isn't nearly enough to appease the insatiable desire burning through my body. I need more.

So much more.

Since he hasn't put the kibosh on what I'm doing, I decide to push the boundary and take it further by tugging at the waistband of his boxers. First one side and then the other, until I've worked the elastic down his narrow hips, and his thick cock springs free.

My eyes widen at the sight of him.

Sure...I'd suspected he was large. I could see the long curve of it beneath the material, but it's considerably bigger than I had assumed. Enamored by the sight, I run the pads of my fingers from the velvety soft head, over the length, to the root, which is buried in a nest of curls. His erection jerks beneath my touch, and another bolt of excitement crashes through me.

I flick my gaze to his and smirk. "Impressive."

His lips twitch at the corners with amusement. "Thanks, I try."

My focus returns to the part of him that holds my attention spellbound. "Oh, there's no *trying* involved."

A snort escapes from him. Beneath his watchful gaze, I inch closer until his masculine scent can assault me.

"What are you doing?" Urgency leaps into his voice as if he's only now become aware of my intentions.

"This." I swipe my tongue across his crown.

He groans, arching his pelvis toward me. *"Demi...do you have any idea what you're doing to me?"*

"If you have to ask, then I guess not." A devious smile dances across my face. It feels so damn good to have him at my mercy. I swirl my tongue over the blunt tip before sucking him into my mouth.

A guttural sound vibrates through his body as his fingers tangle in the length of my hair.

I'm no pro at blow jobs, but I've given enough to know how to do it right. And if his reaction is any indication, then what I'm doing feels pretty damn good. Wanting to give him pleasure, I slowly slide up and down his length. My tongue swirls around the head before I lick my way to his shaft.

"Fuck," he hisses.

The sounds he makes only spur me on. His teeth sink into his lower lip as his eyelids fall shut. Pleasure flashes across his face as I draw him into my mouth until he is able to nudge the back of my throat. When his body tightens, I release him, licking and nibbling at his firm flesh before repeating the process all over again, relentlessly pushing him toward the edge.

It only takes a couple of minutes before his back is arching and his muscles coil tight. His fingers pull at me. "Demi, I'm gonna—"

My suction becomes more voracious. I've only let one other guy come in my mouth. It's not something I normally enjoy, but I want to experience this closeness with him.

More than anything, I want to be the one who snaps his control.

"*Oh, fuck.*" His hips arch off the mattress as he ejaculates. The saltiness gets swallowed down in thirsty gulps. I don't stop milking his cock until every last drop has disappeared, and he softens in my mouth.

When I finally release him, I nuzzle the velvety tip with my lips. This is the first blow job I've ever enjoyed. There's something incredibly intimate about using your mouth to pleasure someone else. There's an exchange of power I never really thought about.

Like everything else with Rowan, this, too, feels different.

A *good* kind of different.

An *addictive* kind of different.

The *best* kind of different.

Chapter Twenty-Five

ROWAN

Holy fuck.

My mind spins out of control. I'm barely able to focus on one thought.

That felt amazing.

No...better than amazing.

fan-fucking-tastic.

I've had girls blow me before, but it was never anything more than a release. This experience couldn't be more different. It was somehow deeper, more meaningful, and that has everything to do with the girl I'm sharing this moment with. The one I've spent years pining for. The one I never thought I'd actually have.

Fuck...would you listen to me?

I don't care if I sound like a lovesick pussy. As my mind clears, my gaze stays pinned to her. Looking away isn't an option. It never was.

Fuck, but she's beautiful. I mean, *really* beautiful. All that messy dark hair falling over her shoulders and cascading down her back. It's spread across my thigh as she stares up at me. Her mouth is so damn close to my cock that every soft inhalation stirs my arousal.

As our eyes lock and hold, all I can think about is returning the favor. I want to press my face against her heat and taste every gorgeous inch. I want to learn every dip and curve of her body. My new mission in life is to discover what gives her pleasure and drives her over the edge. What will make her scream and see stars? Does she like having her lips stroked? Her clit sucked? Her pussy spread wide?

I have no idea, but I'm going to damn well find out.

I want to wreck this girl for all other guys like she's ruined me.

"Fuck, baby," I gasp when I'm finally able to get a handle on myself.

She grins, her chin resting against my thigh as her tongue darts out to swipe over my softened cock like it's a lollipop. If she keeps that up, I'll be stiffening again in no time. This girl turns me on like no other.

Before she can get any more ideas in that pretty little head of hers, I slide my hands beneath her arms and drag her up my body until she's draped over me. My lips slant across hers before plunging inside. The fact that she tastes like me is such a turn-on. I sink into the caress, licking at the inside of her mouth. I could spend days exploring her, our tongues twisted together, teeth scraping. But the need to discover other parts pounds through me like that of a steady drumbeat. I need to taste her. With one smooth movement, I flip us over until she's flat on her back. Then I drag her arms above her head and pin her wrists near the headboard. The delicate pulse in her throat flutters like the wings of a hummingbird as she watches me with wide eyes.

Oh, baby, you have no idea what kind of hungry beast you've unleashed inside me, but you're about to find out.

I lower my face to hers before nipping at that plump lower lip. "And now I get to discover what you taste like."

My fingers loosen from around her wrists before grabbing the hem of her tank top and dragging it up her torso. The material is pulled over her head and tossed to the floor. Excitement rushes through me as I move to the side and stare down at her. A topless Demi is a glorious sight to behold.

But a naked Demi?

Yeah...I've waited too damn long for this moment.

My fingers itch to rip the panties away so that she's completely bared to my sight. I don't want anything standing between us, not even a thin scrap of fabric. Instead of doing that, I will myself to slow my roll. As impatient as I am, I want to savor the moment. It's one I've waited years for. I take a couple of seconds to beat back the raging beast inside me. Once firmly under control, I slip my index fingers beneath the slender elastic band before carefully drawing the material down her body. Anticipation bubbles up inside me.

My whole life has been built around control. There was a time when I didn't have any. I was at the mercy of my father and his whims. It was complete chaos. I never knew from one day to the next if we would have the essentials. Money, food, a roof over our heads. None of it was assured. All that changed once he was locked up. Little by little, I took control back. It's not something I'll ever relinquish. One of the reasons I've worked out and gotten big is so that no one could ever waltz in and take advantage of my mom and me again. I wanted to go to college and play football for a Division I school, and I made sure it happened. The first time I saw Demi, I wanted her. It might have taken years, but I made that happen as well. I could have been getting laid since I was a sophomore in high school. Instead, I exercised that same control, knowing it was all about the long game.

You don't think it takes willpower to turn down every girl who has offered to spread her legs?

It takes a monstrous amount.

Especially when they're crawling buck naked into bed with you, rubbing their hot little pussies against you. It would have been all too easy to bury myself in their tight heat and fuck some of my need for Demi out of me.

But I couldn't do it.

I couldn't sleep with one girl, all the while fantasizing that I was screwing another. It was bad enough I did it when they were blowing me.

When Demi whimpers, I blink back to the present and the girl I've always wanted.

Did I ever think I'd actually see her like this?

Ready and willing?

Crying out for my touch?

I shake those thoughts away and focus on the girl writhing beneath me. Damn, but she's sexy. Way more than I dared to imagine. My tongue darts out to moisten my parched lips as her mound is revealed. The top of her slit comes into view.

Holy fuck...she's completely bare.

Unable to resist the gorgeous sight, I lean down and press a kiss against the delicate folds. She moans, arching against my mouth as if offering herself up to taste. I continue to peel the material down her hips and thighs before untangling them from around her legs and tossing the little scrap of cotton over my shoulder.

Then I settle between her parted thighs, taking in what has been unveiled. "Damn, Demi..."

Barely am I cognizant of the husky words sliding from my lips as I look my fill. It's like staring at the sun. It's almost blinding in its intensity and yet, I can't rip my eyes away. I'm afraid if I do, she'll shimmer and disappear like a mirage.

I've fantasized about this moment for so long, imagining what she looked like beneath her clothes, but nothing could prepare me for the reality of the situation. Her long dark hair is draped across the pillowcase, and her sun-kissed flesh is a sharp contrast to the pale sheets. Her breasts are slightly rounded, topped with pink-tipped nipples that beg to be suckled between my lips. Her waist is narrow, and there's a slight flare to her hips. Tucked between the vee of her thighs is a perfectly bare and silky-smooth pussy. Her mound is plump, and her lips swollen.

With my hands splayed wide against her inner thighs, I push them further apart so I can see each soft pink fold.

"You're so fucking pretty," I whisper, more to myself than to her.

She twitches as I widen her legs. Carefully, I swipe my thumb over her sensitive center. Demi moans, thrusting her hips toward me. All I want to do is spread her wide and lick every delicious inch. I've spent years jerking off to thoughts of her, but nothing compares to reality. My imagination didn't do her justice.

"You're the first girl I've been able to take my time with and really look at." The admission slips free before I can think better of it.

"I am?" Surprise laces her voice.

"Yeah." As embarrassing as it is, I push out the rest, wanting her to know the truth. "I've hooked up with people at parties. But it's usually loud and noisy. Not exactly a place where I could take my time and savor the moment. And I liked it in the dark; it was easier to imagine you were there with me." Heat rises in my cheeks. If I'm not careful, I'll scare this girl away. She might not have thought I was a stalker yesterday, but that could easily change.

The air gets wedged at the back of my throat as I wait for her reaction. When her expression softens, my muscles loosen in relief.

Demi reaches out, snagging my fingers before giving them a light squeeze. "I'm glad you took a chance and told me the truth." There's a pause. "You were always there in the back of my head, but I didn't want to let you in. I was afraid you were every inch the player I'd heard about."

Regret fills me as I shake my head. "That was never the truth. I'm sorry you thought otherwise."

"Keeping you at a distance felt like the safest option."

I've always been aware of the rumors. Maybe I should have put a stop to them a long time ago. But how could I do that?

It was a double-edged sword—out myself or keep it under wraps and save face.

Pushing those thoughts away, I swipe my thumb over her core.

Slowly.

So slowly that she shudders under my touch as need reignites in her eyes.

My voice drops, becoming rough. "Do you still feel the need to keep your distance?"

Her tongue peeks out to moisten her lips as she shakes her head. "No."

"Good." I'm done holding back, and pretending she isn't the reason I draw breath every damn day. Now that I've had a taste of her, there's no going back. Demi is mine. Whether she realizes it or not.

My hand slips free from hers so I can place my thumbs on the side of each pouty lower lip before gently pulling them apart until her pretty little clit is exposed. She gasps as I bury my face against the top of her slit. A whimper escapes as I run the flat of my tongue over her.

Once.

Twice.

Three times.

Her fingers tunnel through my hair as if to lock me in place. Doesn't this girl realize that's not necessary? There's no way in hell I'll willingly leave. Whatever she wants, I'll give her. All she has to do is ask.

The moment I swipe my tongue over her, sweetness explodes in my mouth. Fuck, she tastes so damn good. I'm not sure I'll ever get enough. Need throbs through my veins as my tongue dips between her silken folds. I thrust in and out a few times before lapping at her with the flat of my tongue. My hands drift from her inner thighs to her waist as she writhes beneath me. The more I torture her, the creamier she becomes. I'm so greedy to learn every part of her. My mouth glides upward until I can nibble at her clit. The moment I suck the tiny bundle of nerves into my mouth, her hips jerk, and her back arches off the mattress. When her muscles become impossibly tight and her breathing picks up speed, I realize that she's close to coming. Instead of backing off and trying to draw out the pleasure, I circle my tongue around her until she screams out her orgasm.

My name on her lips is the best fucking sound in the world.

One I plan on hearing more of.

It's only after her body turns limp that I lift my head. A dazed expression fills Demi's face as she stares sightlessly at the ceiling. Pride expands in my chest at the realization that I was able to make her feel so good.

I press one last kiss against her glistening lips before crawling up her sprawled body. As I reach her face, her gaze snaps to mine, and she blinks as if awakening from a long dream. I smack a kiss against her softly parted mouth. "Feel good?"

"Yeah." The sound she emits is more of a satisfied sigh than anything else.

I smirk. She sounds totally out of it. "Better than good?"

"*Way* better than good," she admits.

"That's exactly what I wanted to hear."

A smile curves her lips.

With my arms wrapped around her, I roll onto my back, taking her with me until she's sprawled across my bare chest. A puff of air escapes from her before she settles against me as if she's been there a thousand times before. Silence blankets us, but it's not one that's uncomfortable. Even though this is new, and it happened quickly, it's been a long time in the making.

I strum my fingers over the delicate line of her spine, never expecting the weekend to turn out like this when I stopped to check on her.

Had I hoped for it?

Sure...but I never actually expected something to happen. And now that it has, I don't want anything to ruin it. And I sure as hell don't want her having second thoughts. That's the reason I'm trying to hold off on sex. I want her to be one hundred percent certain about getting involved with me.

"Are you okay?" As much as I want to believe she's fully on board, I need her to verify it. I need to know that she doesn't regret the intimacy we've shared.

Demi lifts her head to meet my gaze. "Yeah."

I sift my fingers through the heavy fall of her hair, pushing it away from her face. I want to see every flicker of emotion as it crosses her expressive features. I want to know every thought that enters her head.

Another silence falls over us before she asks, "What happens now?"

The question is a two-hundred-pound weight sitting in the middle of my chest, making it impossible to suck in mouthfuls of air. At some point, before the weekend ended, the future—if we have one—needed to be discussed. I know what I want. But this is new for Demi. I need to play it cool and not overwhelm her by coming on too strong.

"That's up to you."

She remains silent for a lengthy stretch. It doesn't take long for the stillness to become agonizing. "I'm not sure."

My heart stutters.

Once.

Then again.

"I want to explore this," she whispers, "but there's a reason I don't date football players." For the first time this weekend, uncertainty churns in her eyes, and I'd bet my life that bastard Justin has wiggled his way into her thoughts.

My hands drift to her cheeks. I need to touch her. That's what grounds me.

Slow. I need to take this slow with her.

"We can do whatever you want."

Instead of answering, she nibbles at her lip and glances away. I can almost see the thoughts as they crash through her head. The push and pull. The tug-o-war taking place inside her as we speak. "I'm not sure how my dad would feel about this. It's always been an unwritten rule that I stay away from his players."

Coach.

He's definitely an obstacle that will need to be dealt with in the near future. As much as I don't want to get on his bad side, Demi is well worth the risk. The feelings I have for her aren't going to change anytime soon.

"I don't want people talking about me." Doubt and sadness flicker in her dark eyes, giving them a hollowed-out appearance. As much as I can't blame her, I hate that she's focused on the bullshit that occurred this week.

"I don't give a damn what anyone says," I growl. "Let the fuckers talk. All that matters is you."

Some of the confusion dissipates from her expression as her gaze softens. "I know it's stupid, and I shouldn't care, but I do. It's happened so many times now." Her brow furrows as she glances away. "And Justin..."

Fuck that guy.

I should have beat the piss out of him instead of popping him in the nose. Maybe then, he wouldn't have run his mouth all over campus like a little bitch.

She's waffling. I see it written clearly in her eyes. Demi is scared of the blowback she'll receive when people find out we're together. At some point, her father will discover the truth, and she's afraid of what his reaction will be.

My chest constricts. "If you want to keep this on the downlow for the time being, then that's what we'll do." The words sound wooden and taste like ash on my tongue. "Okay?"

More than anything, I want her to tell me that she doesn't give a crap about the gossip or her father.

Her muscles loosen in relief. "You really don't mind?"

Fuck yeah, I mind, but if that's what she wants, then that's what we'll do. It sucks. I want to yell from the rooftops that Demi is mine. I don't want other guys looking at her without the knowledge that there will be repercussions. And I want the jersey chasers to stop throwing themselves at me. I'm a taken man. There's only one woman I want. Unfortunately, it looks like I'll have to wait a little longer for her to claim me the way I need her to.

"Yeah," I lie, "it's fine."

Now that the future has been settled, she relaxes, stretching her lithe body until she's able to brush her lips against mine. "Thank you."

Even though the situation is far from perfect, a sigh of content-ment fills me.

Demi might not realize it yet, but there's not much I wouldn't do to make her happy or keep her safe.

Chapter Twenty-Six

DEMI

"If we look at this outcome variable—"

Instead of paying attention to the textbook splayed open on the table, Rowan's gaze is fixated on his fingers as they graze my inner thigh. A trail of goose flesh forms in their wake, and I have to stop myself from visibly shuddering. It would only encourage him to keep up his antics.

"Rowan," I growl. Any moment I'm going to self-combust, and I can't afford to fall apart in the library. We're already drawing enough unwanted attention.

All right...Rowan is the one drawing all the attention. Half a dozen girls have already sauntered past, giving him little waves and bright smiles. He acknowledges them without encouraging their behavior.

Am I jealous?

Ha!

Maybe a teensy bit.

I'd like nothing better than to claim him publicly so these girls would back the hell off. But we agreed to keep our relationship quiet for the time being.

When Rowan flicks his eyes at me, I know that I'm in trouble. A smirk simmers across his lips, and I find myself gravitating toward him before snapping to attention with a scowl. Even in the middle of the library, he's able to make me forget myself and the reason we're here.

He cocks a brow and asks innocently, "Is there a problem?"

My attention becomes ensnared by his lips.

You have no idea what the man is capable of with that mouth.

So.

Much.

Pleasure.

It's enough to make my eyes cross.

He wasn't kidding when he said he loves to play south of the border. I'll be completely honest...it's not something I ever thought I'd enjoy. Of course, I've heard girls talk about it. But come on...it seems so intimate. To let someone touch you like that...

And now I can't get enough of it.

I can't get enough of Rowan.

Want to hear something crazy?

I've all but begged him to sleep with me, and he refuses. He keeps telling me that we need to wait. He wants me to be sure.

I am sure, dammit!

I want him.

Now!

All right, maybe not this second. Oh, who am I kidding? If he gave me even the slightest indication he was ready, I'd pack these books up so fast his head would spin. Jeez. I'm worse than a guy. I totally have sex on the brain. It takes effort to clear away those unruly thoughts and focus on the task at hand.

What were we working on again?

Ugh. I'm like a walking hormone.

"You need to focus so we can get through this," I grumble, ignoring his question. We've been at it for almost an hour and only have a couple more problems to plow through. Then we can get out of here. Maybe go back to my place. If Sydney isn't home, I can try to—

"Trust me," his voice drops so low that it strums something inside me, "I'm focused." The calloused pads of his fingers continue to dance across my inner thigh, inching closer to the vee between my legs. "*Laser-focused.*"

There shouldn't be anything sexy about the slide of rough skin against mine, but damn if there isn't. These running shorts were a bad idea. I should have covered myself from head to toe.

At this rate, Rowan will end up flunking statistics.

"Unfortunately, that laser focus isn't where it belongs," I point to the book, "on stats."

"Nope." He leans so close that his warm breath feathers over the outer shell of my ear. Another delicate shiver works its way down my spine. "At the moment, there's something else on my mind."

When his fingers brush against my core, I shift in my seat before cautiously glancing around. We're certainly not alone. Students surround us as they study at nearby tables. Apparently, everyone and their grandmother decided they needed to work at the library this evening. The place is surprisingly packed for a Monday night. When we arrived on the second floor, people were already camped out at our usual table.

"Rowan," I mutter, simultaneously loving and hating the way he drives me crazy.

"We've plowed through most of the assignment. We deserve a break." He waggles his brows. "I'm sure we could find a dark corner to make out in."

I hate to admit how tempting the offer is. It's reluctantly that I pull away until there's a safe distance between us. "You shouldn't touch me like that." I clear my throat and attempt to stomp out the arousal that has flared to life between my legs. "There are too many people watching us."

"Does it really matter?" He toys with my fingers under the table where they're partially hidden.

My teeth sink into my lower lip.

We've been sneaking around for a week, stealing time together when no one is looking. Sydney remains blissfully unaware of our relationship. Which means that Rowan and I can only spend time together at my place when she's at class or with Ethan. Luckily, they're on again this week, so it's worked out perfectly. We can't go to the house Rowan rents off-campus because he lives with a bunch of football players.

It's only been within the last couple of days that the rumors Justin spread around campus have started to die down. The last thing I want is to resurrect them again. Especially, when the gossip would be true.

"I need a little more time." Guilt slices through me as I drop my voice to a whisper. "That's all."

Emotion flares to life in Rowan's eyes, and for a moment, I steel myself for an argument. I can't blame him for wanting our relationship out in the open. It's not like I'm embarrassed to be with him. It's more the fact that I'm the head coach's daughter. And these rumors about me screwing the football team always seem to pop up at the most inopportune times. I don't want people to think that. Rowan doesn't get to fuck me as some kind of bonus for being the star player. Even the thought makes me sick to my stomach.

"Fine." As the tension drains from him, his broad shoulders loosen. "I've waited this long; it won't kill me to wait a little longer."

A burst of relief explodes inside me. I hate that I'm doing this to him, but I'm not ready to out our relationship yet. "Thank you."

He shrugs as a glimmer of mischief leaps into his eyes. "I'll let you make it up to me later."

My brows rise with interest as a smile simmers around the edges of my lips. That's one thing I like about Rowan—he's never bent out of shape for long. It's like a quickly passing summer storm. There and gone before you know it. "And how *exactly* will I do that?"

"I'm sure you'll—"

"Hi, Rowan!"

A chorus of soft female voices has me jerking away. I grit my teeth, tired of this happening. We can't go anywhere without him being bombarded by groupies.

My gaze flies from Rowan to the trio of girls who hover next to us. Two are brunettes, and one is blond. All three are soft and curvy. The dark-haired girls look suspiciously similar. Maybe they're twins. Although, it's difficult to tell because they're all wearing matching T-shirts with sorority letters stamped across their oversized chests and tiny white shorts. Now that I'm scrutinizing them more closely, I realize their hair and makeup look the same. As if there's a strict dress code that needs to be adhered to, or they'll get kicked out of their exclusive club.

I wince at the snarky thought. That's not who I am. I don't hate other girls for being different. I have my priorities, and they have theirs. Neither is right or wrong.

The lack of sex is definitely getting to me.

"Hey." Even though Rowan leans back against the chair, he keeps my fingers firmly ensconced in his beneath the table.

They don't seem to notice. Or maybe they don't care. Since Rowan has never dated one girl specifically, he's been claimed as public property. And these chicks...apparently, don't mind sharing. I, however, am quite territorial. As far as boyfriends are concerned, I don't play well with others.

In a blatant bid to get his attention, one of the girls tucks a strand of hair behind her ear. "We missed you Saturday night at the house." She inches closer to him. "I thought you were going to stop by." Her voice drops, becoming low and sultry. "It's been a while since we partied together."

My brows rise.

Partied together?

I get the feeling she means something else entirely.

"Yeah, sorry." Rowan clears his throat. "I was busy."

This is the downside to dating athletes. They're usually a hot commodity on campus and have a shit ton of options available to them. When I attempt to pull my hand from his, he squeezes my fingers, refusing to relinquish them.

"Do you girls know Demi?"

I'm treated to a chorus of unenthusiastic greetings before their attention returns to Rowan. In approximately three seconds flat, I'm sized up and found lacking. Quite honestly, these are precisely the type of girls I imagined Rowan spending time with.

I look nothing like them.

They probably consider it sacrilegious to leave their sorority house without being fully made up with every hair in place. Hell, they probably have glam squads. I, on the other hand, consider myself ahead of the game if I've thrown my hair up into a ponytail or messy bun. Bonus points if my top matches my bottoms. Which is why I wear a lot of jeans. What doesn't go with denim?

My thoughts exactly.

"Maybe we'll see you tomorrow? Sigma Tau is having another bash." Blondie trails her fingers over his bicep. "It's supposed to be epic."

Oh right...

These girls. They're still here, cooing at Rowan. And there's not a damn thing I can do about it because I told him that I want to keep everything on the down-low. I can't stake a claim just because I'm feeling strangely insecure. The air catches at the back of my throat as I'm struck with the realization. That's exactly what this ugly emotion coursing through me is.

Jealousy.

It takes everything I have inside to bite back the moan of displeasure. I've never liked anyone enough to feel this strongly. Not even when I found Annica with Justin's dick stuffed in her mouth did I feel one iota of possessiveness. Honestly, I didn't care.

"Um, probably not," Rowan says, knocking me out of those disturbing thoughts.

One of the brunettes thrusts out her lower lip into a pout, making her look like a child on the verge of a tantrum. If she's going for sexy, she's completely missed the mark. But then again, maybe this is the kind of behavior guys find attractive. How would I know? It's not like I've ever tried to be alluring. I'm not into acting coy, fluttering my lashes, or sticking my chest out in a bid for attention. That kind of behavior is ridiculous and, quite frankly, beneath me.

"That's too bad. Parties are always more fun when you're there," one of the twins says.

I almost roll my eyes. These girls need to move it along.

As if sensing my annoyance, Rowan clears his throat and points to the textbook on the table. "Sorry, ladies, I hate to cut this short, but we still have a lot of work to plow through."

Instead of taking the hint, one of the girls peers down at the book. "Oh, is that statistics?" Her eyes light up as she bounces on the tips of her toes. "I could help with that! There's no reason for you to pay a tutor."

"Yeah," the other two girls chime in with excitement. "We'll all help!"

Oh lord...

Why do I get the feeling it would be like the blind leading the blind?

Rowan quickly shakes his head. "No, Demi is a great tutor, but thanks."

"Are you sure?" one wheedles.

"Yup, one hundred percent sure."

"All right. If you change your mind, let us know!"

"Will do." Rowan presses his lips together and waits for them to leave.

It takes another five minutes before the trio vacates the area. And even then, they settle at a neighboring table and continue to shoot seductive looks at Rowan.

He squeezes my fingers, drawing my attention to him. "You ready to get out of here?"

"Yeah."

Rowan glances at the girls who perk up and wave before his gaze slides back to mine. "You know I have zero interest in them, right?"

That's the thing...

Why *wouldn't* he be drawn to them? They're all beautiful in that airbrushed sort of way. And clearly, they're sisters who enjoy sharing.

Most guys would be all over that.

Literally.

"Demi?" His voice deepens, and I blink the errant thoughts away. "You know you're the only girl I want, right? It's always been you. And that won't change any time soon."

All of the jealousy eating me up from the inside out dissolves.

When it comes down to it, I *do* know that. Rowan has been nothing if not straightforward and totally honest with me. Unflinchingly so.

I nod, feeling like a jackass. I'm the one who wants to keep this relationship under wraps.

"All you have to do is say the word, and this won't be a secret any longer." As if reading my thoughts, he jerks his head toward his admirers. "They'll be the first ones I tell."

A slight smile tugs at the corners of my lips. "Soon, I promise."

"Fine." He shrugs. "Whenever you're ready."

As tempting as it is to take his face in my hands and smack a kiss against his lips in front of everyone, I hold back. What I've come to realize is that it's getting more and more difficult to keep these feelings to myself.

I want them out in the open.

I want *us* out in the open.

It's only a matter of time before my need for Rowan overtakes the fear I have of going public.

Chapter Twenty-Seven

DEMI

"Shhhh!" I peek my head inside the darkened apartment to see if Sydney is home. I tried to assess the situation through text, but she failed to respond. Half the time, she spends the night at Ethan's place.

When they're not fighting.

A couple of days ago, they got into another spat, but I think they patched things up already. Their relationship gives me whiplash. "You have to be quiet!"

"I *am* being quiet," Rowan whispers, wrapping his arm around my waist and hauling me close to nuzzle my ear.

Before he can distract me from my mission, I fight my way free and continue creeping into the tiny entryway before hitting the kitchen and living area. The rooms are shrouded in darkness. There's a stillness to the place that has me suspecting Sydney is with Ethan.

Which means—drumroll, please—that Rowan and I finally have the place to ourselves.

Yes!

Yes!

Yes!

Other than the weekend we spent at my dad's house; we've only been able to steal time here and there. Sneaking kisses in the library when no one is looking. We can't hold hands on campus, but every once in a while, our fingers will brush. Sparks of sexual tension explode inside me like a firework. When we're sitting in class, his knee will rest against mine. All of these little touches are driving me insane in the membrane, especially since we've yet to have sex.

There hasn't been an opportunity. With any luck, it'll happen tonight. I can't stand to go another day without having him inside me.

Is there a term for lady blue balls?

If so, that's exactly what's going on here. I've never been this revved up.

My muscles loosen as I spin around to face him. "Sydney's gone, which means," I waggle my eyebrows suggestively, "that we're officially alone."

"Excellent." With a grin, his arms slip around me, and this time, I allow myself to sink into the embrace.

As soon as his lips settle on mine, I open under the gentle pressure. My knees weaken as the velvety softness of his tongue brushes against mine. It doesn't take long before my world shrinks, only encompassing the two of us. At that moment, nothing else matters. I wish it could always be like this.

My hands delve under his shirt until they meet warm flesh. His muscles are so rigid, as if chiseled from marble. I could stare at him for days and not get bored by the sight. I gather the material in my fingers before dragging it over washboard abdominals until his upper body is revealed. From somewhere in the background, a choir of angels sing. Even they can appreciate a well-sculpted chest. I pull the fabric over his head before dropping it to the carpeted floor.

"Are you really that impatient?" he asks, a smile simmering in his voice.

"You have no idea." All I want is to get this guy naked. Even the thought is enough to have my panties flooding with heat.

"Can't say that's not sexy as hell."

"You just wait, buddy, and I'll *show* you sexy as hell." Surprise floods through me that I would even say such a thing.

Seriously...who is this girl?

I've never been this horny in my life. And I've certainly never been this vocal about it either. It's kind of a revelation.

"Mmmm, I like the sound of that." His voice turns gruff as if he's as turned on as I am. It strums something deep inside, only making me want him more. My palms rest against the delicious musculature of his chest as I gently push him backward into the hallway.

"Oh?" He raises a brow as he teases, "are we going somewhere?"

"Yup." I give him my best leer. "To my room so I can have my wicked way with you."

It only takes a few steps to get him exactly where I want him. As we reach the threshold of the space, the handle of Sydney's door jangles, breaking the silence of the apartment.

My eyes widen as I realize that we're not as alone as I'd assumed. I quickly shove Rowan into my bedroom and slam the door shut. My heart races as a groggy looking Sydney steps into the darkened hallway and blinks at me. She has the look of an animal on the verge of waking from a long hibernation.

"Hey." She drags a hand through her disheveled blond hair. "What time is it?"

"Ummm," I glance at my phone, "about eight."

"Really?" She rubs her eyes. "I was studying, and then decided to take a short nap. That was two hours ago. Guess I was more tired than I realized."

"Oh. Sorry about waking you. I figured you weren't home."

She shrugs before stifling a yawn. "It's fine. I have a paper to finish up. It's probably good that it happened." She gives me a slight smile before shifting her weight and glancing around the apartment with curiosity. "Is someone else here? I could have sworn I heard voices."

"Ummm...nope!" Well, hell. I really hate lying. Although that doesn't stop me from sliding my cell from my jeans' back pocket and waving it around like evidence. "I was talking on the phone."

"Huh." Her brows draw together in confusion. "That's so weird. I thought I heard a male voice."

"It was my father." There's a pause as my mind whirls, and I add with a bit of a nervous chuckle, "You know how loud he is. Must be all that shouting from the sidelines."

"Yeah," she shrugs, "I guess."

The air gets clogged in my throat. I can't tell if she's buying my story or not. It would probably be for the best if I change the subject rather than dig my hole any deeper. "I figured you would be with Ethan."

Her lips sink into a frown. "We're on another break."

"Oh." I've lost count of how many *breaks* they've taken in the four-plus months they've been together, but it's a lot. Too many.

She rolls her eyes before crossing her arms over her chest and leaning against the door frame. "Yeah, I know. Something has to change. I can't keep doing this anymore."

I hate to say it, but I've heard this song and dance from Sydney before. Inevitably, she'll get back together with Ethan, and the ugly cycle will begin all over again. She never does anything to break the pattern.

When I remain silent, she straightens and switches gears. "I'm starving. I slept right through dinner. Did you eat already?"

"Not yet." I point to the kitchen and improvise. "I was about to make a PB&J."

She scrunches her nose. "What are you? Like five? Let's go out and grab something."

"Oh." Ignoring the jab at my favorite sandwich, I glance at my closed bedroom door. There's no way I can tell Sydney that Rowan is standing on the other side. I mean, I could...but I'm not ready to do that yet. "Um—"

"Please!" She steeples her hands in front of her. "I need you to talk me out of this relationship!"

That's not possible.

"Please, please, please! I need your wisdom now more than ever."

My shoulders collapse. "Fine." Sydney has always been there when I've needed her. How can I not do the same?

A big smile lights up her face. "Yay! I miss spending time with you. It feels like you've been so busy this past week, and I don't even know what you've been up to."

Remorse pricks at my conscience. I've been spending all my free time sneaking around with Rowan. Honestly, I didn't think Sydney would notice my absence.

"Let me change, and we can go."

Before I can respond, she swings away, closing the bedroom door behind her.

There's a beat of silence before mine is cracked open, and Rowan peers out. "Is the coast clear?"

"Yeah." Disappointment floods through me. I was really looking forward to spending a little one-on-one time with him.

As if reading my thoughts, his lips twitch. "Guess we'll have to take a raincheck."

"It looks that way," I say with a pout. I'm going to self-combust if I don't get laid soon.

He points to the wadded-up shirt on the living room floor. "I'm gonna need that before I take off."

"I like you better without it on," I tell him.

"You mean like this?" With a grin, he flexes his biceps, and I go a little weak in the knees. I could stare at him for hours. Unfortunately, now's not the time to get caught up in his body. I scramble to grab the shirt from the floor and toss it to him. He tugs it over his head and covers his chest. Then he smacks a kiss against my lips. "Call me later?"

"As soon as I get back."

"It's a date." And then he's gone, disappearing almost soundlessly through the apartment door.

As if on cue, Sydney strolls out of her room with her purse in hand. "Ready to go?"

"Yup."

"Want to grab Chinese? I could really go for chicken fried rice."

My belly rumbles in agreement. I guess if I can't satiate one appetite, I can at least satisfy the other. "That sounds good."

As we leave the apartment, she throws an arm around my shoulders and tugs me close. "I guess if it doesn't work out with Ethan, we can be single and ready to mingle together."

I hoist my smile. "Yeah."

Except...I'm not as single as she thinks I am.

And sooner rather than later, I need to come clean about that.

Chapter Twenty-Eight

DEMI

Annica knocks into me as I jog to the other side of the field. When I throw a glance over my shoulder, she narrows her eyes and glares. I roll mine and dismiss her like the pesky fruit fly she is. That girl needs to get over herself and move on. I refuse to engage in this petty behavior and divide our team any further than it is.

Clearly, Annica has other ideas. She's like a rat terrier constantly nipping at my heels. If she's not careful, she's going to get a swift kick in the ass. When she doesn't get the expected rise out of me, she swings away. Her cronies flank her as they head off in the opposite direction.

"Maybe you should tell Coach what's going on," Sydney grumbles before pursing her lips and shooting the auburn-haired girl a death glare.

"He's aware of the situation and wants us to act like the adults we're supposed to be and handle it on our own."

She plants her fists on her hips. "Punch her in the face. *Boom*. Then it's handled."

A chuckle gurgles up in my throat. As much as I like the idea, that would probably make matters worse.

After another thirty minutes of scrimmaging, Coach blows his whistle. We huddle up before going over a few plays that need work, and then he releases us for the afternoon.

As Sydney and I head to the locker room, my mind is full of Annica. She won't be happy until she rips this team apart and me with it. I need to figure out a way to stop her. I'm not sure what else to do. I've tried talking to her, and she refuses to listen. If anything, it's only pissed her off more.

"Hey," Sydney says, interrupting the whirl of my thoughts, "isn't that Rowan hanging out by the fence?" Her voice turns speculative. "He must be sleeping with one of the dirty bitches on our team." There's a pause before she mutters, "Lucky girl."

All thoughts of Annica disappear as my gaze arrows to the chain-link fence surrounding the perimeter of the field. Sure enough, there he is, leaning casually against one of the metal poles. Our gazes catch and hold. The force of his stare is almost enough to have me stumbling to a halt.

The sensations that career around inside me are almost shocking in their intensity. It's almost enough to knock the air from my lungs. Never could I have imagined that it would be like this between us. I spent so much time pretending I felt nothing for Rowan. Now that I'm no longer fighting myself, I'm practically drowning in emotion.

The noise of the field fades as he pushes away from the fence and walks toward me. As corny as it sounds, it's as if there's an invisible string pulling us toward one another. I've never felt this with anyone else. Until now, I didn't believe something like this even existed. A smile curves the edges of my lips. As much as I want to play it cool, that's no longer a possibility. The sight of him makes me feel like a goofy teenager. Like there are red and pink hearts dancing over my head. Someone needs to smack me before this can spiral any further out of control.

Sydney continues to chatter away, but I have no idea what she's saying. Her voice is like the insistent drone of bees in my ears. Rowan is the only person I'm able to focus on.

An answering smile lifts his lips, and my heart spasms.

He looks so damn good in a maroon-colored T-shirt that hugs every delicious inch of his chest and biceps. His jeans sit low on his waist and mold to his muscular thighs. A punch of arousal hits me in the gut before settling in my core.

Why am I holding all this in and pretending we're not together?

I've been so insistent that we keep this on the down-low and sneak around like we're doing something wrong when nothing could be further from the truth. I'm not ashamed to be seen with him. Why do I care what a bunch of gossips have to say?

It takes less than thirty seconds to close the distance between us. When he's about five feet away, Rowan's footsteps slow. He glances at Sydney before raising a tentative hand in my direction. Only now do I realize that he stopped because he's unsure how to greet me in front of my teammates. He's trying to do as I've asked. All of a sudden, I feel like a jerk for forcing him to keep our relationship a secret.

Three strides bring me to him, and I slide my arms around his neck. His brows shoot up when he realizes my intent. From my periphery, I catch Sydney's reaction. Her mouth drops open, and her eyes pop wide. A choking sound escapes from her. Instead of admitting my attraction for Rowan, I've always gone out of my way to insist that I didn't like him. It was as if by repeating it enough times, I could convince myself it was the truth. Clearly, that plan backfired. Sydney has never been able to understand my intense disdain for the quarterback. Little does she realize that I was lying to both of us.

As soon as his lips collide with mine, I open under the firm pressure. His tongue sweeps inside my mouth and tangles with my own. His arms band around me, pulling me close. I've never been one for PDA, but at the moment, I don't give a damn who sees us together.

"Oh, my freaking god, *you're* the dirty bitch!" Sydney screeches at a decibel that hurts my ears. "I think I'm losing my ever-loving mind!"

My lips tremble at the corners as I pull away enough to meet his gaze.

"Well, the cat is definitely out of the bag," he murmurs with a grin. "There's no going back now."

A mixture of relief and giddiness flood through me.

"It'll spread across campus like wildfire." He pauses, carefully searching my eyes for remorse. "Are you ready for that?"

"Yeah, let them talk. I don't care." I have no idea when that changed, and I started feeling differently. All I know is that the shift has everything to do with Rowan. Instead of pushing me into a relationship I wasn't ready for, he waited patiently and gave me the time I needed to get there on my own. And now that I have, I couldn't be happier.

His mouth lingers over mine. "Good. Let them run their mouths. It's all a bunch of white noise."

Yes, that's exactly what it is.

"Looks like it's Rowan's turn to take a ride on the coach's daughter."

Annica's obnoxious voice is like a bucket of cold water dumped over my head. And yet, it's still not enough to douse the joy blooming to life inside me.

"Listen here, you little bi—" Sydney growls, taking a menacing step toward our auburn-haired teammate.

I break apart from Rowan in time to grab the back of my friend's practice jersey and stop her from doing any damage. "Ignore her, Syd. She's not worth it."

Annica smirks as if this is yet another battle she's won. I'm really tired of this girl's antics. I refuse to let her ruin this for me.

"Actually," my best friend says with a glower, "it would be *entirely* worth it."

She scowls at Annica until the other girl and her buddies move it along. Only then does the rage filling her green eyes dissipate before they bounce speculatively from me to Rowan and then back again.

"Is this really happening?" She shakes her head as if she must be dreaming. "Someone needs to pinch me." Before I can respond, she throws her arms wide. "How could you keep a juicy morsel like this from me?" She pauses long enough to draw in a sharp breath before firing off another question. "Exactly how long has this been going on for?"

Rowan tilts his head as if giving the question serious consideration. "Two weeks."

"*What!*" Her brows skyrocket into her hairline, and I can almost see the wheels spinning in her head. "Wait a minute...last Thursday when I found you in the hallway and thought you were talking to someone..."

she straightens to her full height and drills a painful finger into my chest. "I knew it! I *knew* someone was there! My Spidey senses were tingling like crazy, and you totally lied to me!"

I wince as guilt creeps in at the edges.

Rowan wraps his arm around my shoulders and tugs me close before dropping a light kiss against the top of my head. "Don't be too hard on her. She needed a little time before we went public with this."

Unmoved by the comment, Sydney folds her arms and glares. "I'm not one of these loudmouth assholes on campus." She presses a hand to her chest. "I'm your *best* friend. I've always been there for you." She stabs a finger toward the locker room. "I have zero problem kicking any of their asses if I have to."

"I'm sorry, Syd. It was never my intention to keep this from you." I pause for a beat. My gaze drifts to Rowan before glancing back at my best friend. "After everything with Justin and all the rumors that were flying around, I wanted to give it a little time to die down."

Some of the rigidity leaks from her shoulders as she glances toward the locker room again. "You didn't need to keep the truth from me. I would have backed you up no matter what."

Regret slices through me. Ever since Sydney and I met in training camp before freshman year, we've been thick as thieves. She's become a solid presence in my life, and I can't imagine college or soccer without her. She's my sister from another mister, and nothing will ever change that no matter where life takes us next year. Instead of sneaking around behind her back, I should have been honest with her.

Needing to make this right, I slip from Rowan's arms before wrapping mine around my bestie and tugging her close. "Sorry, girl. You're the last person I should have worried about."

"I forgive you." Sydney squeezes me in a bone-crushing embrace. As she releases me and steps away, her gaze returns to the handsome football player. "This must be the real deal if you've decided to break your own rules."

I glance at him. "Yeah, it is." Even though it's still early, the feelings I have for Rowan are deeper than anything I've ever experienced before. Maybe that's because he's been a steady presence in my life for so many years.

With her arm wrapped around my waist, Sydney's gaze narrows at him before her expression turns threatening. "I'm warning you upfront that I'll kick your ass if you do anything to hurt my girl."

His lips hitch as he raises his palms in a gesture of surrender. "You don't have anything to worry about from me."

Sydney shoots another glance toward the locker room. "And stay far away from that red-headed viper. If I know that bitch, she'll make a play for you in order to hurt Demi."

The smile dissolves from Rowan's face as his attention shifts to the squat building. Understanding dawns across his expression. "Is that the girl you found with Justin?"

"Yup." Sydney beats me to the punch. "It's not the first time she's gone after someone Demi has been with."

Rowan's troubled gaze slides to mine. "Is she still giving you problems?"

I shrug. I suppose that would depend on your definition of a problem.

"She's jealous that our girl is not only a better player but is a starter. Annica wants her position. Demi is competition, and if she can't wipe her from the field, then she'll destroy her off it." Sydney's expression hardens. "That chick is a real piece of work."

"There's got to be more to it than that." I roll my eyes as heat suffuses my cheeks. "Annica is a good player."

"You're right, she is. But she's nowhere as dedicated as you are. Maybe if she put half the amount of time into improving her skills as she does running her mouth, she'd get more playtime on the field."

Before I can argue with Sydney's assessment of the situation, she untangles herself from me and hitches a thumb toward the locker room. "I need to grab a shower. I'm meeting up with Ethan for dinner." Her lips twitch. "Guess there's no longer a need to sneak around the apartment, huh?"

Now that everything is out in the open, it's like a huge weight has been lifted from my shoulders. Not even Annica can ruin this for me.

"Nope." Rowan's gaze holds mine.

With that, Sydney takes off at a slow jog, leaving us alone on the field.

Rowan closes the distance between us before reaching out and tugging me into his arms. I tilt my head until I can meet his gaze.

"Any regrets?" he asks softly.

It's not even a question in my head. "None."

"Good." His lips drift across mine. "I didn't like sneaking around. I want everyone to know you belong to me."

The possessive sentiment sends a thrill shooting through me. "I like the sound of that."

For one glorious moment, all feels right in the world.

Rowan shatters that peace when he says, "You know we're going to have to talk to Coach, right?"

My heart hitches.

Dad.

Somehow, in the chaos of the moment, I forgot about him. Is it too late to put this under wraps again? How about we consider filling him in after graduation?

Rowan's lips quirk. "Think I'll get benched for the rest of the season?"

I really hope not.

Then again, with my father, anything is possible.

Chapter Twenty-Nine

DEMI

"You need to relax." Rowan squeezes my fingers as he drags me up the sidewalk of my childhood home. Even though we've been doing this since the first week of college, nothing about this particular dinner feels normal. I'm a ball of pent-up anxiety. "Everything will be fine."

I press my other hand to my lower abdomen as if that will calm the sickness roiling inside me. "Are you sure about that?"

"Yup." He lifts our entwined hands to his mouth before brushing a soft kiss against my knuckles. "Pretty sure."

"I don't know." Dad and I have an unspoken arrangement regarding the Wildcat players. It makes it easier for everyone involved. Not once, in all these years, have I been tempted to cross that line.

Rowan has turned out to be the exception.

I'm unsure how Dad will react to this new development.

Will it be with shock?

Anger?

Disappointment?

The last two are what scares me the most. There has never been a time in my life when I didn't toe the line. Why wouldn't I? I had a happy home. Even with the divorce, I knew my parents loved me. Some kids want to push the boundaries and flirt with danger. I never felt the need to do that. I was too focused on soccer and school to get into mischief, or date boys who I knew would be trouble.

Even though I have no idea what to expect from him, I can't see Dad being hunky-dory with his one and only daughter dating his star quarterback. The very same guy he took under his wing, welcomed into our house, and treated as if he was part of the family.

The only good thing that will come out of this evening is that I can finally come clean and get everything out in the open. My father and I have always been close. I don't like sneaking around and keeping secrets from him. There have been two dinners since we spent the weekend together, and I barely survived either without blurting out the truth. I laughed a little too loudly and kept jumping up, fluttering nervously around the kitchen and living room. Dad jokingly asked if I had ants in my pants.

Little does he know that it's Rowan who is in my pants.

Well, not literally. We *still* haven't slept together, and it's driving me bonkers.

As Rowan reaches for the door handle, I slip my hand from his to smooth down my outfit. I'm not a girl who usually wears skirts, but I wanted to look nice this evening. All right...so maybe Sydney got her hands on me before I could walk out the door. I was informed that athletic shorts and a T-shirt are not considered dress code appropriate when you're announcing a new relationship to your father. I'm wearing a pale, blue-colored skirt that hits mid-thigh and a tan, light V-neck sweater that hugs my curves.

As much as I fought Sydney on the outfit change, I'm kind of glad she strongarmed me into it. Rowan's expression was well worth the hassle. His eyes nearly popped out of his head when he caught sight of me.

Who knows...maybe tonight will be the lucky night.

I almost snort.

A girl can dream, right?

He pauses before pushing open the front door. "Did I tell you how amazing you look?"

My lips bow up at the corners. "Only about a dozen times."

"Just wanted to make sure." He gives me a wink along with a quick kiss before swinging the door wide. Barely do I have enough time to collect myself before Dad peeks into the entryway from around the kitchen corner.

"Hey, guys!" He holds up an overflowing platter of uncooked hamburgers and hot dogs. "It's so nice out that I thought we could grill for dinner."

"Sounds good, Dad," I respond in an overly enthusiastic voice. Jeez. I really need to settle down and play this cool.

"Hey, Coach." Rowan lifts a hand to wave. "Need any help?"

"Nope, it's all good. The corn is ready to boil, and the fries are in the oven." He glances between the pair of us. "Did you two ride over together?"

Shoot. Maybe we should have taken separate vehicles. Does he already suspect that we've been seeing each other? Is he going to stomp into his home office and take out his gun in an attempt to scare Rowan away?

I have to swallow down the nerves attempting to fight their way out.

Before I can wrap my lips around an answer, Rowan says in an offhanded manner, "Yup. There didn't seem to be any point in wasting gas when we're both going to the same place."

Dad nods as if that makes perfect sense, and I release the pent-up air from my lungs in a rush. I've only been here for two minutes, and already I know that I won't make it through an hour without blurting out the truth.

My father's gaze returns to me. "Wow, hun, you look nice." His lips sink into a frown. "Is tonight a special occasion? It's not your birthday, is it?"

"No."

"Good. I'd feel terrible if I forgot." He studies me a little more closely. "Well, you certainly look beautiful. Rowan is a lucky guy."

My muscles tense, and my eyes widen. "What do you mean?" Damn Sydney and her meddling ways. I *knew* I should have stuck with athletic shorts and a T-shirt.

He points to my outfit. "Just that Rowan is fortunate to be escorting such a beautiful girl this evening."

Rowan's lips tremble at the corners. "That's exactly what I told her, Coach."

"I don't think you've worn a skirt in years." Silently he racks his brain. "Maybe for high school graduation?"

I force out a laugh. "Oh, come on. That can't be true." Although now that I'm thinking about it, it probably is. "It was Sydney's idea," I grumble. "You can blame her for this."

Dad gives me a questioning look. "Why would I do that? I like it. You should wear them more often. Right, Row?"

"Yup," barely contained laughter simmers in his deep voice, "she looks great."

Unaware of the stress practically choking the life out of me, Dad waves a hand. "Let's get this meat on the grill so we can eat. I'm starving." With that, he heads out the slider door and onto the patio.

"You really need to chill out," Rowan whispers in my ear when we're alone.

"Yeah, that's not going to happen." Not until the air is cleared.

"If you're not ready, we don't have to do this tonight. There's no hurry."

As tempting as the offer is, I shake my head. Even though there's nothing in his expression or voice to give away his true feelings, I know he would be hurt if I chickened out and didn't fill my father in. I don't want Rowan to think I'm embarrassed to be with him. "I'm nervous," I admit. "I'm not sure how Dad will react. I've never dated one of his players before."

"In the end, everything will be fine." He shrugs as if unconcerned with how the evening will turn out. "And if it's not, then we'll deal with it. There's no reason to get worked up before we know how everything will play out. It's a waste of energy."

Under normal circumstances, I would wholeheartedly agree with the statement. But these aren't exactly normal circumstances, now are they?

I release another steady exhalation and try to settle my jangled nerves. When I don't budge from the entryway, Rowan's hand settles on my lower back before giving me a little nudge toward the kitchen. It feels very much like I'm walking to my death.

Thirty minutes later, the hamburgers and hot dogs are ready, and the three of us are sitting at the patio table outside. The oversized umbrella is up, shading us from the evening sun that peeks over the tree line. I grab a hamburger and load it with the works. Rowan and Dad strategize nonstop about the upcoming game. If Rowan weren't an all but surefire draft pick, I think Dad would love to bring him on as an assistant coach.

It's kind of funny. In the past, their banter and closeness annoyed me. Their relationship is easy. Maybe I was even a little jealous of it. Dad and Rowan can talk about football until the cows come home. Then they can talk about it some more.

Sure, I love the sport. I grew up with a football in my hands before it was swapped out for a soccer ball. That being said, there's only so much I can talk about it before my eyes glaze over.

"Is something wrong?" Dad cuts into my thoughts when he points to my untouched plate. "You've barely eaten a bite."

"Oh." I suck my lower lip between my teeth and shrug. It's on the tip of my tongue to blurt out the truth, but the words refuse to budge. "I guess I'm not very hungry."

With a frown, he studies me more closely. "Are you feeling okay? Burgers are one of your favorites."

I shake my head, feeling like the world's biggest chicken for wimping out. "I ate a big lunch."

"Huh." He takes a bite of his burger before chewing and swallowing it.

I pick up my water and guzzle down half the glass. My throat is parched. If I'm lucky, it'll wash away all of the anxiety eating me alive, and I'll find the nerve to tell him what's really going on.

"So," Dad says conversationally, "you've been here for more than an hour. When were you two planning on spilling the beans about your relationship?"

The water goes down the wrong pipe, and I sputter before spitting it all over my plate. Tears fill my eyes as I have a coughing fit. Dad reaches over and gives my back a few good whacks, which doesn't help alleviate the situation. A full sixty seconds tick by before I'm able to catch my breath. "What did you say?" I wheeze.

"You heard me." Dad sits back and folds his arms across his chest. He's wearing a black polo with a Wildcats emblem in the left upper corner. A matching black ball cap sits low over his eyes. "When were you gonna tell me that you two are seeing each other?"

"Ummm." My wide gaze skitters to Rowan before I clear my throat. "We were going to tell you tonight."

Dad's gaze bounces between the two of us. I have no idea what he's thinking. My father has spent years on the sidelines perfecting his poker face, and right now, it's all but killing me.

"Coach—"

Dad turns his attention to Rowan, and I brace myself for all hell to break loose. "You made a move on my daughter?"

Oh, shit.

The younger man inhales before forcing it out and straightening his shoulders. "I did, sir."

"Well, I didn't think that would ever happen."

Rowan's brows draw together as if he didn't hear him correctly. "I'm...sorry?"

A slow grin moves across my father's face. He flicks his gaze in my direction and shocks the hell out of me when he asks, "You've liked her for a while, haven't you?"

There is no hesitation from Rowan. "Since the very beginning."

"That's what I thought."

Even though my heart is galloping uncomfortably under my breast, a mixture of joy and relief bursts through me like a firework. It never occurs to me not to reach out and slip Rowan's fingers into mine. When I squeeze them, he glances over and flashes a smile. The tension that had settled in his shoulders evaporates.

"All I have to say is that you better treat my daughter better than some of the other knuckleheads she's been out with, or you'll answer to me." My father's tone might be mild, but there's an underlying threat buried beneath the surface.

Rowan's lips twitch as mine do the same. "You don't have anything to worry about in that regard."

"Yeah," Dad takes a pull from his bottle of beer, "I don't think so either, but I have to issue the warning nevertheless."

"Fair enough," Rowan says.

"How did you find out?" It's only been a few days since we went public, and we've tried to be so careful. I figured we had some time before we needed to tell him.

My father grins before sitting back and readjusting the ball cap on his head. "Haven't you learned over the years that not much gets past me?"

I roll my eyes to show him exactly what I think about that statement. Give me a break. I could have easily snuck around when I was a teenager, and I didn't. He's always been so preoccupied with football or at the field with the guys. Hell, Mom was gone for a couple of days before he finally noticed and asked where she was. And that was only because he ran out of clean clothes to wear. If he had more of a wardrobe, it might have taken longer.

"I'm serious." Now that my father knows and is apparently okay with our relationship, my appetite comes back full force, and I pick up a fry to nibble on. "How did you figure it out?"

A cagey look enters his eyes as a grin simmers around the corners of his lips. "Did you forget about the doorbell camera out front?"

My mouth drops open as my eyes widen.

Well, shit. Guess I did.

He nods, accurately gauging the dismay on my face. "I knew Rowan was here the entire weekend I was recruiting." He pauses before clearing his throat. "I assume, of course, you two slept in separate bedrooms?"

And just like that, awkwardness descends.

When neither of us jump in to tackle that particular question, Dad hastily throws up his hands. "You know what? Never mind. I don't want to know. *Like ever.*" He shoots to his feet and grabs our plates before hauling ass to the kitchen as if he can't get away from us fast enough.

Once he disappears through the sliding door, I glance at Rowan and shake my head. I'm pretty sure my face is moments away from going up in flames.

He knew Rowan spent the weekend...

Oh, the horror of it all.

Rowan rotates his hand until he can envelope my fingers before giving them a gentle squeeze. "Overall, the conversation went better than expected."

"You realize," I point out in case he missed it, "that my father thinks we're knocking boots."

His shoulders shake as he laughs. "Kind of ironic since we haven't, huh?"

"Yeah," I grumble, "ironic."

He shrugs. "If you'd like, I'd be more than happy to set him straight."

No, thank you.

I'm not sure which is worse—letting my dad think we've already done the deed or telling him the truth.

Can't say I ever thought *that* would be a decision that needed to be made.

Chapter Thirty

ROWAN

I push open the front door to the house I share off-campus with five players from the football team. As soon as I step inside, laughter and good-natured ribbing greet my ears. There are about a dozen or so people crammed into the living room. A few of the guys are playing Madden on the Xbox. Girls are draped over them, staking out their prospects for the evening. It's Monday night, and everyone wants to chill out, play some video games, and have a few beers. If the chicks in various states of undress are any indication, getting laid will probably be high on the agenda. For obvious reasons, that's never been my thing, but I'm certainly not going to hold it against my friends if that's what they choose to do.

To each their own.

There have been times when I've thought it might be nice to live by myself or with another person, but I've never been able to afford that kind of luxury. The more people there are to share rent with, the easier it is to make the money I earn over the summer stretch throughout the year. My athletic and academic scholarships cover tuition, room and board but not much else. So, I have to be careful. Once I make it to the NFL, life will be so much easier. Not only for me but my mom as well. I've worked damn hard to make sure those dreams become a reality. I have to make this season the best of my college career and see what happens in the spring.

"Hey, Michaels, grab a cold one and join us. It's been a while since I kicked your ass in Madden."

"Please, Kendricks. I don't think you've ever kicked my ass unless it was in your dreams. And I told you before, I don't swing that way. So keep me out of them."

When he snorts and gives me the finger, letting me know that I'm number one, I blow him a kiss.

"Yo, Michaels!"

My gaze slides to Asher Stevens. "Yeah?" He's a tight end—one of the best to come through Western's program in a good decade. There's no way he won't be a first-round draft pick. The funny thing is that he could be even better, but the guy parties like it's his job in life.

We finished practice a little less than an hour ago, and already he looks three sheets to the wind. Nothing unusual there. This is a guy who likes to burn the candle at both ends. I keep waiting for him to crash and burn but he continues to surprise me by breaking records on the field and staying academically compliant.

The girl straddling his lap is wearing a thong and nothing else.

Upon closer inspection, I realize she's not the only one who has already shed her clothing. Looks like shit is about to get wild around here, which only makes me wish for the umpteenth time that I had my own place. When I agreed to live with these guys, I'd figured most would be over all the drinking, partying, and fucking.

Turns out that's not the case.

Hell, some are more into it now than ever before. Kind of like it's their final hoorah. Every damn night. Even in the middle of our season. If I thought for one moment that it affected our level of play or the outcome of games, I'd put the kibosh on it. But we're doing pretty well. If that changes, I'll be the first one on their asses.

"A letter came for you in the mail." He points to the dilapidated table in the dining room. "It's over there."

A letter?

Weird. Since I change addresses almost every year, most of my mail goes to my mom's apartment.

"Thanks." I turn away from the orgy that's about to break loose and head into the dining room to sift through a pile of mostly advertisements and junk before finding a plain white envelope with my name and address scrawled across the front of it.

Even though there's no return address in the top left-hand corner, my muscles tense, recognizing the handwriting. Everything stills inside me as I stare at the correspondence in my hands. I don't realize they're shaking until my name blurs. It takes a concerted effort to still them. This is stupid. I need to open it and see what the motherfucker wants. Or...maybe I should toss it in the trash where it belongs, and pretend I never saw it.

Except that's not how I tackle problems. I meet them head-on. I learned at an early age that it's the only way to deal with shit. And make no mistake, that would be an accurate description of my father.

Always has been.

Always will be.

Thank fuck there's no return address. I glance uneasily at my teammates, who are laughing and screwing around in the living room. None of them are aware that my father is a current resident of the state penitentiary. I've done everything in my power to keep my past separate from the life I created for myself at Western University. And if I have my way, that's how it'll stay when I turn pro.

Fury surges through me as I stare blindly at the envelope.

Doesn't this guy realize the best thing he can do is to leave me the hell alone? Apparently not. Every once in a while, he'll send a letter asking me to visit. I can't resist thinking that he has a lot of fucking nerve. Not once in the ten years that he's been locked up have I ever bothered to respond. After reading it, I'll rip the letter to shreds and toss it in the garbage. It usually takes a couple of days for the unease that settles in the pit of my belly to dissipate as I do my best to forget the man who spawned me until another unmarked letter arrives in the mail months later.

Thankfully, they're far and few in between.

Instead of tossing it directly into the garbage, I carefully open the envelope like it's a bomb seconds away from detonation and unfold the paper from inside. My heart jackhammers a painful staccato as I glance at the sparse lines that are painstakingly written. My father has never been a verbose man. Honestly, I'm not sure if he graduated from high school. He's been a petty thief for most of his life before he got wrapped up in someone else's bigger operation.

And he paid the price for it.

The first line knocks the breath from my lungs. It's as if I've been kicked in the chest by a horse.

Wanted you to know that I've been released.

What the ever-loving fuck?

My head spins at this unexpected news. The prosecutor who put my father away said he would spend twenty years in prison. The guy murdered someone in cold blood. He belongs behind bars, locked up like the animal he is.

Where society is safe from him.

Where Mom is safe from him.

I'd like to see you.

Yeah, there's not a chance in hell of that happening.

Unwilling to read the rest, I crumple the letter in my fist until it's a tightly wadded up ball. I'm tempted to hurtle it across the room but fight back the impulse. That's the difference between me and my old man. I have control and exert it at all times. I never allow myself to be driven by impulse. If I do something rash, it's only because I've given it thought and decided it's worth the risk of consequences.

Like hitting Justin.

Totally worth it.

Don't regret it for a second.

And furthermore, I'd do it again.

I nearly jump out of my skin when delicate hands slide their way around my ribcage. For a heartbeat, I relax, assuming it's Demi. After that fucked up letter, she's exactly what I need. That girl is a balm for the soul. She's the only person capable of making me forget the bull-shit trying to press in at the edges.

Except...when the hands snaked around me come into view, the fingernails are painted bright pink. There is no way Demi would be caught dead wearing that color polish. Hell, I don't think I've ever seen her wear polish. Whoever this girl is, her nails are long and lethal like talons. Demi's are short and blunt. Kind of like mine. It's difficult to play sports with long-ass claws. Especially soccer.

Since I'm not sure who I'm dealing with, I carefully wrap my fingers around slender wrists and pry them from my ribcage before turning around. What I find is a toothy brunette smiling coyly at me. She's wearing a low-cut top that displays a ton of cleavage. Not wanting her to get the wrong impression, I take a hasty step in retreat. She's got a hungry look about her as if she'll devour me whole if I give her the green light to proceed. I'm half-afraid she'll do it regardless.

"Hi, Rowan." She flutters her fingers in a wave. "I was hoping to run into you."

Since I live here, the odds of that happening were stacked in her favor.

"Hey." My athletic bag is still slung across my shoulder. I slide it in front of me as a barrier. This girl is probably a foot shorter than I am and weighs half as much. It's not like I couldn't fight her off if I had to. But there's a determined look in her eyes as if she's a woman on a mission, and I've dealt with enough girls since stepping foot on campus to know which ones are more tenacious and have a harder time taking no for an answer.

I almost shake my head. That sounds crazy. Most guys would be more than happy to take this chick up on anything she's offering for the night.

Guess I'm not most guys.

She steps toward me, closing the small amount of distance I've managed to put between us. Her titties bounce as she moves. I have some serious doubts that she's wearing a bra.

Not that I'm looking.

Fine, so maybe I glanced. It's kind of hard not to.

With a seductive grin, her manicured fingers graze over her flat belly and ribcage before settling on her chest. One pink-tipped finger swirls around her nipple until it hardens. She reaches up with her other hand, plucking at both breasts until the tips are poking out of the front of her T-shirt like headlights.

My tongue darts out to moisten my lips. "Ummm..."

"Trust me, they're even more spectacular up close and personal."

I clear my throat. "I'm, ah, not interested. But thanks." I take another step away before the situation can escalate.

Her fingers go to the hem of her shirt. "Maybe you should see them for yourself."

"No," I shake my head, "that's not really—"

"Or maybe you could pretend to have a little bit of self-respect and take the hint. He's already told you that he's not interested."

Oh, fuck.

Well, this isn't good. Even though I'm relieved to see Demi, the last thing I want is for her to jump to the wrong conclusion. She plasters a smile on her face before turning to the busty brunette who has thankfully released the bottom of her shirt.

The other girl frowns before flicking a long sheath of hair over her shoulder. "Who are you?"

Demi's lips slide into a smile as she threads her arm through mine. "I'm Rowan's girlfriend."

The brunette's eyes widen. She blinks a few times as if she must have heard incorrectly before throwing a frown in my direction. "You have a girlfriend?"

"Yup." I grin, thrilled that Demi has admitted the truth. "I sure do." I smack a kiss on her cheek for good measure.

"You didn't mention it," she says with a pout.

"I'm sure he was," Demi's gaze drops to the other girl's breasts, "*distracted*."

The brunette smiles as if given a compliment. "Thank you!" She reaches up and brushes her fingers over her breasts until her nips are once again standing at attention. "They're amazing, aren't they?"

Demi's brow furrows as she openly stares at the other girl's boobs as if seriously considering the question. I'm going to be totally honest here...I'm not sure what's going on.

I'm a little uncomfortable.

And turned on.

This is so wrong.

"Yeah, they are," she finally admits.

The other girl drops her voice as she sidles closer to her. "Any chance you're interested in a threesome?"

"Sorry," Demi shakes her head, "I'm not into sharing."

"Yeah," she sighs, her gaze lingering on me as if undressing me with her eyes. "I can understand why you would feel that way. My name is Cassie." She winks. "If you change your mind, come find me. I'll totally make it worth your while." With that proposal thrown out there, she saunters off toward the living room.

It takes a moment to realize my eyebrows are somewhere in the vicinity of my hairline as I meet Demi's widened gaze.

"I don't even know what to say to that," she murmurs with a slight frown.

Her reaction makes my lips twitch. It takes a lot to knock Demi off-balance. "Sorry."

Genuine confusion laces her voice as she waves a hand toward the living room. "How did you ever hang on to your virginity?"

I shrug. "Guess the right girl never came along and propositioned me."

"Oh, really?" Now it's her turn to hike a brow. "I think we both know that's not true."

A chuckle escapes from my lips. Well, she's got me there. The girl has been coming at me hard for three weeks, and I've been fending off her advances at every turn. Kind of like a superhero. Apparently, remaining a virgin is my superpower. Just kidding. I've wanted her for years, and now that she's finally mine, it's important to take it slow.

When I don't respond, she points to my hand. "What's that?"

I glance at the crumpled paper and blink back to awareness as the past crashes down on me like a twenty-story building.

"Nothing. Just garbage." I clear my throat, wanting to steer the conversation in a different direction. "You ready to study?"

"Yup." We have a stats test tomorrow, and I need to go over the material one more time. I need to get that grade up, or the possibility of my ass getting benched is a very real one. I can't afford to let that happen. Not with the upcoming draft. Every time I step onto the field, all eyes are on me.

I grab her hand and tow her past the living room. Before we reach the first tread, a couple of guys call out greetings to her. Asher and

Brayden grin like Cheshire cats with bird feathers sticking out from between their teeth.

Honestly...they're like a bunch of fucking children.

When I glare, the smiles fall from their faces, and they look away. Once we reach the second floor, I shutter us in my room. The music and boisterous voices fade. Instead of mentioning the orgy that's about to go down, Demi glances around the undecorated space. There's a queen-sized bed that dominates the room, a tall dresser and a matching desk that I picked up at the Salvation Army last year when I moved off-campus. Both have seen better days, but they'll get me through the rest of this year, and that's what matters.

She glances at the mattress. "Well, I suppose this is one way to get you into bed."

"Maybe it would be better if we worked at the library. I'm not sure if you're going to be able to keep your hands to yourself."

A slow smile spreads across her face, and it hits me like a punch to the gut. "I guess that's a chance you're gonna have to take."

I suppose it is. I've been holding Demi off, but I don't have the strength to keep it up for much longer. It's not only her that I'm battling, but myself as well.

An hour later, we're settled in the middle of the bed with a statistics book splayed open in front of us. Demi pelts me nonstop with questions. The girl is relentless. It's only one of the things I like about her.

"Ahhh..." I rack my brain for an answer. When one doesn't immediately come to mind, I pull something from my ass and hope for the best. "I'll take simple conditional probabilities for five hundred dollars, Alex."

Demi narrows her eyes. "Wrong. It's the 'at least one rule'."

I drag a hand over my face. "My brain is fried. I can't do this anymore."

Her expression softens as she reaches out and strokes a hand over my cheek. "You're doing great. You'll pull off a B for sure."

"Um, hello? There's no *pulling off* involved here. You've crammed all this useless information into my head. It has nowhere else to go but onto that test."

She glances at the sports watch adorning her wrist. "We should study for at least another hour. It's always better to be overprepared."

I really hope she's joking. That sounds fairly hellish. There's only so much statistics I can take, and I've already reached my quota for the day. Probably the week. One look at her face tells me this girl is as serious as a heart attack.

A groan leaves my lips as I steeple my hands. "I'm begging you. No more. This is torture. Whatever you want to know, I'll tell you. Please...no more statistics."

She grows silent, almost contemplative, before offering an alternative. "Fine, how about we make this interesting?"

"Ha! Make stats interesting?" There's a beat of silence. "Surely you jest." I stretch out on the bed and fold my arms behind my head. "Let's hear it. What do you have in mind?"

My muscles tense when a sparkle enters her eyes.

"How about, for every answer you get right, I'll take off one item of clothing, and for every wrong one, you remove a piece. Whoever has the most at the end of ten questions wins."

A grin slides across my face. "This sounds like a win-win situation for me."

She arches a dark brow. "Guess we'll find out, won't we?"

"Yes, we definitely will." I wipe the smile from my face and attempt to look serious as I get my game on. "All right, fire away."

"How do you calculate the probability of combinations?"

I blow out a steady exhalation and search the dark recesses of my gray matter. After the last hour, it's a pile of slush. But still...we're talking about getting Demi naked here, so I need to dig deep and find my second wind. A full minute slides by as I carefully consider the merits of a few different answers before eventually discarding them.

"If you don't know—"

"Give me a moment," I grumble, unwilling to be rushed.

Damn, this is difficult.

Wait...I think I got it. "You need to consider the number of favorable outcomes over the number of total outcomes." Right? That's it...right? Or is it the other way around?

Shit. Now I'm not so sure.

"Yay!" A proud smile lights up Demi's face. "You got it!"

Damn right, I did. Was there ever any doubt?

Don't answer that.

I rub my hands together before pointing a finger at her. "Strip."

She reaches for the elastic band that holds her hair in a ponytail.

"Oh, hell, no! You owe me one article of clothing! And that, my friend, is technically not considered clothing. It's a thingy ma-bob."

"A thingy ma-bob?"

"Yup, it's a technical term."

"Hmmm. Is that what we agreed to?" She narrows her eyes and taps her index finger against her lips. "Funny...I don't remember that being specified in the rules."

I narrow my eyes right back at her. Two can play this game. "You gonna renege already? Is that really how we're going to start off?"

"Fine," she grumbles, fingers drifting to the hem of her T-shirt before lifting it slowly up her toned belly. It's enough to make my mouth go dry. The material rises until a hint of her black sports bra comes into view and then—

She drops the shirt back into place. When my questioning gaze flicks to hers, a grin flashes across her face as she lifts her hands, circling her nipples with her fingers until the little buds stand firmly at attention.

My eyes widen.

Holy fuck that is hot.

When she gives them a little pinch, my cock becomes unbearably hard, and I groan. "If stats doesn't kill me, you will."

A wicked smile curves her lips as her fingers fall to the hem of her shirt before yanking it off and dropping it onto the bed. "Ready for the next question?"

I couldn't be more ready.

The sexy little maneuver replays in my head as I stare at her tits. What Demi did was way more tantalizing than the girl downstairs. "Yes, I am." If I have my way, that sports bra will be the next to go.

I got this. I'm riding high off that first question.

"How do you calculate the probability of permutations?"

Well, hell. After a few silent moments, I rattle off an answer, already knowing I bombed it.

She makes a buzzer-sounding noise deep in her throat. "Wrong!"

"You don't need to sound so gleeful."

Demi grins, pointing at my chest. "I want the shirt."

With a shrug, I sit up. The girl wants me to shed my clothing?

I'm delighted to oblige.

I grab the back of my T-shirt before dragging it up my body and over my head. Then I toss it onto hers. Apparently, that's going to be the loser pile. Right now, we're evenly tied.

The way her gaze drifts over my body is almost like a physical caress. I've had girls eat me up with their eyes, but it's different with Demi. I flex my muscles, wanting to give her a little something to drool over. Then I lick my thumbs and forefingers before circling my nipples like she did. When I give them a good pinch, she bursts out laughing.

I can't help but grin. Is there anything better than sexy times mixed in with laughter?

Nope.

"All right, hit me with the next question."

She rattles off another one, and I snap out the answer without having to overthink it. Instead of shedding her bra, she takes off her athletic shorts. Damn, but Demi has an amazing body. She's lean and muscular, and that is such a turn-on.

We go through a couple more questions. I end up peeling off my shorts which leaves me in nothing more than my boxer briefs, and she pulls off her socks. Things are starting to get interesting around here. Although, let's hope I get the next one correct or I'll be studying statistics buck naked. Can't say I ever thought that would happen.

"What is a combination?"

Yes!

I know this!

I clear my throat as if what I have to say is of the utmost importance. "A combination is an arrangement of objects where order does not matter."

"You got it! Awesome job!"

Already salivating, I point to the bra. "Take it off."

Instead of following the command, she says, "Should we end this and call it a draw?"

"No way in hell. Take it off. Stop trying to cheat your way out of our agreement."

"Fine." With that, Demi reaches around her back and unsnaps the clasp. As soon as the stretchy material loosens, the straps slide down her shoulders, revealing a glimpse of tantalizing flesh. Without a self-conscious bone in her body, she shrugs out of the bra and tosses it onto the growing pile of clothing.

Demi sits back, allowing me to look my fill. She has no problem with her breasts being on display. Her confidence is so damn sexy. It's only one of the things that draw me to her like a moth to a flickering flame. It's been that way since I first laid eyes on her. It might have taken me time to capture her interest the same way she caught mine, but now that I have it, I won't be letting it go anytime soon.

"Should we finish this?" Her lips lift at the corners. We're both down to our underwear. "One more question will determine the victor."

"Oh, you bet your sweet ass we're finishing this."

"All right. Final question for the win..." My muscles coil tight as she pauses. "What is statistics the study and interpretation of?"

She's joking, right? That can't be the question. This has to be some kind of sly bit of trickery on her part. I narrow my eyes, but her expression remains inscrutable.

All right, I'm going for it.

"Data." I mumble out the answer. Surely, it can't be that straight-forward.

Her lips lift. "Ding, ding, ding...we have a winner."

No fricking way.

That was *way* too easy.

Without me asking, Demi slides her thumbs into the elastic band of her panties and slips them over narrow hips and muscular thighs before kicking them off. And then she's gloriously bare.

A wicked glint enters her eyes as she stretches out on the bed.

Hot damn.

My gaze drops to the part of her I've become obsessed with.

So fucking gorgeous.

"Be straight with me—did you throw the last question?"

Instead of answering, she spreads her thighs wide before trailing her fingers over the lips of her splayed pussy. "Now why would I do a thing like that?"

My mouth turns cottony as my eyes widen.

"What's wrong?" She smirks. "See something you like?"

Ummm...

"Yeah." Barely is the word able to escape.

"Then get over here and do something about it."

She doesn't need to tell me twice. I toss the statistics book off the bed. The heavy tomb lands on the carpeted floor with a loud thud. Then I'm crawling across the mattress and squeezing my shoulders between her thighs. With heavy-lidded eyes, I stare up at her before lowering my mouth. A whimper slides from her as I make contact with her delicate flesh.

The way she's stretched out on the bed with her elbows propping her up, head thrown back, and lips softly parted makes my cock throb with painful awareness. Demi is the sexiest girl I've ever laid eyes on.

I lick my way from the bottom of her pink slit to the very top. When I get to her clit, I circle it with my tongue before sucking the little bundle of nerves into my mouth. She whimpers, arching her back off the bed as if trying to get closer.

Who would have ever thought that studying statistics could be such a turn-on?

We might have to do this more often.

A lot more often.

When her body tightens, I realize she's moments away from orgasming, and it only drives me on. I want to give her more pleasure than she's ever experienced.

"Rowan," she whimpers.

"What, baby?" I whisper against damp flesh.

"I want you inside me."

"That's exactly where I am." To prove this is true, I spear my tongue inside her heat.

"No, I want your cock." She sucks in a shuddering breath. "I need you...*please.*"

This feels like a dream. Is Demi Richards really begging for my dick? I'm almost afraid that I'll wake up and none of this will be real. She'll still be keeping me at a firm distance, pretending I don't exist. Now that I've sampled her sweetness, there's no way I can go back to the way it's always been between us.

I lift my head and stare into her dazed eyes. So much need swirls around inside them. Damn if I don't want to give her everything she desires. "Are you sure?"

She nods.

I chew my lower lip and contemplate the situation at hand.

Here's my problem...

I'm pretty worked up, if you know what I mean. If I attempt to get inside her in this condition, I'll come within thirty seconds. Probably quicker than that. It was embarrassing enough to admit that I'm still a virgin at age twenty-one, to blow my load after a few strokes would be the ultimate humiliation.

Like...*change my name, forget about football, and transfer to another college* embarrassing.

"Rowan?"

I drag a hand through my hair and try to keep the tortured expression off my face. It's not like I planned for tonight to turn out like this. Hell, I thought we'd be knee deep in stats. And that's the least sexy thing in the world.

Or so I'd thought...

Had I suspected this was the direction the evening would swerve in, I would have rubbed one out...or maybe three in preparation.

Before I realize what's happening, Demi rolls up to a seated position. Her hands go to my cheeks, cradling them in her hands. My head is still between her spread thighs. "I want *this*, and I want *you.*"

"Yeah," I gulp, trying to figure out how to best verbalize my problem, "I feel the same way. It's just..." As my voice trails off, realization dawns in her eyes.

"Turn over."

When I don't immediately comply, she drops her hands from my face and pushes at my shoulders. I scramble up before rolling onto my back. As soon as I hit the mattress, she's crawling up my body and pressing her lips against mine. Oh-so-slowly she moves down my chest, peppering kisses and soft nips over hard muscle until she reaches the waistband of my boxers. She tugs the material down an inch before flicking her eyes at me and pressing a caress against the newly revealed flesh.

I clear my throat as my erection throbs painfully. "You realize that you're not helping matters, right?"

Her expression turns seductive as she torments me with her mouth until I'm shifting beneath her, trying to hold it together. I'm hard as steel. There's an excellent possibility I won't make it inside her before I come like a geyser.

You've heard of a two-pump chump?

I can only hope to make it twice.

This isn't good.

Actually, it's much *too* good, and that's the problem.

Once my dick springs free from the stretchy fabric, I grit my teeth. The way she stares with focused determination only makes matters worse. She swipes her tongue over the head of my cock before licking at the damned thing like it's a lollipop. Sure, I've fantasized about her doing this a million times but at the moment, it will be my undoing. I'm like some prepubescent teenager ready to come all over the place at the drop of a hat.

It's embarrassing as hell.

"If you keep that up much longer, I'm going to come," I ground out, voice scraped raw with need.

She lifts her head enough to smirk. "Yeah, that's kind of the point."

When Demi sucks the crown of my dick into her mouth with tight suction, I know it's game over. There's no holding back. I bury my fingers in her hair as she moves up and down my rigid length.

Goddamn that feels amazing...

I arch my hips and enjoy each wave of intense pleasure as it crashes over me, dragging me to the bottom of the ocean. I don't think anything has ever felt so damn good. It's only when I'm softening in her mouth that she releases me with an audible pop before crawling up my body and kissing my lips. When I open, her tongue slips inside to tangle with my own.

"Feel better?"

"Fuck, yeah," I practically slur.

Her lips tremble against mine. "Good. I aim to please."

Mission accomplished.

With one final kiss, she pulls away before sitting up and straddling me so that her pussy is spread wide against my abdominals. I thrust my hips until her naked body can slide against mine. My hands drift from her thighs, over gently flared hips, to her ribcage before wandering to her breasts and palming the soft weight. Her eyelids feather closed as she arches her back, pressing herself into my hands.

God, I love her tits. Anything more would be a complete waste.

"You're so fucking perfect," I murmur, captivated by the sight of her. She looks so wanton, sitting astride me naked, like the goddess she is. She has no idea how significant this moment is for me. I've waited so long to be with her. If I dwell on it, I'll freak myself out.

Even though I just came, my cock is already stiffening up. I groan as she flexes her hips, brushing against me. My dick slides through her silky folds until I'm once again clenching my teeth. Demi rearranges herself so that the head of my cock is poised at her entrance.

It takes every ounce of my willpower not to thrust deep inside her and bury myself to the hilt. "I need a condom."

"It's okay." She pauses, her movements stilling. "I'm on the pill and haven't had sex in six months."

My eyes nearly cross at the thought of being inside her tight heat without anything between us. "Are you sure?"

"Yeah." As if to prove the point, she lowers herself onto my erection.

Holy fuuuuck!

"God, that feels so good," she groans, her eyes closing as if to savor the feeling of us finally coming together.

"Yeah," I mutter, "praise the Lord."

Her lips twitch. "Let's not talk about God at a time like this."

"You're the one who brought religion into it," I point out.

"Rowan..." She opens her eyes only to narrow them before shooting me an exasperated look.

"Yup, got it." A hiss escapes from me as she slides down my length until fully seated.

My gaze shifts to where we are now connected in the most intimate way possible. I can't envision anything more erotic. Sure, I've seen porn. Who hasn't? And I've wacked off to the images, but nothing compares to the sight of Demi riding my dick.

My hands fall from her pebbled nipples to her hips before wrapping around them as if to anchor her to me. Maybe that's exactly what I'm trying to do. This is the best damn feeling in the world, and I want it to last forever.

Although, I think we all know that's not going to happen.

Unable to stand another moment of this stillness, I flex my hips, sliding from her tight heat before thrusting inside. As I do, a heavy wave of pleasure crashes over me. She tips her face toward the ceiling as a moan slides from her. Even though I came ten minutes ago, I won't last much longer. The pleasure rushing through every fiber of my being is much too intense. It's almost unbearable.

But...I can't get off again without her orgasming first.

Whatever I do, I need to keep it together. I lock my jaw and focus on the upcoming game and how challenging it will be. Mentally, I breakdown the film I've been watching and focus on weaknesses that can be exploited. I run through each play, thrusting my hips and driving inside her tight sheath.

As much as I try to distract myself, I can't help but think about how perfectly we fit together. As if she was made for me. Every time I surge forward, Demi meets my upstroke. We're in perfect rhythm, which makes holding onto the last shred of my control almost impossible.

The delicate sounds that escape from her will be my undoing. My willpower is being stripped away with each one. Up until this point, I've always taken pride in my self-discipline. I've pushed my body to the limits and denied myself temptation. As an athlete, that's the name of the game. You can never give in to the pain. You have to be constantly pushing past your limits. If this continues much longer, this one-hundred-and-twenty-pound girl will be the one who ultimately breaks me.

And that, I will not allow.

When I've run through every play in the book, my mind turns back to statistics. I mean, come on, how could that *not* turn me off?

Except...when I concentrate on the probability of independent events, I conjure up an image of Demi as she removes a piece of clothing and that only makes me harder. How messed up is that?

"I'm going to come," she whimpers, breaking into my thoughts.

Thank fuck!

No, seriously. I mean that with all sincerity. Thirty seconds more, and I would have embarrassed myself.

Instead of speeding up the way my body insists, I hold a steady pace. My balls tighten as her cries grow louder. There's a distinct possibility the tip of my cock is going to explode. What I've learned from this experience is that a blow job is good, but sex is fan-fucking-tastic.

Or maybe, more specifically, it's sex with Demi that's so amazing. I'm not sure, although I suspect it might be the latter.

When she cries out my name, her pussy spasms, strangling my cock, and I totally lose it, coming with a vengeance. It's like the floodgates have opened, and there's no holding back. Stars burst behind my eyelids, and there's an excellent possibility I blacked out for a moment. When I finally come to again, Demi is leaning over me with a smug grin wreathing her face. My fingers bite into her hips, wanting to keep her seated on my dick.

"So," she asks, satisfaction dripping from her voice, "what did you think?"

What did I think?

What did I think?

I think I could fuck this girl for the rest of my life.

Damn. That's a scary thought. And yet...not really. I'm not quite sure what to make of it, so I push it aside for the time being. Then I shutter my expression before shrugging. "It was good. Although, out of curiosity...is that all there is to it? Like, is there anything more?"

Every bit of arrogance filling her expression vanishes as her eyes widen. "*Is...there...anything...more?*" The question gets pushed out slowly as if it's foreign, and she's having a difficult time wrapping her lips around it.

It takes everything I have inside to keep a straight face. "Yeah, you know, like a trick at the end or something?"

A garbled sound gets emitted from deep within her throat. *"A trick?"*

"Yeah. That was a lot of grinding. I expected you to do a little bit more."

When her body stiffens and fire leaps into her dark eyes, I can't stop the laughter from shaking my shoulders as it echoes throughout my body.

"Wait a minute—you're fucking with me?" She sits up and smacks my chest.

I grab her hands before she can inflict any real damage. "Yeah, I'm joking around. You have to know that was amazing."

Her brows jerk together as she grumbles, "Damn right, it was."

I tug her closer before smacking a kiss against her lips. "Nothing I imagined could have prepared me for how spectacular that felt, and that has everything to do with you." I raise my hand to her cheek before stroking my thumb across her lower lip.

Her body softens, turning pliant. "Good."

Quite honestly, I don't know how it could have been any better.

With a sigh, she relaxes against my chest. Her steady inhalations fill the space between us. For the first time in my life, true contentment settles over me. It's as if the last puzzle piece has fallen into place. It's a strange feeling. One I could get used to, if I'm not careful.

Chapter Thirty-One

ROWAN

As I hustle my way across campus to meet Demi for lunch, my phone breaks into the whirl of my thoughts. In case you're wondering, those thoughts have everything to do with the dark-haired soccer player. I'm in so fucking deep with that girl I don't think I'll ever get out. At this point, I don't even want to.

We've been public with our relationship for more than a week, and the talk around campus has finally died down. People are getting used to seeing us together. I'd wondered if the guys on the team would give me a hard time, but other than a few harmless comments, no one has said boo. Now, does that necessarily mean shit isn't being said behind my back?

I'm sure it is. Those dudes gossip like a bunch of old ladies standing around in a church parking lot. At least they're smart enough to keep it out of earshot. They'd get their asses handed to them by yours truly if they didn't. Plus, most of these guys think of Demi as a little sister. They're protective of her and will shut down any bullshit they hear floating around campus.

So yeah, life is pretty damn good at the moment. I don't have any complaints.

I slip the phone from my pocket and stare at the screen.

Mom. Guilt slices through me. I've been so wrapped up in Demi that I haven't checked in to see how everything is going. Normally, we talk a couple of times a week. I should probably stop at home and see how she's doing. Maybe we can grab dinner.

I hit the green button and put the phone to my ear. "Hey, Mom. How's it going?"

There's a slight pause, and I frown, wondering if the connection is bad. Every once in a while, you'll hit a dead spot on campus.

"Hello, son."

Thrown off by the deep male voice that bursts over the line, my footsteps falter before stuttering to a halt.

What the fuck?

I shake my head, clinging to the irrational hope that my brain is playing a trick on me.

"Hello?" he says again before asking, "you there?"

Instead of answering, I rasp, "Why do you have Mom's phone?" A chill slithers down my spine before settling uncomfortably at the base. "Where the hell is she?" My voice rises as I turn panicky. "Put her on the line."

"Calm the fuck down, all right? Your ma is fine." He chuckles before taking his mouth away from the phone. "Say hi, babe. Your son is worried about you."

My muscles coil tight as I wait for the sound of my mother's voice. I swear to fucking God if he's done something to her, I'll be on the phone with his parole officer so fast, his damn head will spin.

"Hi, sweetie," comes Mom's soft voice from somewhere in the nearby vicinity.

Everything in me loosens. "Give her the phone," I snap, wanting to talk privately with her and get to the bottom of what's going on. Why would she be anywhere near him?

Disregarding the demand, he says mildly, "Good news. Your ma and I have decided to give it another whirl." My belly crashes to the bottom of my toes. "Aren't you excited?"

Is that a joke?

It's the worst possible news. After my father was sent away, it took months, if not years, to evict him from my mother's head. She had to practically be deprogrammed. And now he's back. The last thing she needs is him fucking up her life again.

Goddamn it!

"Now that I'm out, we can be one big happy family."

Like we were ever that. My father has proven time and time again that he doesn't give a rat's ass about us.

"I gotta go." I don't have time for this bullshit. I don't want him in my life, and I sure as shit don't want him anywhere near Mom. I'm not the same kid he left behind a decade ago who was easily intimidated. I'm a grown man. I wasn't able to protect my mother from him before, but I sure as shit will do it now.

"Don't you dare hang up!" His voice deepens, cracking like thunder over the line. Some of his nice guy façade falls away like I suspected it would. It only reconfirms my suspicions that he's trying to run a game on me.

"Why? There's nothing for us to talk about."

"We have ten years to catch up on."

"No, *Scott*, we don't."

"You always were a mouthy little bastard, weren't you?" he chuckles, although it sounds like he's holding on to his patience by a thread. I can almost imagine him tightening his hand before flexing it and cracking the knuckles. That sound always meant trouble.

"There's no reason we can't sit down and hash out our shit. You're my son, we're family. I want to see you. It's like I've always told ya— you can pick your friends, and you can pick your nose, but you can't pick your family."

I almost snort.

Is that rationale really supposed to win me over?

"Wish I could." *Not.* "But I've got a lot going on."

As I'm about to stab the disconnect button, he says, "Well, I got your address. Maybe a surprise reunion will be more fun."

That not so subtle threat has my blood running cold. I don't want him anywhere near campus.

Fuck.

Fuck.

Fuck.

I plow my fingers through my hair and quickly decide what to do. There's always the possibility that it's an empty threat. Although...do I really want to take that chance? With my luck, the bastard will show up on my doorstep.

"When do you want to meet?" I gnash my teeth together so hard they feel as if they're in imminent danger of shattering.

"Now works for me."

No way in hell.

"Sorry, I can't—"

"Look, I'll make it easy on you. There's a truck stop on the outskirts of town, right off highway eighteen and county ten. I'll be there in an hour."

Before I can open my mouth, the line goes dead. A cold sweat pops out across my brow at the thought of coming face-to-face with my father after all these years. As much as I don't want to cancel my plans with Demi, there isn't a choice in the matter. The thought of lying to her leaves a bad taste in my mouth, but there's no way in hell I can tell her the truth.

Hey, remember when you asked about my parents? Well, guess what? Pops was released early from prison, where he was serving a twenty-year sentence. That's right, I've got the blood of a murderer running through my veins.

Can you imagine the look of horror and disgust that would come over her face?

I shake my head as if the movement alone will banish the ugly thought from my brain.

It doesn't work.

I fire off a quick text explaining that something came up, and I can't meet her for lunch after all. It's not exactly a lie. It's just not the unvarnished truth. Within moments, a sad face emoji pops up on my screen followed by a bunch of hearts and kisses. It's almost enough to bring a smile to my face.

I slide my phone into my back pocket and take off for home. An hour later, I'm parked in the gravel lot outside a seedy truck stop along the highway. There's a peeling sign that advertises massages.

Yeah right...

My guess is that they're offering a lot more than that—more like a rub and a tug. It shouldn't come as any surprise that my father is familiar with a place like this. I still can't believe he's a free man. In all honesty, after he was incarcerated, I never imagined seeing him again. I had high hopes of him rotting in prison. Do you have any idea how comforting that thought was? And now it's all been blown to shit. The same sick feeling I used to get when I was a kid settles in the pit of my belly. I hate that he's still able to tie me up into knots.

My muscles stiffen as I sit in my truck and watch mostly men come and go from the establishment. There's a ball cap pulled low over my eyes. So far, I haven't caught sight of my father. Is it too much to ask that he doesn't show up? Although, deep down, I know he will. The only reason he contacted me is because he wants something. And contrary to the garbage he spewed earlier, it's not for us to be a happy family. We were a lot of things, but that was never one of them.

I glance impatiently at my sports watch, only wanting to get this over with. Once I shut him down, I won't have to think about him again. Maybe this is for the best. I can get him out of my life once and for all.

Another ten minutes tick by without any sign of Scott. As I consider starting up the engine and getting the hell out of here, a beat-up Chevy pulls into the lot. I squint, trying to get a good look at the driver. Even though I can't see the guy's profile clearly, the fine hair at the back of my neck stands at attention. It's like déjà vu. That's exactly what would happen when I was a kid, and he'd come home drunk, spoiling for a fight. It pisses me off that after a decade, I still have a sixth sense where he's concerned. My gaze stays pinned to the driver's side door.

The man who unfolds himself from inside the vehicle only vaguely resembles the one who was hauled away by the police in cuffs a decade ago. His blond hair is cropped short. Almost as if he walked into a barbershop and told them to buzz it with a number one. And he's more jacked than I remember. My gaze drops to his belly. No longer is there a beer gut hanging over his belt. The sleeves of his black T-shirt are wrapped tightly around bulging biceps. Looks like someone made good use of the prison workout room. That was probably more of a survival tactic than anything else. I study his face carefully and notice the roadmap of new lines.

The years have not been kind to my father.

It's almost like he can sense my scrutiny. He squints, glancing around the half-filled parking lot before taking a drag from his cigarette. The cherry at the end glows bright red as he inhales. My immediate response is to fold in on myself as his gaze coasts over my truck. The moment I realize what I'm doing, I straighten my shoulders.

Fuck that. No matter what he thinks, I'm not the same timid kid he left behind.

As soon as he's done with the smoke, he flicks it onto the gravel and saunters toward the diner. A chime over the door rings out faintly as he steps over the threshold. I force out the lungful of air that is lodged in my throat.

My fight or flight instincts kick in, screaming at me to start up the truck and get the hell out of here while the getting is still good. It only proves you can never escape from your past. And rewiring your brain—even after a decade—is more difficult than you'd think.

As tempting as it is to cut and run, I know there's no point. He'll make damn good on his threat to come looking for me, and I don't want him anywhere near Western University.

Or Demi.

My mouth dries.

Especially Demi.

It takes another ten minutes before I work up the courage to leave the safety of my vehicle. As I stalk toward the rundown restaurant and whatever-the-hell-goes-on-here, it's like I'm walking toward certain death. I pull open the door and step inside. Maybe I'm a mess of nerves, but I'll be damned if I show him anything but strength. My gaze scans the faded red vinyl booths that have seen better days—more like better decades—until it lands on a man buried in the far corner. A waitress who looks as worn as her surroundings sets a cup of coffee in front of him. I blow out a steady puff and force myself to eat up the distance that separates us. I'm halfway across the room when he senses my presence and glances up, his light blue eyes landing on me.

They flare slightly with surprise before the emotion is quickly masked. The corners of his lips twitch with a forced smile as he rises to his feet. "It's good to see you, son."

The endearment rings false and grates against my nerves.

"Don't call me that," I snap, unable to rein in my irritation.

There is no love lost between us. When I was a kid, he couldn't be bothered to treat me with an ounce of kindness. I was nothing more than a nuisance. His lips would twist with disgust, and he'd snap at me to stop hiding behind my mother's skirt and act like a man, not a little pussy. That's probably the best memory I have of him. Actually, watching him get hauled away by the police is my fondest recollection.

It's only when I'm standing a few feet away that I realize he has to tilt his chin to hold my steady gaze. As a child, my father loomed over me, always seeming larger than life. A powerhouse of physical force and brute strength he used to strongarm Mom into giving him what he wanted.

That's not the case anymore.

I straighten to my full height and lower my shoulders, hoping to intimidate him the same way he used to do to us. Instead, he does the unexpected and opens his arms as if this is a happy reunion, and I wasn't threatened into making an appearance. I recoil at the thought of touching him and drop into the booth instead.

He stands there for a moment. Annoyance flickers in his eyes before he slides in across from me. "What? No hug for the old man?"

I sit back and fold my arms across my chest. "My guess is that you didn't come here for hugs."

His lips twist. The slight semblance of a smile doesn't reach the coolness of his eyes. Instead of answering, he says, "Aw, come on. It doesn't have to be like this. We're family." There's a pause as if he's assessing the effect of his words. "Tell me what you've been up to."

I lived with him until I was eleven years old, and not once could the guy be bothered to ask how my day at school went. If there wasn't a way for me to be useful, it was like I didn't exist. And now he wants to be filled in with all the details?

I don't think so. He can get bent for all I care.

"Can we drop the façade?" Rather pointedly, I glance at my watch. "I don't have a lot of time."

The look in his eyes sharpens, turning just this side of feral. I tense, immediately recognizing the reaction. It brings me straight back to my childhood and makes me send up a little prayer of gratitude he was sent away before he could inflict any real damage. Who would I be if he hadn't pulled the trigger? Would he have sucked me into his orbit? Gotten me involved with his petty con games? There are nights when I lay awake and try to imagine an alternate future. Thank fuck that was never my reality. If it had been, it's doubtful I'd be where I am today.

The waitress stops by our table. On closer inspection, I realize she's not as old as I pegged her to be from a distance. It's like this place has sucked the youth right out of her.

"What can I get for you, hun?"

I hold up a hand. "Nothing. I won't be staying long."

She raises a brow in surprise before her gaze slides to my father. "Need a refill, sugar?" When her lips pull back, I notice that she's missing a tooth.

My father shakes his head and flashes her a tobacco-stained smile. "Nah, I'm good."

"Just holler if you need anything," she calls over her shoulder, already moving on to another table.

"What did you want to talk about?" I'm done beating around the bush. "I already told you that I didn't have a lot of time."

"And yet, here you are." A glint of satisfaction enters his eyes. It's as if he's playing a game of cat and mouse. Little does he know I'll never be the mouse again. "I've been away for ten long years. Is it so much to ask that we spend a little time together? I'll be honest, kid, it hurts my feelings that you won't even call me dad like the good old days."

It takes everything I have not to roll my eyes.

Give me a damn break.

"How about you get to the point, *Dad*," I grit between clenched teeth. Acknowledging the piece of shit sitting across from me as anything more than a sperm donor feels like a slap in the face to any man who took the role seriously and helped shape their children into productive human beings.

You know who had that kind of impact on me?

Coach. Without him, I don't know who I would be or what I would be doing. He gave me hope and showed me that life could be different. There's no way I'll ever be able to repay him for giving me a future to believe in.

"See?" If not for the hardening of his eyes, I'd think the sarcasm had gone completely over his head. "Was that so hard?"

Yeah, it was. The man has no idea how sick inside it makes me to know that I'm a biological product of him.

He doesn't bother to wait for a response. "Your mother tells me football is going well, and you'll get drafted this spring."

My belly heaves, twisting painfully. Now it all makes sense. He heard I should be coming into money and wants his slice of the pie, whether he deserves it or not. If there's a potential payday without having to lift a finger, my father will sniff it out. It might be his only true talent.

I jerk my shoulders, wanting to downplay my prospects. Not that it'll do me any good. He's like a bloodhound who has picked up the scent. "Don't know," I mutter, wanting to shut down this line of questioning, "nothing is for certain."

His lips lift into a yellowed smile as if he knows exactly what I'm up to and isn't fooled by my modesty. "Ever since I got home, that's all your ma squawks about. How many teams are looking at you and the kind of money you'll be raking in by next year." He licks his lips as if he can already taste it.

Fuck.

Why hadn't I kept my big trap shut?

I'll tell you why—I'd wanted my mother to be proud of me. She's worked so damn hard to put food on the table, keep a roof over our heads, and pay for football. For the first time in her life, I'd wanted her to know someone would be taking care of her. She could finally stop stressing over the bills. Once I signed that contract, everything would get easier for the both of us. She wouldn't have to work another day. I'd buy the damn restaurant where she's been waitressing if that's what she wanted.

I press my lips together and shift uncomfortably before glancing out the window at my truck in the gravel parking lot. I want to wrap up this little reunion and take off.

He tilts his head and digs for info. "You got an agent?"

"Yup," I say in a clipped tone, offering up nothing further. Where the hell is he going with this?

It doesn't take long to figure out.

"Cause that's something I could do for you." When I stare blankly, he shifts on the bench and continues impatiently. "Negotiate your deal."

My eyes widen, and a gurgle of laughter rises in my throat before I choke it down. He's not joking. The man is as serious as a ninety-nine percent blockage of the arteries.

An image of Greg Abbot, my sports agent, pops into my head. I've never seen him dressed in anything less formal than a pricey suit with a flashy tie. There's never one damn hair out of place. It's pomaded into submission. When he smiles, the whiteness of his teeth almost blinds me. He reminds me of a glossy cardboard cutout.

He's not the type of guy I'd want to hang out with on a Saturday night or grab a beer with while watching a game, but he's the best in the business and has promised to get me a six-figure signing bonus. I have zero doubts that he'll deliver. He's one tenacious motherfucker who knows the ins and outs of the sports world. I'm damn lucky Coach has a relationship with him. That's the only reason a nobody like me ended up with such a well-known agent.

I blink reluctantly back to the conversation. Dollar signs are practically dancing in my father's beady eyes.

He leans toward me, closing as much distance as the Formica table that separates us will allow. "Now that I'm back, I can manage your career. It'll work out perfectly. I'll have a job, and my probation officer will get off my ass."

The more he talks, the faster my heart races until it feels like it will jackhammer right out of my chest. I shake my head, wanting to stop this one-sided discussion in its tracks. "Sorry, I have an agent."

Like I'd let him anywhere near my career?

Is he fucking crazy?

"Fire him." He raps his knuckles on the table as if the decision has already been made. "Let's keep this in the family. There's no reason to give your money away to strangers."

No, he would much prefer I give it all to him. There's not a snowballs chance in hell of that coming to fruition.

"I've already signed a contract. I'm locked in tight." I slide to the edge of the booth, ready to bolt. "So, if that's all you wanted to talk about, I've got to get moving."

Some of his nice guy veneer crumbles as he scowls, stabbing a finger at me. "Sit your ass down. I'm not finished yet."

I glare before begrudgingly dropping back to the seat.

It takes a moment for him to regain his composure. He picks up his mug and takes a sip before grumbling, "Stone cold."

With a wave of his hand, he flags down our waitress and asks for a second cup. This takes a good five minutes. I drum my fingers impatiently on the chipped table as I simmer. What he's doing right now is deliberate. He's purposefully trying to rile me up. All I want is for him to get to the fucking point so I can shoot him down.

Once he has a fresh cup of coffee, he points to me and says in an overly loud voice, "This here is my son, Rowan Michaels. Maybe you recognize him? He plays football for the Western Wildcats."

The waitress narrows eyes that have been made up with an overly heavy hand, inspecting me carefully. "I thought I recognized you." She points to a decrepit TV mounted on the wall. "Hal has the game on every Saturday afternoon."

"Take off your hat, son," Dad says mildly, "let the woman get a good look at you."

I grit my teeth, torn between refusing the directive and not wanting to appear like a total dick in front of this stranger. Manners win out as I drag the ball cap off my head before combing my fingers through my unruly hair. I give her a tight smile and hope I don't come across half as pissed off as I feel.

She whistles. "You sure are a handsome one." Her gaze slides approvingly to my father before she winks at him. "Just like your daddy."

It takes everything I have inside not to throw up in my mouth.

"Yup." The man across from me grins like he's the reason for my success. "You mark my words," he jabs a finger at her, "he's gonna make millions next year."

"Gracious." Her hand flies to her narrow chest as if she had no idea something like that was even possible.

He puffs up, clearly pleased by her reaction. "His mama and I couldn't be any more proud."

"Well, then, I should get your autograph." She shifts, searching her pockets for a pen before grabbing it from where it's tucked in her hair. "Once you turn pro, we can hang it on our wall of fame."

Wall of fame?

I don't even want to know.

"We should probably charge you for it," my father chuckles, sounding lofty. When her wide gaze cuts to him in question, he waves a hand and sits back like he's the Grand Poobah or something like that. "But we'll let it slide this once."

Embarrassment stings my cheeks. If only it were possible to sink into the floorboards and escape from this nightmare.

With that declaration, the waitress shoves a small pad of paper in front of me. I scribble out my name, hoping it's somewhat illegible. Like I want anyone to know I ever stepped foot in this dump that masquerades as a no-tell motel?

It's a relief when another customer flags down the waitress, and she reluctantly takes off in his direction.

"Well," Dad leans against the booth before settling one arm along the torn-up top, "I think it's safe to say you made her day."

Fucker.

I drag a hand over my face and decide to pull the plug rather than allow this to continue a moment longer. "How much do you want?"

He takes a sip of his fresh coffee. It's still steaming. "That's much better." Instead of answering, he inspects the dirt caked under his fingernails. "How much can you spare?"

"Not much," I grunt out bitterly. "Football is my job during the year so I'm not able to work. I live off savings from the summer."

"What? They don't pay you to play ball?" His brows snap together as if he's personally offended on my behalf. "You're practically a professional."

"That's not how college athletics work. I have a scholarship that pays for my tuition."

He shakes his head as if I was stupid enough to get screwed over. I'll tell you who I got fucked over by...

"See? If I'd been around, I would have negotiated better terms for you. Get you paid under the table or something."

Jesus Christ.

"That's illegal. There are strict NCAA rules surrounding that kind of thing."

He waves a hand. "They're all corrupt—"

"How much, Dad?" I pinch the bridge of my nose. There is so much pressure building in my head. Any moment it's going to explode, and then none of this will matter because I'll be dead. "How much do you need?" *How much will it take to make you go away and never come back? Drop a number.*

"A grand."

Well, fuck.

Does he really think I have that kind of money laying around?

I earn a couple thousand during the summer working for a friend's landscaping company. I give Mom some and sock the rest away to carefully dole out through the year. A number of my teammates have beaucoup bucks. Money isn't a concern for them. They're able to go on epic spring break trips to the Bahamas, Mexico, and Costa Rica.

But I can't afford that. If I'm lucky and the weather is nice in March, I can work for the week.

"I need a little something to tide me over until I can find a gig that pays well." When I fail to react, he adds, "I'll pay you back as soon as I can. Although, after this year, you won't need me to. You'll be rolling around in the Benjamins."

"If I give you this money," I pause, carefully contemplating my response, "you need to consider it a parting gift. I don't want to see you again." Surprise flares in his eyes before they narrow. "And I want you to leave Mom alone. She doesn't need you messing up her life again."

"Excuse me? Who the hell do you think you're talking to? Maybe you've forgotten that I'm your pops." He stabs a finger at me as fury flashes across his face. "Don't think you're too old for me to beat some sense into. I should have known that your mother would fuck this up. She put ideas in your head." The smile he gives me is bone-chilling. "I see the way you look at me. Like you're so much better." An ugly glint enters his eyes. "But you know what? We're the same, son."

If I actually thought that was true, I'd shoot myself.

I rise from the booth before glaring down at him. As I do, I feel nothing but anger and resentment. The first, because he's no longer locked up, and the second, because he'll never be anything more than a leech trying to suck me dry. "We are *nothing* alike." Unable to stomach the sight of him, I walk away.

"What about the money?" he snaps from the booth.

I stop but don't turn. "You'll have it by the end of the week."

It takes thirty steps to reach the exit before I'm shoving through the door and into the fresh autumn air. I inhale a breath and hold it captive in my lungs before slowly exhaling. Nausea swirls in the pit of my gut before searching for a way out. Just as I make it to the truck, I puke near the driver's side door, narrowly missing my shoes. Everything I wolfed down this morning makes an encore appearance. As soon as the contents of my belly are emptied, I swipe the back of my hand across my mouth. Only now do I realize it's shaking.

My entire body is shaking.

I grab the keys from my front pocket and click the locks before slumping onto the seat and starting up the engine. Barely do I glance around before peeling out of the parking lot and hightailing it back to Western.

Chapter Thirty-Two

DEMI

I snuggle against Rowan's chest on the couch in my apartment. His arm is around me, and we're chilling out, watching *Mike and Dave Need Wedding Dates.* Zac Efron does something, and a chuckle bursts from my lips. This movie is stupid funny. I've probably seen it a dozen times, and it never gets old. When I realize that I'm the only one laughing, I glance at him to see what's going on. It becomes obvious that Rowan may be physically with me, but his mind is somewhere else. A distant look fills his eyes.

It's one I've never seen before.

Instantly forgetting the movie, I reach up and stroke my fingers across his cheek to capture his attention. "Hey, are you all right?"

The strange expression dissolves as the corners of his lips hitch. "Yeah, I'm fine. Sorry, guess I zoned out for a minute."

"You want to turn off the movie?" I sit up and hunt around for the remote. "We don't have to watch it."

He shakes his head. "Nah. It's all good."

Even though he's denying there's a problem, I get the feeling he's not being truthful with me, and I hate it. Hate that he might—for some reason—be lying. Rowan has never been anything but honest. The realization doesn't sit well with me.

Mike and Dave continue with their slapstick comedy, but I can't get back into it. And I find myself unable to brush aside the suspicions that gnaw at me. "Are you worried about the game tomorrow?"

He jerks his shoulders and shifts on the couch. There's a slight tightening to his jaw. "Not really. Their defense is crap, so we'll turn that to our advantage."

Okay...then what's the problem?

It can't be stats. Rowan aced the last exam. Who would have thought a simple game of strip statistics could make such a huge impact?

It goes to show that with the proper motivation, anything is possible.

After five minutes of silence, I grab the remote and click off the television.

Rowan shoots me a questioning look as his brows draw together. "I thought you wanted to finish the movie?"

"I'm not into it." Anymore. "We can watch it another time."

"All right." Interest ignites in his eyes. "Got something else in mind?"

A smile curves my lips as I twist in his arms before crawling onto his lap. "Hopefully it's something that'll hold your interest more than the movie." I run my fingers through his hair before pressing my lips against his. "What do you think?"

"Umm, yeah." His voice deepens. "I can say with a hundred percent assuredness that this will do the trick."

"Good." I run my tongue across his top lip before giving the same attention to the lower one. Rowan has an amazing mouth. Soft and plump. Perfectly kissable.

Why did it take so long to acknowledge my attraction to him?

Now that I've given in to the need coursing through me, there's no going back.

He groans as I keep up the sweet torture. Whatever is going on in his mind, I want to banish it. His cock stiffens beneath his athletic shorts as I grind against him.

"You're killing me, Demi."

The funny thing is that I'm not just torturing him, I'm doing the same damn thing to myself. I've never felt this way before. Sure, I've always enjoyed sex. Most of the time it felt good. A couple of the guys I've been with made sure to prime the pump before diving straight in. But those encounters were always hit or miss. It hasn't been that way with Rowan. He always takes his time to make sure I'm practically begging for it when he slides inside me.

Sex has dominated my thoughts more in the last month than ever before. That has everything to do with Rowan and how he makes me feel. Not only physically, but emotionally. This relationship is unlike anything I've ever experienced. It's on a whole different level. A deeper one. We have so much more in common than I allowed myself to believe.

And I'm not going to lie—his smoking hot body doesn't hurt either. I'm obsessed with running my hands over all those perfectly sculpted muscles. He's turned me into a complete hornball. It's almost embarrassing.

My fingers itch to touch him. Giving in to the need, I grab the hem of his shirt before dragging it over his torso and tossing it to the floor.

"You have an amazing chest," I whisper, fingertips gliding over sinewy muscle.

He tugs at my shirt, quickly divesting me of it. "Trust me, I'm a real fan of yours, too."

My lips lift as he cups my bare breasts. I arch into his palms, loving the feel of him holding me. His touch is always reverent.

"Is Sydney going to be home anytime soon?"

"Nope. She and Ethan were planning to hit a party and then spend the night at his place." I grin. "Which means we have the apartment all to ourselves."

A matching smile lights up his face. "Guess I won't have to muffle your screams of pleasure."

"Don't get cocky." I roll my eyes as a punch of heat slams into my cheeks. "It was one time, all right?"

"Please, woman," he grumbles, "it's a point of pride. Just let me have it."

I chuckle and press my lips against his. "Fine. You're a stud."

His eyes narrow. "Why do I get the feeling you're placating me?"

"What? *Me?* No way." The moment my fingers settle on his thick length, he thrusts against them. I'm about to pull the material down when the apartment door crashes open, and loud voices fill the quiet space.

"If that's the kind of girl you want, then you can have her! We're through!" There's a pause before Sydney snaps, *"And this time, I mean it!"*

I yelp, my fingers tightening around Rowan's dick.

He grunts with a wince. "Damn girl, I'd like to use that appendage in the future."

"Sorry!" I release him, hands flying to my naked breasts as the apartment is flooded with light.

Sydney stalks into the tiny living room, grinding to a halt when she spots us on the couch. Her eyes widen in surprise. Ethan slams into her back, and she pitches forward a couple of steps.

"Why did you—"

His voice falls off as he takes in the sight before him. The tension filling his face vanishes only to be replaced by one of amusement. "Oh." A chuckle escapes. "Sorry, man, looks like we've interrupted your Friday night."

Rowan drags a hand through his hair. "It's not a problem."

Really?

I'm perched on his lap.

Topless.

This definitely seems like a problem...an embarrassing one.

Sydney spins around to face her boyfriend. Or maybe ex-boyfriend. It changes on the daily and is difficult to keep track of.

"You should go. Not only have you ruined my night," she thrusts a hand in our direction, "but you've ruined theirs as well!"

Ethan's lips sink into a frown as the humor from moments ago evaporates from his eyes. He folds his arms across his chest. "I'm not going anywhere until we hash this out. As usual, you're overreacting."

Her brows skyrocket into her hairline.

I almost shake my head. That's the wrong thing to say to a girl who is already pissed off.

"As usual?" Her voice rises a couple hundred decibels until it could shatter glass. "What does that mean?"

You can see the exact moment Ethan realizes the error of his ways as he drags a hand over his face. "That's not what I meant," he mumbles.

"All right." She plants her fists on her hips. Ethan should quit while he's already behind. If he continues, this won't end well for him. "What exactly *did* you mean then?"

He presses his lips together before throwing a pleading look in our direction as if it's possible for us to save him from himself.

Sorry buddy, you're on your own with this one.

"We need to get out of here," Rowan mutters, "before it turns ugly."

I glance at my naked breasts which are still shielded by my arms. "Any ideas as to how we accomplish that?"

"Yup."

Before I can ask any further questions, Rowan wraps his arms around me and rises swiftly to his feet. I bury my face against the hollow of his neck and hang on for dear life.

"We're, ah, gonna give you guys some privacy to talk," he says by way of explanation for our hasty retreat.

Let's hope it's more talking and less yelling. Although I wouldn't lay money on it.

Neither respond as Rowan moves swiftly toward my bedroom, firmly shutting the door behind him. Once he settles on my bed, I lift my face to meet his gaze. A smile curves his lips, and I find my mouth bowing up at the corners. A chuckle slips free before his shoulders quake, and then we're both dying of laughter.

"So," he says, "you still interested in continuing this or..."

"Or," I quickly reply. "*Definitely or.*"

"My thoughts exactly."

Chapter Thirty-Three

DEMI

Students scatter like rats fleeing a sinking ship as Professor Peters releases us for the day with a reminder that there will be a not-so-pop quiz on Friday.

Rowan groans, joining the chorus of other less than thrilled students. I shoot him a smile before elbowing him in the side. "Oh, come on, you did awesome on the last one. Pretty soon, you won't need my help."

"Maybe I should consider tanking this quiz on purpose so I can keep getting your special brand of assistance." Humor ignites in his voice.

"Don't you dare!" I roll my eyes as a grin simmers at the corners of my lips. Ever since Rowan and I got together, I've been over-the-top, ridiculously happy. It's like I'm living in my own real-life version of a Disney movie. It wouldn't surprise me in the least if I woke up to woodland creatures singing on my windowsill. Not even Annica's snarky comments are enough to bring me down. Her antics are like that of a pesky fruit fly. Easily ignored.

Once our bags are packed up, we head into the crowded corridor. Rowan snags my fingers as we make our way out of the building. People call out his name, greeting him as if he's a celebrity. I never noticed all the attention he garners. I was too busy trying to avoid him. A lot of guys in his position would soak it up as if it were their due and bask in the adoration, but he doesn't seem to give a damn about the notoriety. He simply goes about his business as if it's normal. The way he handles himself only makes me fall harder for him. He's nothing like what I assumed. Or maybe what I talked myself into believing.

Thank goodness he never gave up on me. I would have missed out on getting to know a great guy as well as a meaningful relationship.

Rowan holds open the door as we step into the bright autumn sunshine. There's a hint of crispness to the air as the breeze wafts over us. As much as I love summer, sweater weather is my favorite time of year.

"Want to grab a coffee before your next class?"

See how well he knows me?

I shoot him a grateful look. "You read my mind. I'm dying for a Frappuccino." My next class is even more boring than stats. Imagine *that* if you can. I'm going to need all the caffeinated help I can get to make it through the morning.

We're not more than a few steps down the cement walkway when Rowan's name is shouted. I glance around, not immediately spotting the individual. Rowan's fingers stiffen as he picks up his pace. He must not realize someone is trying to grab his attention. If he did, he'd stop. He's always so gracious when fans want to talk about football or snap a selfie with him.

I shrug it off as we make our way along the path.

"Hey, Rowan Michaels!"

This time, the name booms over the crowd. Several people crane their necks, glancing at us before searching the surrounding vicinity. When Rowan's fingers bite into mine, I wince, flicking my gaze to him. I'm surprised to find that his expression is pinched. Even under the bright sun filtering down, his skin tone has turned ashen. He looks moments away from being sick.

"Rowan," I murmur, "you're hurting me."

"Sorry." He immediately releases my fingers as we grind to a halt.

I peer around, trying to find the person shouting his name. After a moment of combing the throng, my gaze lands on a man pushing his way through student traffic in an attempt to reach us. I'm not sure who I was expecting, but it wasn't an older dude who looks to be in his late forties or maybe early fifties. It's difficult to tell with the ball cap pulled low over his eyes. From what I can see, his face is creased with lines. He doesn't strike me as someone who works for the university. His appearance is a little too...*rough*.

Unease slithers down my spine as my gaze stays pinned to the guy walking toward us. For reasons I don't understand, I'm afraid to take my eyes off him. As if he's a predator I need to be cautious of, which is strange; we're in the middle of campus, there are swarms of students, and it's broad daylight. Nothing is going to happen. But still...there's this little buzz at the back of my brain screaming—*danger!* No matter how hard I try, I can't shake the disconcerting sensation.

Even though we're standing side by side, I edge closer, needing the comfort of his body next to mine. "Do you know him?"

Rowan watches the older man carefully as if he too, senses that something is off. It only reinforces my initial feeling of concern.

Instead of answering the question, he mutters, "Why don't you grab your coffee, and I'll catch up to you in a couple of minutes."

And leave him alone with this strange dude?

No way. Not that I'll be any help if this situation turns sideways, but still...I refuse to leave Rowan's side.

"I'll skip the coffee, it's not a big deal."

"*Demi—*"

A strange urgency fills his voice. Rowan doesn't get a chance to bite out anything more before the guy following us stops a few feet from where we stand.

His pale blue gaze bounces between the two of us before fastening on Rowan. "I was afraid you didn't hear me."

A crack of anger flashes across Rowan's face before it's tucked away behind a steely mask. "Sorry, there's a lot of noise."

I'm not sure who this guy is or what he wants, but I know Rowan isn't telling the truth. The moment he heard this man's voice, his fingers tightened almost painfully around mine. His entire demeanor changed, becoming more anxious. As those thoughts circle through my head, I realize that Rowan must know him.

"What are you doing here?"

The older man shrugs as his lips twist into a thin smile. "Just thought I'd swing by campus and check the place out." There's a beat of awkward silence. "It's not like you've returned my calls."

That statement only confirms my suspicions. They definitely know one another. But how?

Rowan's jaw locks. A mixture of nerves and anger vibrate off him in suffocating waves.

Who is this guy?

When it becomes apparent that neither will fill me in, I step forward and thrust out my hand. "Hello, I'm Demi." I hesitate before tacking on, "Rowan's girlfriend."

The man's piercing gaze flicks to me before sliding over my body in an assessing manner that makes me feel as if I've been stripped bare. Another bolt of unease shoots through me when his rough skin comes in contact with mine.

"Girlfriend, huh?" His brows rise under the brim of his hat. "Seems like you're doing pretty well for yourself, huh, Row?"

Row. With the exception of my father, no one else calls him that.

"Who are—"

"Demi," Rowan cuts me off before I can spit out the rest, "why don't you head to class, and I'll meet up with you later."

A fresh wave of tension rolls through me as my narrowed gaze bounces between the two men. Now that I've had time to study them side-by-side, I realize there's a likeness between them. They have the same sharp cheekbones and straight nose. Rowan is taller by a handful of inches, but they both have the same broad set of shoulders.

Is it possible they're related?

It's an unsettling thought.

"Umm..." It's on the tip of my tongue to argue. Even if they are family, I'm still loath to leave Rowan alone with this guy. The hair at the back of my neck prickles with unease.

"Demi," his voice drops, "please."

I'm unsure what to do. If Rowan wants me to take off, I should go. But still...

My instincts are screaming for me to stay.

"Demi," he growls, impatience simmering in his voice.

"Are you sure?"

"Yeah, I'll catch up with you after your next class."

"Fine." My focus shifts from Rowan to the man silently watching our exchange with amusement. I don't like it. Not one damn bit. It's as if he's won some sort of game. This entire interaction can only be chalked up as bizarre.

For a split second, I consider brushing a kiss across his lips, but don't want to do that with this stranger looking on. Instead, I give a hesitant wave before taking off. Rowan's expression turns to one of relief as I step away—which is odd. He's never happy when we part ways, and he always tugs me in for a kiss. Even when we're in public. Rowan has turned out to be surprisingly affectionate. I can't say that I don't love it.

"Bye."

Rowan gives me an abrupt nod, only meeting my gaze for a moment before his attention shifts back to the man.

It's almost difficult to turn my back on him and walk away, but it's obvious he doesn't want me to stick around. When I'm about twenty feet away, I glance over my shoulder and catch a glimpse of the thunderous expression on Rowan's face.

I don't know what this is about, but I'm going to figure it out.

One way or another.

Chapter Thirty-Four

ROWAN

Relief pumps through me as Demi takes off. I know she was hesitant to leave and wanted to argue but thankfully changed her mind at the last minute. I don't want her anywhere near my father. And I sure as shit don't want him sniffing around her either. If I had my way, he wouldn't even know she existed.

Unfortunately, it's too damn late for that. He's already sizing her up and assessing the situation. If he can use her to squeeze me, he'll do it in a heartbeat. It doesn't matter if I'm his own flesh and blood.

He cocks his head and watches her walk away. "Pretty girl you got there."

"Don't talk about her," I growl, taking a step closer and forcing his gaze to me.

"What?" he says with a chuckle. "You're a chip off the old block when it comes to the ladies."

That thought fills me with revulsion. I don't want to be like him in any regard. I've done my best to be the polar opposite. I try to live my life with integrity and discipline. My father knows nothing about that. He's always taken the easy way out instead of working hard for what he wants.

"What the hell are you doing here?" My jaw is clenched so tightly that it aches.

A smug smile simmers around the corners of his lips. I'm so tempted to punch it off his face. I have to keep my arms locked at my sides in order to not give in to the impulse. I'm much too cognizant of the audience that surrounds us. Even now, people are calling out greetings and waving. Whatever I do will spread through campus like wildfire. I'm sure that's why he chose such a public place to ambush me. My father might be a lazy piece of shit, but he's not stupid.

He jerks his shoulders as if he doesn't understand why I'm upset when in reality, this is all a game, more like a warning. He's not afraid to insert himself where he doesn't belong. And he wants me to understand it. "Like I said before, you haven't been answering my calls."

"That's because we have nothing to talk about," I snap with frustration. "You asked me for money," more like demanded it, "and I gave you everything I had. We agreed you wouldn't contact me again."

"Hmmm. Is that what we decided?" He purses his lips all the while pretending to look thoughtful. "I can't remember."

A growl explodes from my lips as I propel myself forward, eating up a chunk of distance between us. I'm so damn tempted to strangle the life out of him and put us both out of our misery.

As soon as the thought pops into my head, I rein myself back in. I won't allow him to crawl under my skin and burrow there. That's exactly what he's trying to do. Drag me down to his level, and I won't allow him to fuck with me or my destiny.

"You know damn well what—"

"Hey, Michaels," a voice calls out, interrupting our terse conversation, "do we have film review at three?"

I flick my gaze in Brayden's direction and give him a tight smile. "Yup."

He points toward the student union. "You interested in grabbing an early lunch?"

"Nah." I shake my head. "Can't. I've got class."

His focus shifts to my father. Curiosity fills his eyes. Before he can ask any more questions, I say, "I'll catch you at three."

He jerks his head into a nod and takes the hint. "Yup. Later."

Relief escapes from my lungs as he leaves. People continue to walk past and stare. A few girls giggle and wave when I catch their gaze. I really need to take this conversation someplace a little less public.

"Not sure why you would tie yourself down when the pussy is so plentiful around here," my father says with a leer as he watches the girls walk away. "Goddamn, son. You must be drowning in it. Makes me realize how much we've done for you."

My jaw drops to the ground.

Is he fucking delusional?

Rage claws at my insides, searching for an escape.

"I told you before," I mutter, not wanting to be overheard, "I don't have anything else to give."

"Well," he jerks his shoulders and raises his hands as if it can't be helped, "that's gonna be a problem." He pulls off his ball cap and scratches his head. "Who would have thought everything would be so damn expensive? A grand doesn't stretch nearly as far as it used to. I'm going to need a little extra to help get me on my feet."

"There's nothing more I can do."

He purses his lips and glances around the tree-lined campus. "You got a nice set up going here." His hardened gaze flicks to me. "I would hate for anything to ruin it."

I gulp down the rising nausea before it has a chance to explode from my lips. It might be a vague threat, but it's one to take seriously. He doesn't care about making problems for me. He's always been a selfish bastard. Clearly, nothing has changed in that regard.

"I'm cash strapped," I repeat. If I give him anything more from my savings, I don't know how I'll support myself for the rest of the academic year. I still need to eat and pay rent. Now that I'm no longer living in the dorms, scholarship money doesn't cover off-campus housing. Although, with the number of guys I share a place with, it's cheaper than the student residence halls.

"Maybe you can get a loan. It's not like you won't be making millions next year. You're a good investment." His eyes light up, warming to the idea. "In fact, I got a couple of associates who would loan you some money at a fair price."

Loan sharks.

He wants me to take money from guys he got in the hole with. There's no damn way I can get involved with people like that.

"Well, you better figure it out. I'm almost out of cash, and your mother doesn't bring in much."

"Maybe you're the one who needs to get a job." The bitterness shoots from my mouth before I can think better of it.

He would much rather sit on his ass and take money from his wife and kid than actually do something to change his situation. I wish he would get the hell out of our lives and leave us alone once and for all. But he won't. As long as he sees a way to squeeze us for money, he'll stick around. I see it in his eyes. And right now, I'm a cash cow for him.

Anger snaps in his dull blue eyes as he straightens. "What? You too good to help out your old man? After everything I've done for you?"

Done for me?

What a joke. The best thing he ever did was get sent to prison. Too fucking bad he couldn't have stayed locked up behind bars where he belongs.

And now he's back.

To ruin my life.

When I remain silent, lost in those depressing thoughts, he steps toward me and smacks my shoulder. "Get me a couple of hundred bucks by the end of the week. That should hold me over for the time being. But you're gonna have to figure something out, kid. Maybe talk to that fancy agent you got and see if he can slip you something." Then he says what I've been dreading but know deep in my soul is the truth. "I ain't going away."

He's right about that.

He'll *never* go away.

He'll continue to suck off me until I die.

For the first time in a decade, I feel hopelessness rush through me, filling up every space inside as it threatens to suck me under.

Chapter Thirty-Five

ROWAN

"I'm not going to lie, North Carolina will be a tough one, but we're prepared. They have a powerhouse of a defensive line. As long as our guys give you a pocket to do your thing, we'll be good."

Coach's voice barely penetrates the thick haze clouding my thoughts. I startle when he jumps to his feet before clapping his hands and pointing to his daughter on the field. "Way to go, honey! Keep up the pressure!"

I follow suit and refocus my attention on the game. Demi is in her zone today, kicking ass and taking names. If there's action on the field, she's involved in it. There's only been a handful of times when she's come out for a break and that was to guzzle down water before her coach sent her right back in. My heart swells with more love than I ever imagined possible. As soon as that realization enters my mind, my breath hitches, and everything inside me goes eerily silent.

I don't bother trying to convince myself those thoughts aren't true. That's exactly the way I feel about her.

My gaze stays pinned to Demi as she races toward their opponent's goal. She is so single-minded and determined. I've never met anyone who has so much heart for the game. How could I not fall for a girl with so much passion burning inside her?

Now that I've gotten to know Demi on a deeper level, the feelings that have always been simmering beneath the surface have taken root. All I want to do is wrap her up in my arms and protect her. Not that she needs me to do that. Demi is more than capable of fighting her own battles.

Everything would be perfect if not for my father's unwanted presence. Even the idea of him is enough to make me feel like there is a thousand-pound weight sitting on my chest, crushing the very life out of me. He won't be happy until he sucks me dry like an emotional vampire. And there is nothing I can do to get rid of him. There's not enough money in the world to satiate him.

Those thoughts have me dragging a hand over my face.

What the hell am I going to do?

I glance at the man next to me. As close as we are, he has no idea what I'm struggling with. Coach has helped me in so many ways. Am I really going to repay all that by bringing my ex-con of a father into his life?

Into his daughter's life?

There's no way I can do that to either of them. I need to keep Scott Michaels as far away from Demi as possible.

"Rowan?" There's a pause. "Have you heard one damn word I've said?"

I snap to attention and glance at Coach. "Yeah, sorry. Just thinking about the game on Saturday."

His large hand drops onto my shoulder, and he gives it a squeeze. "Now's not the time to get in your head."

Even though we're talking about different things, it's much too late for that.

"Is there something else going on?" He searches my face. "You're not acting like yourself."

Fuck.

As much as it pains me to lie to Coach, there's no way I can tell him the truth. I can't drag him into my shit. That's exactly what this situation is—a shit sandwich I'll have to swallow down on my own, one disgusting bite at a time.

"Nope, it's all good. I'm going over everything in my head and hoping Kendricks catches what I throw his way."

He flashes me a grin. "You two are solid this season. No reason to think it won't continue."

He's right. Brayden and I are in the zone. It's like he can't *not* catch what I throw. We've totally gelled on the field. He seems to move into position before the ball explodes from my hand. I'm going to miss him next year.

I glance at the man beside me. Out of everyone on the team, he's the one I'll miss most. Nick Richards has been like a father to me since he strode into my life the summer before ninth grade. There's no way I would be where I am today without his guiding hand. Unbeknownst to him, he stepped in and filled the gaping hole my father never could. He's always led by example, demonstrating how to be a man. He's taught me invaluable life lessons along the way. Ones that I will carry with me forever.

How do you repay the one person who has altered the course of your life and made you a better human being?

I'll tell you what you don't do—you sure as shit don't bring your deadbeat father around him or his daughter.

The air held captive in my lungs burns as I release it back into the world and watch Demi race up the field before scoring her third goal of the game. That girl is unstoppable. She's a force of nature to be reckoned with. The two of us jump to our feet and clap our hands. He sticks his fingers between his lips and lets out a loud whistle. A few other spectators blow air horns. Sure, women's soccer doesn't bring in the same kind of fanatic crowd that football does, but there are still a good number of fans filling the soccer arena.

We sit in silence for a few minutes, watching the fast-paced action on the field before Coach says, "I think she has a damn good chance of getting picked up by the NWSL. A few scouts have contacted her, expressing interest."

That would be amazing for Demi. She's talked about playing professional soccer, but I also know that she's not pinning her hopes on it either. She has a backup plan in mind. My girl is so damn smart.

She's as talented as she is beautiful.

Demi Richards is the total package.

The girl of my dreams.

Which is exactly why I won't be the one who stands in her way. I won't allow my past to alter her future. My heart lurches as the realization of what I need to do sinks inside me like a boulder. I spent all these years trying to get close to Demi and now that she's mine, I have to let her go.

She deserves the best, and I'm not it.

When the buzzer sounds, signaling the end of the game, I blink back to the present. The Wildcats have pulled off their third win in a row. This was the most challenging team they've taken on this season. A few players surround Demi, hugging her before they line up and congratulate the other team on a good game.

Demi's gaze seeks mine out in the crowd of spectators before she flashes me a grin. That one smile is enough to have everything stilling inside me.

How the hell am I going to cut this girl loose?

Not only will I break her heart, I'll shatter my own in the process.

Chapter Thirty-Six

DEMI

Tonight's the night.

I'm going to tell Rowan what's in my heart. The feelings that have taken root inside me have come on so hard and fast. It's almost enough to make my head spin. In the beginning, I held them in because I wanted to be sure they were real. Over the last couple of weeks, they've managed to multiply, growing out of control and intensifying rapidly. Now that I've come to terms with my own emotions, I don't see a reason to hold them inside any longer. I want Rowan to know how much he means to me.

This is a massive step. I've never told anyone other than my parents that I love them. It's as thrilling as it is scary.

The plan for tonight is to meet up at a party. The Wildcats won this afternoon's football game, and everyone will be out celebrating like their lives depend on it. It's kind of cool that we both won our respective games this week. How often does something like that happen? Adding to the celebratory mood is Rowan's statistics grade. It's sitting at a solid B. He's worked so hard to get it there. We both deserve to relax and have some fun tonight.

There's a light knock against my bedroom door. Before I can call out a response, Sydney pushes it open and pokes her head inside.

Her gaze roves over me as I hold out my arms and do a little twirl. "What do you think?"

"That you look hot, and you'll definitely be getting laid this evening."

My lips quirk as a gurgle of laughter breaks loose. "I certainly hope so." I haven't been able to spend much time with Rowan this week. We've both been busy, and I've noticed that he's been a little preoccupied. Now that today's game is won, I think he'll loosen up. If not, I'll have to get him there, and I know exactly how to do that.

Sydney grins and takes another step inside the room. "I wasn't kidding, girl. You look seriously hot." She raises a brow. "Special occasion?"

A flutter of nerves wing their way to life inside the pit of my belly. I chew my lower lip before shrugging. "Just want to look nice."

"Mission accomplished. Rowan won't be able to keep his hands off you."

That would happen regardless. But this sexy little skirt and cleavage-baring top should clinch the deal. I glance at the mirror and scrutinize my reflection before turning one way and then the other to get a better look at my ass. I've never felt so far out of my comfort zone. I'm almost tempted to tear the clothing from my body and throw on a comfy sweater and a pair of well-worn jeans.

Needing to get my mind off how momentous tonight feels, I say, "You never told me what happened with Ethan." Which, now that I think about it, is odd. Usually, Sydney gives me a blow-by-blow of their relationship status. She's the queen of oversharing.

"We're still broken up."

I meet her gaze in the full-length mirror. It's been a week. Their usual pattern is to work everything out within a couple of days. So, this is odd. I twirl around to search her face. "I'm sorry. Do you think you'll get back together again?"

She jerks her slender shoulders as a wave of sadness crashes over her features. "I think we're both tired of the drama. It's become soul-sucking, and I don't have the energy for it anymore."

Holy shit. This is the first time I've heard her say that. Sydney had crushed on Ethan all last year, and when they finally got together this summer, it seemed like they were really happy.

At first.

And then the bickering started, followed by the constant whirlwind of breakups and makeups. It was exhausting, and I was the one sitting on the sidelines.

"Wow." I have to admit that I'm shocked by the sudden turn of events. Although...let's see if it sticks. Those two are like magnets. They're either pulling at each other or forcing the other away.

"I know." She nods, understanding my reaction. "I think it'll be good to be on my own for a while."

Woah. Talk about another curveball. Sydney has been a serial dater since I met her. She hops from one guy to the next without blinking her eyes. I rack my brain, trying to figure out if I've ever known a single Sydney. This will be a first.

"I agree. It almost sounds like," I pause for a moment, "you're making a mature decision."

Laughter bubbles up in her throat. "I know, right?" It doesn't take long before she sobers again. "I really do like Ethan..." her voice trails off, and her brow furrows as if she's trying to work out a complicated math equation in her head.

"But?" I prompt when she remains silent.

She blinks, and her gaze refocuses on me. "I don't think we're very good together."

That is the understatement of the year. And the thing is, they're great people on their own, just not as a couple. For reasons I don't understand, they bring out the worst in each other.

With any luck, the breakup will stick this time.

"I really am sorry." Even when you're the one making the decision to walk away, the demise of a relationship is still painful. "Are you sure about going out tonight? We could always chill here. Rent a few movies, order pizza, and dive headfirst into cartons of chocolate ice cream. You know, all the things that are supposed to help you move on."

She snorts before shaking her head. "No, I need to get out and get my mind off of it. If I sit at home, all I'll do is mope and eat. It'll turn into an ugly cycle." She pats her behind. "My ass can't take that."

"Please." I roll my eyes. "Your ass is amazing."

She waves a hand in my direction. "Plus, you're dressed to slay. There's no way in hell we're wasting *that*."

As much as I want to see Rowan tonight, if Sydney needed to stay in, I'd do it in a heartbeat. She's always stood staunchly by my side. How could I not be there for her in her moment of need?

"Are you absolutely sure?" I search her gaze. "I don't mind."

"Nope, it's all good." She heads for the door. "Let me throw on something party-appropriate, and we can hit the road. I'm sure Rowan has already texted you half a dozen times, wondering where you're at."

My brows draw together as I glance at my cell on the nightstand. It's been strangely silent for the last couple of hours. No chirping or dinging to speak of. I swipe it from the small table and glance at the dark screen. Rowan hasn't texted or called at all today. I'm the one who reached out earlier to firm up our plans, and his reply was abnormally brief.

I stare at my phone as a kernel of unease settles in the pit of my belly before quickly pushing it away.

What am I worrying about?

So what if he hasn't checked-in?

Just because we're going out doesn't mean we're attached at the hip. Even when I'm in a relationship, I've always maintained my independence. I've never been one of those girls who loses themselves in a guy. And I don't want to start now. It takes effort to shake away the concern that has taken root inside my brain. As soon as I see him, everything will fall back into place.

I add a little bit of coppery eyeshadow and shimmery lip gloss before checking myself out one last time in the mirror. Normally, I throw my hair up into a ponytail because it's easy. I'm all about low maintenance. But tonight, I've straight ironed my long lengths, so they fall down my back in a shiny dark curtain.

Even I have to admit that I'm looking pretty damn good. Sydney's right—I am *so* getting laid tonight.

Twenty minutes later, we walk arm in arm up the front steps of the house that Rowan shares with a bunch of guys from the football team. Sydney has pulled out all the stops. Her long blond hair has been curled and falls in soft waves around her shoulders. She's wearing a dark green shirt that hugs her curves and makes her emerald-colored eyes pop. The short denim skirt barely covers her ass as the black leather boots stretch over her calves.

She commented earlier that I looked smoking hot. Well, she doesn't look so shabby herself. I wouldn't be surprised if she leaves the party with someone. Just as long as it's not Ethan. Everything she admitted earlier rings true. It would be best for all involved if they went their separate ways.

"This place is packed," Sydney shouts in my ear, in an attempt to be heard over the pumping music that emanates from inside the house.

It's like everyone and their mother showed up to help the Wildcats celebrate another victory. So far, they're ranked number one in their conference. If the team keeps playing this well, they'll take home another championship. It would be the perfect way for Rowan and the rest of the seniors to end their college football careers. I hope the soccer team can do the same. Unlike Rowan, I have no idea if I'll go on to play professional sports. My athletic career might be over at the end of this season. It's a depressing thought, but one I've been preparing myself for.

One of the freshman football players loiters outside on the front porch, manning the door. Guess we know who drew the short straw this evening. He straightens to his full height as his drunk gaze crawls over Sydney. She's got the girls out on full display this evening, and this guy has definitely taken notice. I recognize him but don't remember his name. Barely is he able to rip his gaze away from my bestie long enough to glance at me. Sydney has that effect on the male sex. After three years of friendship, I'm used to it.

Before I can interrupt his intense perusal, a voice shatters the moment.

"Let them in, Sausage. Don't you recognize Coach's daughter?"

Sausage?

That's an odd nickname. Let's hope that's all it is. If not, it's a bummer of a first name.

My gaze slices to the tall, dark-haired football player. At the sound of Brayden's voice, Sydney stiffens. If I weren't standing so close to her, I would have probably missed the reaction.

"Hi, Bray," I say with a wave.

He gives me a chin lift in greeting before his attention deviates to my roommate. A sexy smile lifts his lips as he takes his sweet damn time eyeing her up and down. "Looking good, Sydney."

It's a well-known fact around campus that Brayden is a huge flirt. And Sydney can be just as friendly. Her normal reaction to a guy checking her out is to turn up the wattage of her charm. So, you can imagine my surprise when she does the opposite and bares her teeth before growling like a feral animal.

What the hell?

She only reinforces the depth of her disdain when she adds in a none too polite tone, "Bite me, Kendricks."

His smile turns into more of a full-blown smirk. "Is that an invitation, sweetheart? I think we both know that I'd like to do more than bite." He takes his gaze off her long enough to glance around. "Where's the boyfriend?"

"He'll be here shortly," she snaps. "Now go away."

My wide gaze bounces between them as I try to figure out what's going on. There's a strange combustible energy sizzling in the air. It's practically choking me alive.

Sydney and Brayden know each other. But not that well. Certainly not well enough for Sydney to want to rip his throat out. Which is exactly how she looks at the moment.

He ignores the last comment and focuses on the first. "That's too bad."

With a snort, she attempts to push past him. But Brayden has other ideas. Before Sydney is able to make a clean getaway, he grabs her upper arm and drags her close. Then he whispers something in her ear. There's no way to hear what's being said. My brows shoot up when Sydney rips her arm away, practically hisses, and leaves him in her dust. Amusement lights up his face as if that's exactly the reaction he was going for.

As tempted as I am to give Brayden the third degree, there's no time. I don't want to lose Sydney in this crowd. I send him a quizzical look before hurrying after my friend. It takes approximately thirty seconds to catch up to her. She finally slows her pace when I tug on her arm.

"What was that all about?" I shout over the music.

Tension vibrates off her in heavy suffocating waves. She jerks her shoulders before attempting to smooth out her features. It's not a battle she's going to win. "Umm, what are you talking about?"

A chuckle of disbelief slides from my lips as I jerk my thumb toward the front door, and the guy she couldn't get away from fast enough. "What's the deal with Brayden? Is there a problem?"

"Not really," she grunts, pressing her lips into a tight line.

"Not really?"

A beat of silence passes before she grumbles, "It's nothing." She huffs and glances away. "We have a class together, and we've been partnered up for a project." Another scowl moves across her pretty features. "Do you have any idea what a conceited jackass the guy is?"

Ummm...no? I shake my head.

Her brows jerk up. "Really? I can't stand him."

Brayden is many things, but I never thought he was an arrogant jerk. Is he a player? Guilty as charged. But there's a lot of them at Western. That being said, he's always struck me as a nice guy. One who likes to sleep around. The last time I checked, that wasn't a crime. It's more or less something to be wary of.

I tilt my head, searching her gaze carefully in the darkness. She definitely has a burr up her ass. Although I'm not sure what it is. "Did something happen between you two?"

Guilt flickers across her face before it vanishes, making me wonder if I glimpsed it in the first place. "Of course not."

"Hmmm." Strangely enough, I don't believe her. But then again, Sydney has never lied to me. She's always been an open book about what's going on in her life. Sometimes a little too open.

Before I can come at her with anymore questions, she points toward the living room. "I think I see your man."

Rowan!

A fresh burst of nerves explodes inside me and, just like that, I forget all about the weird interaction with Brayden. This is it. It's do or die time. I follow behind her as she blazes a trail through clumps of people before grinding to an abrupt halt. Unprepared for the sudden stop, I slam into Sydney's back. She stumbles forward a couple of steps before swinging around.

There's a grimness to her expression that catches me off guard. "Let's detour to the kitchen and grab a couple of drinks first."

"What?" Confusion spirals through me at the abrupt change in plans. "I thought you spotted Rowan."

Her gaze darts around before flitting toward me again. "Drinks first, then we'll find him."

Sydney has always been something of a wildcard, but this behavior doesn't quite fit the pattern. The unease I'd felt earlier this evening slams back into me full force.

"What's going on?" I try to peek around her, but she quickly shifts to block my line of sight.

What the hell?

"Trust me, all right?" Her voice rises. "Let's grab a drink instead."

Wait a minute...is Sydney trying to prevent me from seeing something in the living room?

Why would she do that?

Only one reason comes to mind. I need to see if my suspicions are correct. I fake a move to the left. When she attempts to sidestep me, I lunge to the right. The moment Sydney is no longer shielding my view, my gaze lands on him.

Or maybe I should say *them*.

All of the oxygen gets sucked from the room as paralysis sets in. My feet freeze to the floor, rendering me incapable of movement.

A tentative hand lands on my shoulder. "Demi—"

I blink away the shock and wait for the image to shimmer and disappear as if it's a figment of my imagination, but it remains solid. My heartbeat thunders in my ears, drowning out the loud music as I try to make sense of the scene unfolding in front of me. There's no mistaking Annica. Her body is pressed against Rowan. Her head is tipped back, a cascade of auburn-colored hair falling down her back as she grins up at him.

What bothers me most is the way he's smiling at her. His arm is wrapped loosely around her body. He's certainly not making any attempt to push her away. In fact, he looks to be enjoying the attention.

I don't understand.

It feels like my lungs will burst when he glances over, and our gazes collide. I expect the easygoing smile he always flashes at me to cross his expression. Something that will tell me I've jumped to the wrong conclusion, and this isn't what it looks like. But his face never transforms. It remains strangely devoid of emotion.

"You need to talk to him and figure out what the hell he's doing with that viper." Anger bleeds through every whipped-out word.

A gurgle of laughter rises in my throat.

Talk to him?

There's no way in hell I'm going to stomp over there and get into a wicked fight with a captive audience watching. Especially when the girl he's with is none other than my nemesis. He's well aware of the problems we've had. Clearly, there's nothing for us to talk about. The fact that he's staring at me, making no attempt to untangle himself from her, speaks volumes.

Decision made, I straighten my shoulders and spin around before stalking toward the front door. The beginning of this relationship caught me by surprise and turned my world upside down.

It seems like the end, unfortunately, has done very much the same.

Chapter Thirty-Seven

ROWAN

As soon as Demi disappears through the crowd, I push Annica away. I've never felt so sick to my stomach. Every instinct is screaming at me to run after the only girl I've ever cared about and apologize for causing her even an ounce of pain.

That had never been my intention.

All right, so maybe it was.

What's become clear over the last couple of days is that I needed a clean break from Demi. If our relationship had lingered even for a day or two, there was the distinct possibility I wouldn't have been able to go through with the breakup. I couldn't allow that to happen. There's no way I could permit Demi to get sucked into my bullshit. I'd assumed that once my father had been sent to prison, I would be free of him, but that hasn't turned out to be the case. He'll continue to suck off me like a leech, and nothing short of death will ever get rid of him. He soils and destroys everything he comes in contact with. I only have to look at my mom to see the truth of that. I don't want him anywhere near Demi.

In the end, cutting her loose was the only way to protect her. No matter how much pain it causes me. She might not realize it right now, but I'm doing her a massive favor.

"Hey," Annica stares up at me with lust-filled eyes, "I thought we were going to hookup."

Thankfully, she has no idea Demi saw us together. I'm sure this girl would only use it as another way to inflict pain on her teammate. "Sorry, not tonight."

Or, more than likely, ever.

Her smile turns seductive. As if she's used to getting what she wants from the opposite sex. "Are you sure about that?" When she reaches out to trail her fingers over my chest, she's yanked away.

"*Ow*," the redhead howls as Sydney buries one hand in her hair, dragging her back a few steps. "*Get off me!*"

The blonde gives her a vicious shake. "Someone needs to put you in your place, and if Demi won't do it, then I sure as hell will!"

Annica winces, her lips twisting into a snarl as she tries to free herself. "Let me go, you crazy bitch!"

"You have no idea how crazy I can be, but you're about to find out! You should know better. You mess with my girl, you mess with me!"

As I consider jumping between them, arms wrap around Sydney from behind. The blonde struggles, attempting to fight her way free. Annica screams again as her head is jerked one way and then another. Brayden whispers something in Sydney's ear before her body goes limp, and she reluctantly releases the other girl.

"You fucking psycho!" With a glare, Annica lurches a few steps before righting herself. One hand goes to the back of her head to gingerly rub at the spot. "I think you pulled some of my hair out!" Her lips curl. "You're as talentless as your stupid friend!"

The insult renews Sydney's fight. It's like a light switch being flipped as she tries to break free from the tight grip Brayden has on her wiggling body.

"Get the hell out of here," Brayden barks to Annica, "before I let her loose. I doubt that's something you want to happen."

Annica's eyes widen before narrowing. Without another word, she swings away, shoving through the crowd. If she's got any brains whatsoever, she'll leave the party. My gaze slides to Sydney with renewed appreciation. That girl is definitely a fighter. I'm not going to lie, I'm kind of frightened.

I glance at Brayden who still has Sydney held captive in his arms.

"You can let go now," she growls, attempting another escape.

"You sure about that, killer?" Brayden asks with a grin. He doesn't seem to be in any hurry to turn her loose. A moment later, Sydney drives her elbow into his ribs, and he releases her with a grunt. "Fine," he chuckles, "have it your way."

Sydney takes a moment to straighten her clothes before turning and shooting him a withering glare. I'm almost surprised when his balls don't shrivel up and fall off his body. Then she swings around.

Sparks of fury flash in her green eyes as she advances, shoving the palms of her hands against my chest. "What the hell were you doing with that viper? Actually, a better question would be—what the hell are you doing with *any* girl?"

Brayden's brows jerk up as something hardens in his eyes. "Were you fucking around on Coach's daughter?"

I glower at my wide receiver. Like I need shit from him? He needs to stay the hell out of my business. "I wasn't fucking around on anybody."

"That's not the way it looked to me. And more importantly," Sydney snaps, "that's not how it appeared to Demi."

I jerk my shoulders and attempt to lock down all the turbulent emotions fighting to break free under the surface. "It doesn't matter what it looked like. I did what needed to be done."

She plants her fists on her hips before tilting her head. "And why *exactly* did you need to hurt her?"

I drag a hand through my hair and shoot Brayden a pleading look. I shouldn't have to explain myself to Demi's friend. When Bray cocks a brow as if also waiting for an answer, I realize that he won't be any help whatsoever.

Fucker.

"It wasn't going to work out in the long run. Better to pull the plug now than down the road when we're both invested."

Disgust fills Sydney's expression as her upper lip curls. "I can't believe how wrong I was about you." She jabs a finger into my chest. "Congratulations, you're no better than that asshat Justin."

The comparison stings. As much as I want to reveal the reason it was necessary to cut Demi loose, the truth stays trapped behind my teeth where it belongs.

When I remain silent, she stalks away without another word to either of us.

I stare after her retreating figure for a long moment, torn between ending this charade and letting it die a long slow death. I knew this would be painful, but I never imagined it would hurt this much. It's almost as if I've severed a limb. I get the feeling that the phantom pain will stay with me for the rest of my life.

When Brayden clears his throat, my gaze jerks to him.

"I've known you for more than three years, and my guess is that you've always had a thing for that girl." He searches my eyes as if he's able to inspect everything I'm hiding inside. "I'm not sure why you purposefully jacked up this relationship, but I sure as hell hope for your sake you made the right decision."

Yeah...that makes two of us.

Chapter Thirty-Eight

DEMI

Dad and I sit quietly at the kitchen table as I use my fork to pick at the chicken divine casserole he whipped up for dinner. It's something Mom used to make before the divorce, and it's comforting as hell. Right now, I need as much solace as possible.

After five full minutes of silence, Dad clears his throat, "So...anything new going on?"

As soon as the question erupts from his mouth, he winces. I pause with my fork mid-air, my widened gaze cutting to his. "Sorry," he mumbles, "I meant anything else *besides* that."

My utensil falls back to my plate with a clatter. As much as I want to eat, I can't. My appetite has pulled a vanishing act. My belly has been in knots since Saturday night. Out of all the girls I could have found Rowan with, it had to be her.

Annica.

Ugh.

Honestly, this is the kind of behavior I've come to expect from her. The girl has turned out to be a real supervillain. I'm sure she's hunkered down in her lair somewhere, rubbing her hands together and chuckling malevolently at my expense.

But Rowan?

Not in a million years did I imagine he was capable of inflicting this kind of damage. It makes me wonder if our entire relationship was a lie. Or maybe a game. How do you treat someone you supposedly care about with such cruelty? Someone you claim to have wanted for years?

It doesn't make sense.

For the first day or so, I'd held out hope that Rowan would show up at my door and demand I give him a chance to explain his side of the story. That never happened. As hurtful as it is, his silence speaks volumes that can't be ignored.

The second slap in the face was when he walked into stats Monday morning. He didn't even glance in my direction, but he must have sensed my presence. For the first time since school began in August, he chose to sit as far from me as humanly possible. The girls in the class were thrilled and immediately swarmed him. A few actually sent triumphant looks at me.

If those telltale signs hadn't been enough of a tip-off, Rowan bailing on Wednesday night dinner with Dad was the final blow. I'd thought maybe...

Maybe he would show up, and we could finally talk. Or, at the very least, he could explain how we ended up at this place. Maybe we've moved past the point of trying to pick up the shattered pieces and glue them back together, but we could at least part ways as friends. That would be the mature thing to do considering he's practically family.

Instead, he chickened out at the last minute and gave Dad some random bullshit story.

For the first time in more than three years, my father and I are dining alone for our weekly dinner. I don't think Rowan has missed one since freshman year. There were so many times when I wished he would stop coming around, and now that he has, I'm eaten alive by sorrow and grief.

How stupid am I for thinking we'd found something special?

After Justin, I should have known better than to get involved with another athlete. One would have thought I'd learned my lesson, but apparently not.

"Demi?"

I blink out of those thoughts, before refocusing on my father. "Yeah?"

"I'm sorry about Rowan." He shifts uncomfortably on his chair. "Do you want to talk about it?"

With my father?

As much as I appreciate him asking, I'll take a hard pass.

When I shake my head, relief floods his expression. It's almost comical. Except there's nothing funny about the situation.

Dad changes the conversation to a safer topic. "You got a big game coming up tomorrow."

Right...soccer.

I focus my attention on the team we'll be versing. It's a conference rival game. We've lost to this team as many times as we've won. There's no doubt in my mind that it'll be a challenging match. This is exactly what I should be concentrating on.

Instead, my mind circles back to the sudden death of my relationship. Unfortunately, the autopsy is inconclusive. I can't figure out what went wrong. Even in retrospect, there's nothing that sticks out in my mind. One minute we were riding high and it seemed like we might actually have a shot at a future after graduation, and the next, the entire thing is exploding upon impact.

Only Rowan knows what happened, and he isn't willing to share that information. It would be so much easier to move on if he would give me some answers.

But he refuses to do that.

Chapter Thirty-Nine

ROWAN

The pass I throw spirals fifty yards through the air before landing in Brayden's arms like a heat seeking missile. Coach blows his whistle, signaling the end of practice. As soon as he does, Demi pushes her way relentlessly into my thoughts. Out on the field is the only time I can forget about her and concentrate on something else. If I could stay out here twenty-four/seven, I would do it in a heartbeat. It would be so much easier than the constant thoughts of her that swirl through my brain.

But that's not possible.

Brayden grins as he jogs toward me with the football tucked in his arms. I'll miss playing ball with him next year. Whatever team he goes to will be damned lucky to have him. He's ranked number one in the country for college receivers.

When he's about ten yards away, he tosses the ball, and I catch it easily in my hands.

"Good practice." He unsnaps the chinstrap and yanks off his helmet before shaking out his damp hair like a dog.

My attention meanders to the stands where there is a small group of girls sitting in a line. As soon as Brayden glances their way, they wave frantically. He grins and returns the gesture with a little more subtlety. Each girl has one letter of his name stamped across her chest.

And people have the audacity to say that *I'm* a player?

Please...this guy has an entire fan club dedicated solely to him. Surprisingly, Brayden hasn't let all the female attention go to his head.

"Looks like you have plans after practice," I say with a smirk, nodding in their direction.

"Nah." He shakes his head. "Not interested."

Well, this is certainly news. Brayden goes through girls like most people go through underwear. He's one of those guys who could talk a baby out of candy. Or...a girl out of her panties for the evening.

He's a charming bastard...when he wants to be.

"Can't say I ever thought that would come out of your mouth."

"Yeah, me neither." A slight smile curls around the edges of his lips. "I like being single and playing the field." He glances at the girls. "That's what college is all about, right?"

Maybe for other guys. I've never been interested in banging as many chicks as I can get my hands on. There was one girl, and she was all I could see. It was like I was blinded to everyone else.

He tilts his head and narrows his eyes. "But it was never like that for you, was it?"

The words might be arranged in the format of a question, but I get the feeling we both know the answer without me having to confirm it. Unwilling to have this conversation turned around on me, I lift my chin toward his fan club. "They'll be disappointed."

He flicks a glance toward the stands. "Not really my problem. I've got to head over to the library after this."

Now he's really starting to scare me. Brayden is going to turn down pussy to study at the library? I squint at the sky. "Have I somehow entered a parallel universe where up is down and down is up?"

With a grin, he knocks his shoulder into mine. "Shut the fuck up. It's more of a study date if you catch my drift."

"Well, that makes a little bit more sense." I guess.

As we reach the tunnel where the locker rooms are located, a prickle of unease slithers down my spine. I have the strange sensation of being watched. As I glance up, my gaze sweeps over the stands until it fastens on pale blue eyes. My heartbeat stutters before pounding into overdrive. Even though my footsteps falter, I keep moving.

Brayden stays at my side. He continues to talk, but his voice doesn't penetrate the thick haze that has descended.

My father is here...

At the stadium.

One side of Dad's mouth hitches into a nasty smile. He knows I don't want him anywhere near the university.

A potent mixture of rage and nerves rush through my veins. Hopelessness swiftly follows, overriding all other emotions trying to take root because I know deep-down, he'll never leave me alone. I'll admit I've been having second thoughts about pushing Demi away, but seeing him here only reconfirms that I made the right decision. There is no way I could saddle her with my past. It's like having a fucking anchor shackled around my neck. No matter how much I fight against the constriction, it'll eventually drag me to the bottom of the ocean.

I don't realize my feet have stopped moving until Brayden interrupts the frantic whirl of my thoughts.

"You coming or what?"

Dread pools inside my gut. "No, go on without me." The fewer people that see us together, the better. I don't know how to make it any clearer that he can't keep popping up on campus like this. Not if he wants more money.

Brayden jerks his shoulders. "Okay, man. Catch you in a few."

"Yup." I blow out a steady breath as he takes off, thankfully disappearing inside the tunnel.

A couple of the other guys jog past. Once the turf has been emptied, I glare at my father who has made his way down to the field.

When I remain silent, he grins, opening his arms wide. "Mighty fine place you got here." He glances around the stadium as if casing the joint. Like this is my personal space, and he's trying to come up with a way to rob me blind.

I clench my hands at my sides in an effort to resist the urge to wrap them around his throat and squeeze. "What do you want?" As if I didn't already know.

After he showed up on campus almost two weeks ago, I scraped together another couple hundred bucks. Now he's back for more. That's the thing about him. He will *always* come back for more. Even when there's nothing for me to give.

A slight chuckle falls from him as he shrugs. "You know how it goes."

Unfortunately, I do. "I thought you were trying to find a job."

"Yeah, I've been looking around." His gaze skitters away, which is a sure sign he's lying. "Even filled out a few applications." Bitterness whips through his eyes, turning them frosty. "Had to show my parole officer."

Right. It's all smoke screens and lies with this guy. He would probably expend less energy taking a part time gig than constantly manufacturing excuses along with applications for jobs he has no intention of accepting.

One quick glance around tells me that we're alone. But still, I step closer and lower my voice. "I told you that I didn't have anything more to give."

"And yet you came up with a little bit more."

"That was the last of it." A towering wave of bitterness crashes over me. "What I make in the summer is all I have to live on during the year."

"I bet if you asked around, someone would loan you the money." He waves a hand, encompassing the stadium. "I saw all the photos that line the walls, you're a big deal around here. People are probably throwing shit your way all the time. It wouldn't surprise me if you could squeeze them for a goddamn car."

I drag a hand over my face. He has no idea how anything works.

"How about that girlfriend of yours?" He shifts his weight and cocks his head. "She'd probably be more than happy to help out."

I recoil at the idea of asking Demi for anything, let alone money for my deadbeat father. "We're not together anymore."

Thank fuck. It's the first time I've had reason to think it. But staring at the man before me, it's a relief to know that she's out of my life for good. He'll never touch her.

"Michaels!"

Shit.

I whip around only to find Nick Richards standing twenty feet away with his clipboard in hand.

"Yeah, Coach?" I straighten my shoulders and pray that he'll rattle off something before disappearing back into the tunnel.

Instead, his gaze darts from me to my father before he eats up the distance between us with a couple of long-legged strides. "Hello, Scott. I didn't realize you'd been released."

What the fuck?

I had no idea that Coach knew anything about my father. It's not something we've ever discussed. It was too embarrassing to admit, even to this man who has been nothing but good to me, that my father was sent to prison for murder.

"What?" Scott stiffens, eyes narrowing to slits. "You keeping tabs on me?"

Coach's lips lift slightly at the corners as his dark eyes harden. "I've been at the last two parole hearings, so I think we both understand that I've made it my business to be involved."

What?

I can't believe what I'm hearing.

My gaze shifts from one man to the other before refocusing on Coach. Barely am I able to find my voice. "You know him?"

He glances at me for a moment before his attention resettles on my father. It's like he understands that it wouldn't be prudent to take his eyes off him, even for a second. "Yup. Made it my business to know."

"Why?" My mind spins out of control. I'm almost dizzy with the sensation.

"You've overcome a lot of challenges and worked hard to get to where you are. I wanted to make sure nothing interfered with that." Nick Richards levels a hard look at my father, and it becomes clear that what he didn't want interfering in my life was this man.

"I spent the last decade rotting in prison," Dad hisses as if answering the silent accusation in the other man's eyes. "Don't you think I've paid my debt to society?"

"That's not my decision to make." Coach shrugs and steps closer to me before settling a hand on my shoulder. The heavy weight of it anchors me to the earth, leaving me to feel less vulnerable. It's the first time in my dad's presence that I've been able to suck in a full breath of air. "Why are you here, Scott?"

My Dad's lips thin before he bites out a response. "I wanted to see my son. It's been a long time. The ungrateful little shit didn't visit me once while I was in prison." He stabs a finger at Coach before hocking a loogie and spitting it at his feet. "I bet you had something to do with that."

"Nope." Nick shakes his head. "Rowan makes his own decisions. You may not realize this, but he had to grow up awfully quick after you got locked up—probably while you were around. And look at him, he's done pretty well for himself." He squeezes my shoulder. "Any man would be proud to call him son." Before my father can respond, Coach continues. "But here's the thing, you only seem to come around when you want something. And I'm guessing that what you want right now is money. I won't put Rowan on the spot by asking him, all I'll say is this —if you truly want to build a relationship with this young man, then you need to make some positive changes in your life, and let him come to you when he's ready. Maybe that won't ever happen. What I do know is that you need to stop coming around campus and harassing him."

My father takes a menacing step in our direction. His hands tighten into fists. "That's not what I'm doing!"

"Isn't it?" Coach raises a brow. Instead of being intimidated, the guy is calm, cool, and collected. "You're a grown man. If you're intent on turning your situation around, you need to prove that to Rowan by standing on your own two feet instead of looking to your twenty-one-year-old son for handouts. Now, if you're ready to make those changes, I would be more than happy to steer you in the right direction as far as jobs go."

"I don't need any charity from the likes of you," Dad snarls.

"Suit yourself," Coach says as if it doesn't make a difference to him one way or the other. "But I think this conversation is over, and it's time for you to leave."

Dad bares his teeth. "You can't tell me what to do!"

"Actually, that's where you're wrong. You step foot on university property again, I'll call campus police and tell them that you've been harassing one of my players. Then I'll personally call your parole officer and fill him in on what's been going on." He pauses for a beat before adding, "Because we both know this isn't the first time you've contacted Rowan."

"You son of a—"

"Yup," he agrees easily, cutting off the tirade, "that's exactly what I am. I've got no problem playing hardball with you."

Dad grits his teeth as rage flashes in his eyes before they slide to me. "You gonna let this asshole talk to me like this?"

Ignoring the question, I say instead, "I don't want you coming around here anymore, and I don't want you calling. If I want to talk, I'll get ahold of you." Although we both know that's not going to happen anytime soon. Whatever bridge could have been tentatively built between us has been destroyed.

Dad opens his mouth to argue when Nick cuts him off. "Your time is up. You can leave on your own volition or," Coach nods toward the tunnel and the security guard who lounges there, "you can be escorted out. The choice is yours."

Scott pales before gnashing his teeth. He looks on the verge of exploding. "Fine, I'm going," he grumbles.

With his lips pressed tightly together, he stalks past us.

When my father is half a dozen feet away, Nick raises his voice. "Chuck, please escort this man off the grounds, and make sure he leaves university property."

The security guard dips his chin. "You got it, Coach."

With that, Chuck ambles after my father as he disappears across the field. When he reaches the other side, I notice a second guard waiting on a glorified golf cart they use to move around the stadium. We watch in silence as my father is followed off the field before disappearing inside the building. Once he vanishes from sight, the tension filling my body drains away, and my shoulders sag in relief. Only then do I become conscious of the suffocating silence that has fallen over us. I shift my stance and clear my throat. Coach and I have spent hundreds of hours hashing out plays and discussing the intricacies of a football game, and yet, right now, my mind is blank. I never wanted these two worlds to collide. "I'm sorry."

"You don't have a goddamn thing to apologize for." He searches my eyes. "I hope you realize that."

I stare at the turf and shrug.

"Hey." When I continue to avoid eye contact, his fingers bite into my shoulder through the thick pads. "Look at me, Rowan."

Forcing my gaze to his is one of the hardest things I've ever had to do. Humiliation gathers in my cheeks, making them burn with heat.

"Your father is in no way a reflection of the person you are."

"His blood runs through my veins." It takes effort to swallow down the rising nausea. "He's a criminal." I force out the ugliest part. "*A murderer.*"

"It doesn't make a damn bit of difference if his DNA is part of your genetic makeup. You are *nothing* like him." He gives my shoulder a good shake before bringing his face close to mine until I have no other choice but to meet the intensity of his gaze. "From the first moment you walked onto that high school football field, I knew you were something special. But it's not your athletic ability that sets you apart from everyone else. It's what's in here." He taps my chest with his fingers. "*This* is what matters. I've never met a player with more heart for the game or life. There aren't many people I would entrust with my daughter. You're one of the few."

I blink away the emotion as it pricks the back of my eyes. This man is more of a father figure to me than mine could ever be. The sentiment he's expressing means more than he'll ever realize. I never wanted Coach to know about my father. I didn't realize he was aware of the situation. Most of the time, I try to forget the man even exists. It was easy enough to do when he was locked away in prison. Nick Richards knowing about my past, accepting me, and continuing to stand by my side, feels like a massive weight lifted from my shoulders.

"You've known this entire time?"

"Yup. Your mom told me everything shortly after we met. I made a promise to her when I took you under my wing that I'd keep an eye on the situation and help steer you in the right direction. That's all I've ever tried to do, Rowan. At the time, I wasn't sure what I was taking on, but you made it easy. Right from the start, you've taken school, and this team seriously. You've walked the straight and narrow. You've grown into a fine young man and a real leader the other guys can look up to. You're someone I'm proud to have coached, and I look forward to what you're going to do with your career, as well as your life."

I glance down, attempting to wrangle my emotions under control. "Thanks, Coach." I want to tuck the words away and play them over and over again in my head. I've spent years idolizing this man. To hear him verbalize his feelings means everything.

"You've got nothing to thank me for. Everything you've achieved has been because of *your* drive and determination. It's your work ethic that will get you everywhere in life. Do you understand that?"

I dip my chin in acknowledgment.

"Good." He smiles. "Now get the hell out of here and hit the showers."

"Okay." With nothing left to say, I jog toward the locker room.

I'm about to disappear through the tunnel, when he calls out my name. "Rowan?"

I grind to a halt before turning around. "Yeah?"

"You hurt my little girl." There's a beat of uncomfortable silence. "I didn't expect that from you."

I suck in a sharp breath, holding it in my lungs until it feels like they might burst from the pressure. "All I was trying to do is protect her. I didn't want Demi getting dragged into this mess."

He squints before cocking his head. "That might be so, but she needs *you* more than she needs your protection."

I shift my weight as a flutter of nerves explodes in the pit of my belly. Maybe I should have been honest with her from the very beginning, instead of trying to hide my past. "She might not forgive me."

"You're right, but you won't know until you try."

With a jerk of my head, I hit the showers. It's a painful admittance to realize that I might have fucked up the best thing in my life, because I was too scared to open up and tell her the truth.

Coach is right. It might be too late to work things out, but I won't know until I try.

The apartment door whips open, and Sydney races inside with excitement dancing in her eyes like it's Christmas morning and her birthday all wrapped up into one. I haven't seen her this ecstatic since...

Well, never. I've *never* seen this level of elation from her. Sydney is usually lowkey. Unless she's angry. Then watch out.

When I raise my brows, she crows, "I have the best flipping news ever!" I don't get a chance to bombard her with questions before the words explode from her tongue. "Annica broke her ankle over the weekend! She's out for the rest of the season!"

My mouth falls open. No matter what I thought she might say, that certainly wasn't it.

Holy crap!

"Yeah," she nods enthusiastically, "I know, *right?* I have to say, I didn't really believe in karma before, but this has totally changed that line of thinking." She drops onto the overstuffed chair across from me before throwing her arms wide. "I'm a big believer now!"

"Then you should be careful," I warn. "I'm pretty sure karma doesn't appreciate when you revel in the misfortune of others."

Sydney makes a big show of rolling her eyes. "Listen, Annica deserves it and karma, that glorious bitch, realizes it as well."

"How did it happen?"

"I guess she was really drunk Saturday night and tripped down someone's front porch steps. When she couldn't put pressure on her foot, her friends made the boneheaded decision to take her to the emergency room." She turns gleeful. Kind of like the Grinch anticipating Whoville's disappointment on Christmas morning. "Get this— not only did she break her ankle, she also got a drinking ticket too, and now has to face sanctions from both Coach and the university. Triple whammy." With a pause, she counts out something on her fingers. "More like quadruple whammy."

My eyes widen. "That's terrible."

"No, *she's* terrible, and you," she stabs a finger in my direction, "of all people should know it."

With a shrug, I glance away. Yeah, Annica has turned out to be a real pain in my ass, but that doesn't mean I wish her any ill will. Fine...maybe a teeny-tiny shred of it. But it sounds like she got the motherload in one fell swoop.

"You know," Sydney says, breaking into the chaotic whirl of my thoughts, "she caused a lot of friction with the team. It's like she thrived on it."

That's true. Annica *did* seem to enjoy the discord. Most people understand that a team can't succeed unless they band together to achieve a collective goal. Does that necessarily mean every player's personality will mesh? Of course not.

Guess that wasn't a lesson that Annica learned early in life like the rest of us.

"With her out for the rest of the season, maybe we can get the team gelling again."

If there's anything good that comes out of the situation, it's that we pull the younger girls back into the fold and get them to buy into the idea of working together to bring home a championship. At this point, it's not too late to turn things around. I think that's what we all want.

Now that Sydney has shared the good tidings, she huffs and rises to her feet. "All right, I've got to head over to the library for a couple of hours."

I perk up. "Want some company? I'm not busy, I can come with you." It would probably be a good idea to get out of the apartment for a little bit. It's been more than a week since the breakup, and I'm still all sad bastard. Even I'm tired of being around myself.

"I wish you could." A scowl twists her pretty face. "Unfortunately, I'm meeting up with Brayden to work on that stupid project."

"Oh." Their strange interaction pops into my head. I've been so focused on my own situation, that I almost forgot about her run in with Brayden. "He's a nice guy, I'm surprised you have such a problem with him."

She straightens to her full height and stares at me like I've grown a horn on my head. "How can you even say that?"

Ummm...

"I don't know." I've never had an issue with the handsome wide receiver. He's always treated me like a little sister. Out of all the guys on the team, he's probably the one I trust most. Clearly, Sydney feels differently—which is strange. As far as I know, nothing has ever happened between them to bring out such animosity in her. "Most girls would be thrilled to be partnered up with him."

A haughty look enters her eyes as she sniffs. "Well, I'm not most girls."

True that.

"I'll be honest, after we ran into him at that party, I kind of wondered if there might be a little something-something going on between you two. You had that whole I-hate-you-but-I-secretly-want-to-sleep-with-you vibe going on." Although now that I think about it, Brayden wasn't acting that way. He was needling her, trying his best to solicit a reaction. Kind of like an elementary school boy would do to a girl he liked.

She makes a choking noise. "I have way too much self-respect to ever get tangled up with such a manwhore, and quite frankly, after the whole Ethan situation, I'm taking a timeout from the dating game. I need to get my head on straight."

In a surprising plot twist, Sydney and Ethan haven't mended their broken relationship. It's been a little more than two weeks. This is the longest they've ever gone without getting back together again.

"That's probably a smart decision."

She chews her lower lip before reluctantly admitting, "I saw him the other day walking to class with another girl."

Ouch. It doesn't matter if she's the one who pulled the plug on the relationship, seeing your ex with another person still stings.

"I'm sorry, Syd," I say gently. "Are you okay? Do you want to talk about it?"

Sadness flashes in her eyes as she shakes her head. "No. The thing is, it hurt to see him but not nearly as much as I assumed it would. It didn't make me want to call him up and get back together again." She pauses, as if thinking about what she's admitted before her gaze refocuses on me. "That's got to mean something, right?"

"I think it means you made the right decision where Ethan is concerned."

"Yeah." A small sigh escapes from her. "You're probably right. For a while, we were really good together. And then we weren't. Now that I'm looking back, I think we hung on for too long. We should have broken up a while ago." She jerks her shoulders as if unsure what the correct answer is. "But it was comfortable, you know? It was easy."

Easy?

That's not the term I would use to describe their relationship.

When I give her a get-the-hell-out-of-town look, her lips twitch, and a few chuckles escape. "All right, maybe not *easy*, but you know what I mean. No matter what, Ethan's a good guy, and I always knew what to expect from him."

"He's definitely a good guy," I agree.

"Just not for me," she tacks on almost regretfully.

I nod, understanding the mix of emotions she's experiencing.

"The plan is to focus on school and soccer for the time being. The last thing I need is a man fucking up the works."

"Sounds smart. We can do it together."

"The celibate sisters," she adds with a grin. "I like it. We'll get T-shirts." Sydney slips her phone out of her pocket and glances at it before the lightheartedness she'd managed to find drains away. "All right, I've got to go meet up with WU's very own manwhore."

"See you later," I call after her as she grabs her bag and heads to the door. "Try not to kill him."

"I'm not making any promises!" she shouts before disappearing into the hallway. Less than a minute later, there's a knock.

I jump from the couch and pad into the tiny entryway before opening the door. "Back already? What did you—"

My voice dies a quick death when I realize it's not my roommate. Instead, I find Rowan standing on the other side of the threshold. The sight of him has me hugging the door frame a little closer to my body.

"Hi." He shoves his hands into the pockets of his khakis. There's a ball cap pulled low over his eyes, and even though there's a definite chill to the air, he's wearing a black T-shirt that hugs his biceps.

In other words, he looks amazing. The magnetic attraction that always hums beneath the surface when we're together explodes to life with a vengeance. It's so tempting to reach out and pull him to me. Instead of giving in to the urge, I squeeze the door a little harder.

"Hey." My heart slams painfully against my ribcage. I've seen him in class and caught glimpses of him around campus, but we haven't been this close in a while. When he remains silent, I clear my throat and attempt to turn off the tangle of emotions slyly wrapping their way around me. "What are you doing here?"

"I was hoping we could talk."

An image of Annica hanging all over him flashes through my head. A pit of nausea blooms at the bottom of my belly, and I force myself to straighten my shoulders. "After more than a week of silence, I don't think we have anything to discuss."

Rowan draws his lower lip into his mouth before chewing on it. A mixture of sorrow and regret fills his expression, and it's almost enough to break my heart.

What the hell is wrong with me?

I want to smack myself for even thinking along those lines. I'm not the one who hurt or betrayed him. It was the other way around.

"I need to explain something to you and then, if you don't want to speak with me again, I'll respect that." When I remain silent, unsure what to do, his voice turns pleading. "Give me five minutes, and then I'll leave. You'll never hear from me again. I promise."

If I were smart, I would slam the door in his face. There is nothing he can say or do to change the way I feel about him. He's the first guy I took a chance on and opened myself up to. I was prepared to lay it all on the line for him. Thank God, I didn't get a chance to do that. It would have only made me feel more pathetic than I already do.

Whoever said—it's better to have loved and lost than never to have loved at all was seriously mistaken. The whole loving-and-losing thing sucks major ass. And quite honestly, I don't see it getting better anytime soon.

"Please, Demi?"

A huff of frustration leaves my lips. I wish I were strong enough to tell him to go to hell. Since I'm not, I begrudgingly move away from the door and wave him in. There's a tiny part of me that's curious about what he has to say.

"Thanks," he murmurs, slipping past me and into the living room where he drops onto the chair. Needing as much distance as possible, I gravitate to the far end of the couch. Regret flickers over his expression as he watches me. It's like he realizes what tactics I'm trying to employ to keep him at a safe distance. His elbows settle on spread thighs as he clasps his hands together in front of him.

An oppressive silence blankets us, and I shift restlessly beneath the heavy weight of his stare. This is more painful than I expected. Only now do I realize that allowing him inside was a mistake. I've changed my mind. No longer do I care what he has to say. His rationale of the situation won't make a difference.

Rowan clears his throat and his gaze falters, falling to his fingers. I don't realize how tightly clasped they are until the knuckles turn bone white. "I want you to know that nothing happened with Annica. That night or any other."

For the second time in a matter of minutes, an image of them flashes unwantedly through my head, and my heart jackhammers a painful staccato against my ribcage. I jerk my shoulders, not wanting him to see how deep his betrayal has cut. "That's not the way it looked."

It's a relief when my voice comes out sounding devoid of emotion. If he thinks he can waltz in here with some half-assed explanation, and I'll fall all over him, Rowan has another thing coming.

"I know." There's a moment of silence before he admits softly, "That was the plan. I wanted you to find us together."

What?

For a beat, maybe two, my mind cartwheels, and all I can do is stare.

He wanted me to find them?

I shake my head as my brows slam together. It's almost impossible to wrap my lips around the question. "You deliberately set out to hurt me?"

My throat grows scratchy as thick emotion wells in the middle of it.

"No." There's a pause before he hastily amends, "I mean, yes." Frustration vibrates off him in suffocating waves as he yanks off his black Wildcats ball cap and drags a hand through his long blond hair. "I wanted to make sure you would be pissed off and never talk to me again."

Un-fucking-believable.

"Well," I force out a mirthless laugh, "you got what you wanted." I rise unsteadily to my feet. "I'm not sure why you felt the need to come here and share this with me, but I think you should leave."

Desperation flares in his eyes as he jumps to his feet. "Please, Demi. Hear me out!" In two long-legged strides, he eats up the distance between us. "I'm doing a shit job of explaining this."

I hold up a hand, not wanting him any closer. "I assume that's because there's no way to justify why you would do something so fucked up."

When I try to move past him, his fingers lock around my wrist. All it takes is one tug to drag me closer. The force of the movement sends me stumbling, and I lose my balance before crashing into him. My hands go to his chest in an attempt to shove my way free. Instead of releasing me, his arms lock around my body until I'm rendered powerless.

"Your five minutes are up. You need to leave." If it were possible to move my leg, I would knee him in the balls. He deserves that and so much more for the pain he's caused. Refusing to make this easy, I struggle against the hold he has on me. Rowan made his choice, and now I'm making mine.

"I thought I was doing the right thing," he says with a grunt, attempting to subdue my movements.

"*Ha!*" Disbelief bubbles up in my throat. How did I not realize Rowan was delusional? "So, let me understand this correctly," I snap, "your idea of *doing the right thing* was to hurt me by messing around with one of my teammates? The very same teammate, I'll remind you, that has been gunning for me both on and off the field. Wow!" Bitterness drips from every word. "How very *thoughtful* of you."

The air deflates from his lungs as he exhales. "Well, when you put it like that, it doesn't sound good."

"No," I agree flatly, "it really doesn't."

"At the end of the day, all I wanted was to protect you." Weariness flashes across his face. "Maybe I went about it the wrong way."

His strange explanation knocks me off-balance, and I still. "Protect me? From what?"

"My past."

"I don't understand." My brows draw together as I search his eyes for clues. "Why would I need protecting from your past?"

Rowan glances away as embarrassment floods his features and darkens his cheeks. "There's a reason I don't talk about my family."

That's something I've noticed. The times I've tried to dig deeper, he immediately shuts down and changes the subject. Instead of pushing the issue, I backed off, assuming Rowan would open up when he was comfortable. That never occurred. I know as much about his personal history now as I did before.

"It's difficult to talk about," he mutters. "I never wanted you to find out about my father."

"Rowan," I say softly, the sharpest parts of my anger dissolving, "you don't have to tell me." This is clearly a painful subject for him. Even though I want to understand how his family impacted our relationship or why he set out to hurt me, maybe it no longer matters. What we need is closure so that we can move on.

"It's important you realize why I pushed you away." He draws in a steady inhalation as if to steel himself for what will come next. "You're the last person I would ever want to cause pain, and I'm sorry for that. I can't say that it wasn't my intention, because it was. I didn't see another way." He pauses for a beat. "Can we please sit down and have this conversation?"

That's when I realize I'm still locked in his arms, held tightly against his chest.

When I nod, he swings toward the couch with me held securely in his arms. I get the feeling he's afraid to let me go, even for a moment. The urge to burrow against his chest thrums through me, but I'm not quite ready to do that. I've missed Rowan more than I allowed myself to acknowledge, even privately. It was so much easier to push him to the outer recesses of my mind and pretend I hadn't already given him my heart. With him standing before me, I can no longer do that.

"Do you remember the older guy we ran into on campus a couple of weeks ago?" When I stare, he adds, "It was after stats class."

I nod as the memory flashes through my head. Something about him had unsettled me. It's as if my body had gone on high alert.

"That was Scott Michaels." There's a pause. "My father."

"Oh." Air gets lodged in my throat as my mind spins. That still doesn't explain why he would feel the need to push me away.

A humorless chuckle escapes from him. "He's been incarcerated for the last ten years for murder."

Murder?

The word echoes in my head.

"Your father was in prison for," I force out the rest, "*murder?*"

He jerks his head into a tight nod before glancing away as if barely able to hold my gaze. "Yeah. He's been a petty criminal my entire life and then he fell in with the wrong people and got in over his head."

I can't begin to fathom how difficult it would be to grow up with a parent like that. My heart clenches painfully knowing there's no way to alleviate the hurt and damage that must have been inflicted. Only now do I understand why Rowan is so closed off when it comes to his family. I wish he would have felt safe enough to open up and share this with me.

"Rowan," I whisper, unsure how to proceed.

He doesn't give me a chance to say anything else. "He'd recently been released from prison, and he started coming around, wanting money from me. The first time it happened, I gave him a good chunk of my savings. I told him that I couldn't give him anymore, and I didn't want to see him again. A week later, he showed up on campus."

"That's when we ran into him after stats class," I murmur. Only now does Rowan's strange reaction make so much more sense.

"Yeah." Humiliation flags his cheeks as I cup the sides of his face with my palms. "As long as he's free, he'll never stop coming around, trying to milk me for everything he can. I didn't want him anywhere near you." He shakes his head. "Maybe I went about it the wrong way, but in the end, all I was trying to do is protect you from the ugliness of my past."

All of the puzzle pieces I couldn't fit together now make perfect sense. I had noticed changes in his behavior but was unable to put my finger on the reason for them. All the times I'd caught him zoning out, he'd been worrying about his father. He didn't want me to know anything about his family. More specifically, his dad. Now that the man was out of prison, Rowan didn't want me exposed to him. And the quickest way to cut ties would have been to—

"So, you made sure I found you with the one girl who would hurt me the most."

His shoulders slump under the weight of my retort. "I was scared and didn't want him anywhere near you. Pushing you away seemed like the easiest way to achieve that. It was stupid. The look on your face," regret fills his eyes as he shakes his head, "I'm sorry for hurting you. I don't expect you to forgive me."

"Why didn't you tell me the truth? I would have understood." There's a beat of silence. "I would have stood by your side."

"I was embarrassed." He quickly amends the statement. "Hell, I'm still embarrassed. My father has always been a drain. Not only on me, but my mom as well. I hate that he's in my life, causing havoc. The last thing I wanted to do was bring him into yours. Coach has been nothing but good to me. How could I repay that kindness by bringing a degenerate into his daughter's life?" His voice dips, sounding scraped raw. "Tell me how I was supposed to do that?"

The heaviness of his emotion shatters my heart into a thousand jagged pieces.

"I wish you had trusted me with the truth."

"It had nothing to do with trust and everything to do with keeping you safe. That's all I wanted to do. *Protect you.*"

With my palms still cupping his cheeks, I bring my forehead to rest against his. "Your father has nothing to do with you. The truth wouldn't have changed my feelings."

"I realize that now. I made a mistake, and I hurt you. I understand if that's something you can't forgive." His gaze clings to mine. "But I hope you will. I love you, Demi. I always have."

"I love you, too."

Air escapes from his lungs in a rush as he tilts his head until his mouth can slant across mine. When his tongue sweeps over the seam of my lips, it never occurs to me to hold back. No one has ever made me feel the way Rowan does. And the truth of the matter is, I don't think anyone ever will again.

What we've found is once in a lifetime.

He breaks away long enough to search my gaze. "From the very beginning, it's been you."

It might have taken me three years to realize that I had feelings for him, but I'm there now. He took the time to break down all of my resistance until I could see the man standing before me with his hand stretched out.

Maybe I didn't want to admit it—even privately to myself, but it's always been Rowan. And if I have my way, that will never change.

EPILOGUE

Rowan

Three years later...

"As you can see, the kitchen is completely stainless steal with brand new marble countertops." The real estate agent beelines from the spacious kitchen with an island so massive, I could probably roll around on it, to the adjoining living room.

Instead of following her, I stay in the kitchen and stare at the island. I can just imagine christening the joint, and that ocean of white marble is the first place I'd start.

"I know exactly what you're thinking," Demi whispers in my ear.

"That's because you're a dirty girl and thinking the exact same thing."

"Only with you," she says, pressing a kiss against my lips.

"Hey, that's my line." I glance at the realtor who stands next to the floor-to-ceiling windows that overlook the white-capped waves of Lake Michigan.

"You have to check out the view!" She pauses for a beat before doing her best impersonation of Vanna White. "Isn't it absolutely *fabulous?*"

Ignoring the woman, I glance around the wide-open space. "What do you think of the place?"

We've been condo hunting in Milwaukee, Wisconsin and have toured a couple dozen buildings. Demi and I have spent the last two years living in separate cities. I ended up getting drafted in the first round by the Milwaukee Mavericks and Demi tried out for the Chicago Suns women's soccer team after graduation and made it. Even though we've been in different cities, we've only been an hour and a half away from each other. As much as it sucks, it could be worse.

The most challenging part has proven to be when we're both in season. My training camp starts mid-July and goes through February, depending on if we're knocked out of the playoffs. Professional soccer runs April through October. It's a constant battle to find time together.

While Demi has enjoyed playing in the NWSL for two years, she's decided to hang up her cleats and attend graduate school for a master's in Exercise Science. She's already been accepted at the University of Milwaukee-Wisconsin and is now moving here permanently.

Demi makes a visual sweep of the kitchen and living area. "I like it."

The place is just shy of three thousand square feet and is located on the thirtieth floor. There are three spacious bedrooms and a study with wood paneling.

"Did I mention there's a rooftop garden?" Cindy, the realtor, takes a step toward us. Her high heels click against the sea of shiny hardwoods. "I'd be happy to show it to you."

The woman is a little pushy for my taste, but she's shown us everything under the sun.

I clear my throat. "Would you mind giving us a little time to talk it over?"

Her eyes sharpen with the thrill of a potential sale. "Of course!" She rushes past us on the way to the foyer. "I'll pop downstairs for a few minutes and speak with the building manager to make sure all of the necessary paperwork is in order."

I dip my chin in acknowledgment. "Great."

"Tootles," she calls out in a sing-song voice, closing the door behind her.

"Finally," I sigh, pulling Demi to me, "alone at last."

Her arms thread around my neck. "Yup. I'm sure we have a good ten minutes to ourselves."

"Unfortunately, that's not nearly enough." I brush my mouth across hers for a quick kiss. "You know I like to take my time."

Her lips bow up against mine. "Yes, I do. And trust me, the effort is always appreciated."

"Damn right it is."

When Demi groans, I reluctantly break away before we ignite a fire that can't be extinguished.

"Give it to me straight. What do you think?" I wrap my arm around her waist and walk us toward the large picture windows to inspect the million-dollar view. I point to the path across the street that winds its way along the shoreline. "How amazing would it be to run along the lake every morning?"

The sexual haze I'd stoked to life moments ago clears from her eyes as she surveys the vast blueness of the water. "That would be nice."

"Plus," I add, "there's a gym on the third floor. If you can't run outside, you can lift weights or use the elliptical."

She narrows her eyes before slanting a look in my direction. "It sounds like you're already sold on the condo."

"Yeah, I like it." It would certainly be the bougiest place I ever lived, that's for damn sure. "But you have to like it, too."

She wraps her arms around my neck again before leaning into me. "I do, it ticks all the boxes."

I squeeze her body to mine before dropping a kiss on the top of her head. "I love you."

A smile wreaths her face as she tips her chin up to meet my gaze. "I love you, too."

"You know what?" I make a big production about looking around the living room and kitchen. "I think there's something missing."

"Really?" The smile disappears as she frowns. "What? This condo has every possible amenity. A gym, amazing views, rooftop garden, security, underground parking, a small convenience store next to the lobby..." Every item is ticked off on her fingers. "What more could you possibly want?"

When she shoots me a perplexed expression, it's all I can do not to grin like a lunatic.

"This." When I drop to one knee, Demi's eyes widen. I slip my hand inside the pocket of my khakis and pull out the signature light blue box with a white bow wrapped around it.

Her hands fly to her gaping mouth as her eyes fill with tears, and she shakes her head. "No."

"Yup." I pull off the silky ribbon and pop open the lid. "You saying yes to being my wife is all that's missing."

"Rowan," she whispers, emotion flooding her features.

"What?" Before she can respond, I say, "I've wanted this for the past two years, but I needed everything to be perfect. I wanted us to be in the same city and state. And now that we are, and we've found the perfect place to call home, I want to make that home with you. I want to marry you, Demi. I want to be your husband and spend the rest of my life with you. What do you say, baby? Will you marry me?"

Her hands fall back to her sides as she presses her lips together and nods. "Yes!" Even though her voice is wobbly, it grows stronger. "Yes, I'll marry you!"

I jump to my feet and take the ring from its plush satin bed before carefully slipping it on her finger.

She stares at her left hand in wonder. "It's gorgeous!"

"I'm glad you like it. Sydney helped pick it out."

"What!" she laughs. "She knew about this and didn't tell me!"

I give a little shrug. "I swore her to secrecy."

Demi throws herself into my arms. "I can't believe this is happening." Tears of joy streak down her face. "I'm so happy that we're finally going to be together."

"Me, too. If you hadn't retired, I would have. The separation was killing me."

"Really?" She grins. "You would have done that?"

Is she kidding?

Damn straight I would have.

"Yup." I smack another kiss against her lips. "You're the most important thing in my life. You always have been, and you always will be."

"I don't know how we made it through the last two years, but I'm glad we did."

"So…" I waggle my brows, "any interest in celebrating our engaged state by christening our new condo?"

"You really think there's time for that?" She throws a cautious look toward the entryway. "Won't Cindy be back any minute?"

"Nope, she's gone. I bought the place last week. Straight up cash, homey. It's ours."

Her eyes widen to the point of falling out of her head. *"What!"*

"Yup."

"I can't believe you did that! What if I had hated it?"

"Then I would have sold it. But I was pretty sure that you'd fall in love with it like I did. The moment Cindy showed me the condo, I knew it was the perfect place for us to start our future together."

She shakes her head. "I can't believe you had this all planned out."

I can only grin before telling her the rest. She's probably had enough surprises for one day. "We've got enough time to make this place ours, and then we're meeting Sydney, Brayden, your dad, and a few of the guys from the team to celebrate our engagement."

For about the dozenth time in the last ten minutes, her mouth drops open and a wave of shock washes over her. *"Are you serious?"*

I smack another kiss against her parted lips. She's adorable when she's thrown off-kilter, and this has definitely done the trick. There haven't been many times when I've been able to keep anything from her. Demi is way too smart for that. And apparently, I'm bad at keeping secrets. Especially from her. "Yup. I planned a little celebratory party so you can show off that giant rock on your finger."

Her gaze falls to the ring before her features soften. She holds out her hand to admire the massive sapphire surrounded by diamonds. "It really is spectacular." Her gaze flicks to me. "And you did an amazing job picking it out."

"I want you to be happy."

She places her palms against my chest before sliding them toward my shoulders and wrapping them around my neck. "*You* make me happy. I can't imagine my life without you in it."

Unable to resist the lure of her mouth, I dive in for another kiss. "Guess it's a good thing you'll never have to worry about that."

With a sigh, her lips part, and my tongue sweeps inside to tangle with hers.

After a couple of heated moments, she pulls away enough to ask, "Aren't we going to christen the place?"

She squeaks in surprise when my palms settle on her ass, and I hoist her into my arms. Thirty steps later, I'm setting her on the marble island. Her hands go to my shirt, untucking it from the khakis before yanking it over my head and tossing it to the hardwoods. It doesn't take long before we're both naked. As I sink inside her tight heat, I'm hit with the realization that as much as this condo will be our new home, it's this right here, buried deep inside the warmth of her body, is where I belong.

As long as Demi and I are together, it doesn't matter where we are or what city we live in.

My home is with her.

It will always be with her.

ABOUT THE AUTHOR

Jennifer Sucevic is a USA Today bestselling author who has published nineteen New Adult and Mature Young Adult novels. Her work has been translated into German, Dutch, and Italian. Jen has a bachelor's degree in History and a master's degree in Educational Psychology. Both are from the University of Wisconsin-Milwaukee. She started out her career as a high school counselor, which she loved. She lives in the Midwest with her husband, four kids, and a menagerie of animals. If you would like to receive regular updates regarding new releases, please subscribe to her newsletter here- Jennifer Sucevic Newsletter (subscribepage.com)
Or contact Jen through email, at her website, or on Facebook.
sucevicjennifer@gmail.com
Want to join her reader group? Do it here -)
J Sucevic's Book Boyfriends | Facebook
Social media links-
https://www.tiktok.com/@jennifersucevicauthor
www.jennifersucevic.com
https://www.instagram.com/jennifersucevicauthor
https://www.facebook.com/jennifer.sucevic
Amazon.com: Jennifer Sucevic: Books, Biography, Blog, Audiobooks, Kindle
Jennifer Sucevic Books - BookBub
https://www.tumblr.com/blog/jsucevic
https://www.pinterest.com/jmolitor6/

Made in the USA
Monee, IL
29 December 2023

50774927R00178